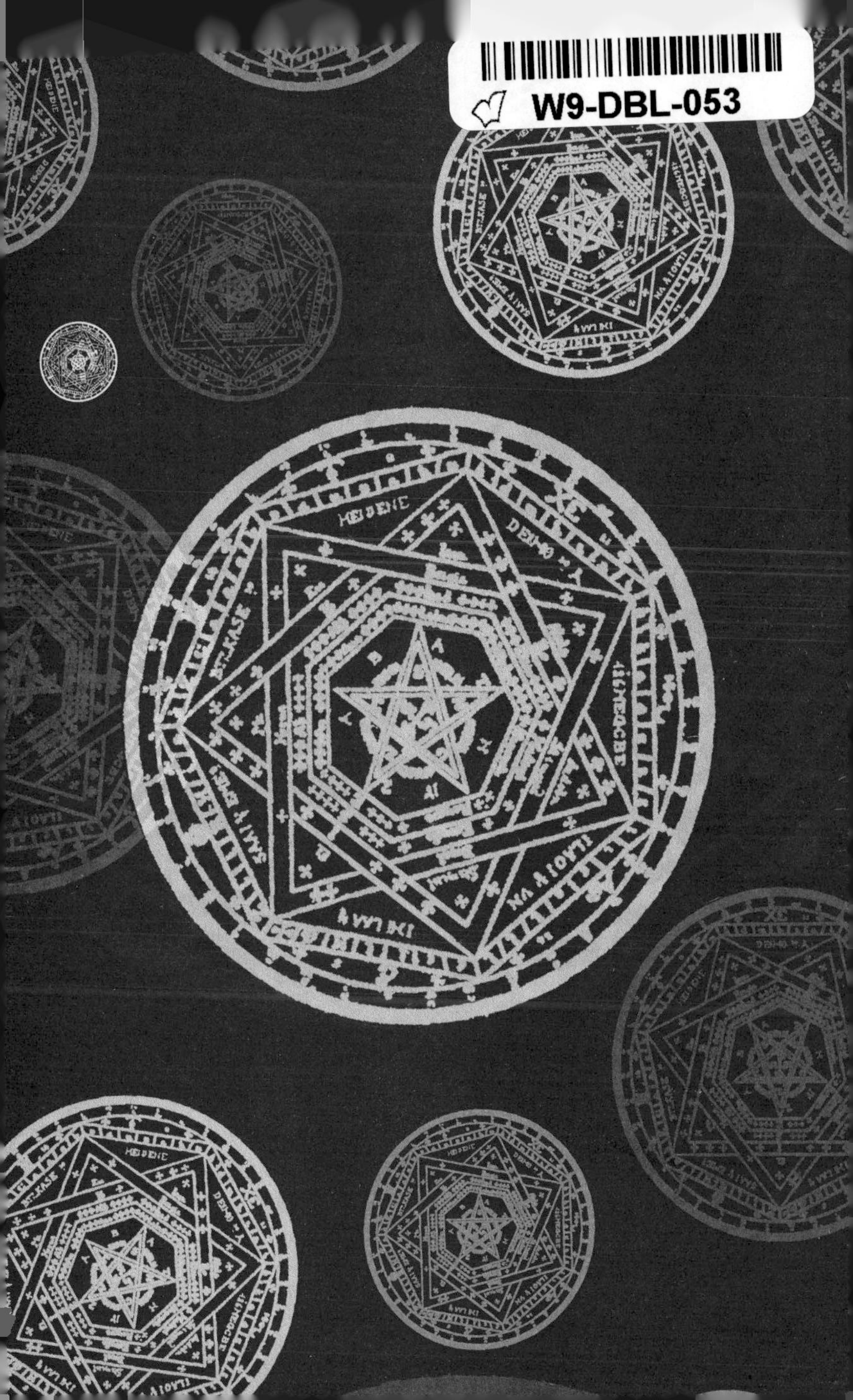

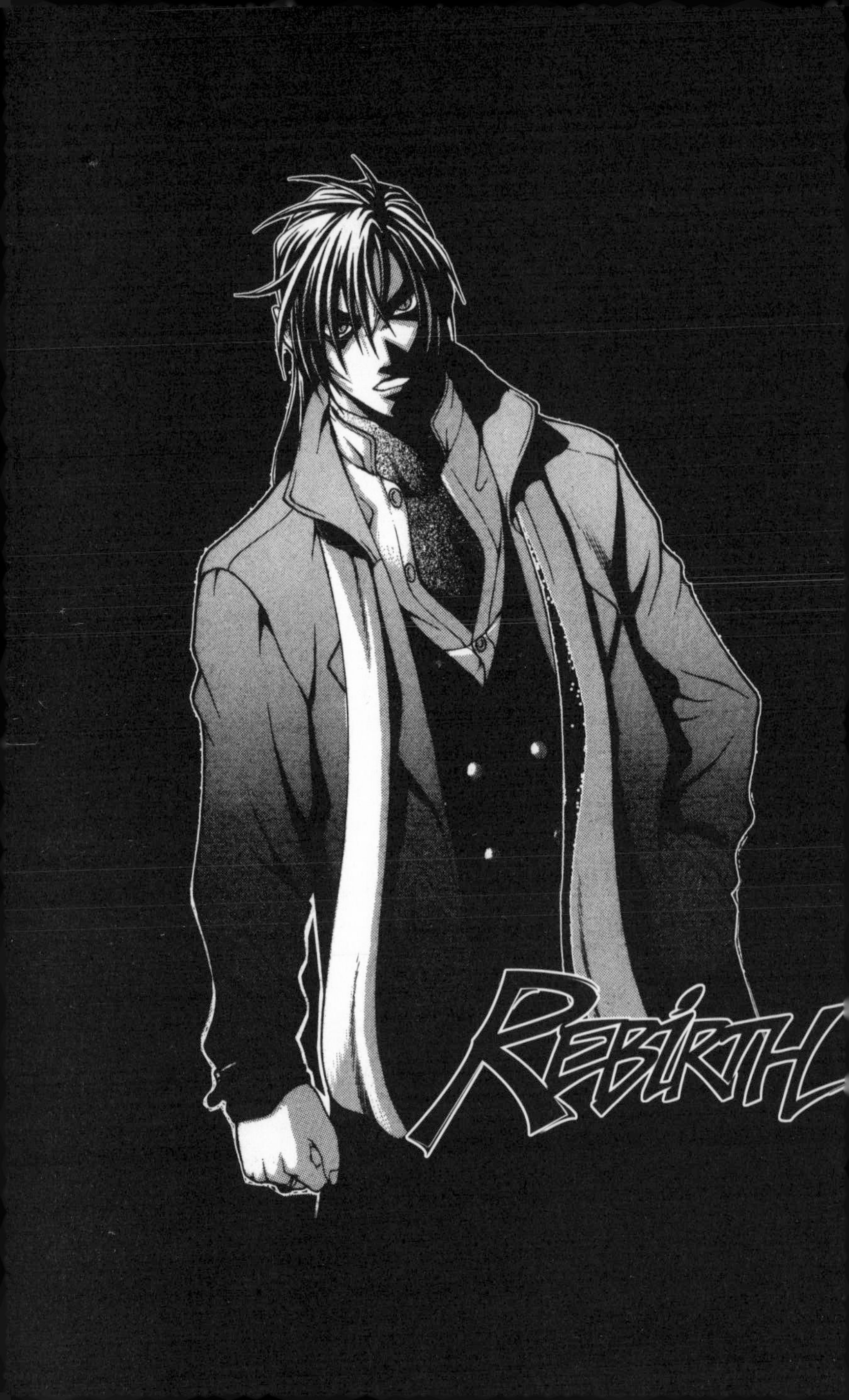
REBIRTH

VOLUME 6

STORY AND ART BY WOO

LOS ANGELES • TOKYO • LONDON

Translator - Youngju Ryu
English Adaptation - Bryce P. Coleman and Taliesin Jaffe
Associate Editor - Bryce P. Coleman
Retouch and Lettering - Caren McCaleb
Cover Layout - Patrick Hook

Editor - Luis Reyes
Managing Editor - Jill Freshney
Production Coordinator - Antonio DePietro
Production Manager - Mutsumi Miyazaki
Art Director - Matt Alford
Editorial Director - Jeremy Ross
VP of Production - Ron Klamert
President & C.O.O. - John Parker
Publisher & C.E.O. - Stuart Levy

Email: editor@TOKYOPOP.com
Come visit us online at www.TOKYOPOP.com

A  Manga

TOKYOPOP Inc.
5900 Wilshire Blvd. Suite 2000
Los Angeles, CA 90036

Rebirth Vol. 6

ISBN: 1-59182-524-5

First TOKYOPOP® printing: February 2004

10 9 8 7 6 5 4 3 2 1

Printed in the USA

STORY THUS FAR

Betrayed by his closest friend, the vampire Deshwitat has for centuries lain in a state of limbo, a plain of non-existence, neither dead nor alive. Until now...

While conducting a paranormal investigation, Professor Do, his daughter Remi, and the exorcist Millenear Shephild unwittingly release Deshwitat back into the world. It is a mistake that would have cost the Professor his life had not his fearless daughter struck a deal with the vengeful vampire to assist him in his quest to find and destroy the sorcerer Kalutika. In order to battle Kal, Deshwitat must first learn the secrets of "light-magic" — a pursuit that leads the unlikely group to an ancient Buddhist monastery. There, Deshwitat is reunited with his old comrade, Rett, who himself has been cursed with immortality by Kal. Joined by Rett and the enigmatic Beryun, the team's search for knowledge leads them to the Vatican and into a deadly trap engineered by the maniacal Bishop Bernard. Deshwitat is nearly destroyed by the religious zealot whose dreams of messiahdom have driven him insane. In a daring rescue attempt, the group puts an end to Bernard's apocalyptic machinations, destroying half the Vatican in the process.

Now, as Millenear pores over an ancient text retrieved from the Vatican Archives, we learn the untold histories of Deshwitat and Kalutika. The following pages recount the tragic events that would change two lives...and the fate of the world...forever

REBIRTH

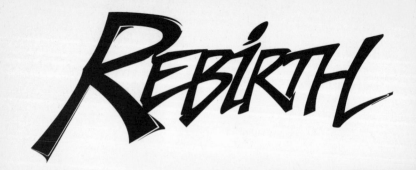

Vol 6

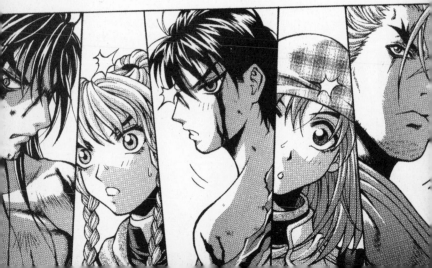

CHAPTER 22: INTO THE PAST

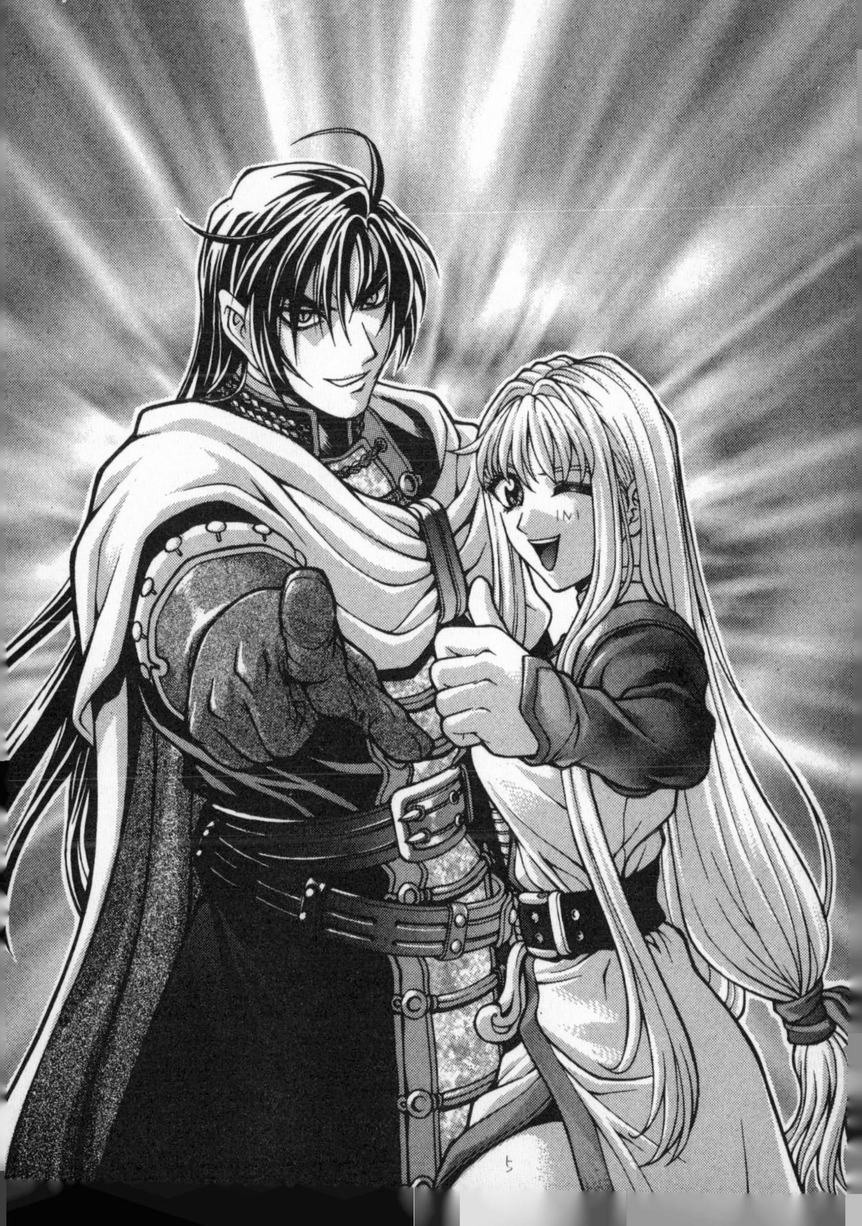

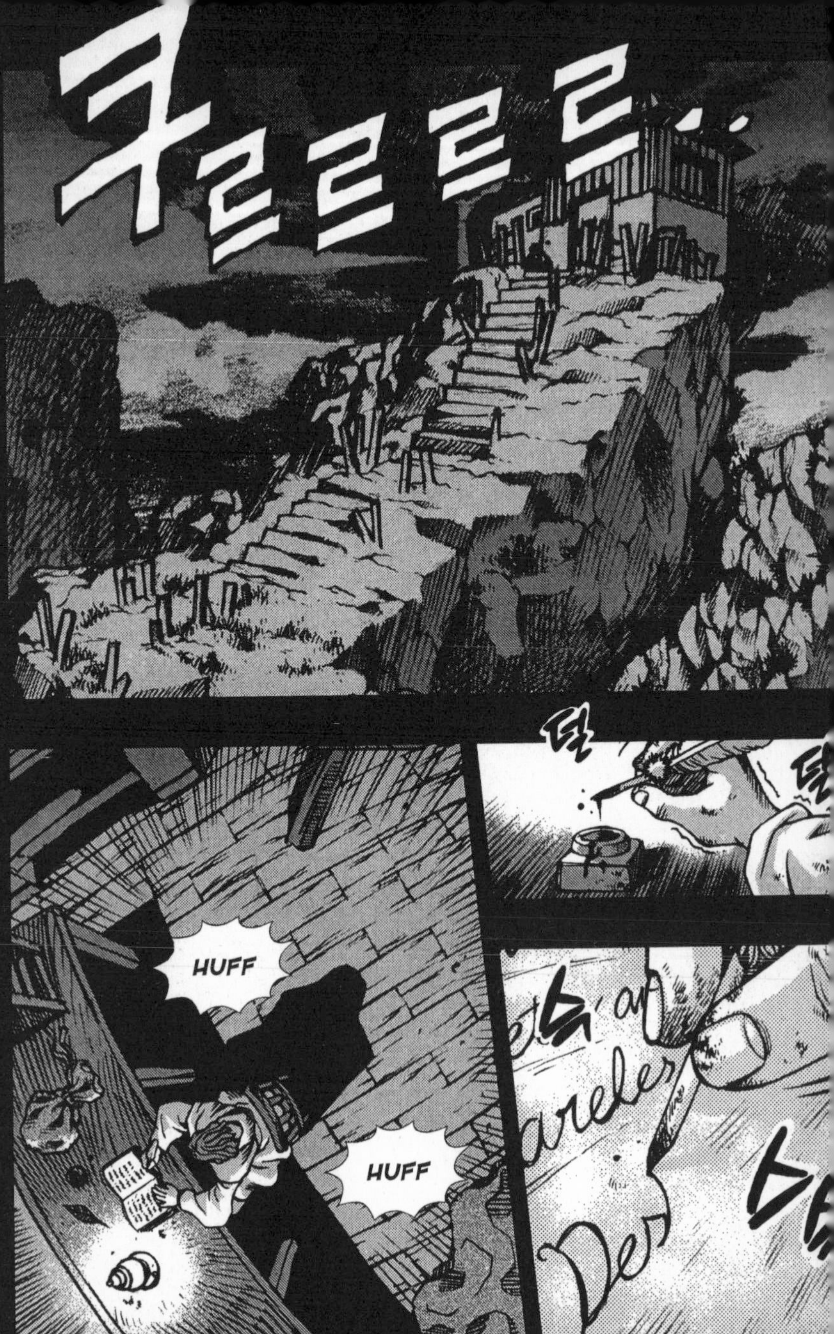
쿠르르르...
HUFF
HUFF
털

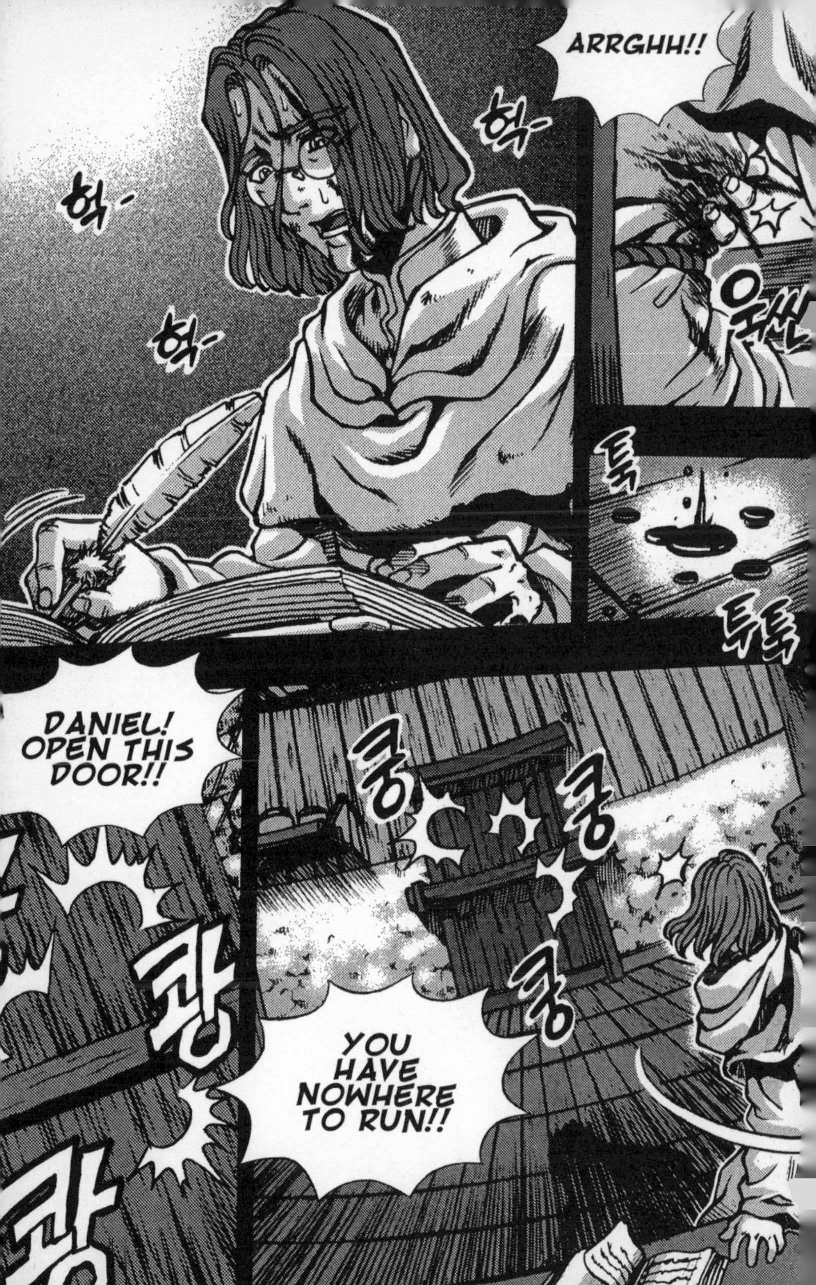
헉-
헉-
헉-
ARRGHH!!
툭
투툭
DANIEL! OPEN THIS DOOR!!
쾅
쾅
쿵
쿵
쿵
YOU HAVE NOWHERE TO RUN!!

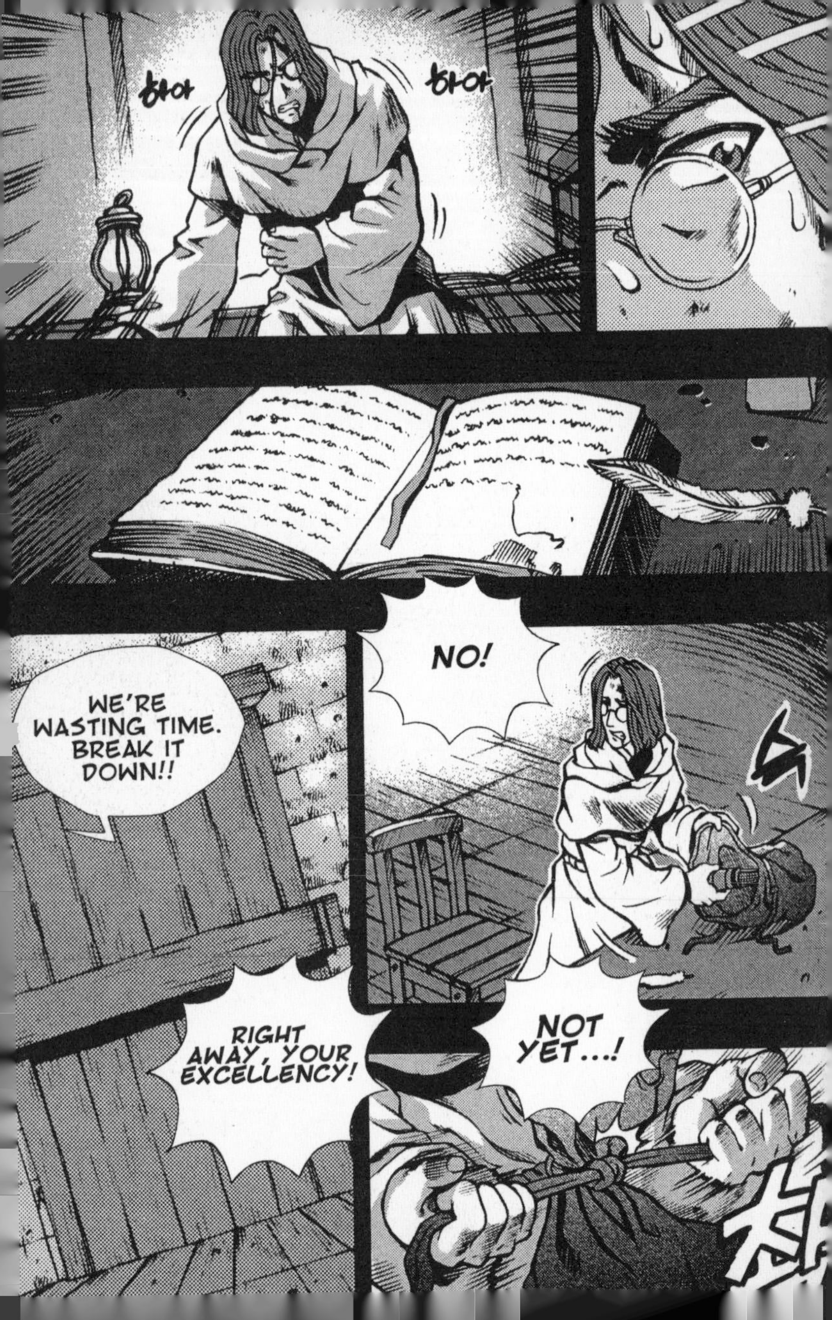
하아
하아
WE'RE WASTING TIME. BREAK IT DOWN!!
RIGHT AWAY, YOUR EXCELLENCY!
NO!
NOT YET...!

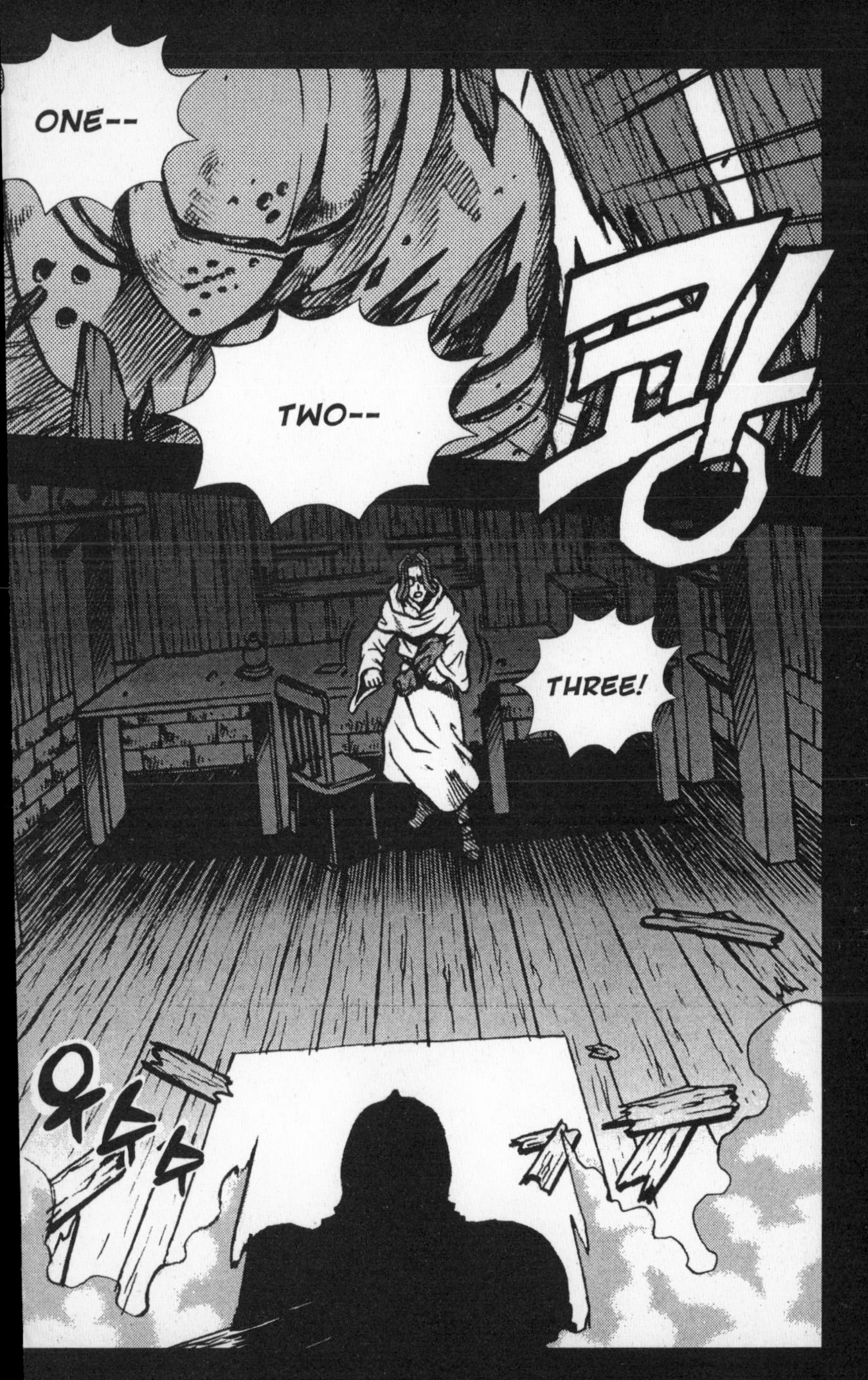
ONE--
TWO--
THREE!

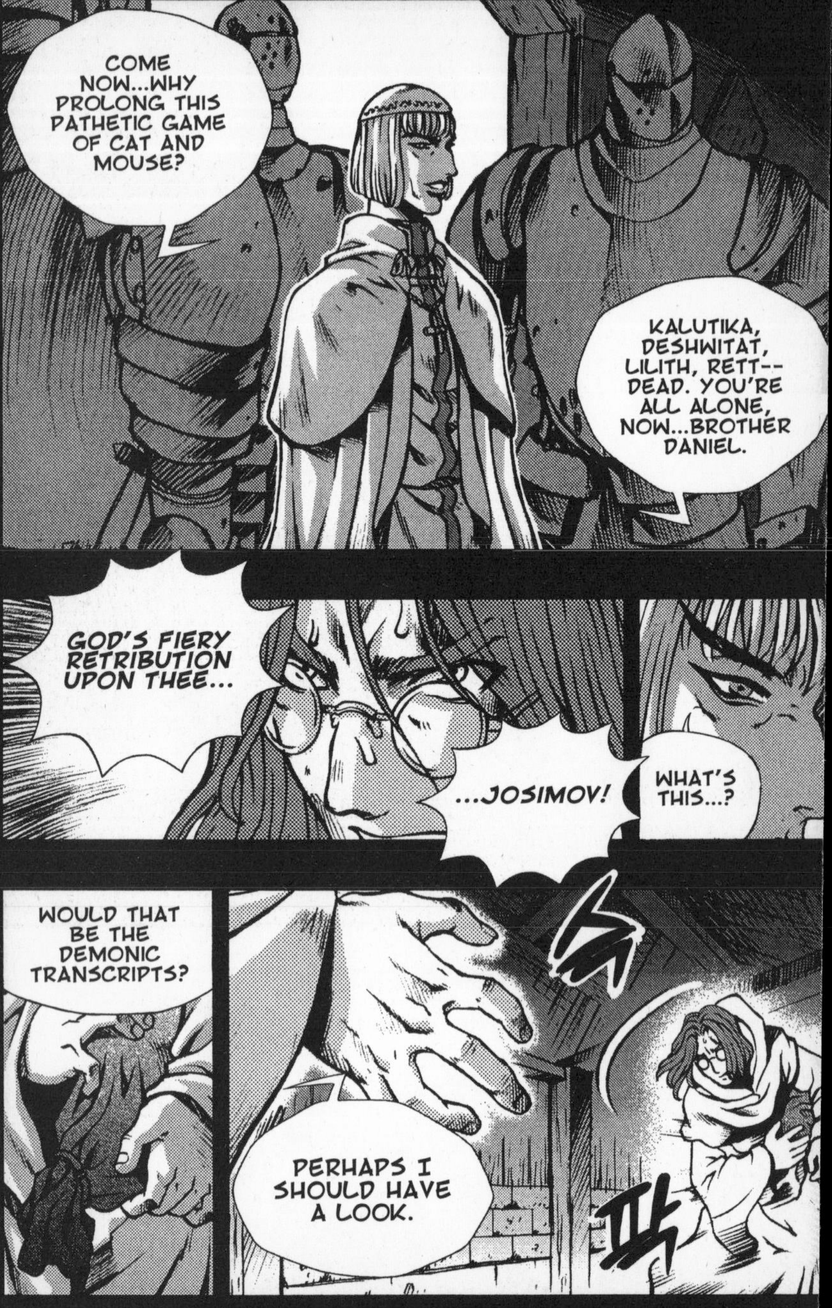
COME NOW...WHY PROLONG THIS PATHETIC GAME OF CAT AND MOUSE?
KALUTIKA, DESHWITAT, LILITH, RETT--DEAD. YOU'RE ALL ALONE, NOW...BROTHER DANIEL.
GOD'S FIERY RETRIBUTION UPON THEE...
...JOSIMOV!
WHAT'S THIS...?
WOULD THAT BE THE DEMONIC TRANSCRIPTS?
PERHAPS I SHOULD HAVE A LOOK.

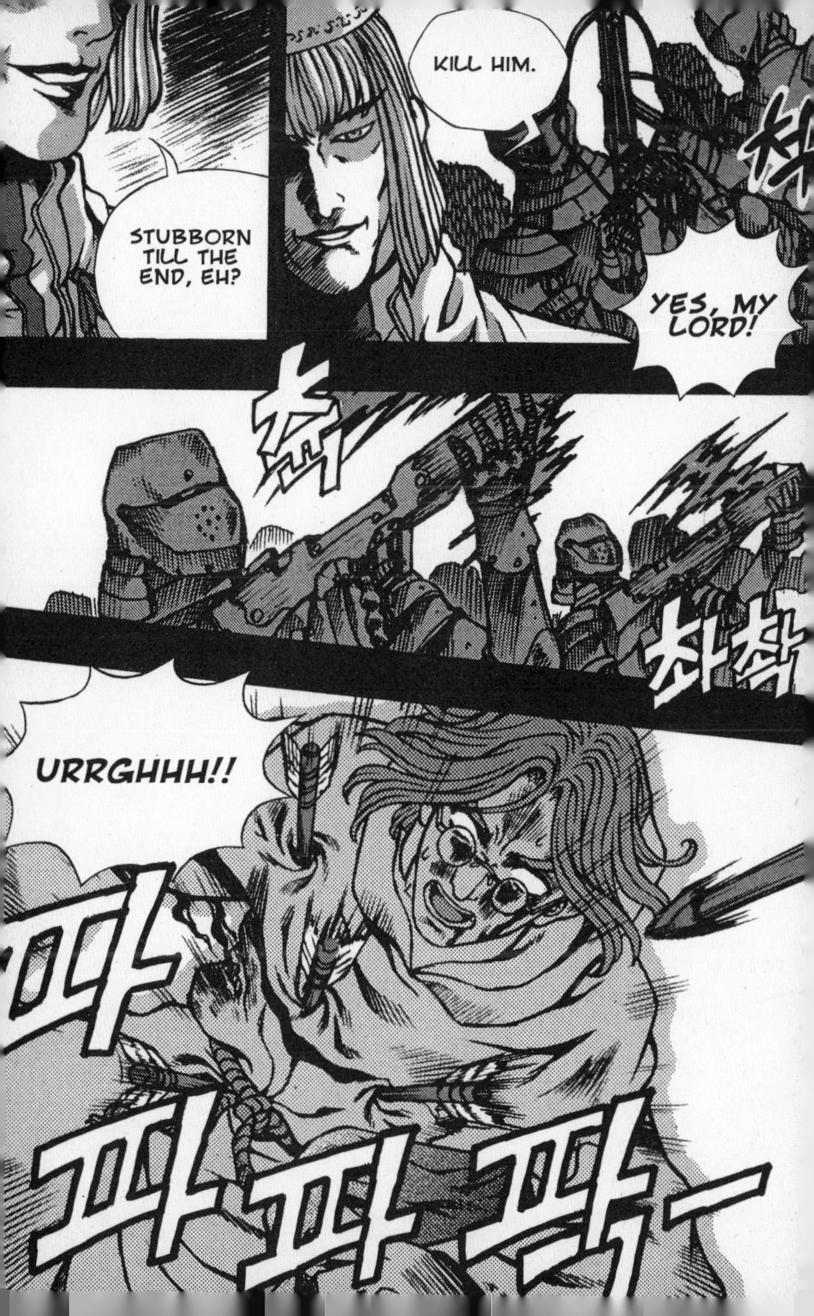
STUBBORN TILL THE END, EH?
KILL HIM.
YES, MY LORD!
착착
URRGHHH!!

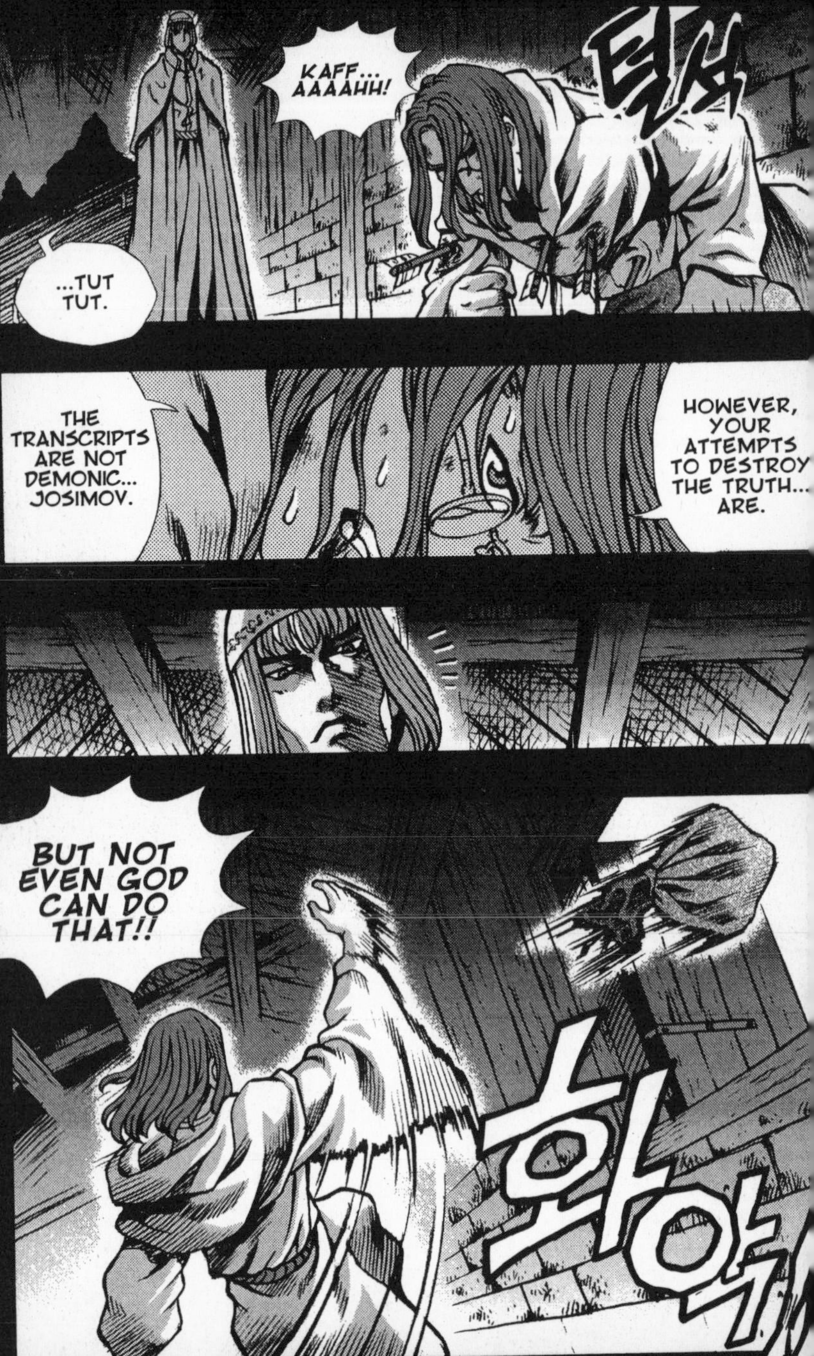
KAFF... AAAAHH!
...TUT TUT.
THE TRANSCRIPTS ARE NOT DEMONIC... JOSIMOV.
HOWEVER, YOUR ATTEMPTS TO DESTROY THE TRUTH... ARE.
BUT NOT EVEN GOD CAN DO THAT!!

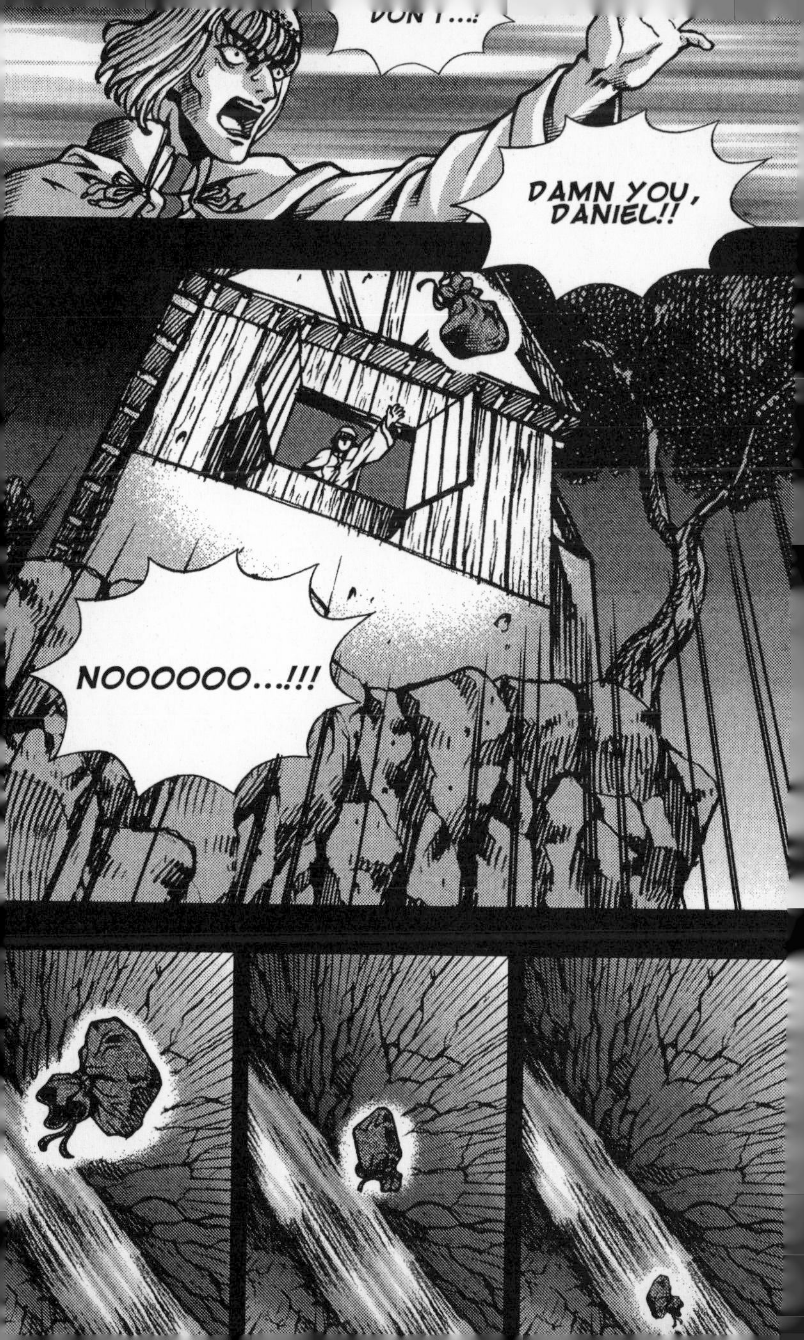
DON'T...!
DAMN YOU, DANIEL!!
NOOOOOO...!!!

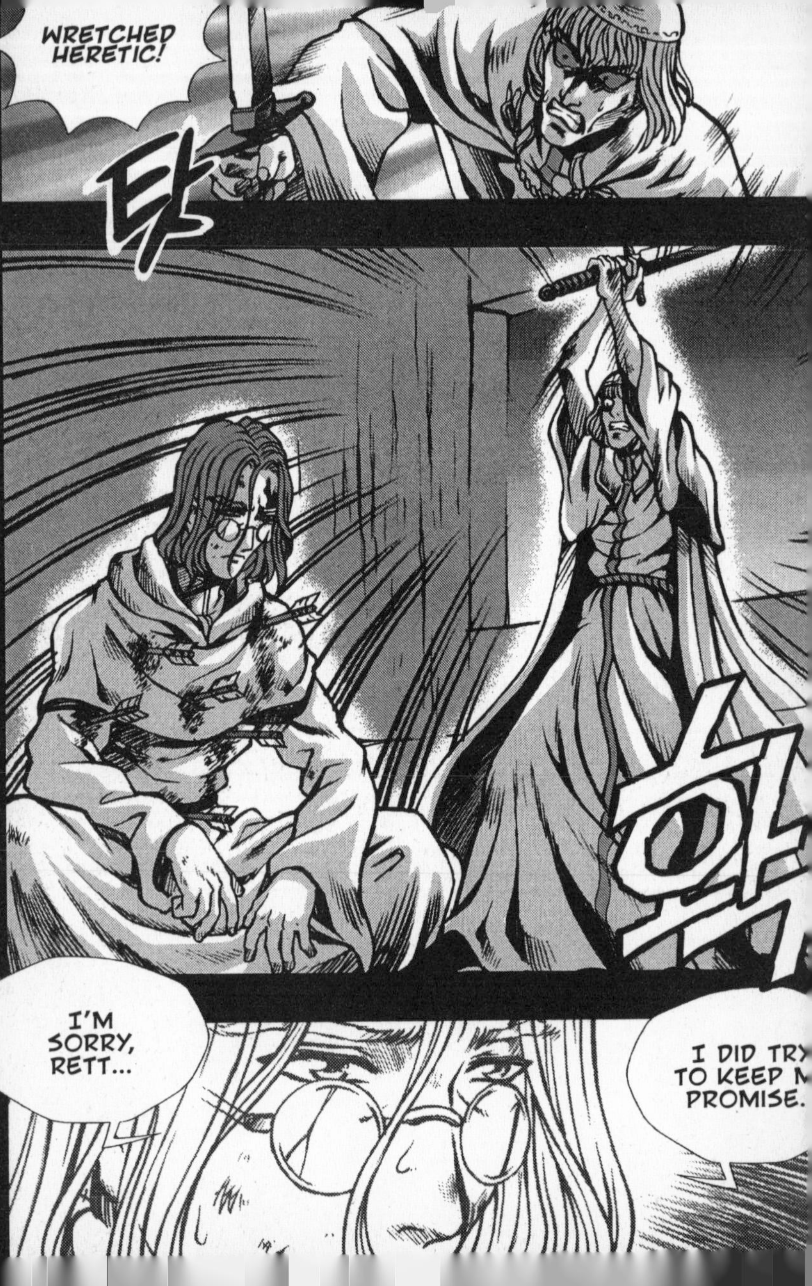
WRETCHED HERETIC!
I'M SORRY, RETT...
I DID TRY TO KEEP M PROMISE.

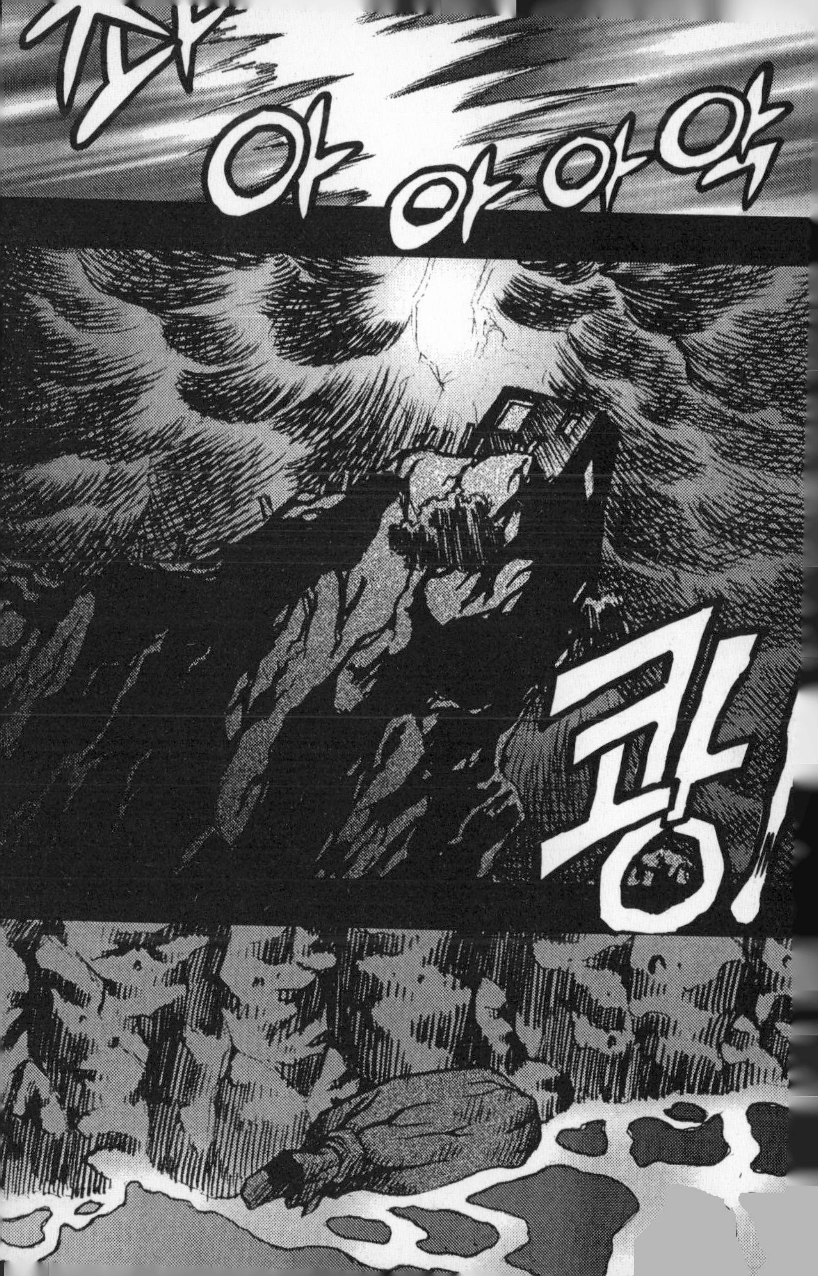
꺄아아아악
쾅!

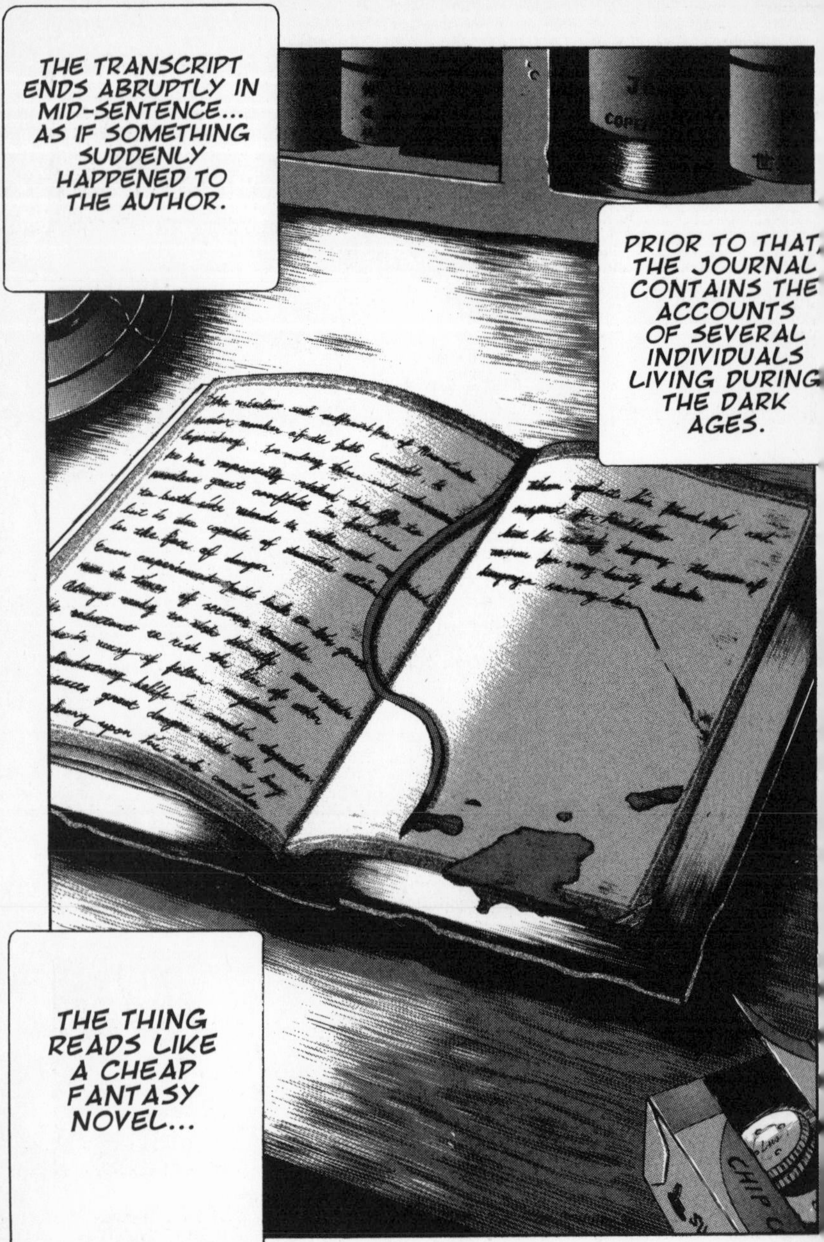
THE TRANSCRIPT ENDS ABRUPTLY IN MID-SENTENCE... AS IF SOMETHING SUDDENLY HAPPENED TO THE AUTHOR.
PRIOR TO THAT, THE JOURNAL CONTAINS THE ACCOUNTS OF SEVERAL INDIVIDUALS LIVING DURING THE DARK AGES.
THE THING READS LIKE A CHEAP FANTASY NOVEL...

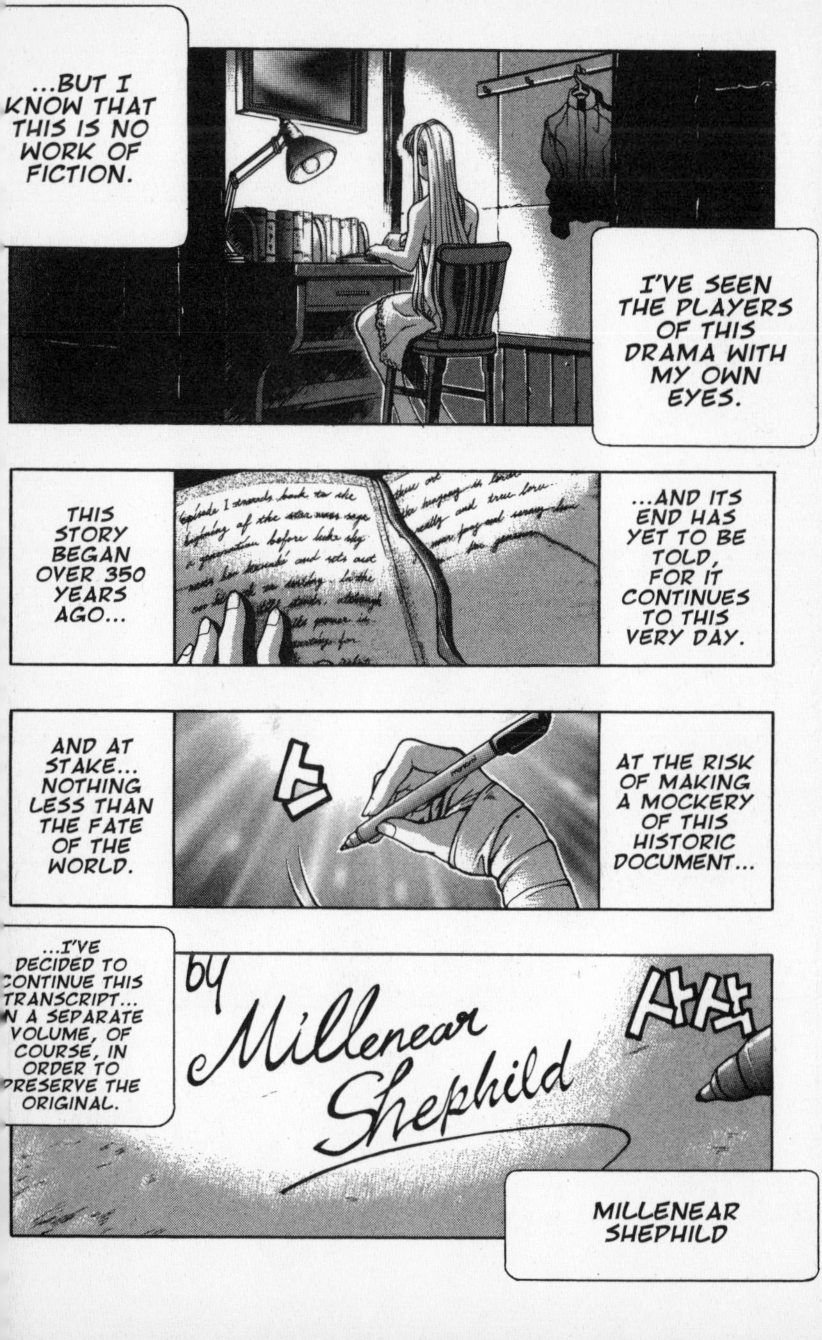
...BUT I KNOW THAT THIS IS NO WORK OF FICTION.
I'VE SEEN THE PLAYERS OF THIS DRAMA WITH MY OWN EYES.
THIS STORY BEGAN OVER 350 YEARS AGO...
...AND ITS END HAS YET TO BE TOLD, FOR IT CONTINUES TO THIS VERY DAY.
AND AT STAKE... NOTHING LESS THAN THE FATE OF THE WORLD.
AT THE RISK OF MAKING A MOCKERY OF THIS HISTORIC DOCUMENT...
...I'VE DECIDED TO CONTINUE THIS TRANSCRIPT... IN A SEPARATE VOLUME, OF COURSE, IN ORDER TO PRESERVE THE ORIGINAL.
by Millenear Shephild
MILLENEAR SHEPHILD

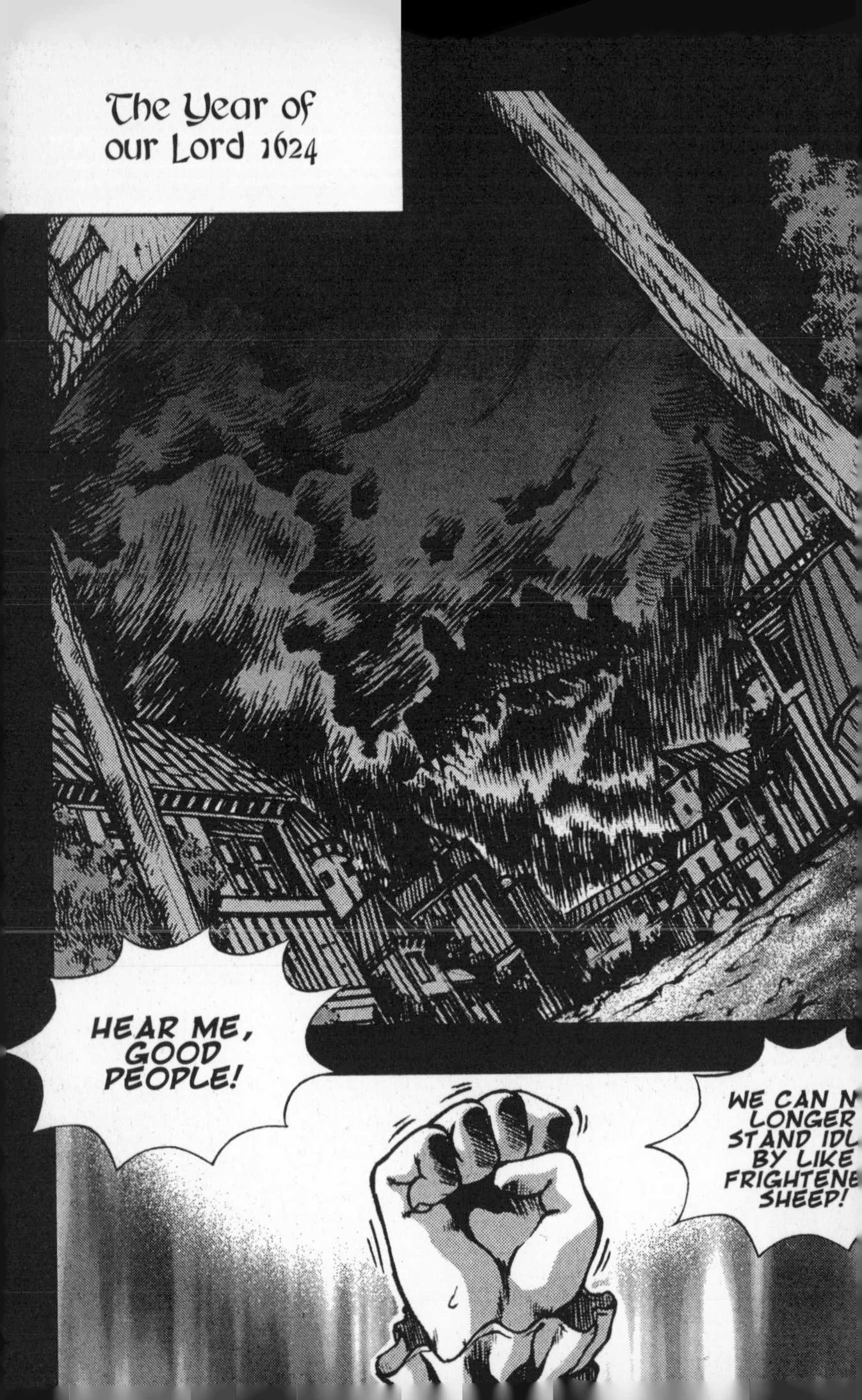
The Year of our Lord 1624
HEAR ME, GOOD PEOPLE!
WE CAN N LONGER STAND IDL BY LIKE FRIGHTENE SHEEP!

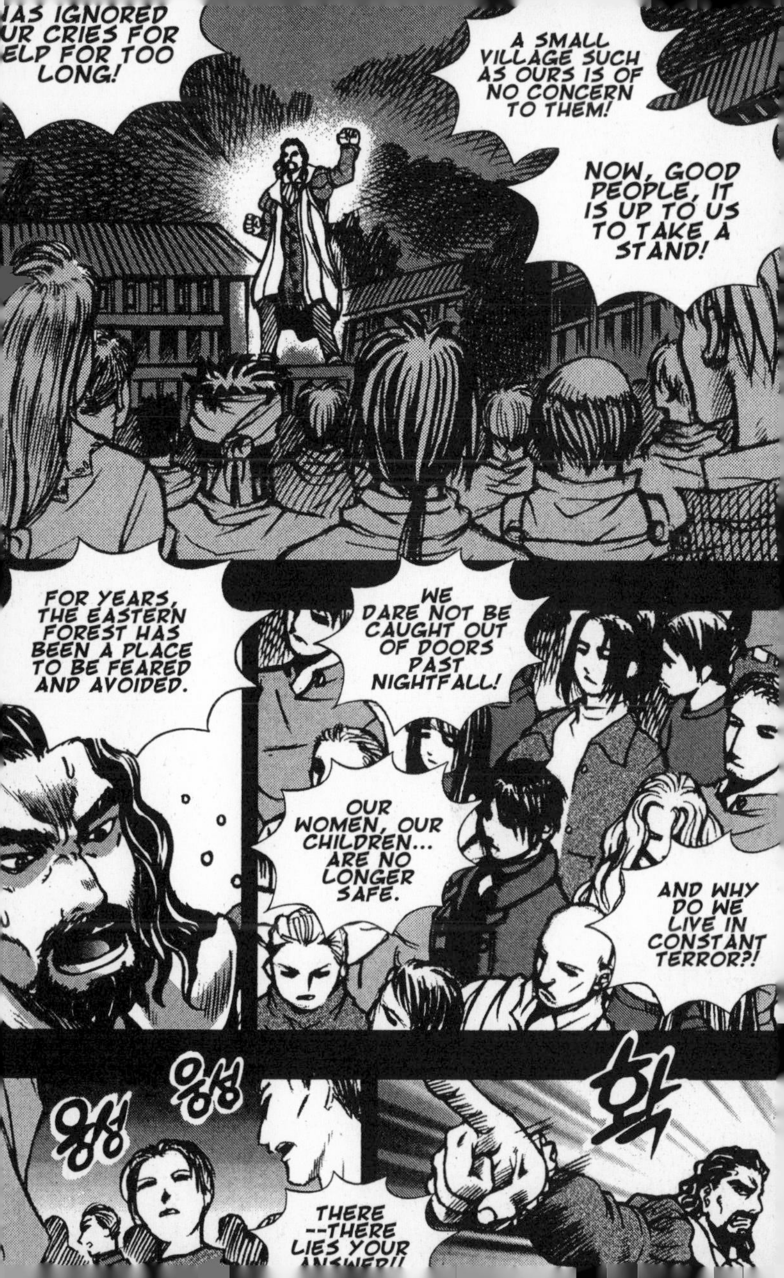

IAS IGNORED UR CRIES FOR ELP FOR TOO LONG!
A SMALL VILLAGE SUCH AS OURS IS OF NO CONCERN TO THEM!
NOW, GOOD PEOPLE, IT IS UP TO US TO TAKE A STAND!
FOR YEARS, THE EASTERN FOREST HAS BEEN A PLACE TO BE FEARED AND AVOIDED.
WE DARE NOT BE CAUGHT OUT OF DOORS PAST NIGHTFALL!
OUR WOMEN, OUR CHILDREN... ARE NO LONGER SAFE.
AND WHY DO WE LIVE IN CONSTANT TERROR?!
웅성
웅성
확
THERE --THERE LIES YOUR

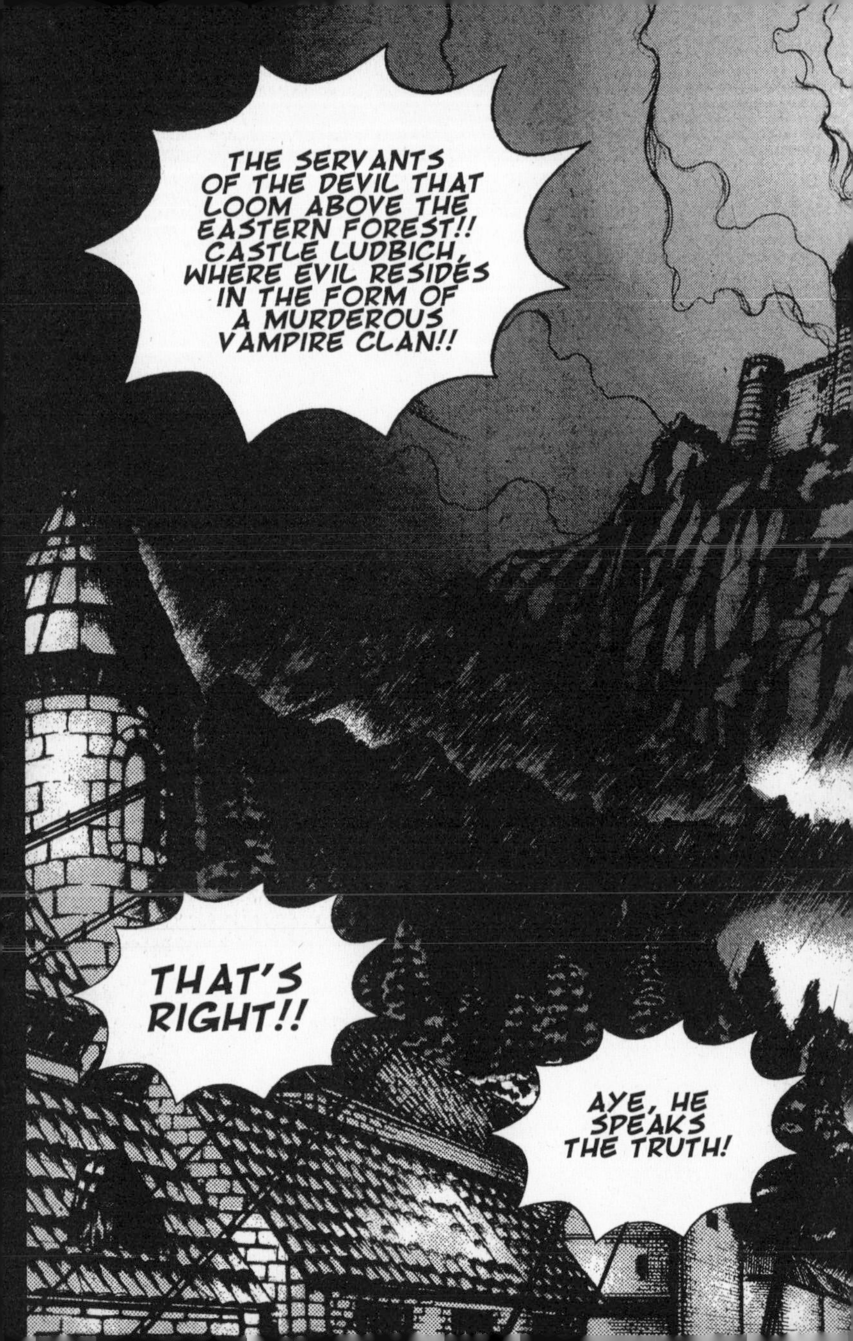
THE SERVANTS OF THE DEVIL THAT LOOM ABOVE THE EASTERN FOREST!! CASTLE LUDBICH, WHERE EVIL RESIDES IN THE FORM OF A MURDEROUS VAMPIRE CLAN!!
THAT'S RIGHT!!
AYE, HE SPEAKS THE TRUTH!

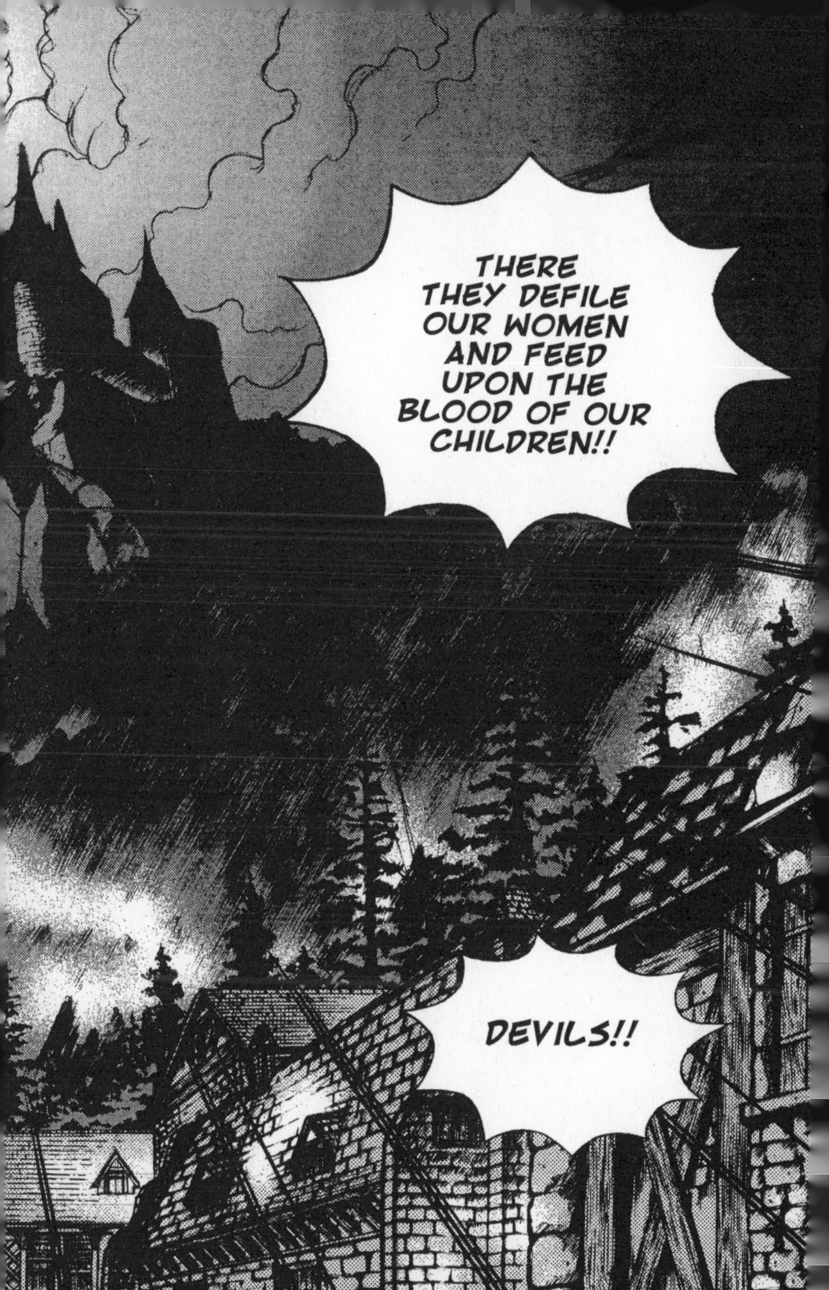
THERE THEY DEFILE OUR WOMEN AND FEED UPON THE BLOOD OF OUR CHILDREN!!
DEVILS!!

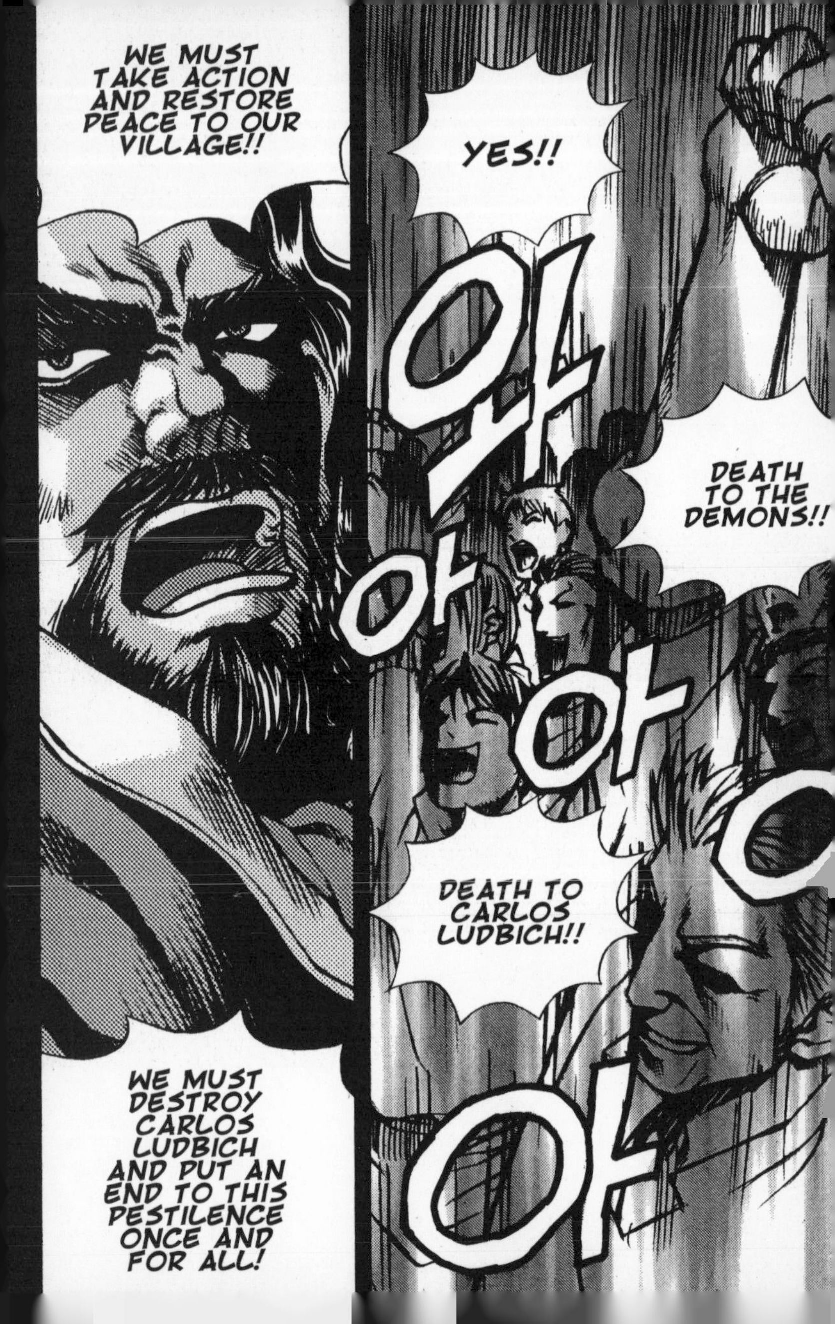
WE MUST TAKE ACTION AND RESTORE PEACE TO OUR VILLAGE!!
WE MUST DESTROY CARLOS LUDBICH AND PUT AN END TO THIS PESTILENCE ONCE AND FOR ALL!
YES!!
DEATH TO THE DEMONS!!
DEATH TO CARLOS LUDBICH!!

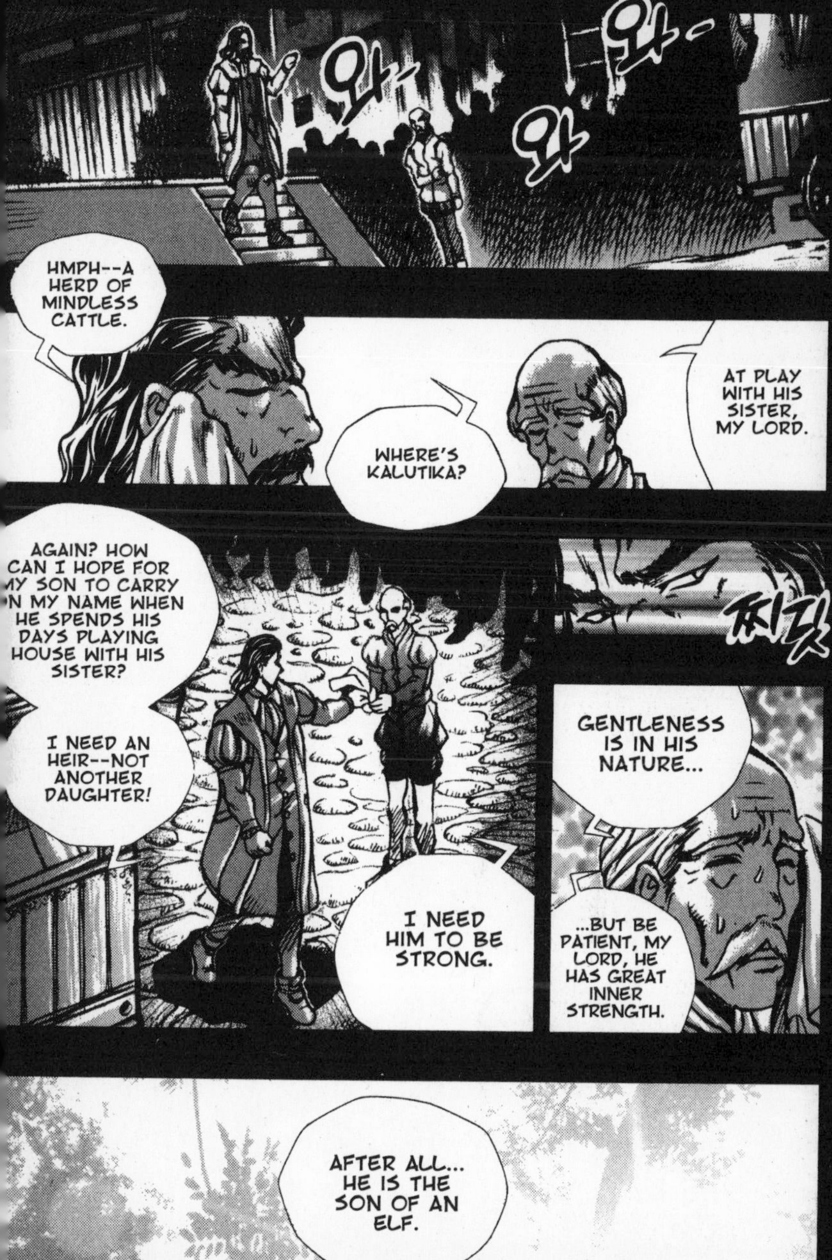
HMPH--A HERD OF MINDLESS CATTLE.
WHERE'S KALUTIKA?
AT PLAY WITH HIS SISTER, MY LORD.
AGAIN? HOW CAN I HOPE FOR MY SON TO CARRY ON MY NAME WHEN HE SPENDS HIS DAYS PLAYING HOUSE WITH HIS SISTER?
I NEED AN HEIR--NOT ANOTHER DAUGHTER!
I NEED HIM TO BE STRONG.
GENTLENESS IS IN HIS NATURE...
...BUT BE PATIENT, MY LORD, HE HAS GREAT INNER STRENGTH.
AFTER ALL... HE IS THE SON OF AN ELF.

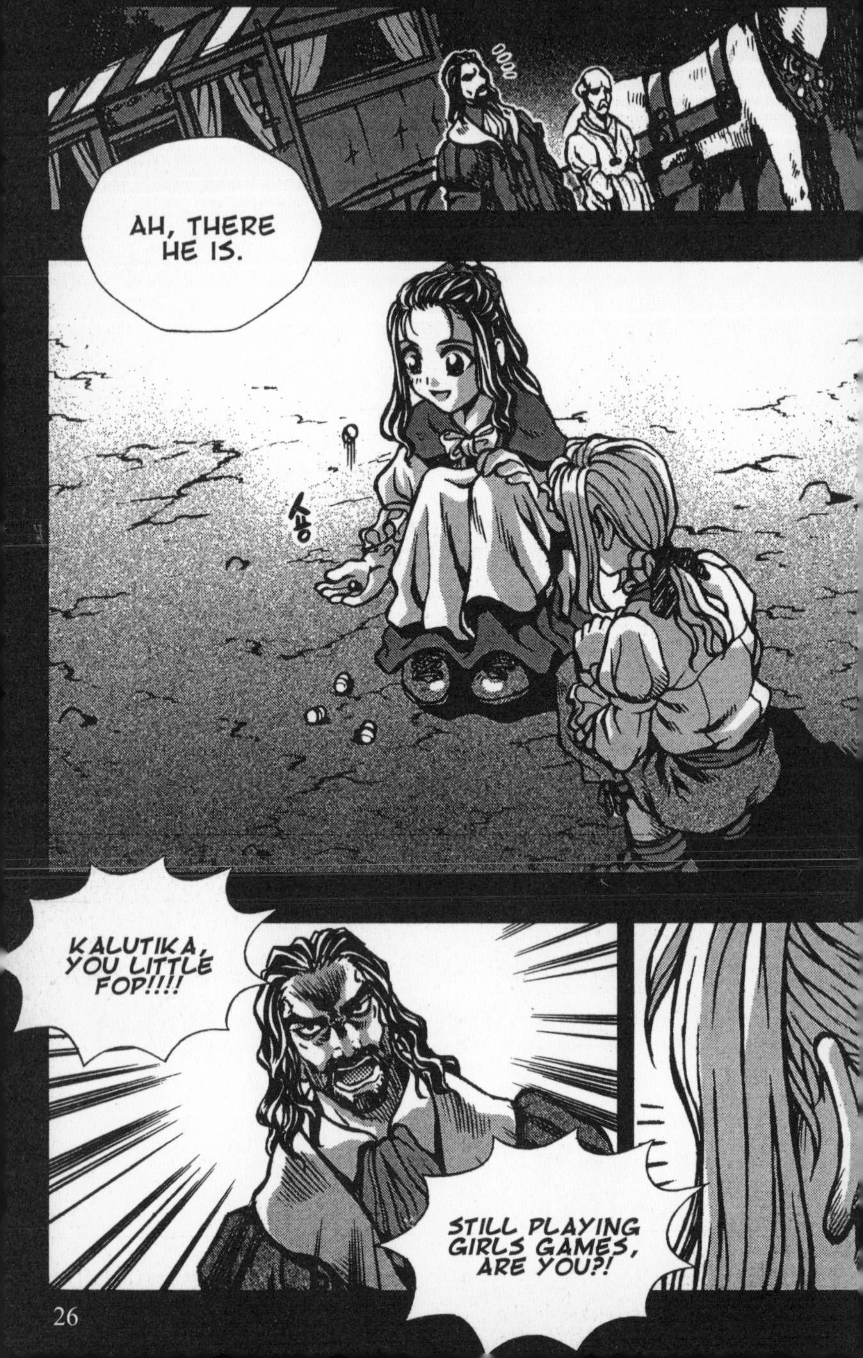
AH, THERE HE IS.
슝
KALUTIKA, YOU LITTLE FOP!!!!
STILL PLAYING GIRLS GAMES, ARE YOU?!

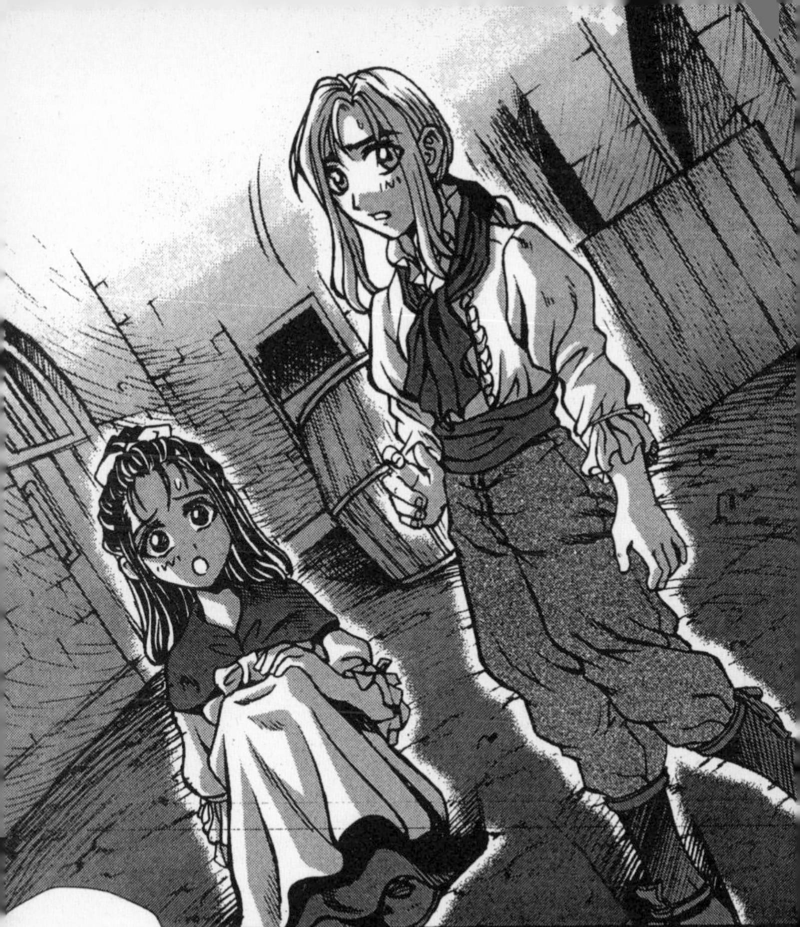

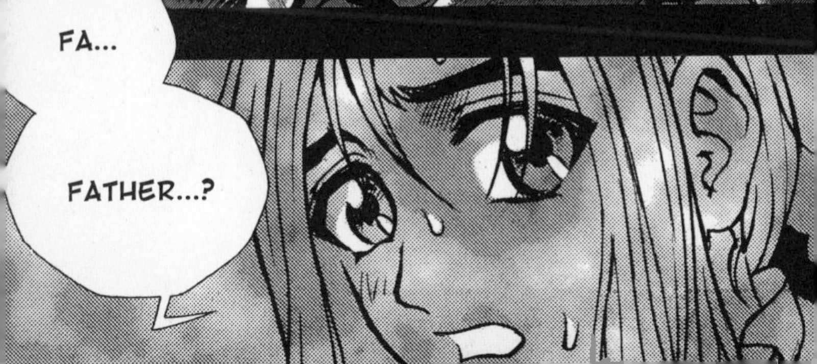
FA...
FATHER...?

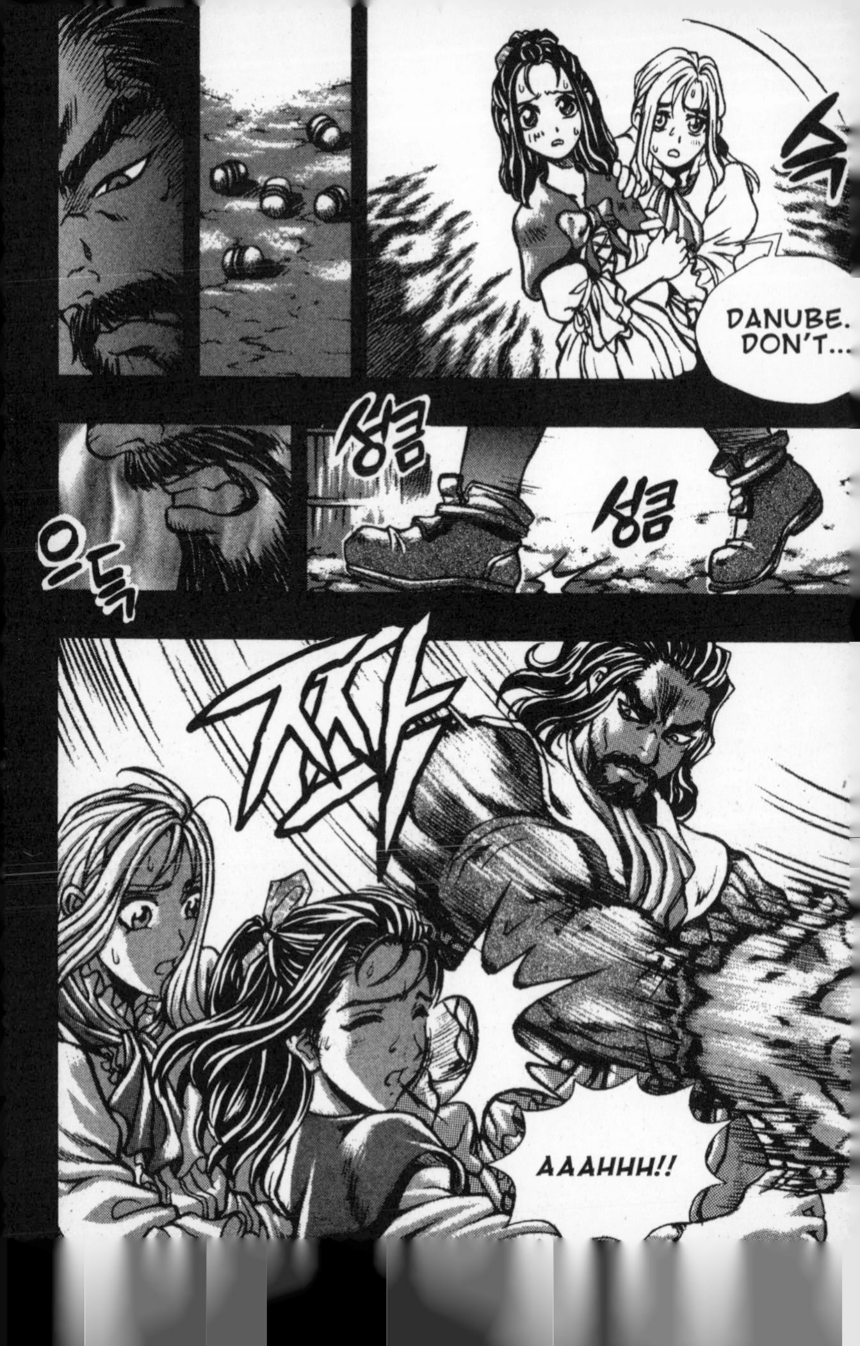
슥
DANUBE. DON'T...
으득
성큼
성큼
AAAHHH!!

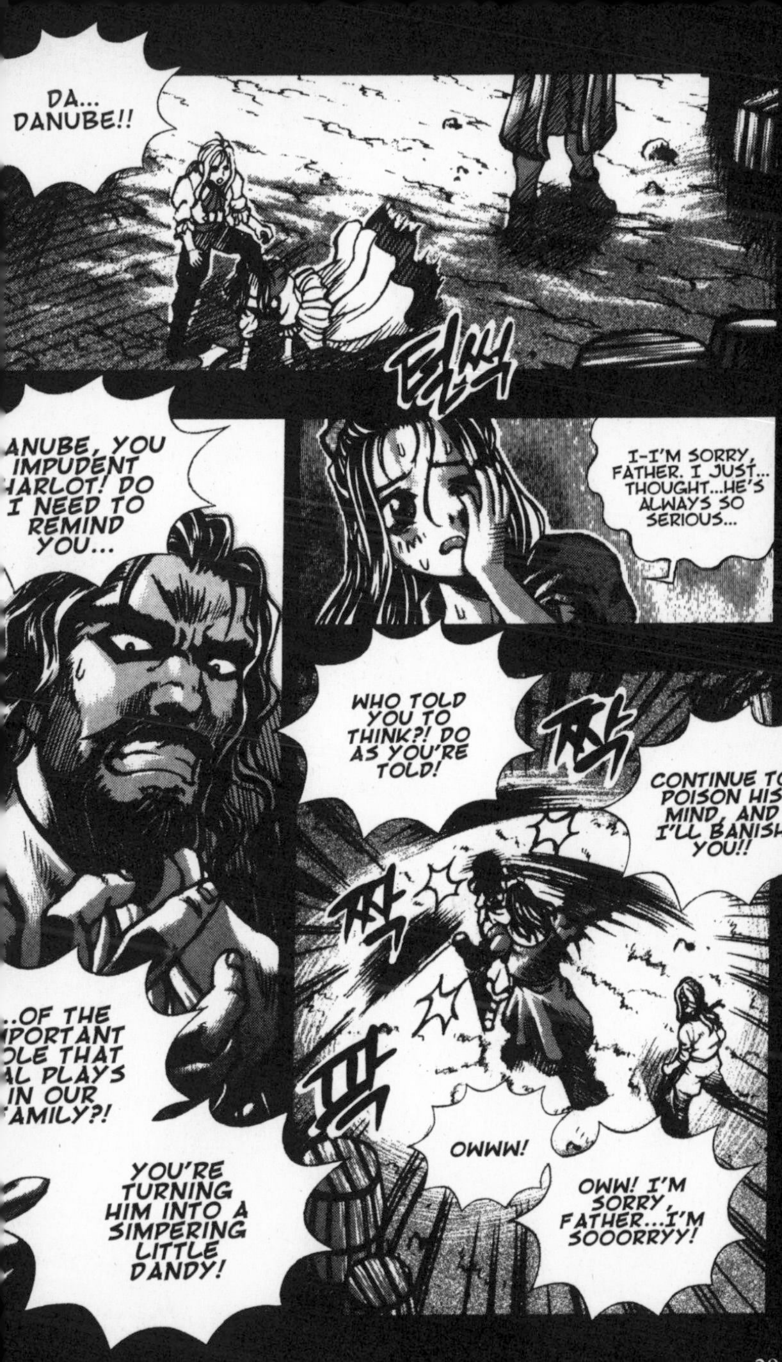
DA... DANUBE!!
ANUBE, YOU IMPUDENT HARLOT! DO I NEED TO REMIND YOU...
..OF THE PORTANT OLE THAT AL PLAYS IN OUR AMILY?!
I-I'M SORRY, FATHER. I JUST... THOUGHT...HE'S ALWAYS SO SERIOUS...
WHO TOLD YOU TO THINK?! DO AS YOU'RE TOLD!
CONTINUE TO POISON HIS MIND, AND I'LL BANISH YOU!!
YOU'RE TURNING HIM INTO A SIMPERING LITTLE DANDY!
OWWW!
OWW! I'M SORRY, FATHER...I'M SOOORRYY!

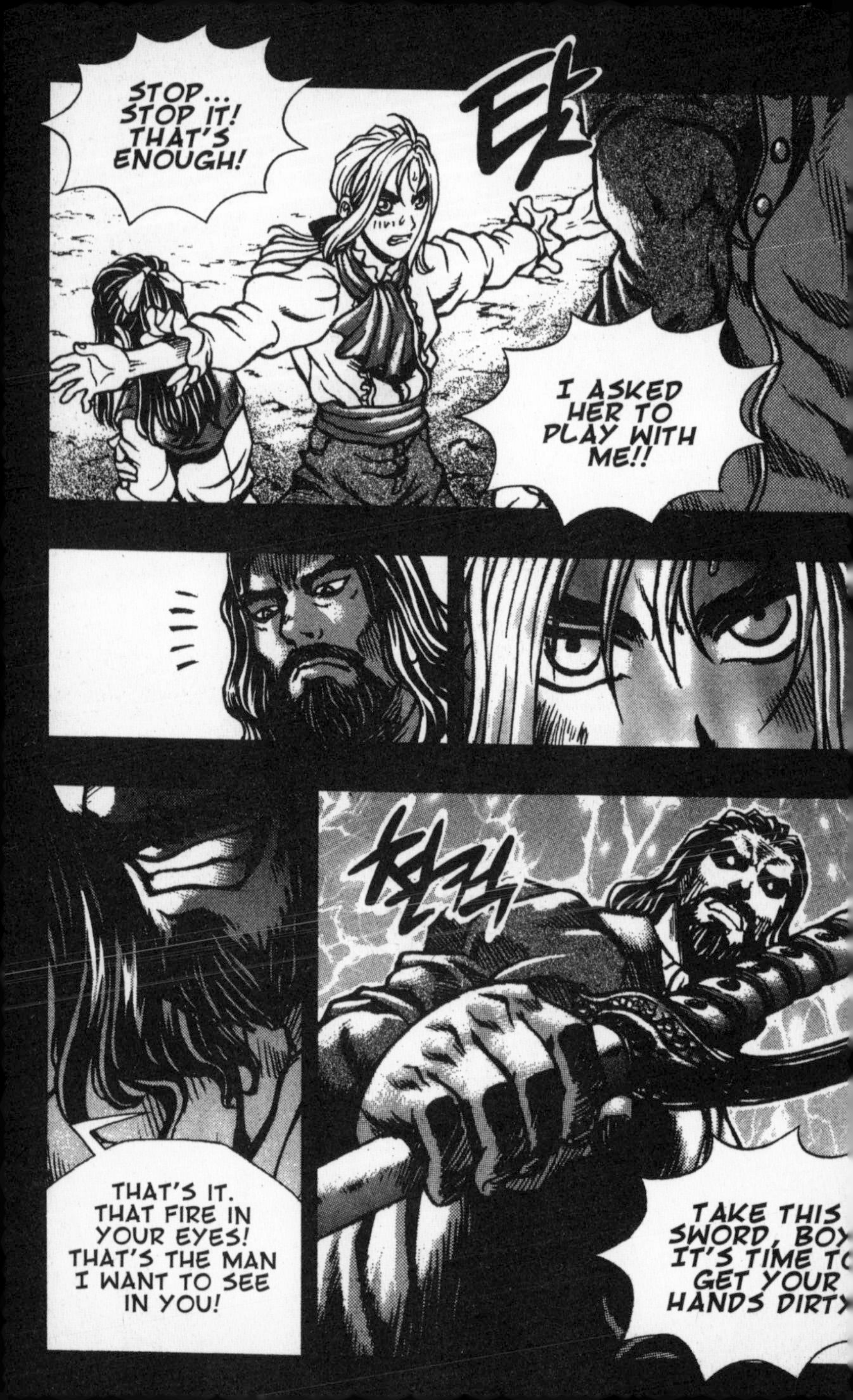
STOP... STOP IT! THAT'S ENOUGH!
탁
I ASKED HER TO PLAY WITH ME!!
THAT'S IT. THAT FIRE IN YOUR EYES! THAT'S THE MAN I WANT TO SEE IN YOU!
TAKE THIS SWORD, BOY IT'S TIME TO GET YOUR HANDS DIRTY

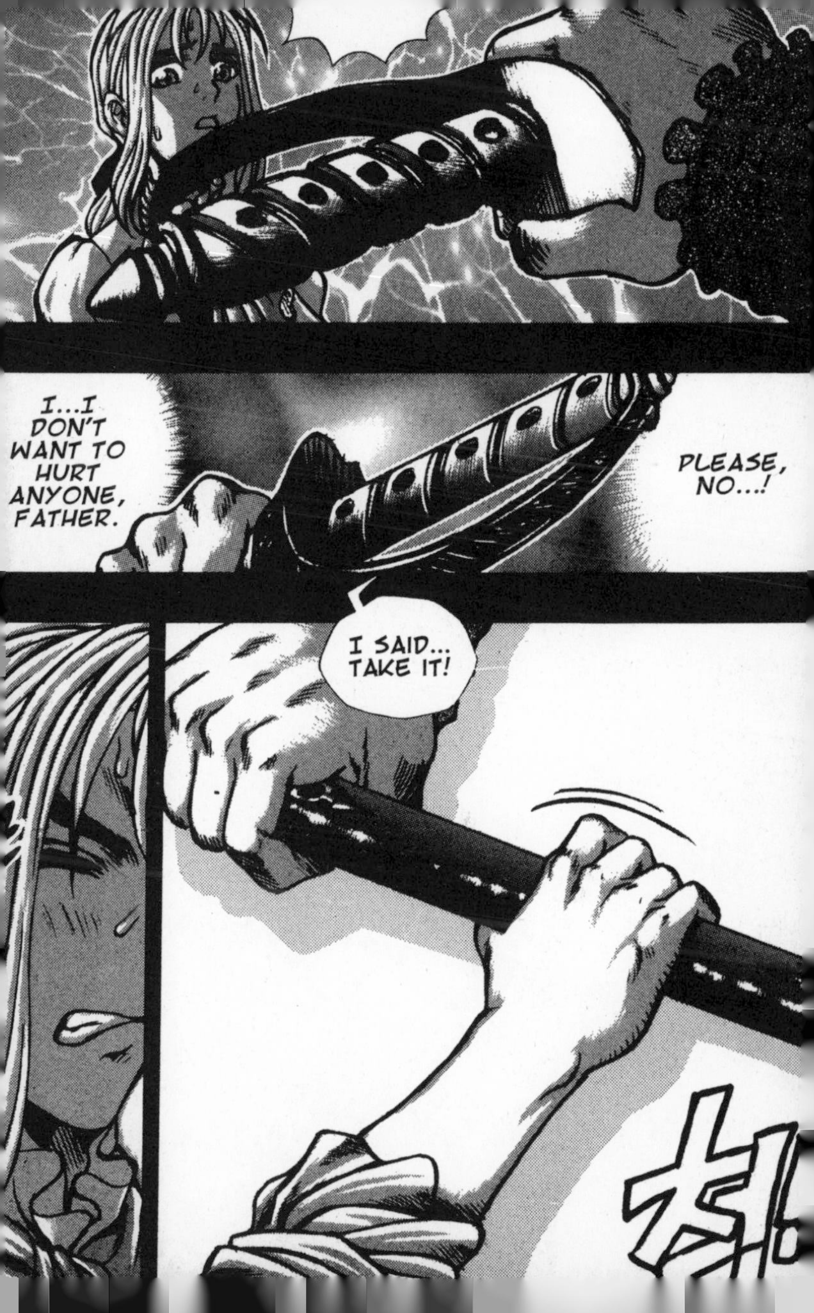
PLEASE, NO...!
I...I DON'T WANT TO HURT ANYONE, FATHER.
I SAID... TAKE IT!

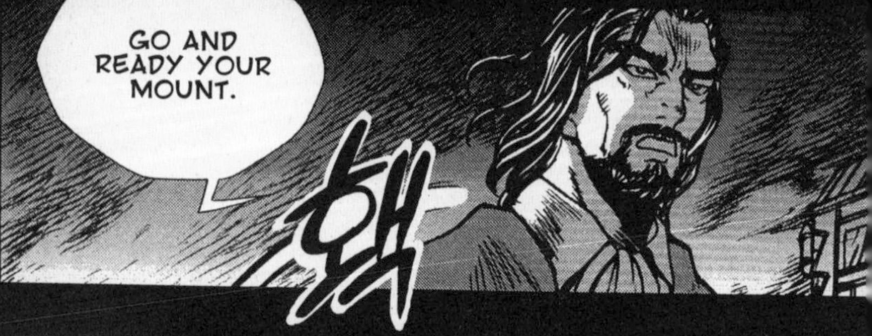
GO AND READY YOUR MOUNT.

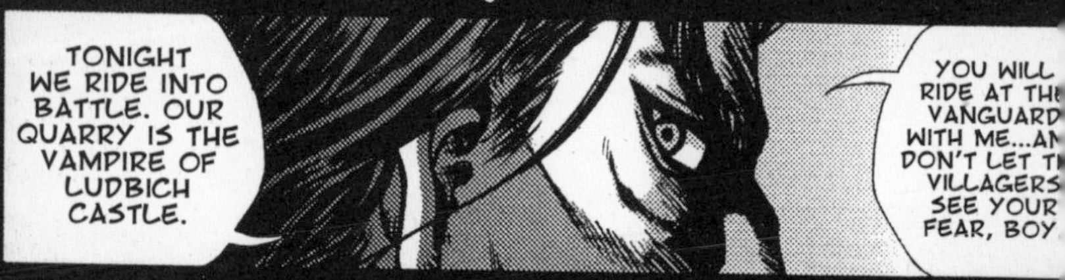
TONIGHT WE RIDE INTO BATTLE. OUR QUARRY IS THE VAMPIRE OF LUDBICH CASTLE.
YOU WILL RIDE AT TH VANGUARD WITH ME...AN DON'T LET T VILLAGERS SEE YOUR FEAR, BOY.

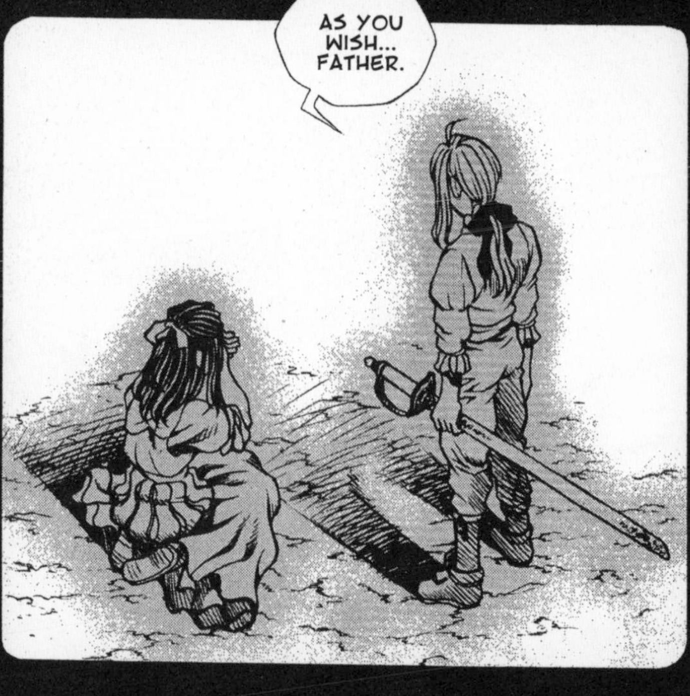
AS YOU WISH... FATHER.

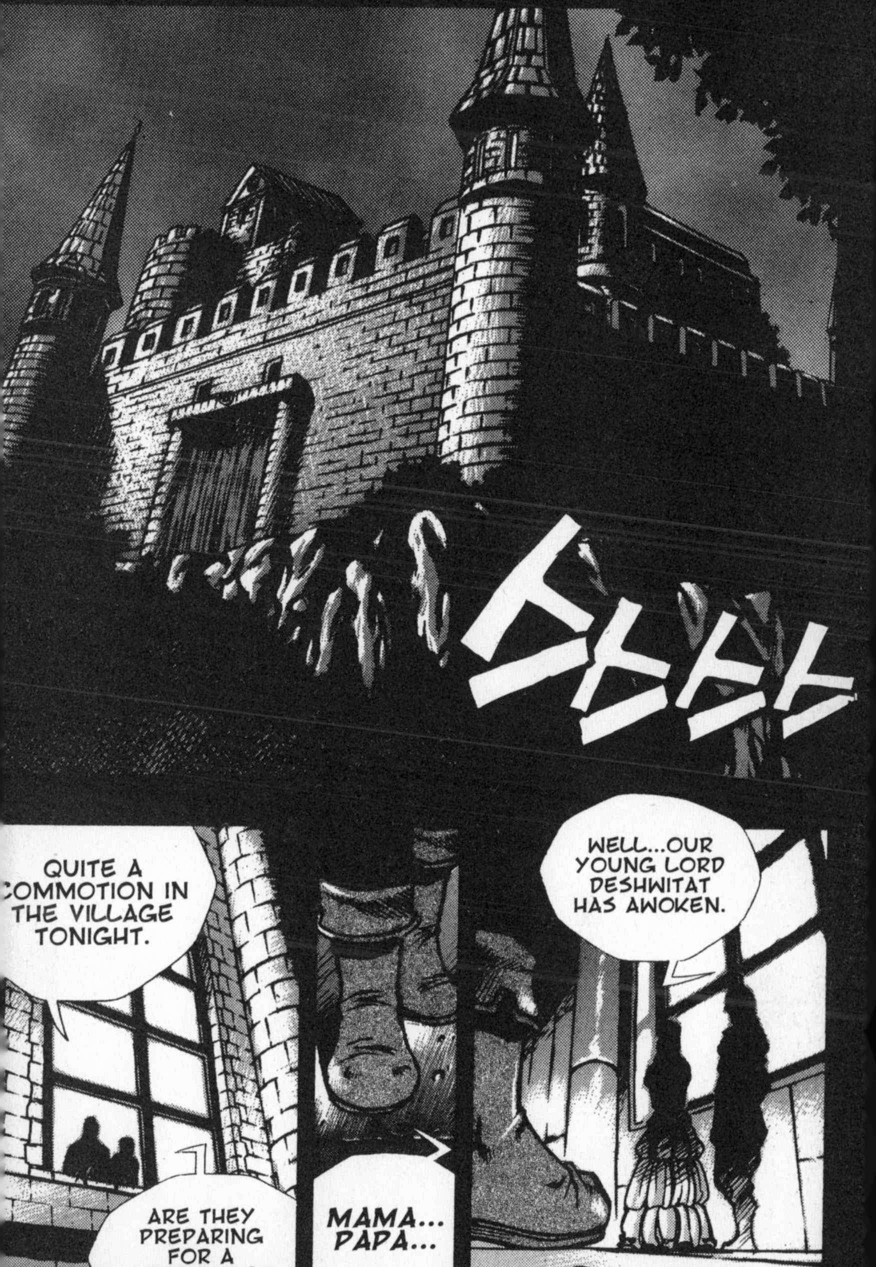
トトトト
QUITE A COMMOTION IN THE VILLAGE TONIGHT.
ARE THEY PREPARING FOR A FESTIVAL?
MAMA... PAPA...
WELL...OUR YOUNG LORD DESHWITAT HAS AWOKEN.

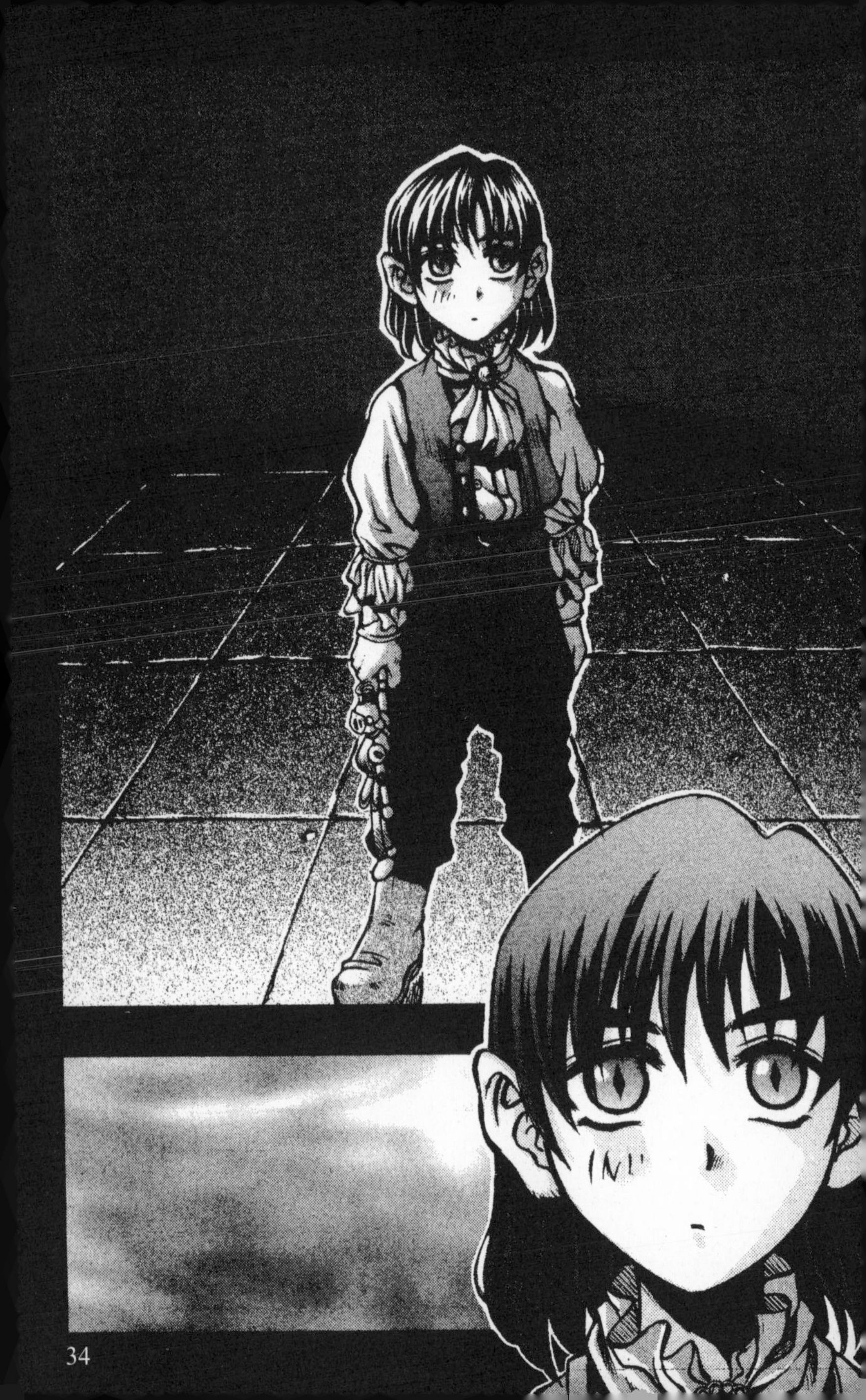

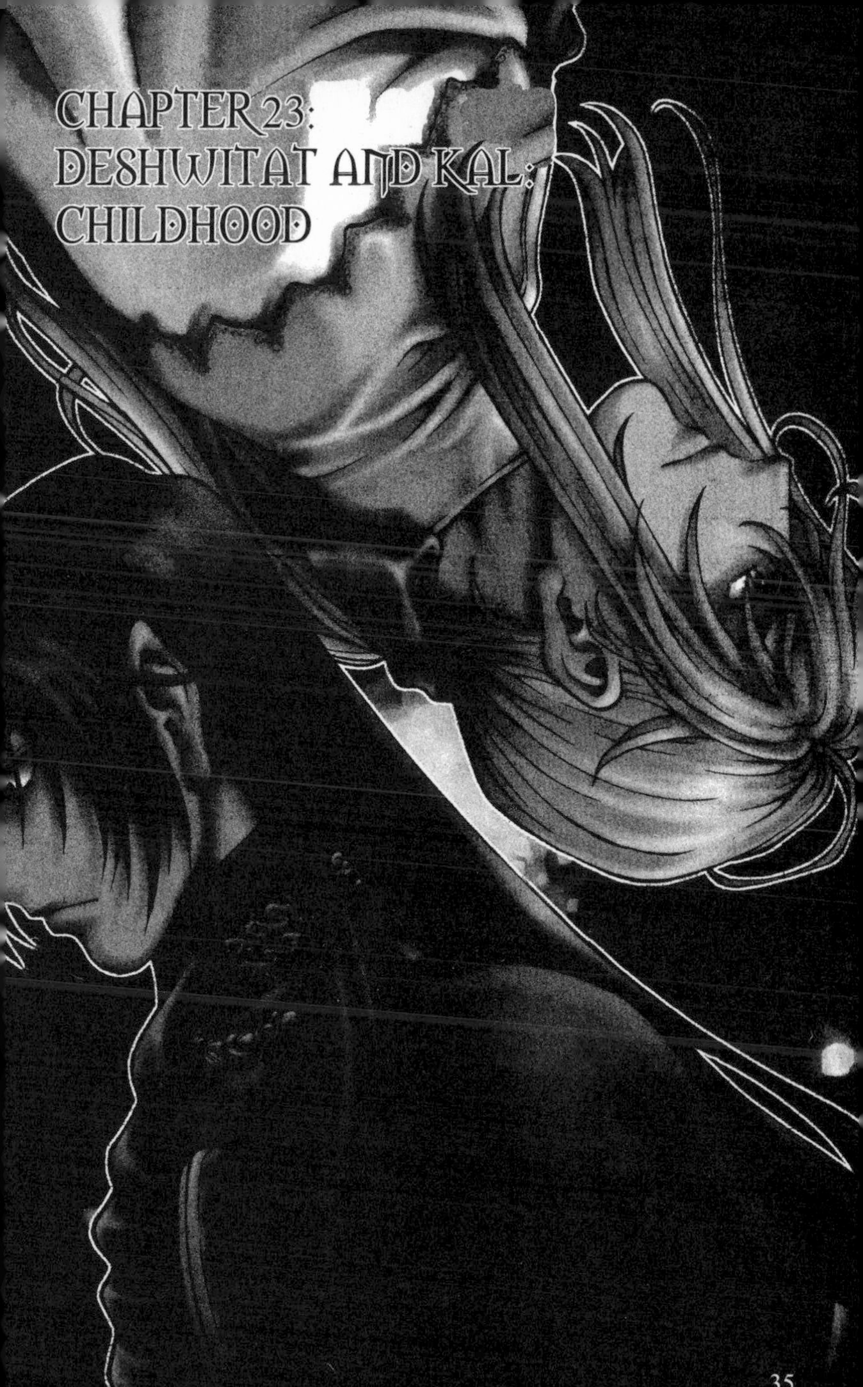
CHAPTER 23:
DESHWITAT AND KAL:
CHILDHOOD

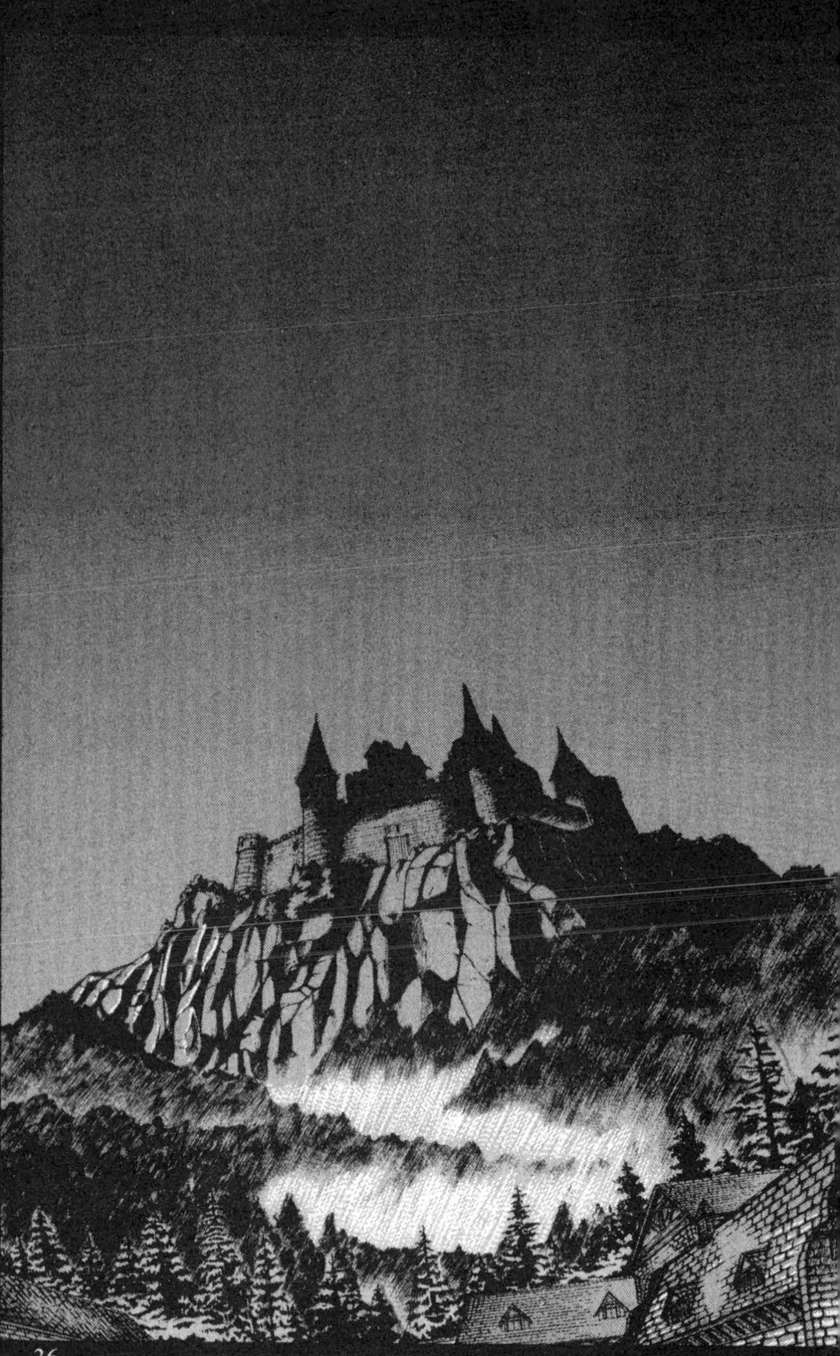

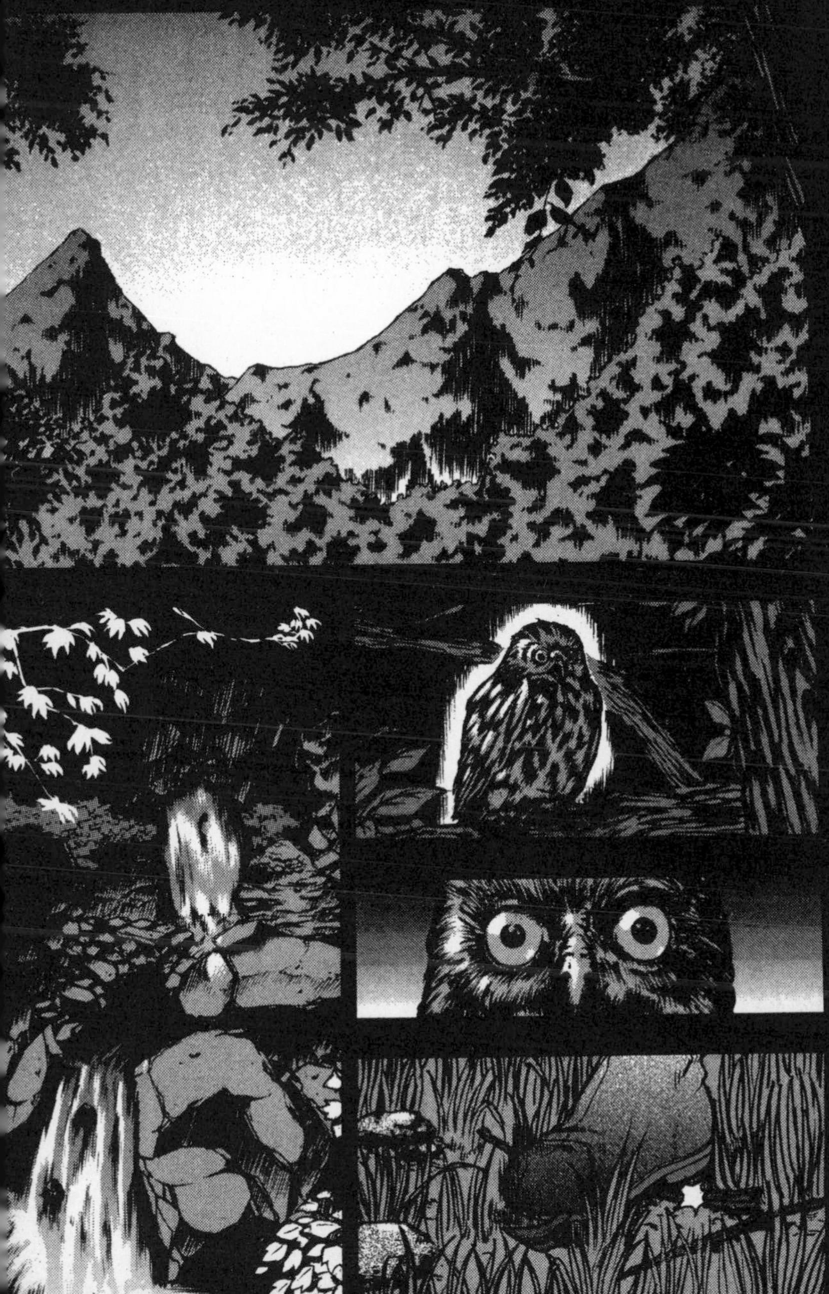

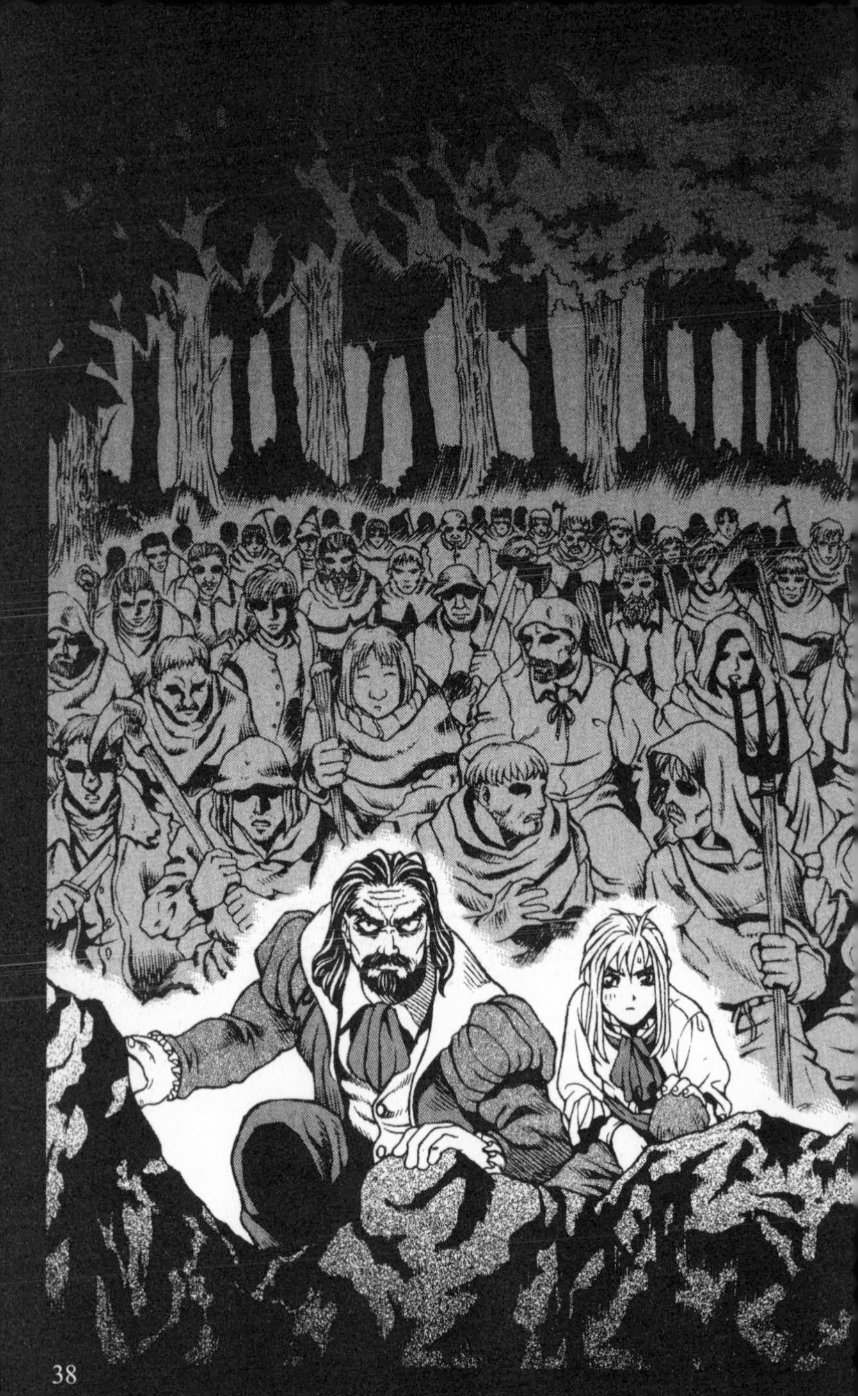

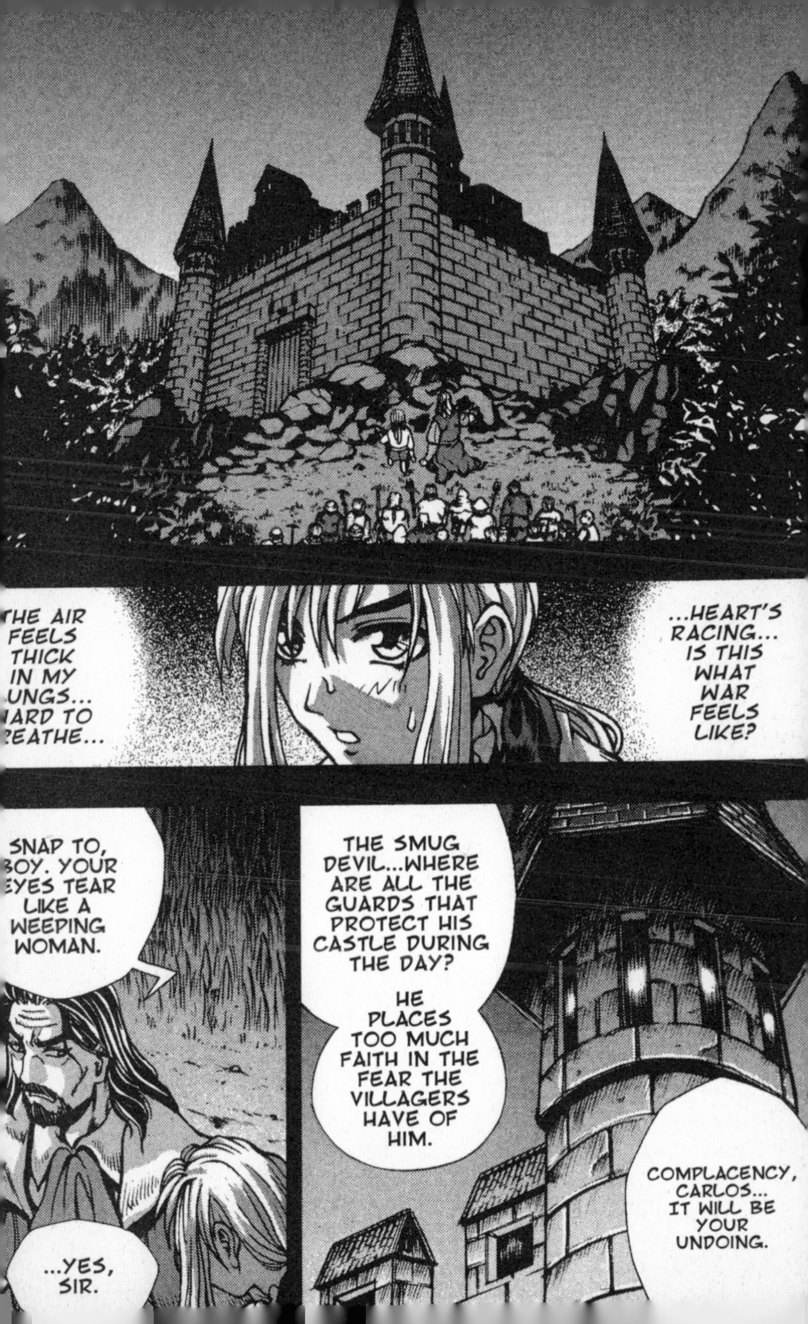
THE AIR FEELS THICK IN MY UNGS... ARD TO EATHE...
...HEART'S RACING... IS THIS WHAT WAR FEELS LIKE?
SNAP TO, BOY. YOUR EYES TEAR LIKE A WEEPING WOMAN.
...YES, SIR.
THE SMUG DEVIL...WHERE ARE ALL THE GUARDS THAT PROTECT HIS CASTLE DURING THE DAY?
HE PLACES TOO MUCH FAITH IN THE FEAR THE VILLAGERS HAVE OF HIM.
COMPLACENCY, CARLOS... IT WILL BE YOUR UNDOING.

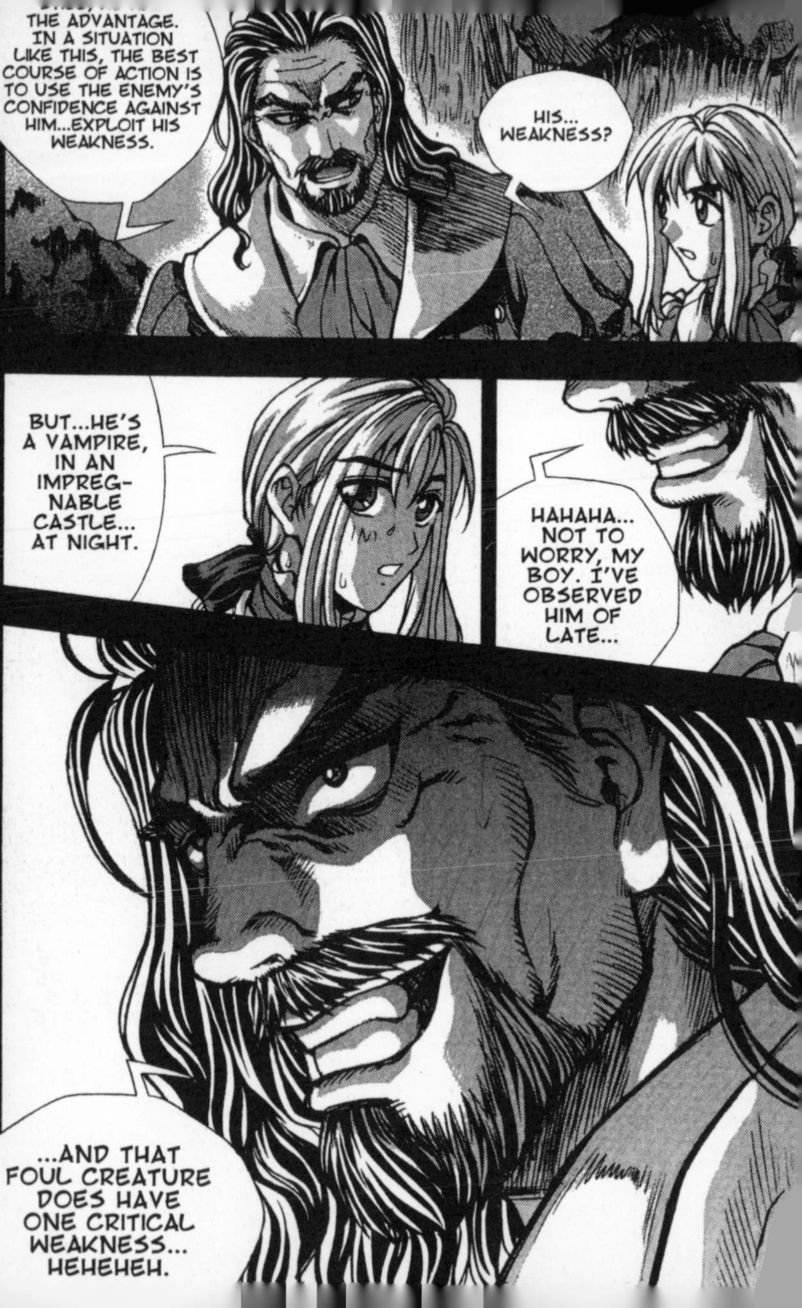
THE ADVANTAGE. IN A SITUATION LIKE THIS, THE BEST COURSE OF ACTION IS TO USE THE ENEMY'S CONFIDENCE AGAINST HIM...EXPLOIT HIS WEAKNESS.
HIS... WEAKNESS?
BUT...HE'S A VAMPIRE, IN AN IMPREG-NABLE CASTLE... AT NIGHT.
HAHAHA... NOT TO WORRY, MY BOY. I'VE OBSERVED HIM OF LATE...
...AND THAT FOUL CREATURE DOES HAVE ONE CRITICAL WEAKNESS... HEHEHEH.

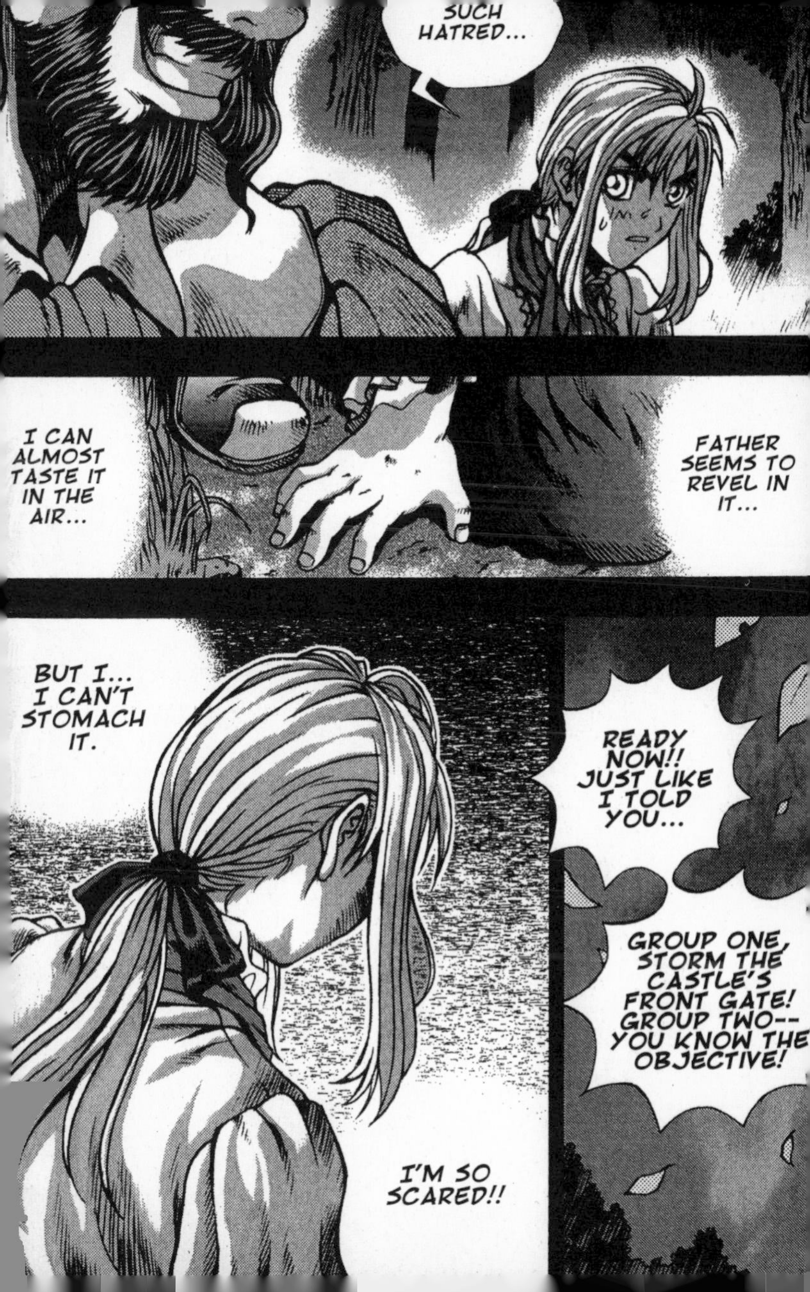
SUCH HATRED...
I CAN ALMOST TASTE IT IN THE AIR...
FATHER SEEMS TO REVEL IN IT...
BUT I... I CAN'T STOMACH IT.
I'M SO SCARED!!
READY NOW!! JUST LIKE I TOLD YOU...
GROUP ONE, STORM THE CASTLE'S FRONT GATE! GROUP TWO-- YOU KNOW THE OBJECTIVE!

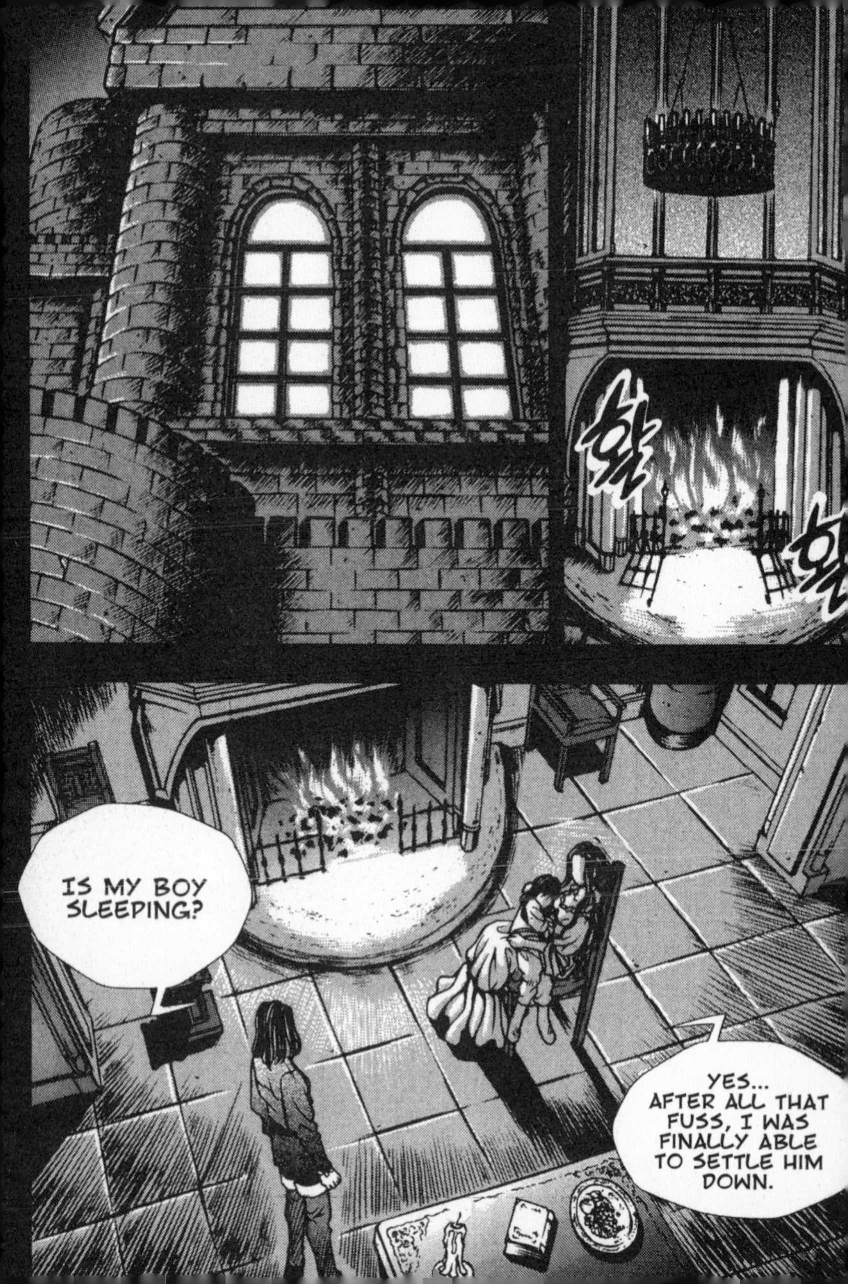
IS MY BOY SLEEPING?
YES... AFTER ALL THAT FUSS, I WAS FINALLY ABLE TO SETTLE HIM DOWN.

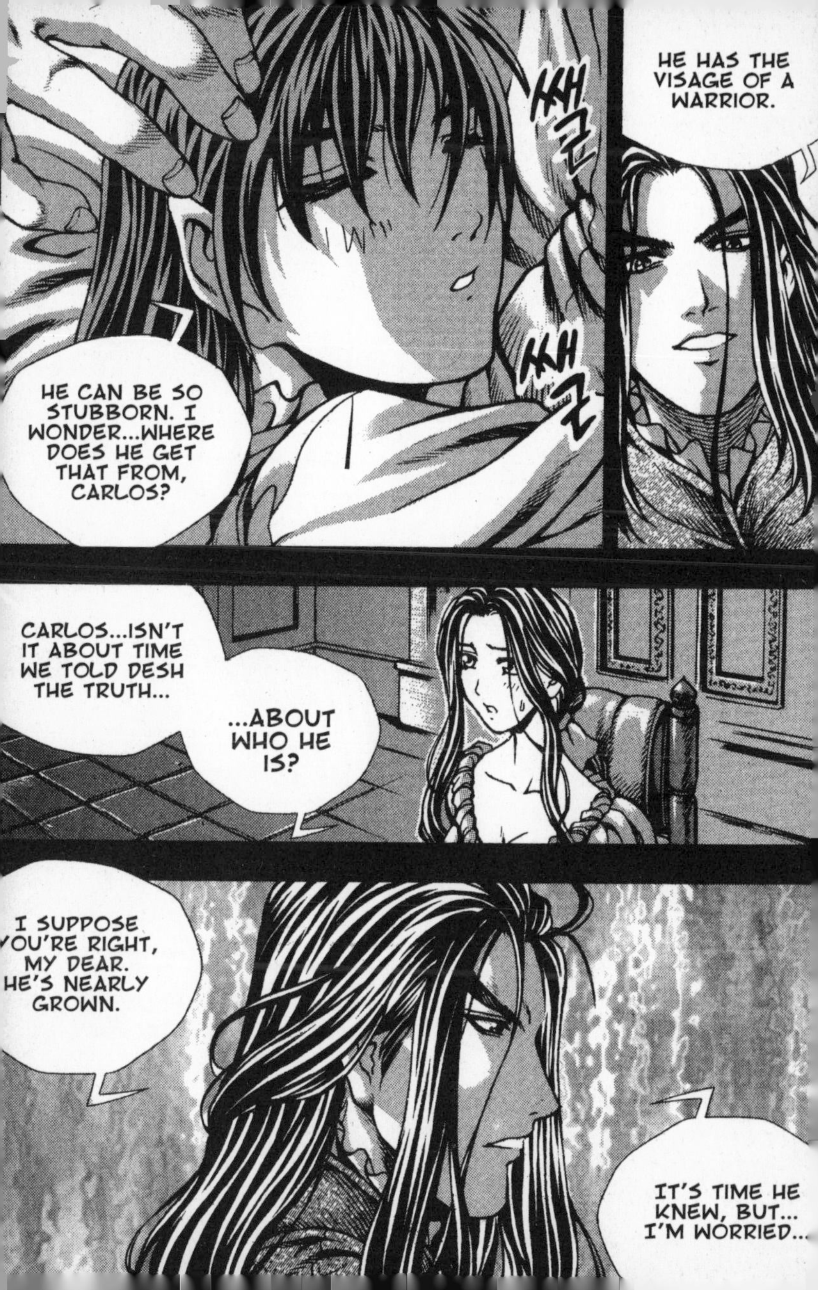
HE HAS THE VISAGE OF A WARRIOR.
HE CAN BE SO STUBBORN. I WONDER...WHERE DOES HE GET THAT FROM, CARLOS?
CARLOS...ISN'T IT ABOUT TIME WE TOLD DESH THE TRUTH...
...ABOUT WHO HE IS?
I SUPPOSE YOU'RE RIGHT, MY DEAR. HE'S NEARLY GROWN.
IT'S TIME HE KNEW, BUT... I'M WORRIED...

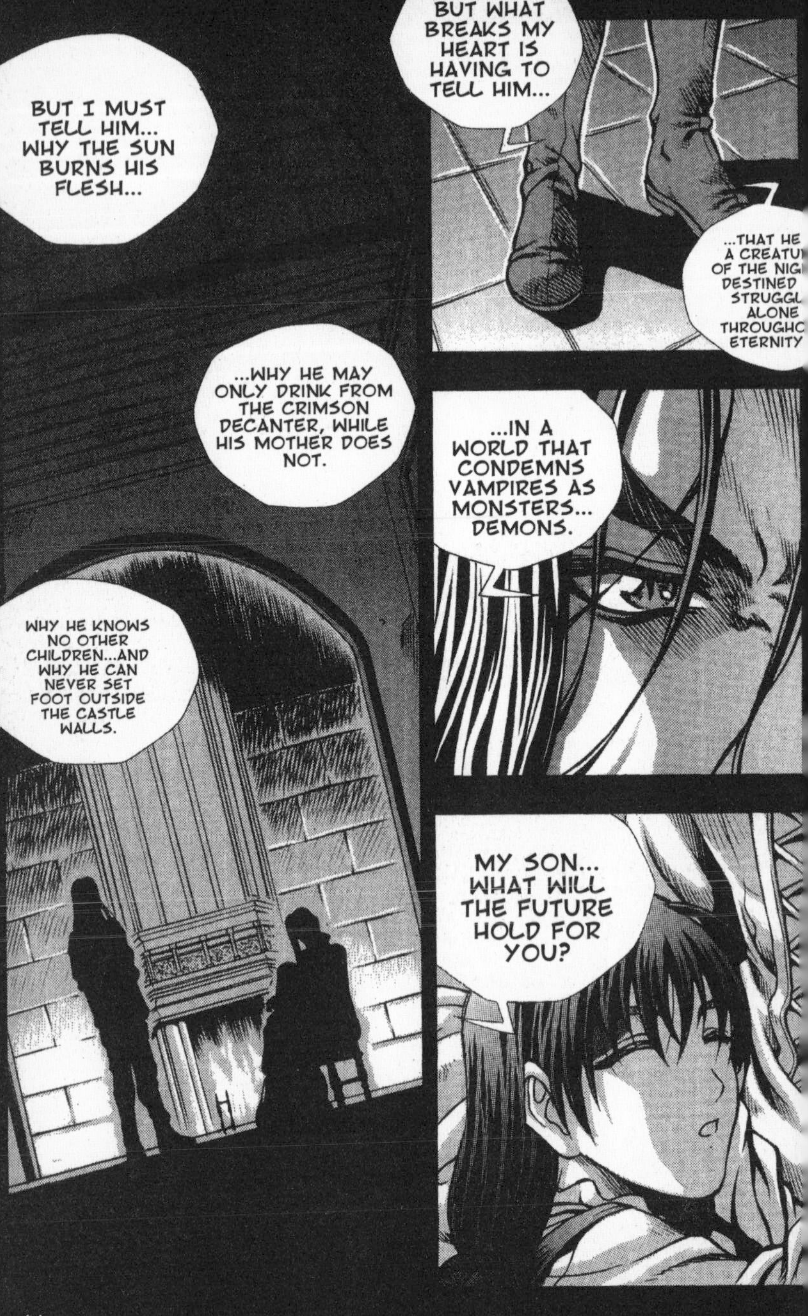
BUT I MUST TELL HIM... WHY THE SUN BURNS HIS FLESH...
...WHY HE MAY ONLY DRINK FROM THE CRIMSON DECANTER, WHILE HIS MOTHER DOES NOT.
WHY HE KNOWS NO OTHER CHILDREN...AND WHY HE CAN NEVER SET FOOT OUTSIDE THE CASTLE WALLS.
BUT WHAT BREAKS MY HEART IS HAVING TO TELL HIM...
...THAT HE A CREATU OF THE NIG DESTINED STRUGG ALONE THROUGHC ETERNITY
...IN A WORLD THAT CONDEMNS VAMPIRES AS MONSTERS... DEMONS.
MY SON... WHAT WILL THE FUTURE HOLD FOR YOU?

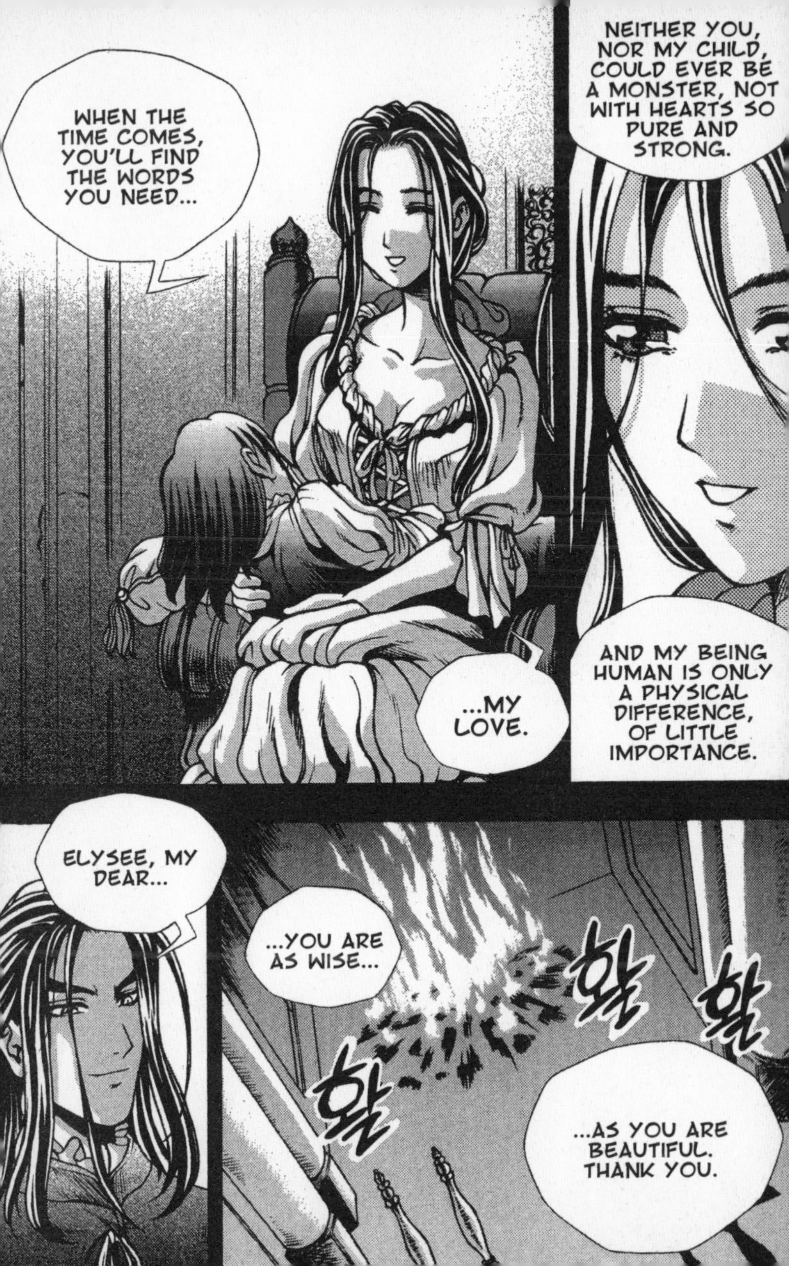
WHEN THE TIME COMES, YOU'LL FIND THE WORDS YOU NEED...
...MY LOVE.
NEITHER YOU, NOR MY CHILD, COULD EVER BE A MONSTER, NOT WITH HEARTS SO PURE AND STRONG.
AND MY BEING HUMAN IS ONLY A PHYSICAL DIFFERENCE, OF LITTLE IMPORTANCE.
ELYSEE, MY DEAR...
...YOU ARE AS WISE...
활
활
활
...AS YOU ARE BEAUTIFUL. THANK YOU.

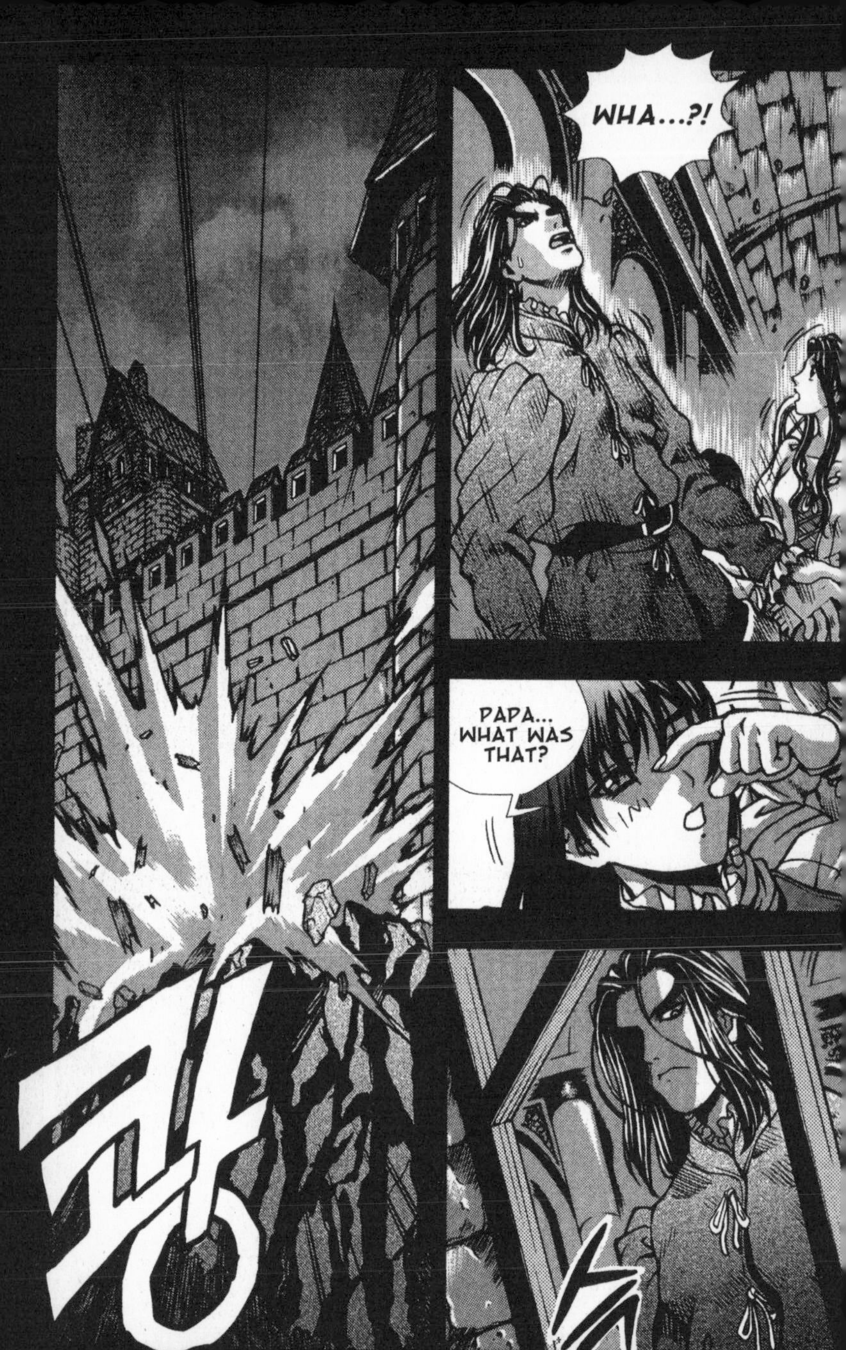
WHA...?!
PAPA... WHAT WAS THAT?

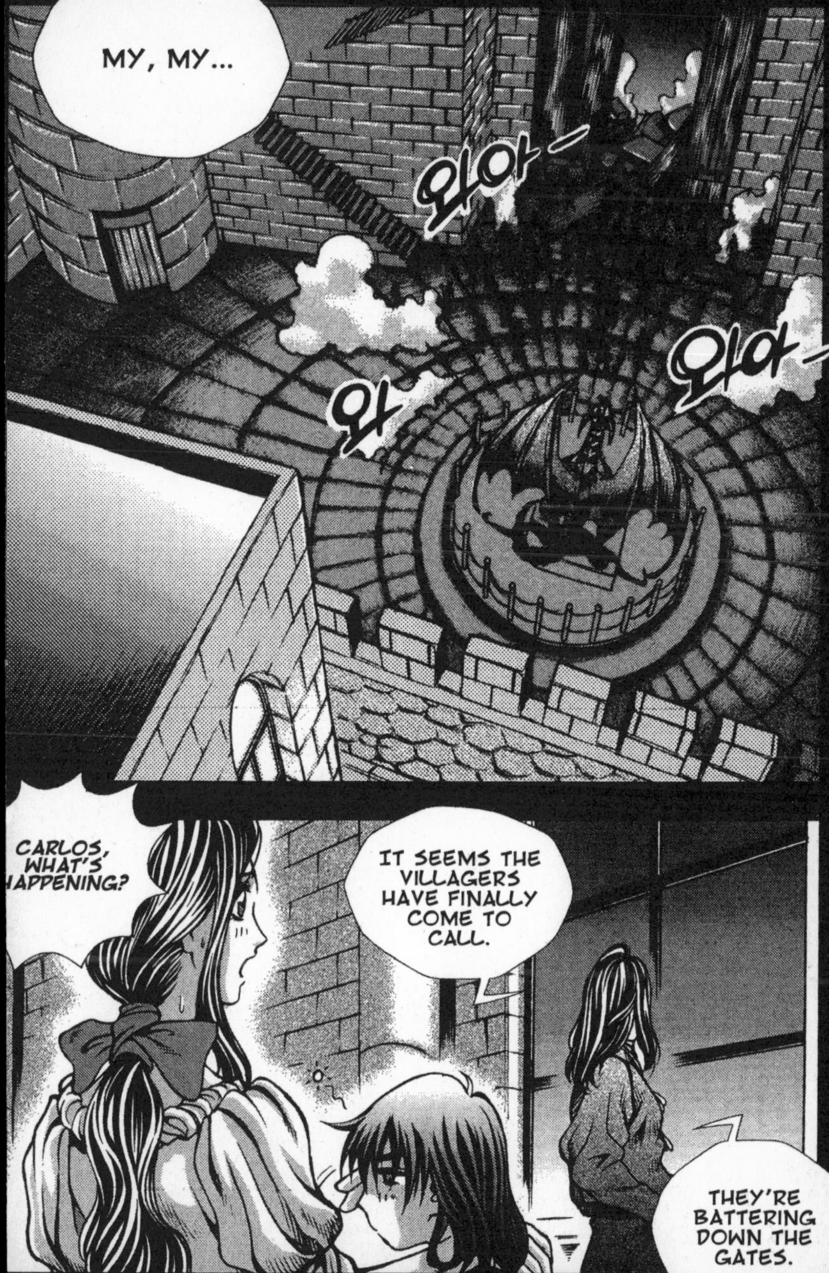
MY, MY...
와아-
와
와아-
CARLOS, WHAT'S HAPPENING?
IT SEEMS THE VILLAGERS HAVE FINALLY COME TO CALL.
THEY'RE BATTERING DOWN THE GATES.

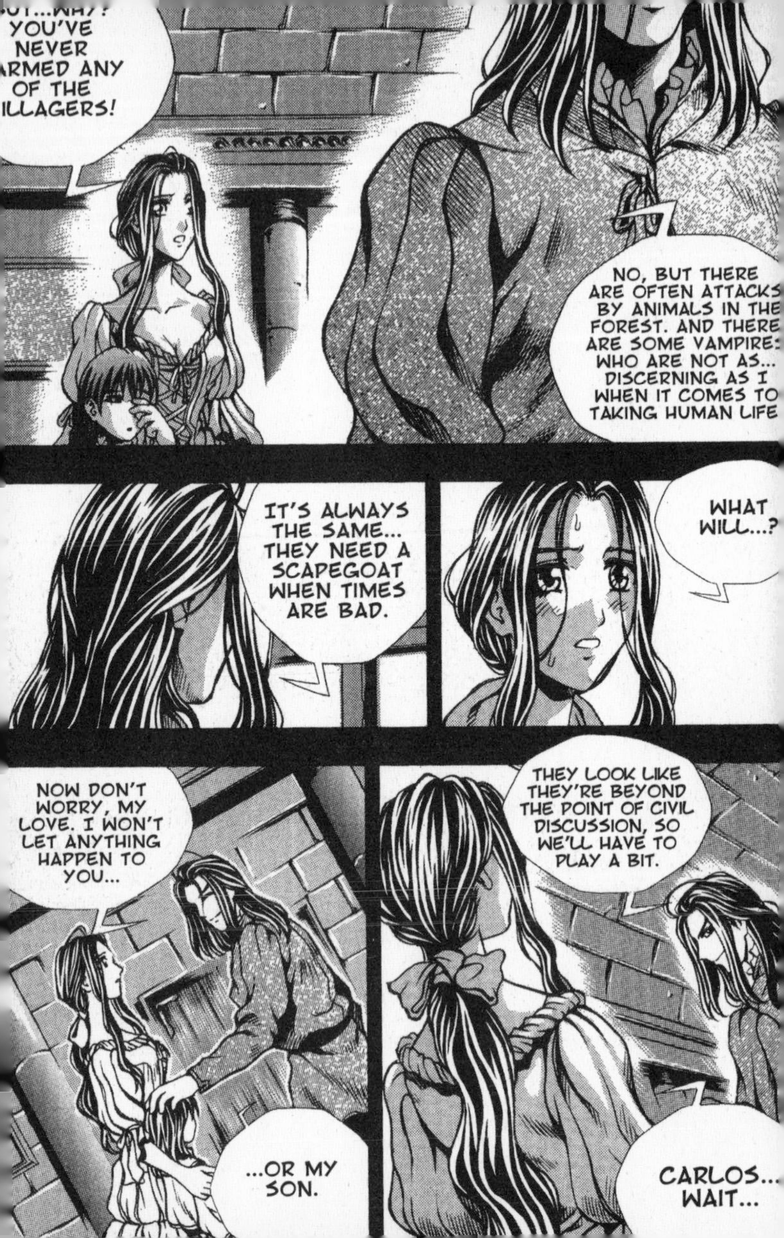
YOU'VE NEVER ARMED ANY OF THE ILLAGERS!
NO, BUT THERE ARE OFTEN ATTACKS BY ANIMALS IN THE FOREST. AND THERE ARE SOME VAMPIRE WHO ARE NOT AS... DISCERNING AS I WHEN IT COMES TO TAKING HUMAN LIFE
IT'S ALWAYS THE SAME... THEY NEED A SCAPEGOAT WHEN TIMES ARE BAD.
WHAT WILL...?
NOW DON'T WORRY, MY LOVE. I WON'T LET ANYTHING HAPPEN TO YOU...
...OR MY SON.
THEY LOOK LIKE THEY'RE BEYOND THE POINT OF CIVIL DISCUSSION, SO WE'LL HAVE TO PLAY A BIT.
CARLOS... WAIT...

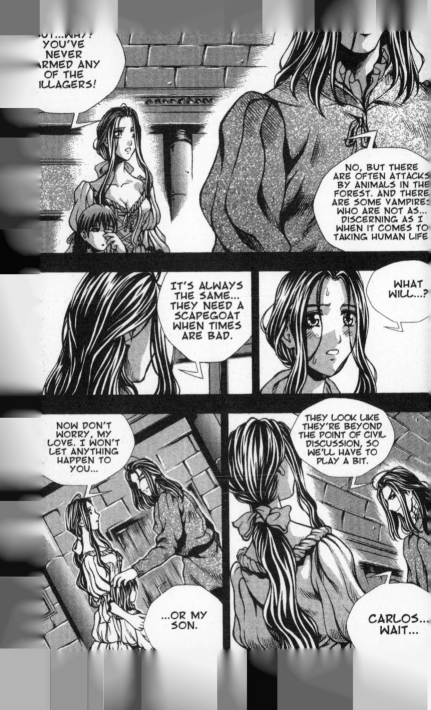

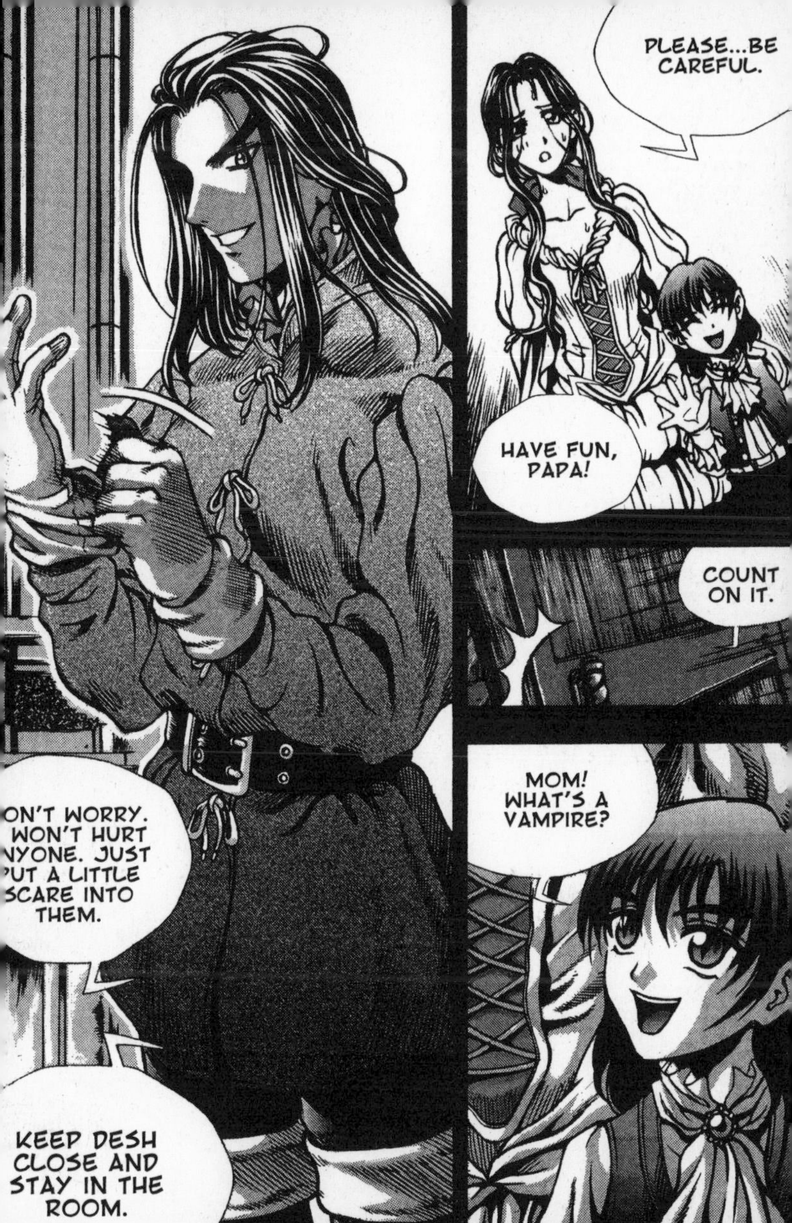
PLEASE...BE CAREFUL.
HAVE FUN, PAPA!
COUNT ON IT.
MOM! WHAT'S A VAMPIRE?
ON'T WORRY. WON'T HURT NYONE. JUST PUT A LITTLE SCARE INTO THEM.
KEEP DESH CLOSE AND STAY IN THE ROOM.

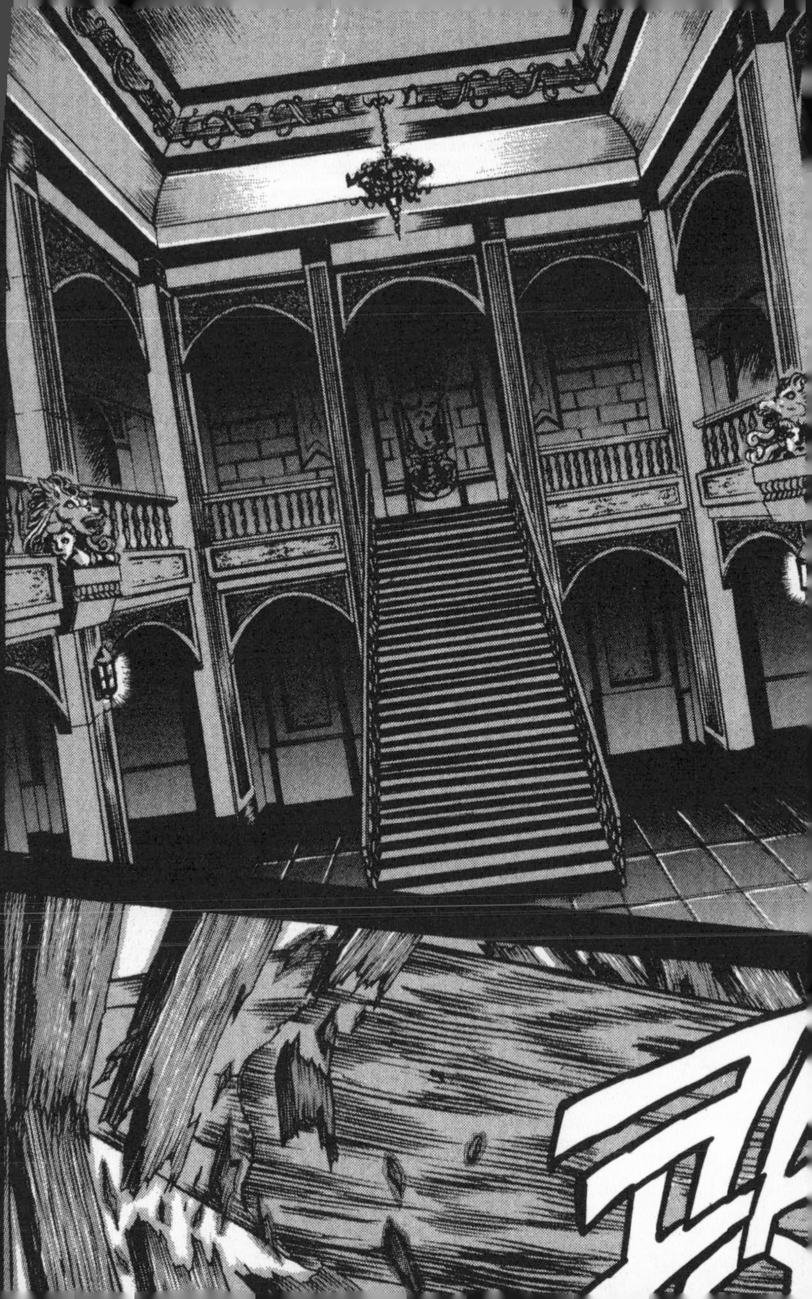

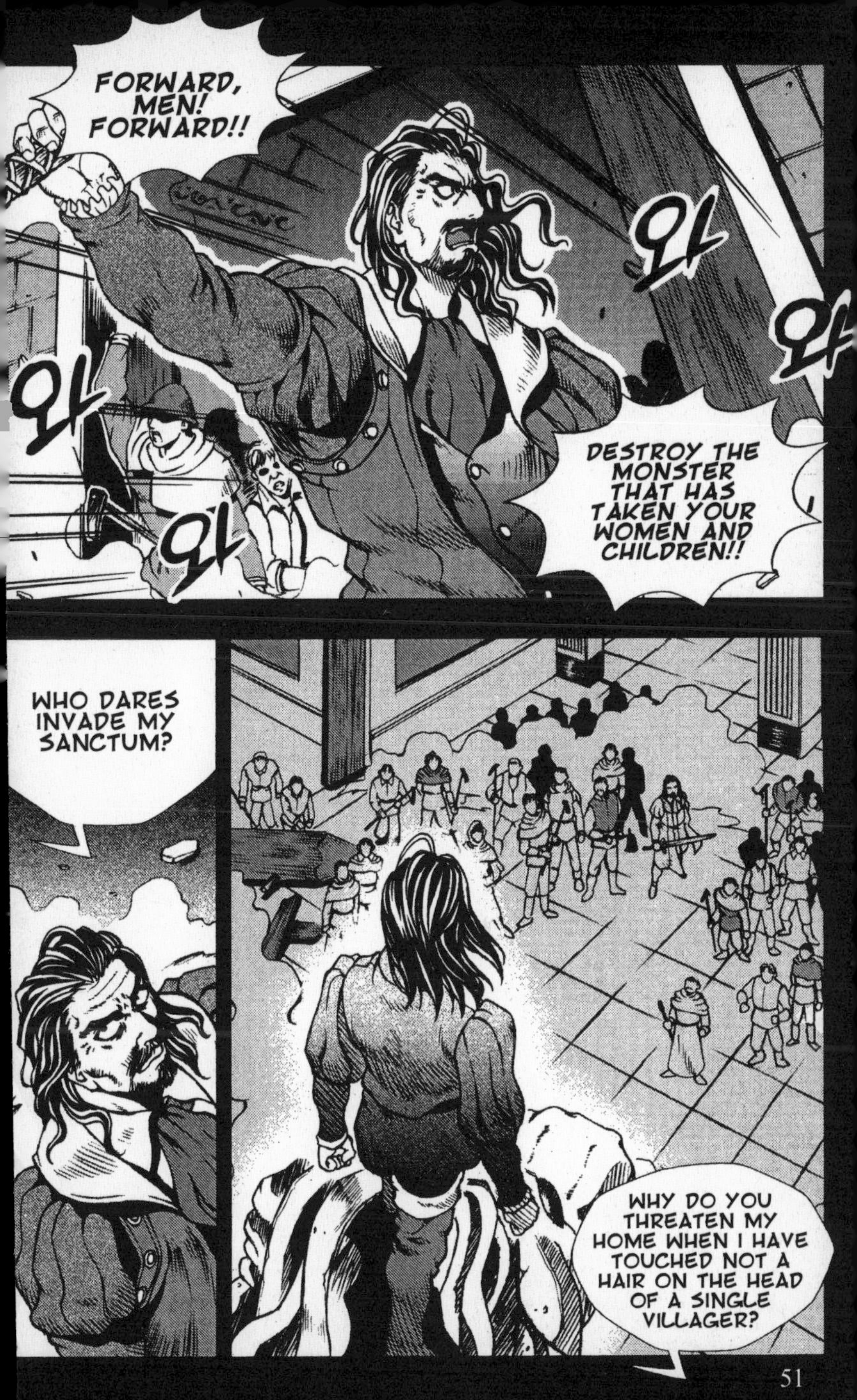
FORWARD, MEN! FORWARD!!
DESTROY THE MONSTER THAT HAS TAKEN YOUR WOMEN AND CHILDREN!!
WHO DARES INVADE MY SANCTUM?
WHY DO YOU THREATEN MY HOME WHEN I HAVE TOUCHED NOT A HAIR ON THE HEAD OF A SINGLE VILLAGER?

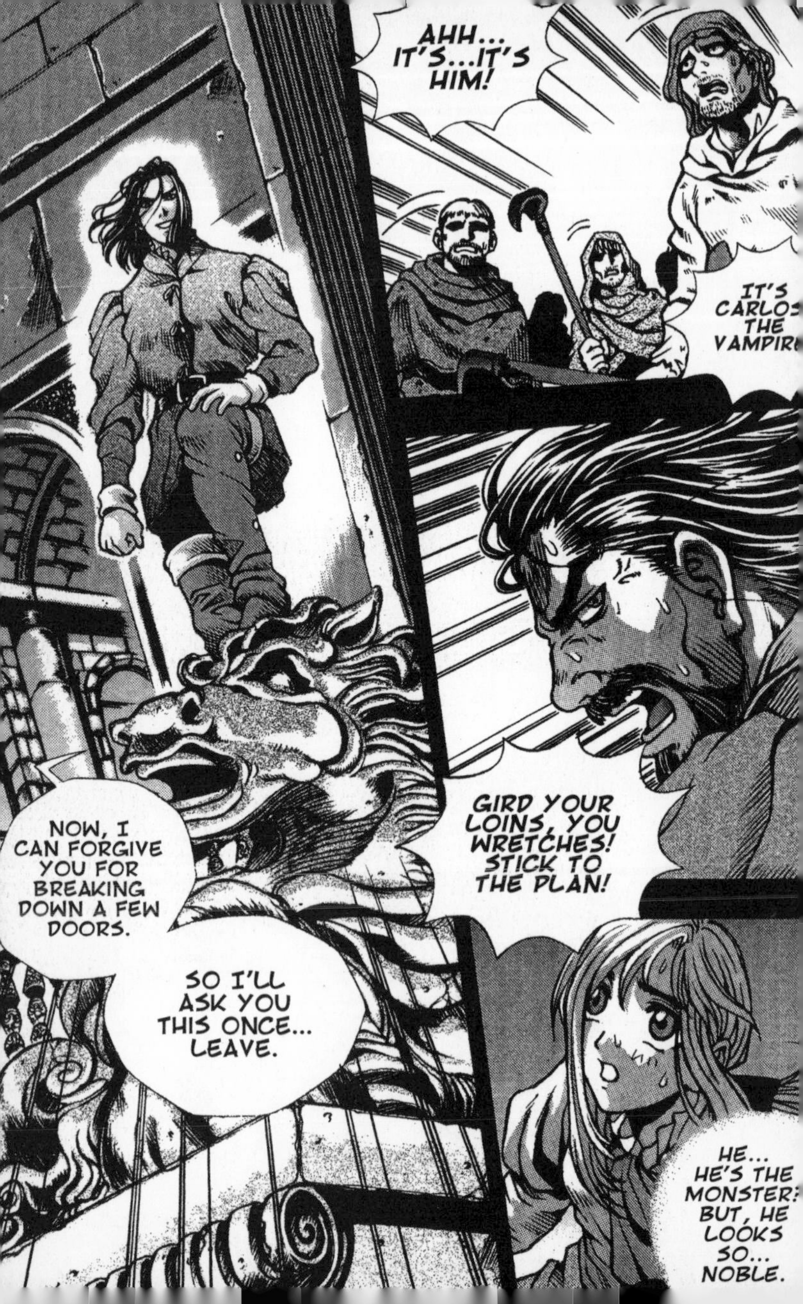
AHH... IT'S...IT'S HIM!
IT'S CARLOS THE VAMPIR
GIRD YOUR LOINS, YOU WRETCHES! STICK TO THE PLAN!
HE... HE'S THE MONSTER BUT, HE LOOKS SO... NOBLE.
NOW, I CAN FORGIVE YOU FOR BREAKING DOWN A FEW DOORS.
SO I'LL ASK YOU THIS ONCE... LEAVE.

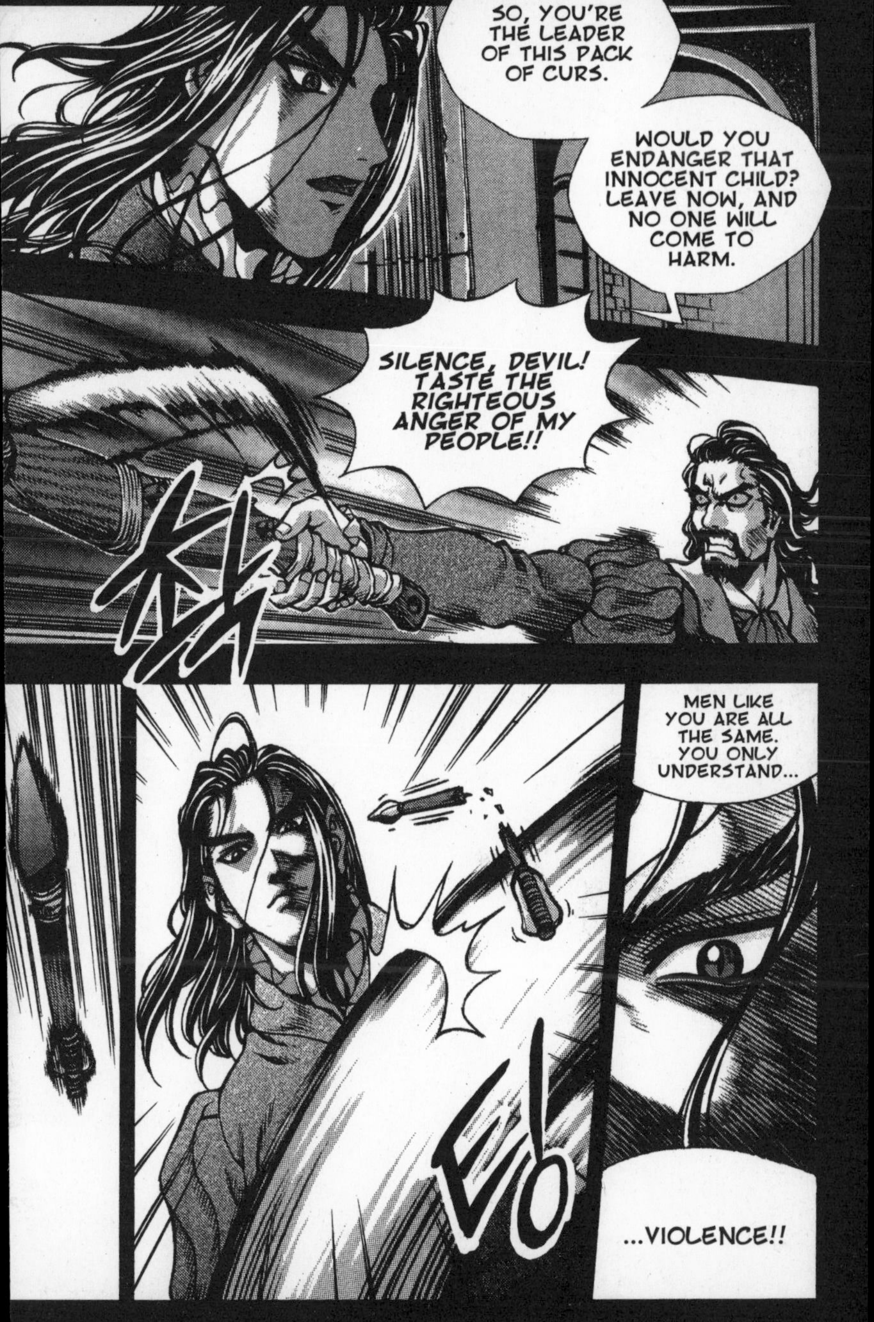
SO, YOU'RE THE LEADER OF THIS PACK OF CURS.
WOULD YOU ENDANGER THAT INNOCENT CHILD? LEAVE NOW, AND NO ONE WILL COME TO HARM.
SILENCE, DEVIL! TASTE THE RIGHTEOUS ANGER OF MY PEOPLE!!
MEN LIKE YOU ARE ALL THE SAME. YOU ONLY UNDERSTAND...
...VIOLENCE!!

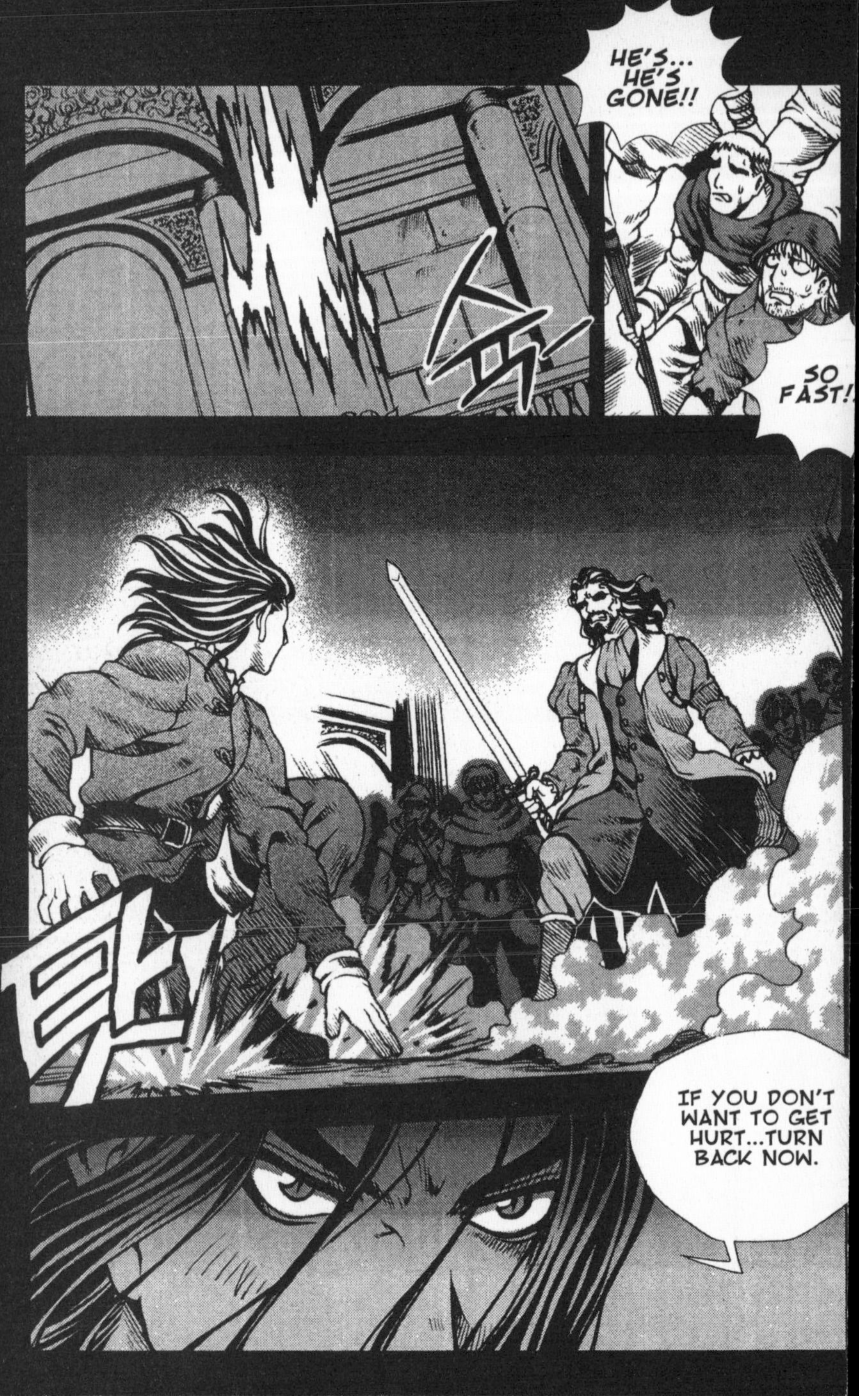
HE'S... HE'S GONE!!
SO FAST!!
IF YOU DON'T WANT TO GET HURT...TURN BACK NOW.

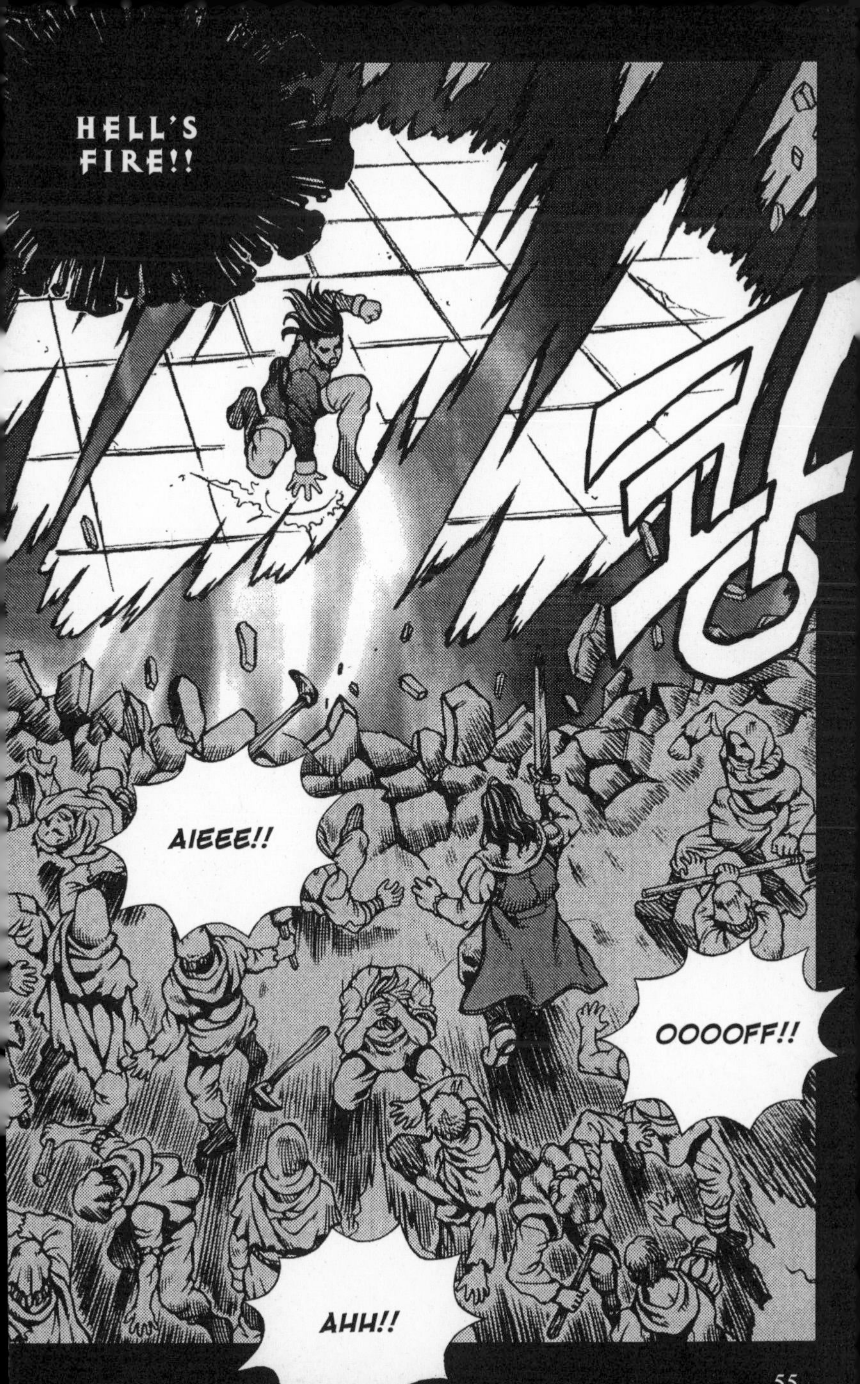
HELL'S FIRE!!
AIEEE!!
OOOOFF!!
AHH!!

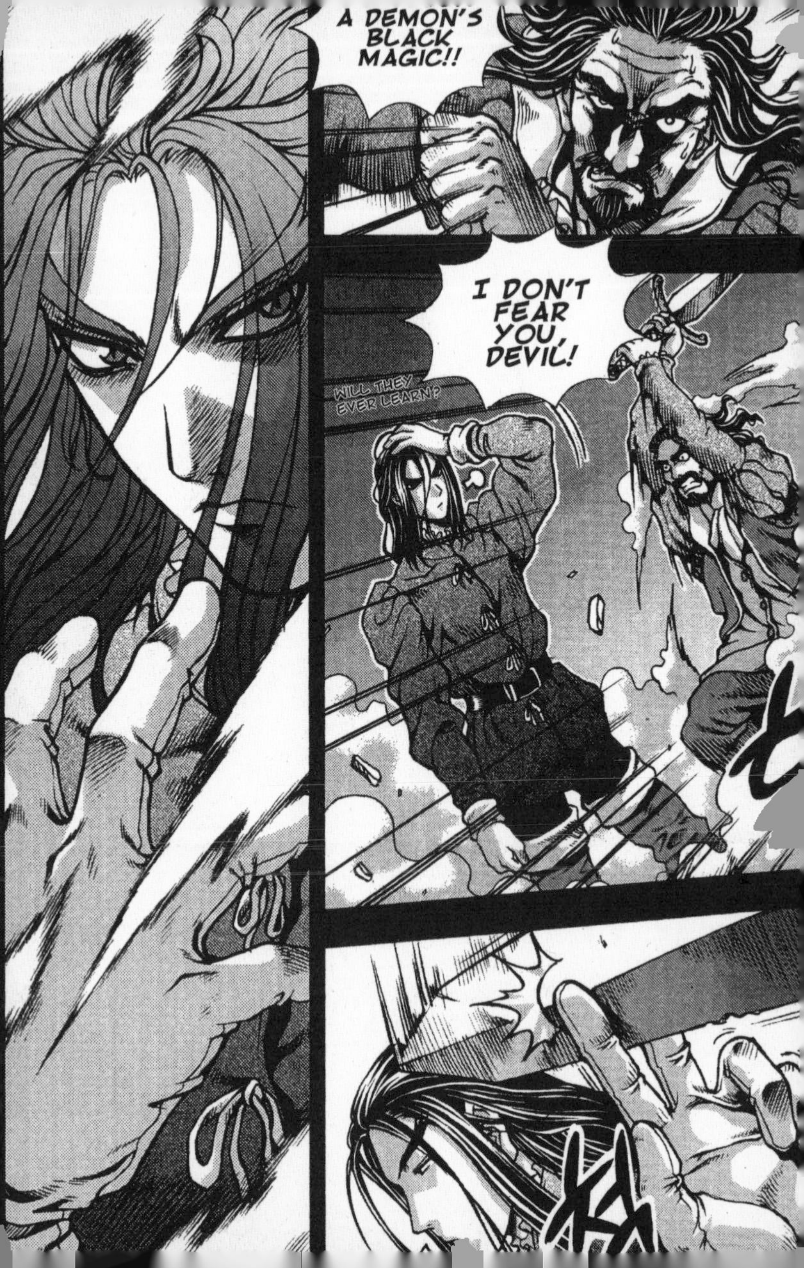
A DEMON'S BLACK MAGIC!!
I DON'T FEAR YOU, DEVIL!
WILL THEY EVER LEARN?

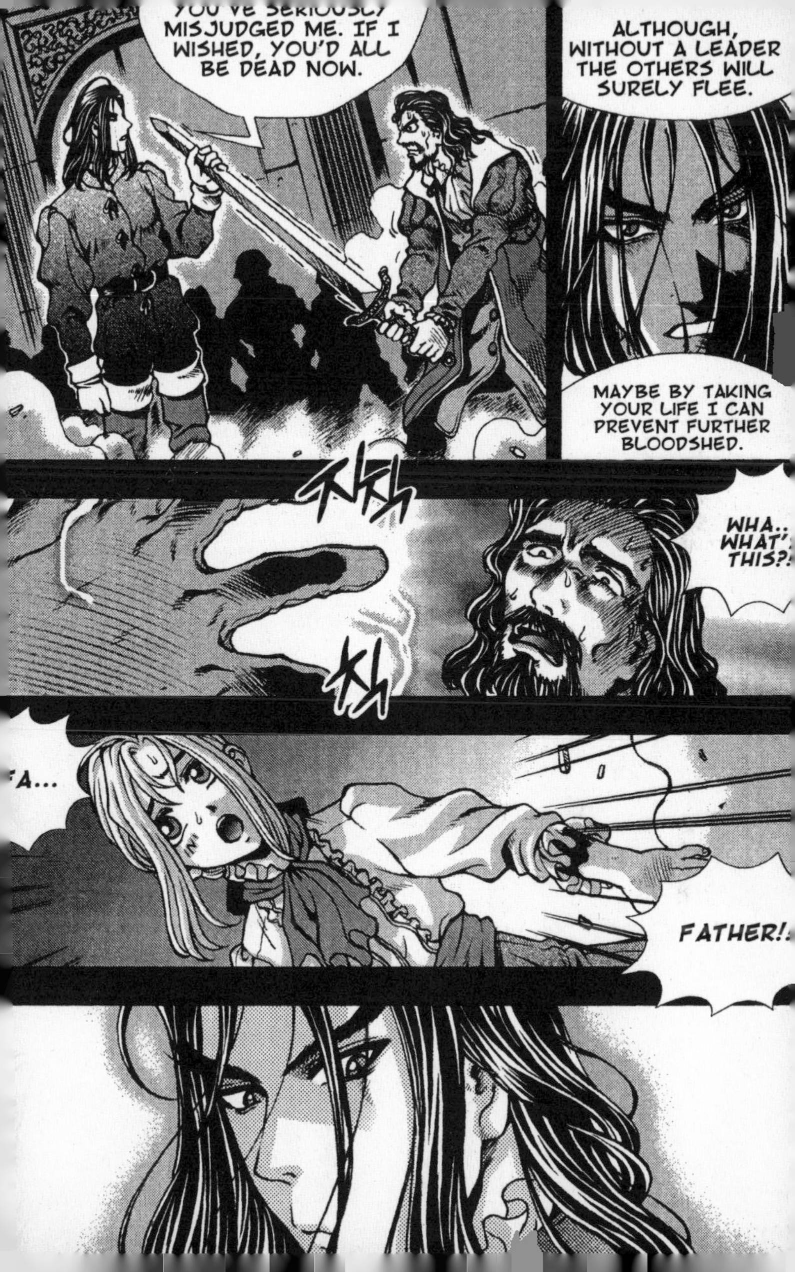
YOU'VE SERIOUSLY MISJUDGED ME. IF I WISHED, YOU'D ALL BE DEAD NOW.
ALTHOUGH, WITHOUT A LEADER THE OTHERS WILL SURELY FLEE.
MAYBE BY TAKING YOUR LIFE I CAN PREVENT FURTHER BLOODSHED.
WHA.. WHAT'S THIS?!
FA...
FATHER!!

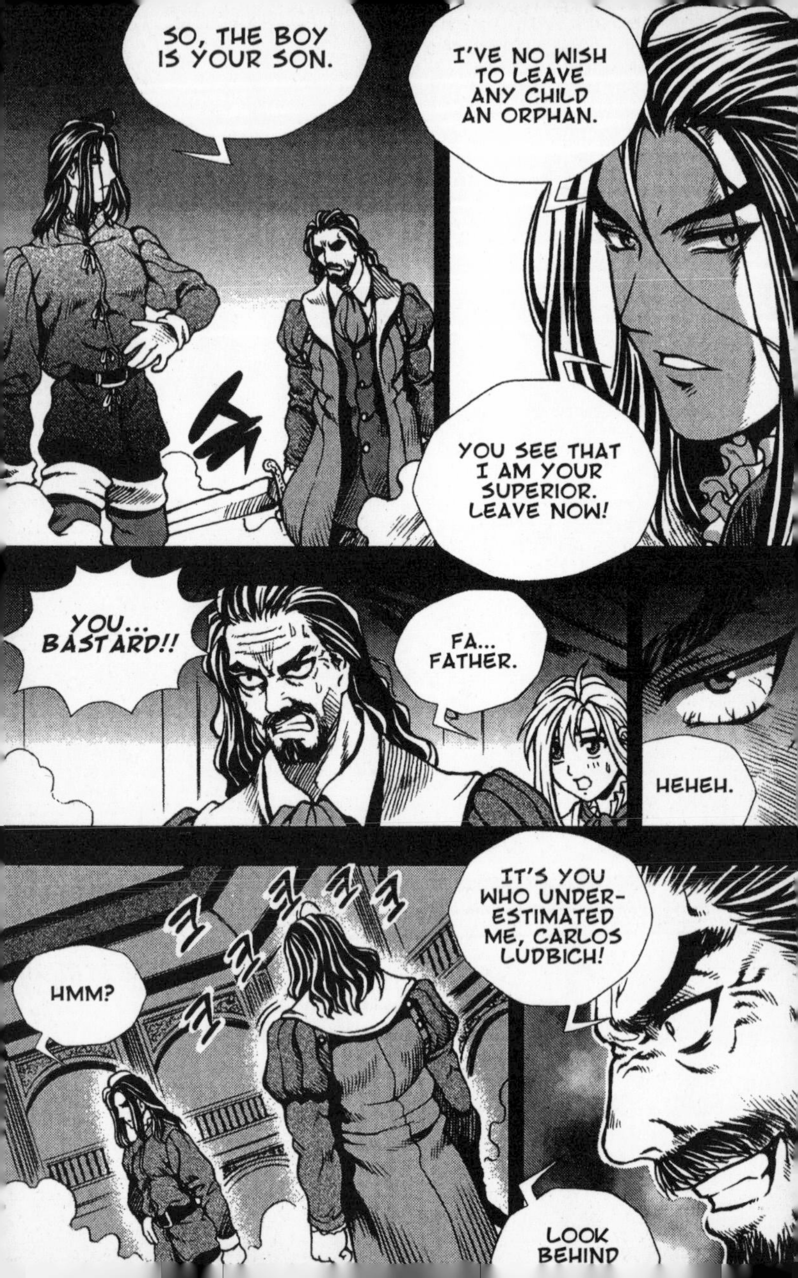
SO, THE BOY IS YOUR SON.
I'VE NO WISH TO LEAVE ANY CHILD AN ORPHAN.
YOU SEE THAT I AM YOUR SUPERIOR. LEAVE NOW!
YOU... BASTARD!!
FA... FATHER.
HEHEH.
HMM?
IT'S YOU WHO UNDER-ESTIMATED ME, CARLOS LUDBICH!
LOOK BEHIND

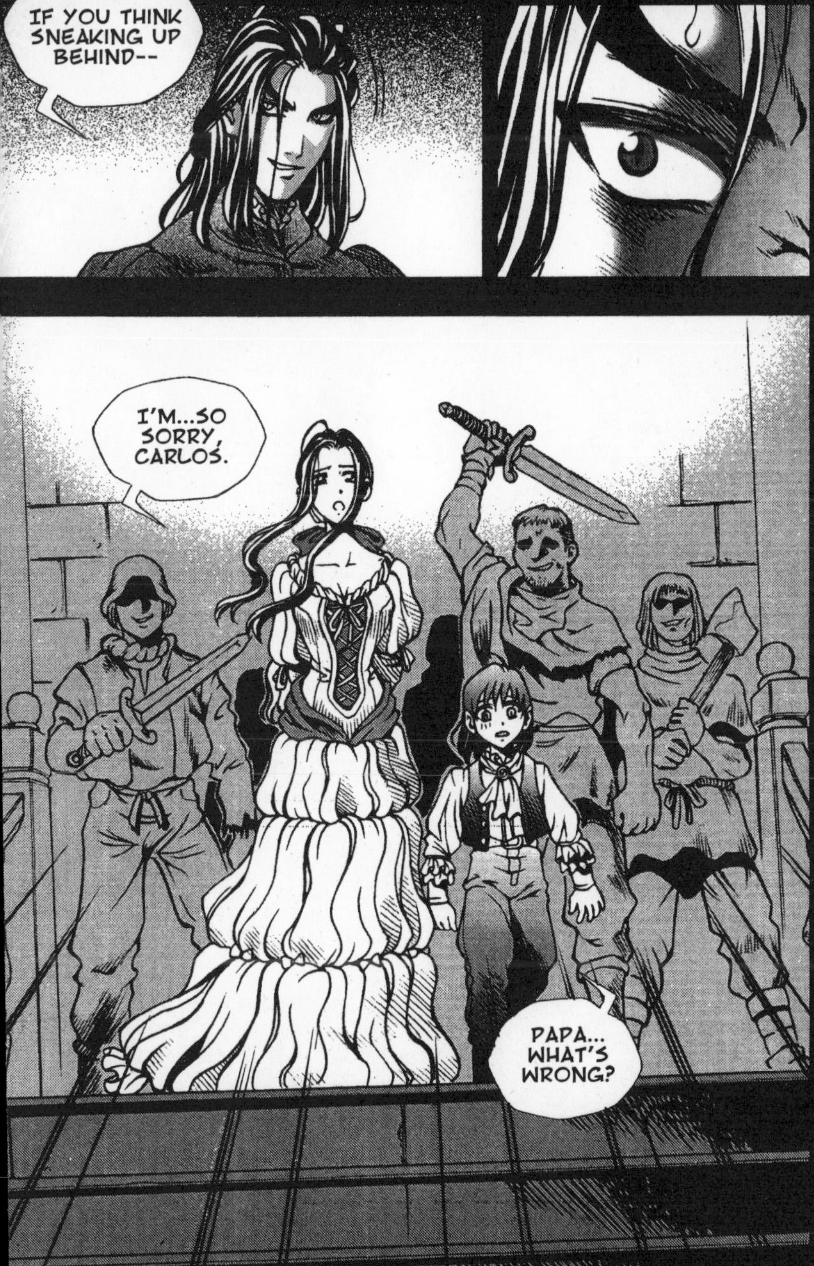
IF YOU THINK SNEAKING UP BEHIND--
I'M...SO SORRY, CARLOS.
PAPA... WHAT'S WRONG?

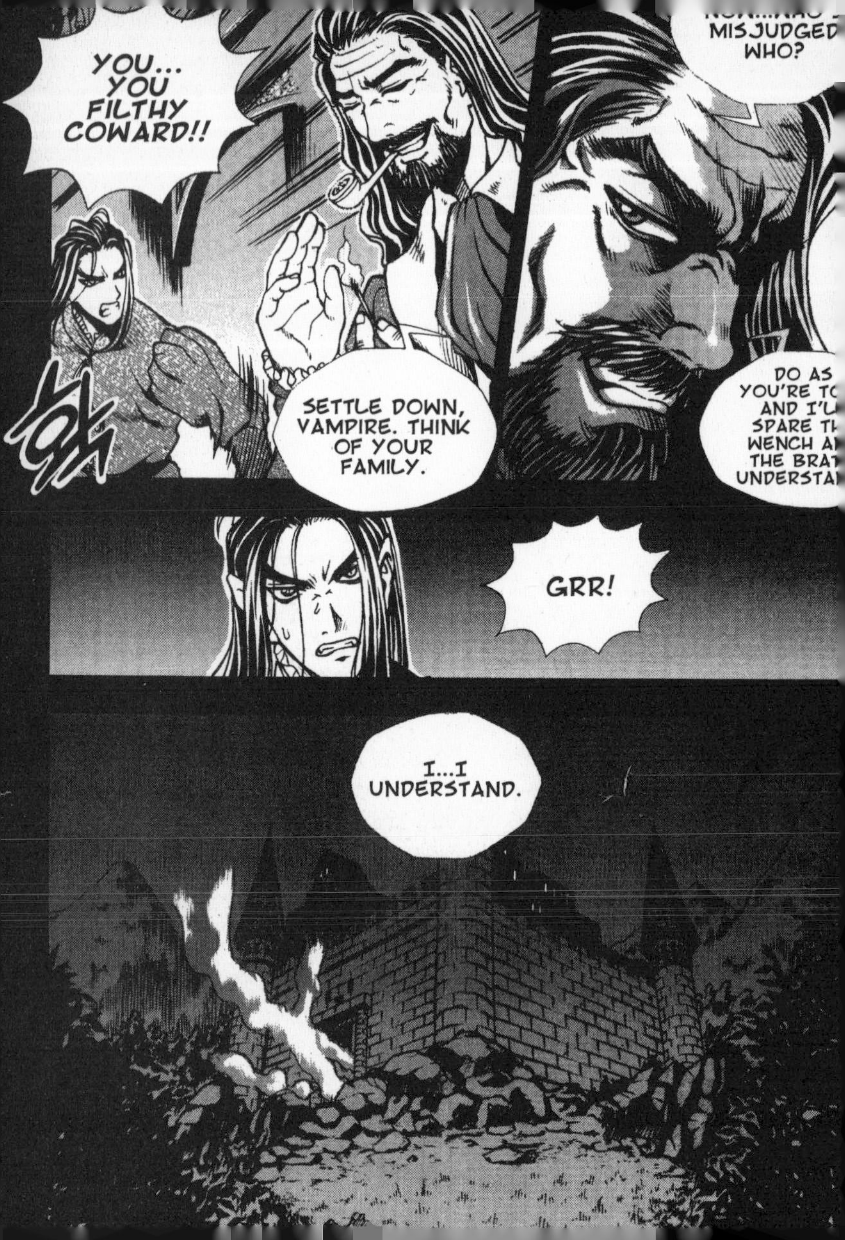

MISJUDGED WHO?
DO AS YOU'RE TO AND I'L SPARE TH WENCH A THE BRA UNDERSTA
YOU... YOU FILTHY COWARD!!
SETTLE DOWN, VAMPIRE. THINK OF YOUR FAMILY.
GRR!
I...I UNDERSTAND.

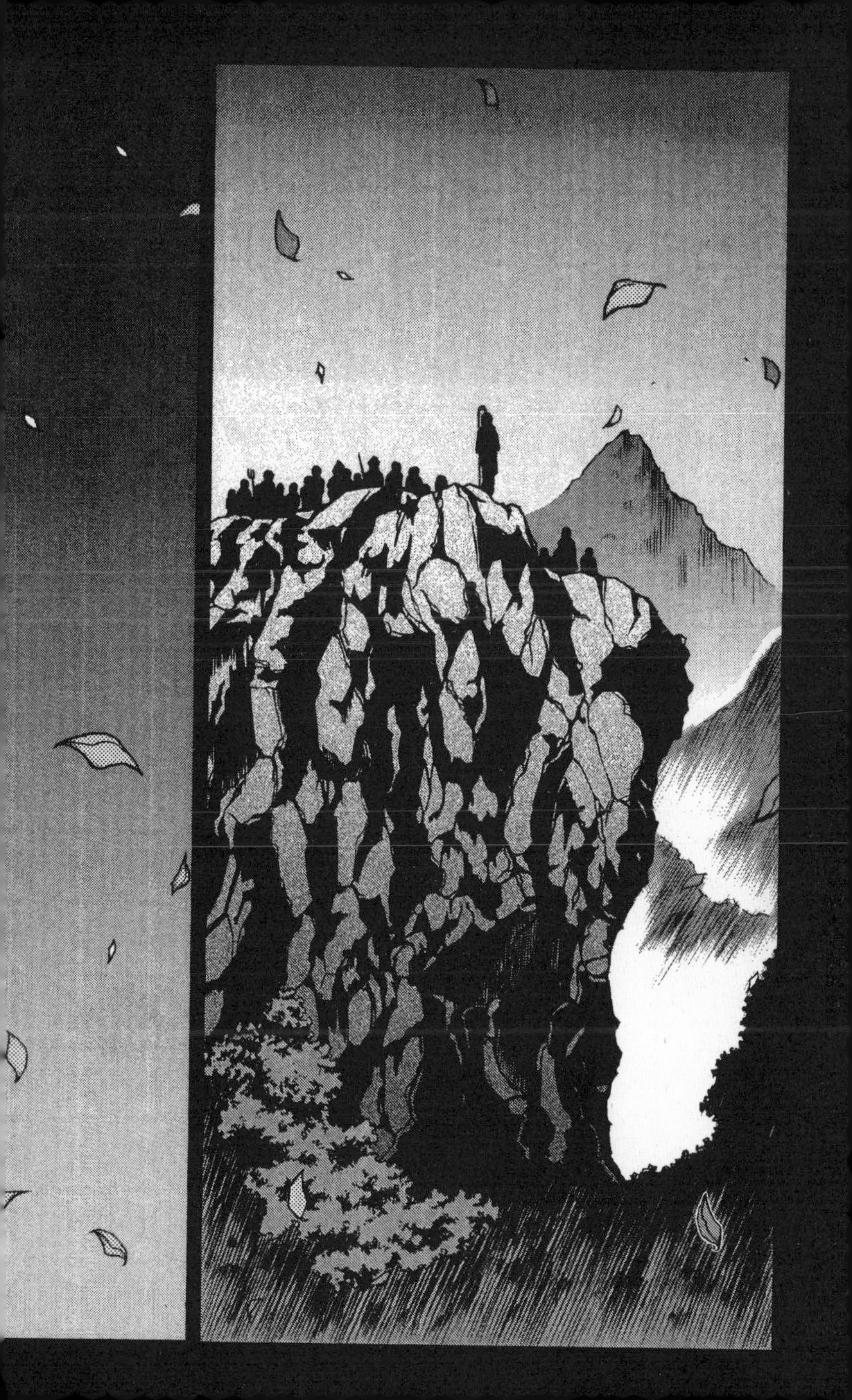

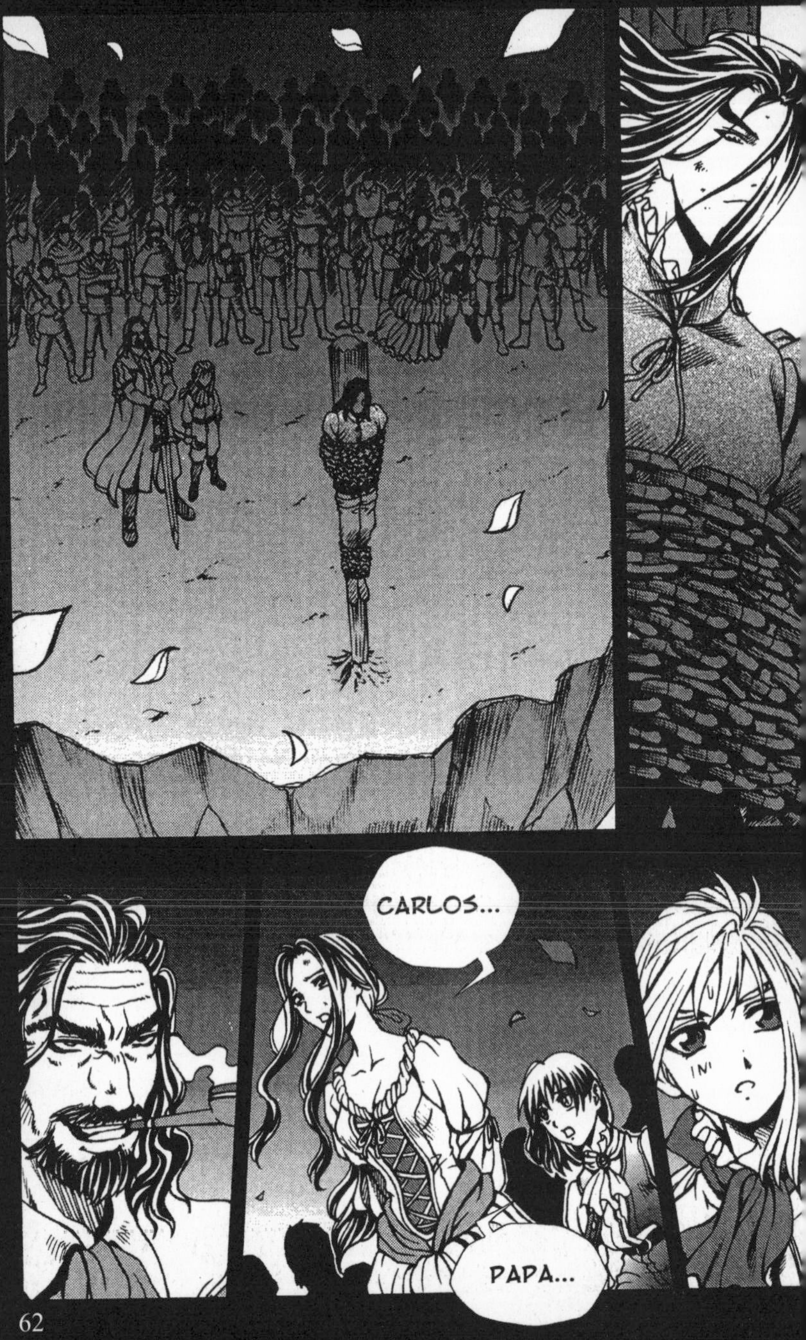
CARLOS...
PAPA...

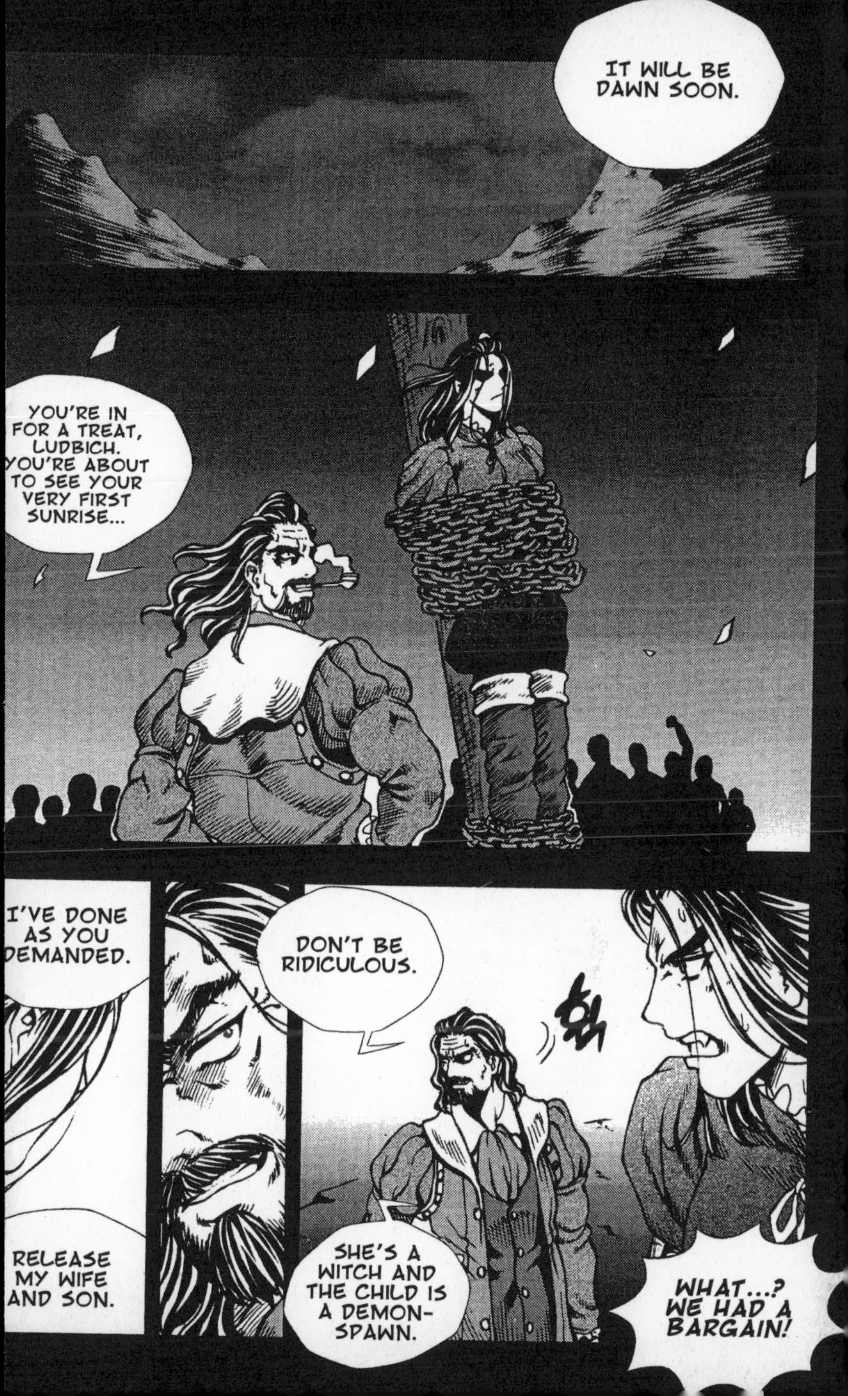
IT WILL BE DAWN SOON.
YOU'RE IN FOR A TREAT, LUDBICH. YOU'RE ABOUT TO SEE YOUR VERY FIRST SUNRISE...
I'VE DONE AS YOU DEMANDED.
RELEASE MY WIFE AND SON.
DON'T BE RIDICULOUS.
SHE'S A WITCH AND THE CHILD IS A DEMON-SPAWN.
WHAT...? WE HAD A BARGAIN!

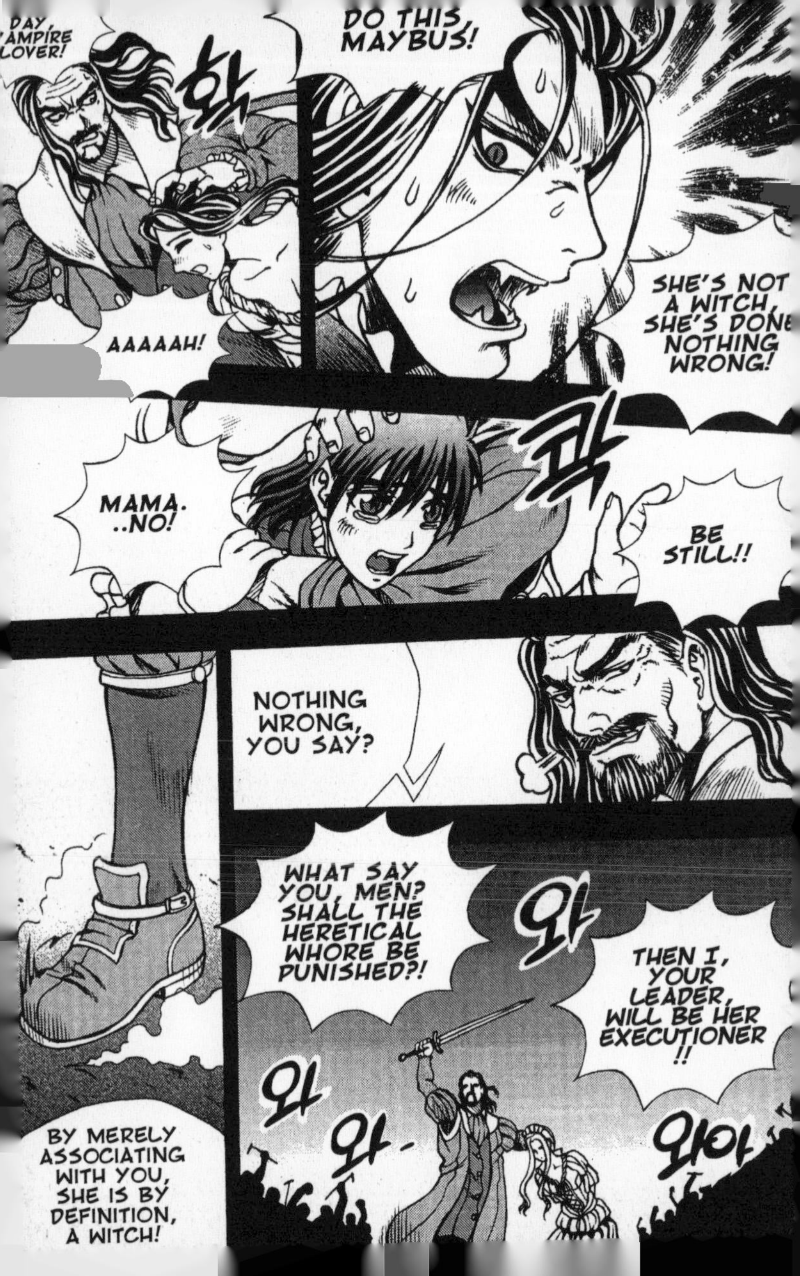
DAY, AMPIRE LOVER!
AAAAAH!
DO THIS, MAYBUS!
SHE'S NOT A WITCH, SHE'S DONE NOTHING WRONG!
MAMA. ..NO!
BE STILL!!
NOTHING WRONG, YOU SAY?
BY MERELY ASSOCIATING WITH YOU, SHE IS BY DEFINITION, A WITCH!
WHAT SAY YOU, MEN? SHALL THE HERETICAL WHORE BE PUNISHED?!
THEN I, YOUR LEADER, WILL BE HER EXECUTIONER !!

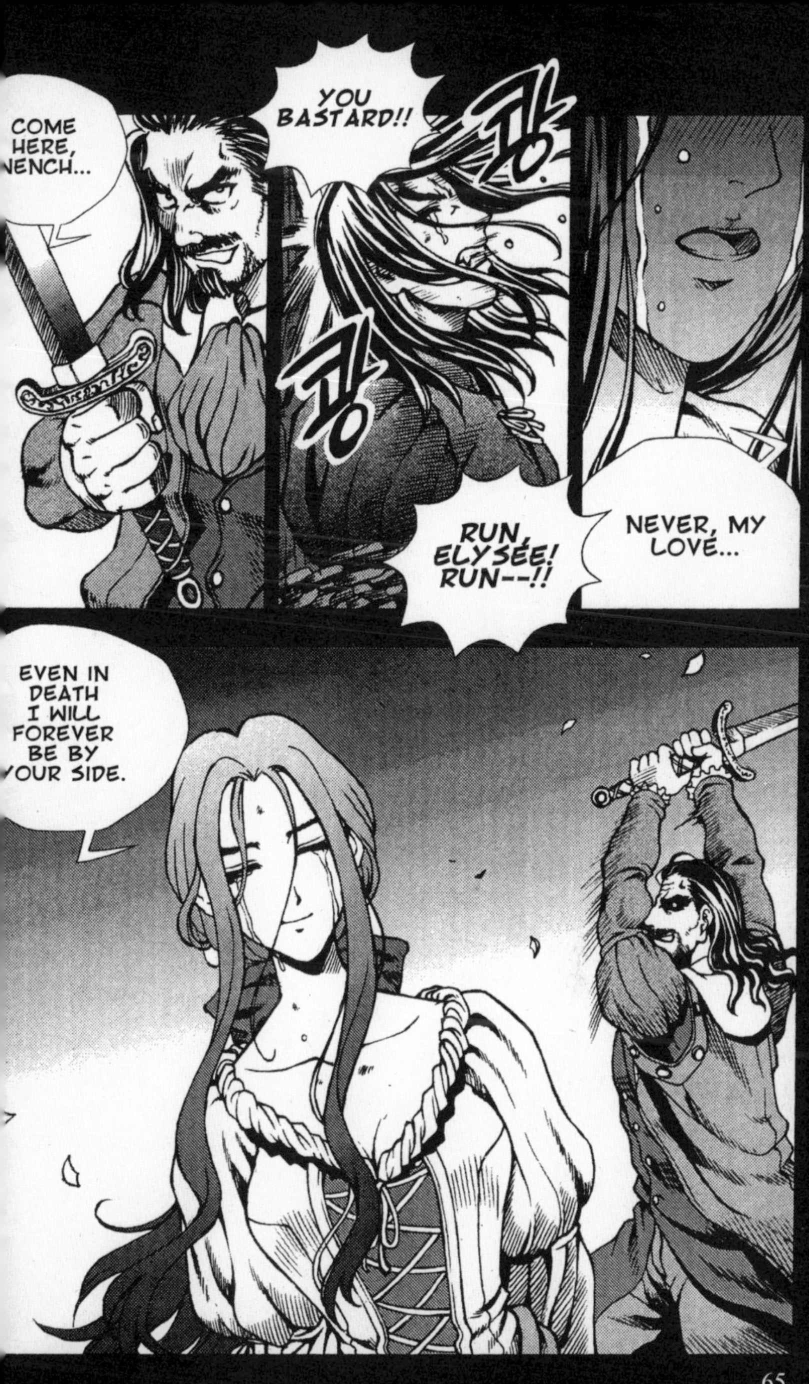
COME HERE, WENCH...
YOU BASTARD!!
RUN, ELYSÉE! RUN--!!
NEVER, MY LOVE...
EVEN IN DEATH I WILL FOREVER BE BY YOUR SIDE.

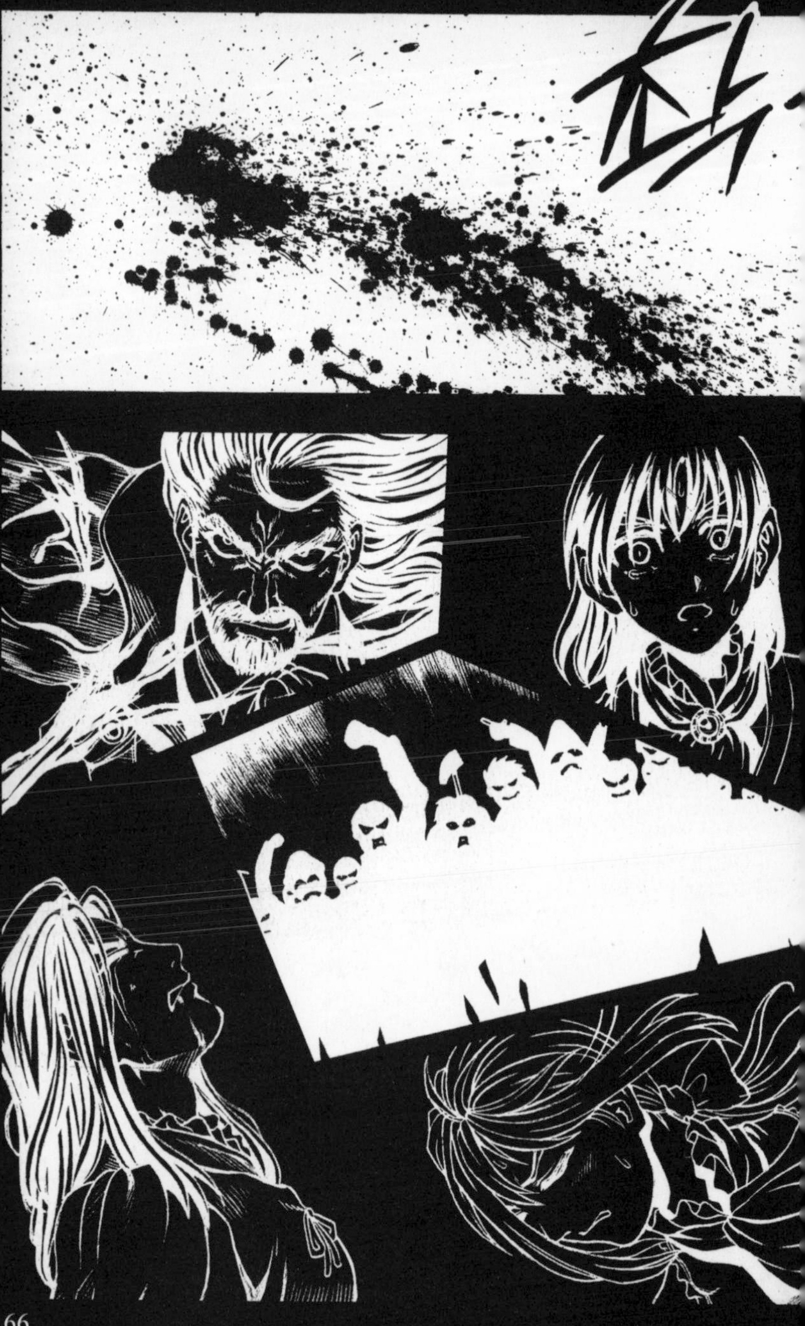

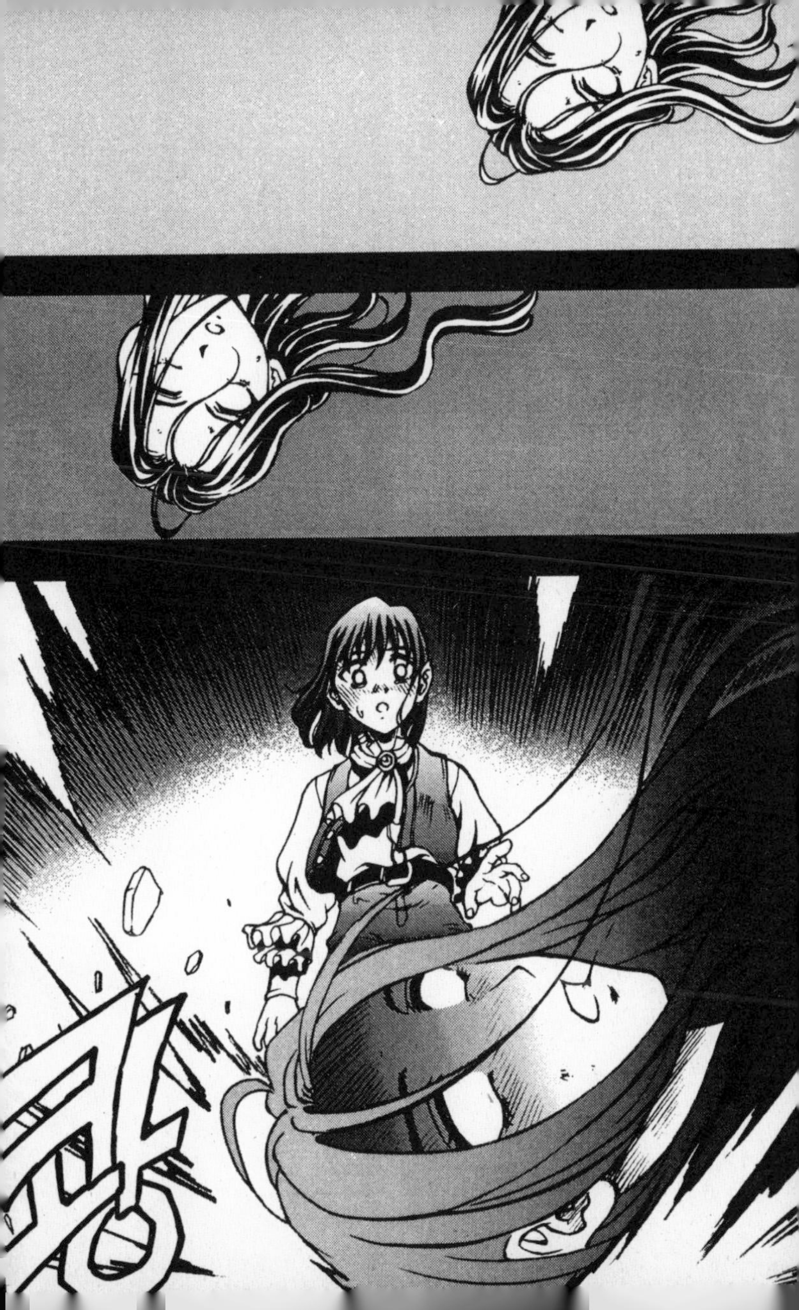

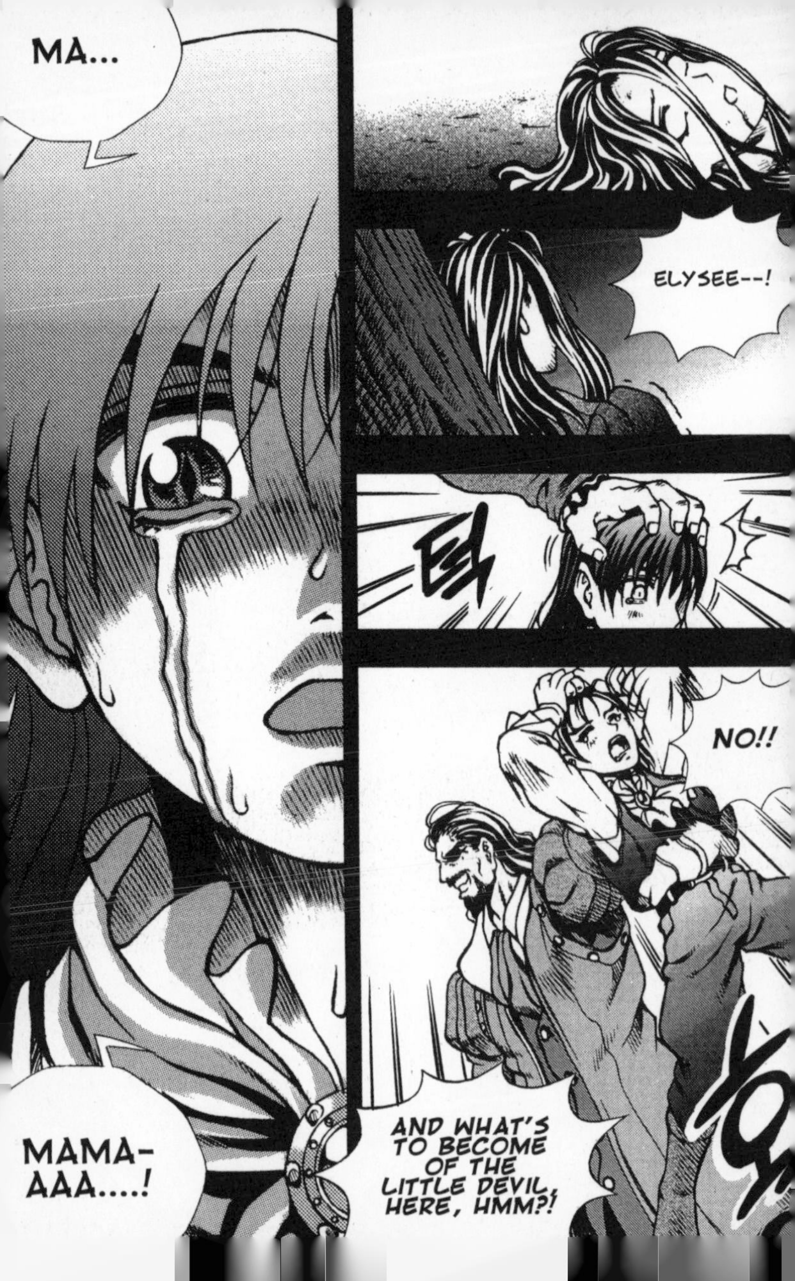
ELYSEE--!
NO!!
AND WHAT'S TO BECOME OF THE LITTLE DEVIL HERE, HMM?!
MA...
MAMA-AAA....!

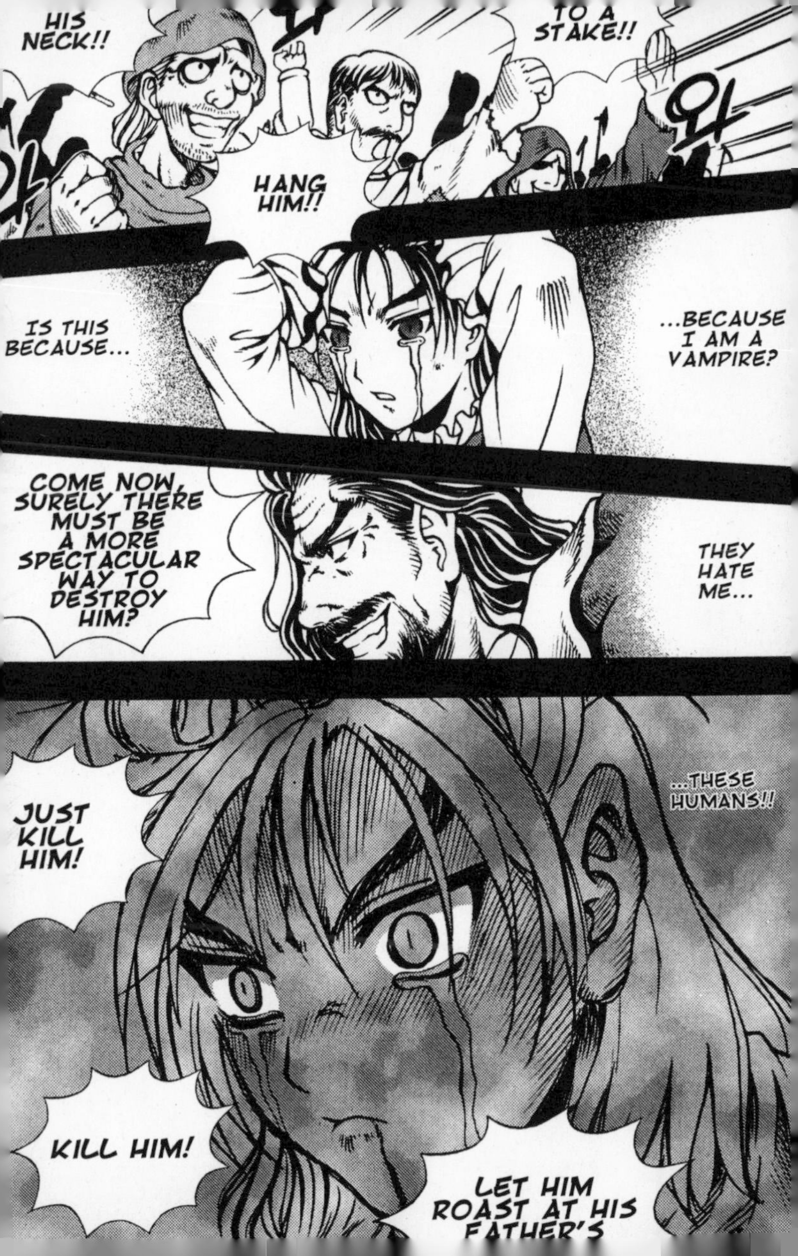
HIS NECK!!
HANG HIM!!
TO A STAKE!!
IS THIS BECAUSE...
...BECAUSE I AM A VAMPIRE?
COME NOW, SURELY THERE MUST BE A MORE SPECTACULAR WAY TO DESTROY HIM?
THEY HATE ME...
JUST KILL HIM!
...THESE HUMANS!!
KILL HIM!
LET HIM ROAST AT HIS FATHER'S

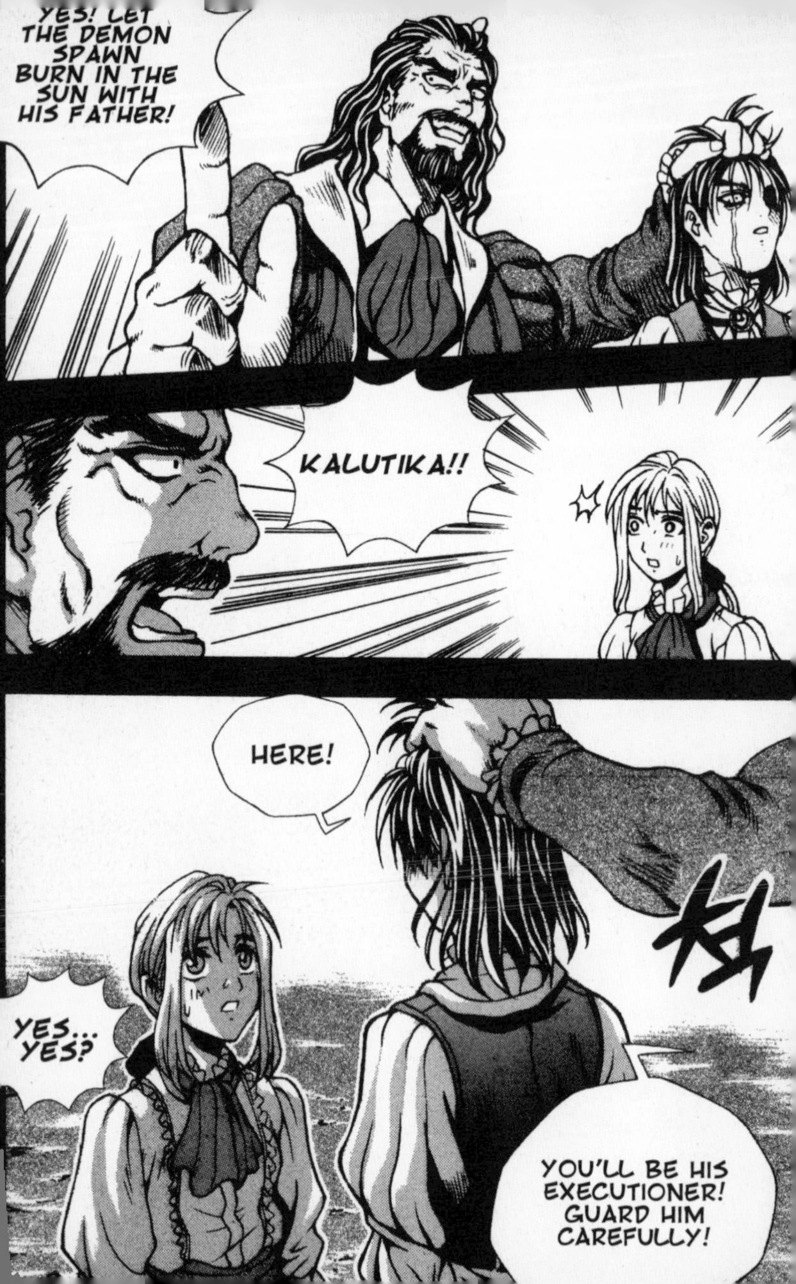
YES! LET THE DEMON SPAWN BURN IN THE SUN WITH HIS FATHER!
KALUTIKA!!
YES... YES?
HERE!
YOU'LL BE HIS EXECUTIONER! GUARD HIM CAREFULLY!

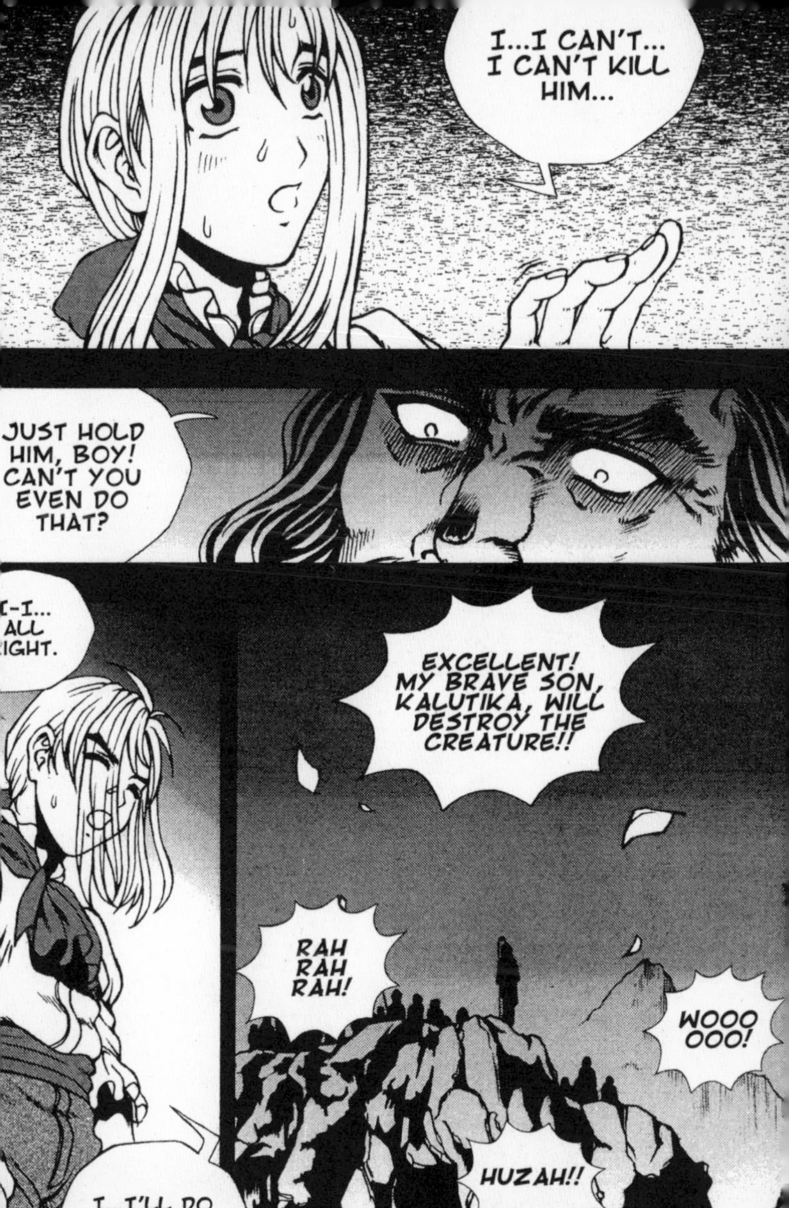
I...I CAN'T... I CAN'T KILL HIM...
JUST HOLD HIM, BOY! CAN'T YOU EVEN DO THAT?
-I... ALL IGHT.
I...I'LL DO IT, FATHER.
EXCELLENT! MY BRAVE SON, KALUTIKA, WILL DESTROY THE CREATURE!!
WOOO OOO!
RAH RAH RAH!
HUZAH!!

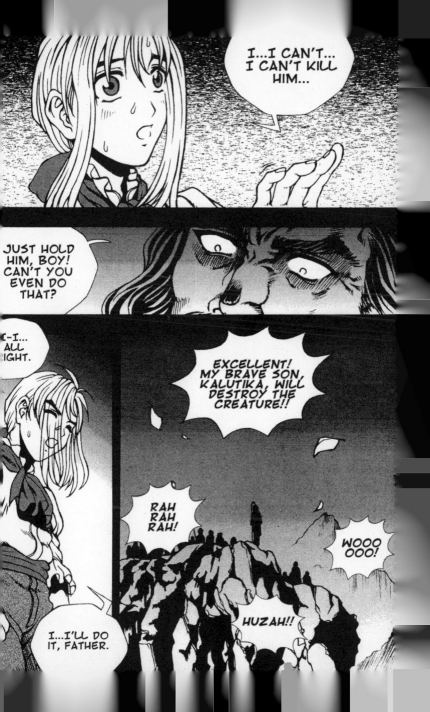

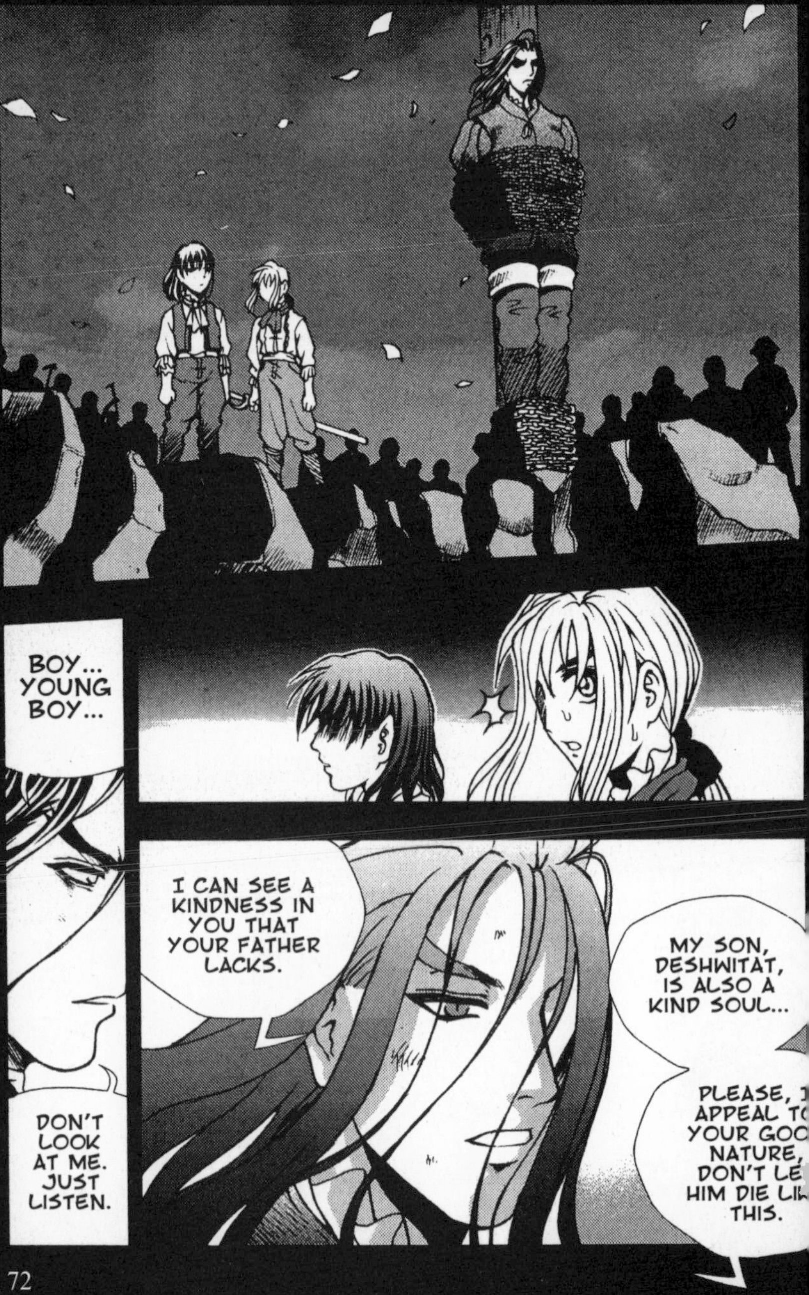
BOY... YOUNG BOY...
DON'T LOOK AT ME. JUST LISTEN.
I CAN SEE A KINDNESS IN YOU THAT YOUR FATHER LACKS.
MY SON, DESHWITAT, IS ALSO A KIND SOUL...
PLEASE, I APPEAL TO YOUR GOO NATURE, DON'T LE HIM DIE LI THIS.

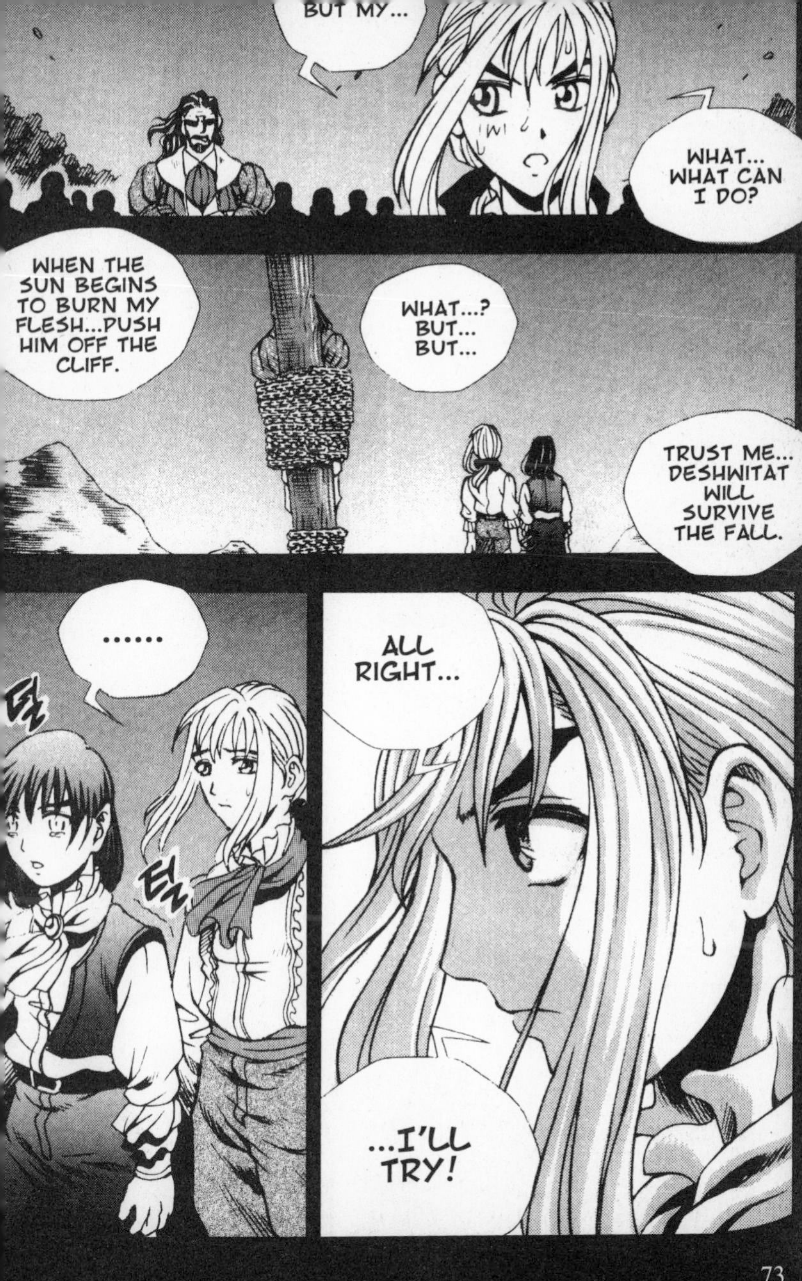
BUT MY...
WHAT... WHAT CAN I DO?
WHEN THE SUN BEGINS TO BURN MY FLESH...PUSH HIM OFF THE CLIFF.
WHAT...? BUT... BUT...
TRUST ME... DESHWITAT WILL SURVIVE THE FALL.
......
ALL RIGHT...
...I'LL TRY!

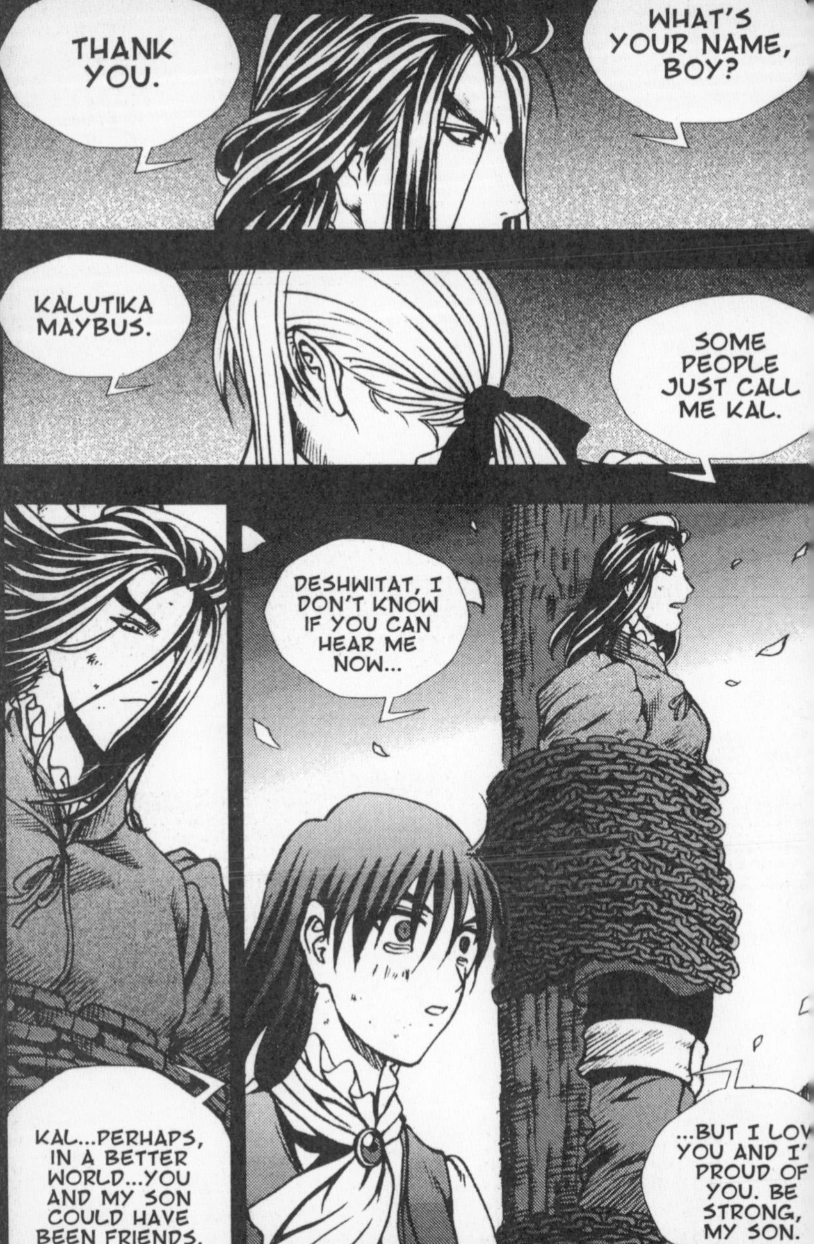
THANK YOU.
WHAT'S YOUR NAME, BOY?
KALUTIKA MAYBUS.
SOME PEOPLE JUST CALL ME KAL.
DESHWITAT, I DON'T KNOW IF YOU CAN HEAR ME NOW...
...BUT I LOV YOU AND I' PROUD OF YOU. BE STRONG, MY SON.
KAL...PERHAPS, IN A BETTER WORLD...YOU AND MY SON COULD HAVE BEEN FRIENDS.

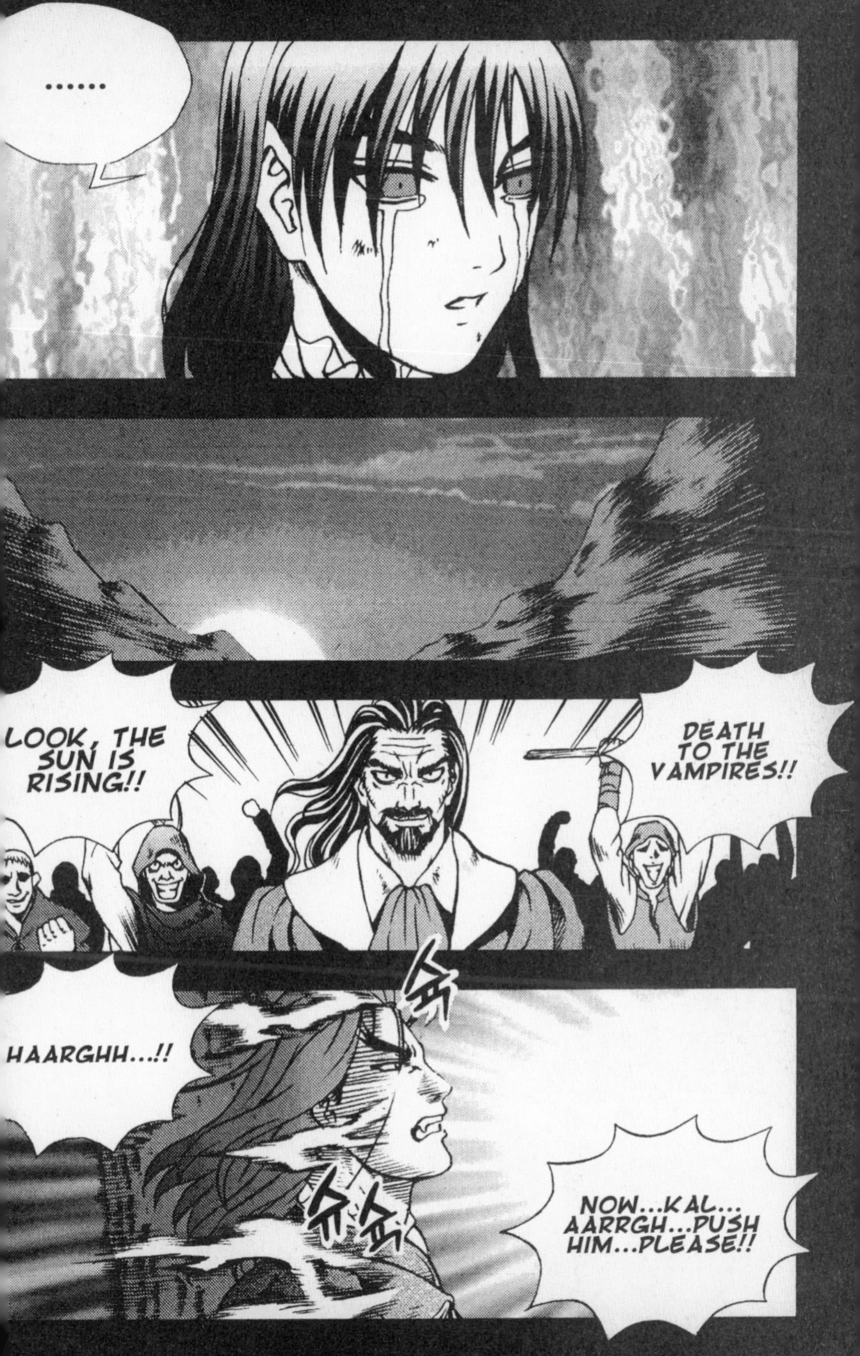
......
DEATH TO THE VAMPIRES!!
LOOK, THE SUN IS RISING!!
HAARGHH...!!
NOW...KAL... AARRGH...PUSH HIM...PLEASE!!

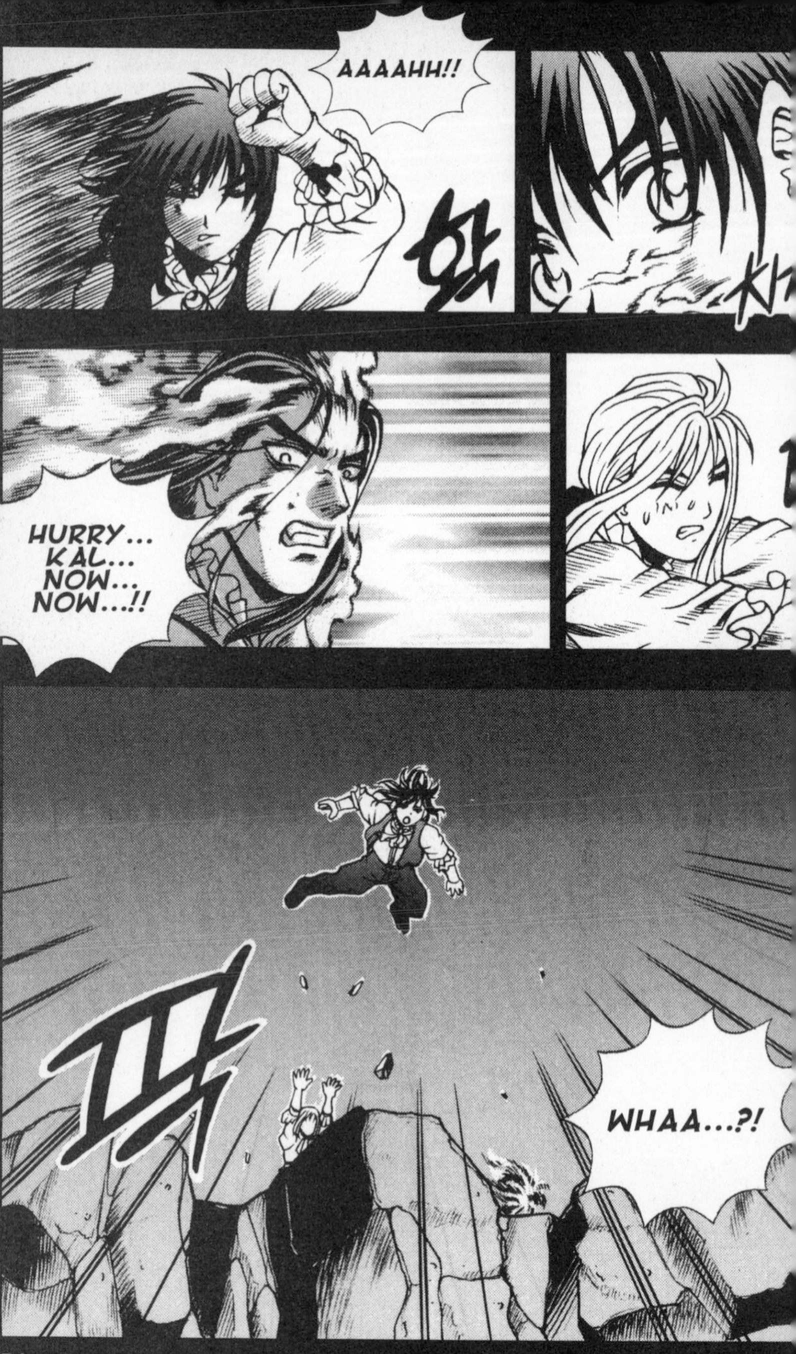
AAAAHH!!
HURRY... KAL... NOW... NOW...!!
WHAA...?!

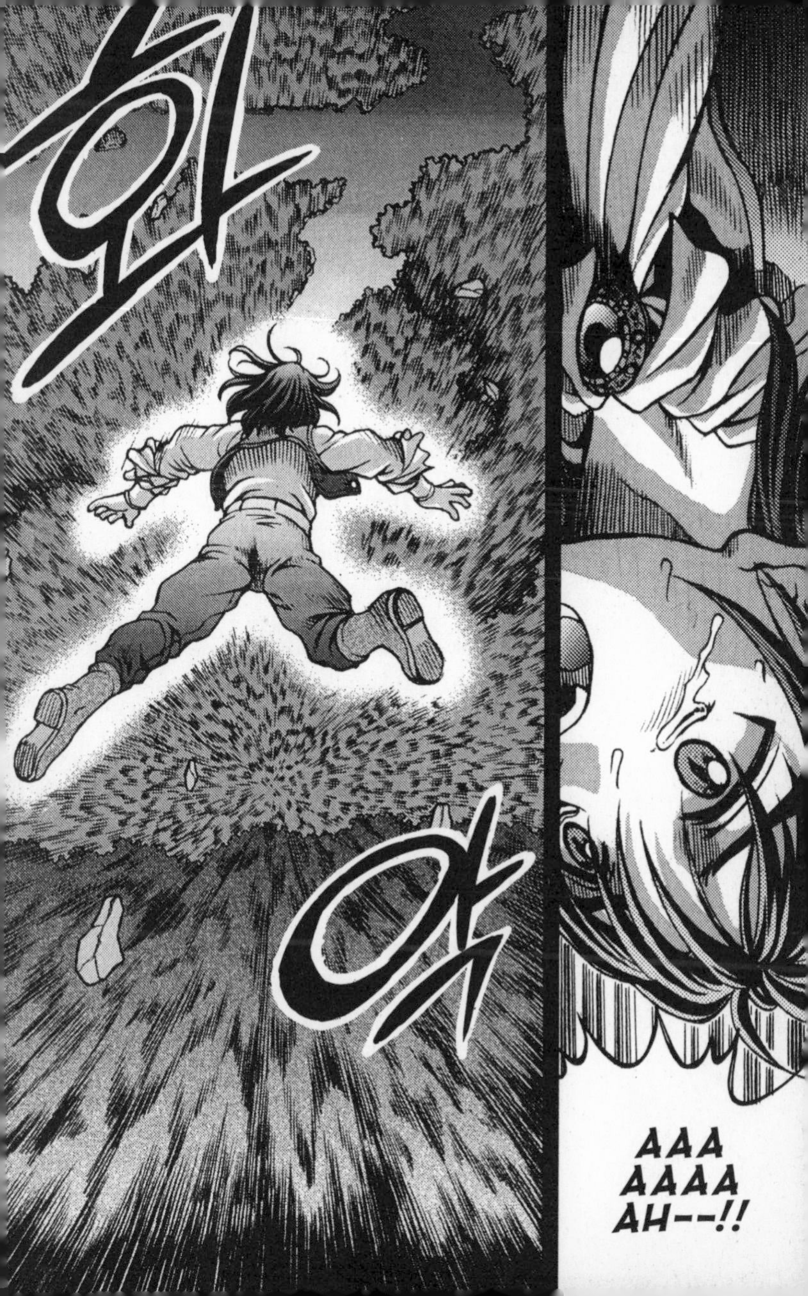
AAA
AAAA
AH--!!

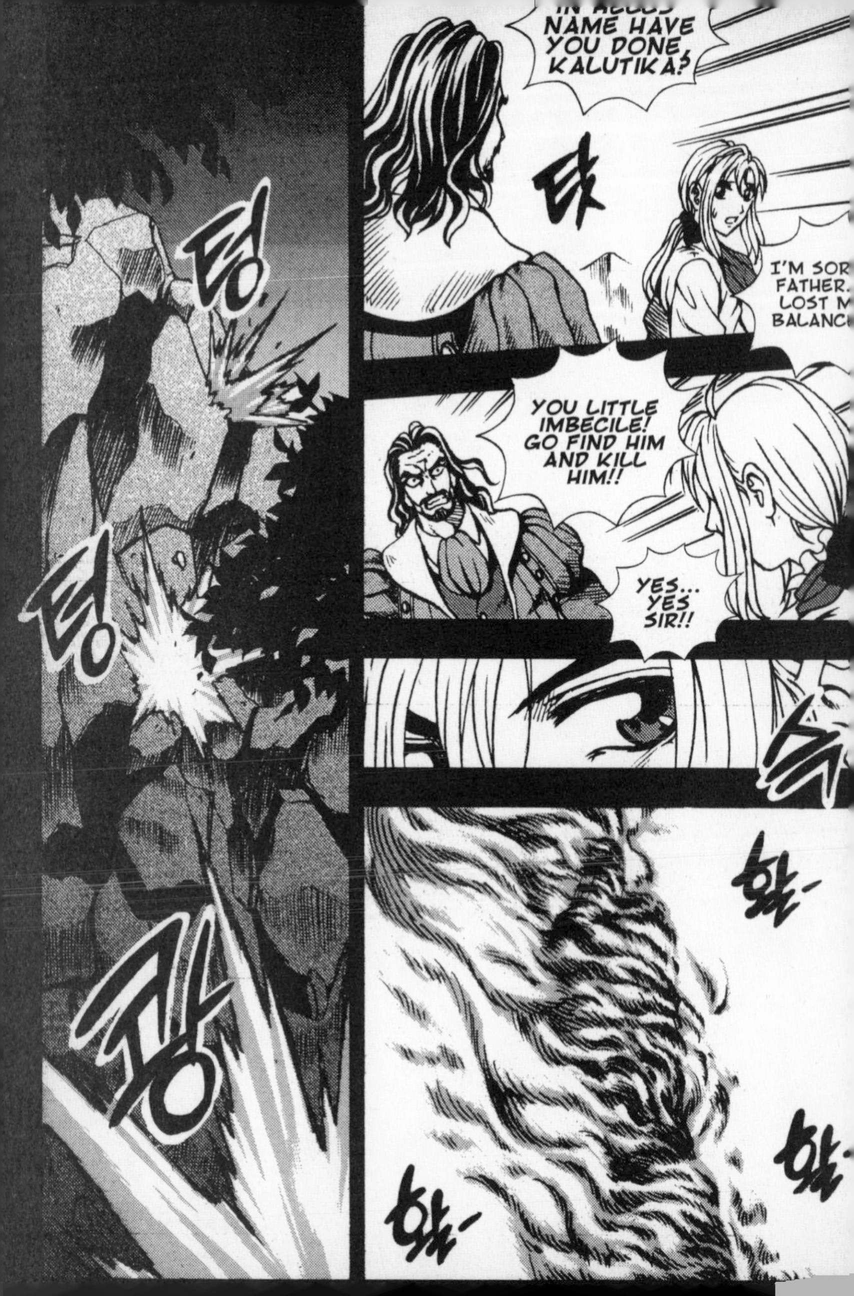
NAME HAVE YOU DONE, KALUTIKA?
I'M SOR FATHER. LOST M BALANC
YOU LITTLE IMBECILE! GO FIND HIM AND KILL HIM!!
YES... YES SIR!!

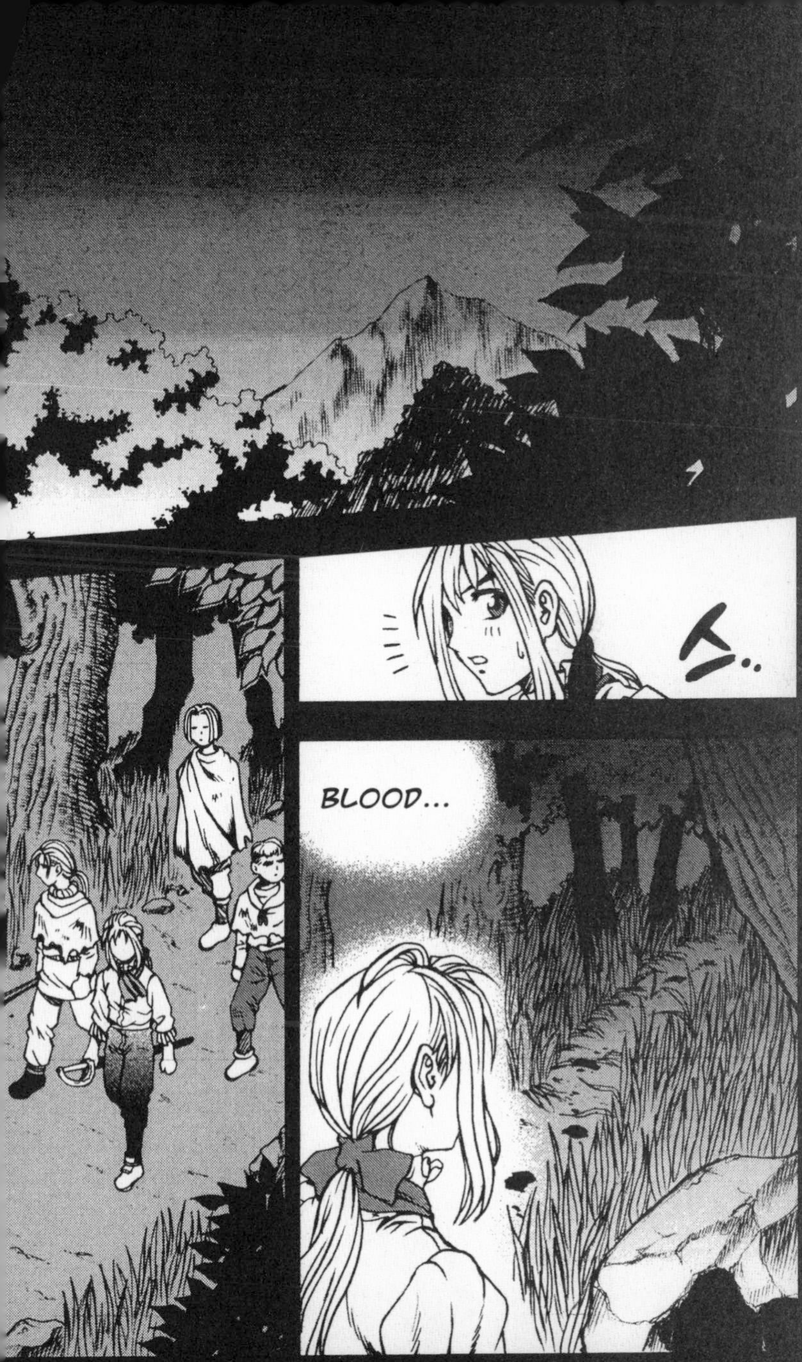
BLOOD...

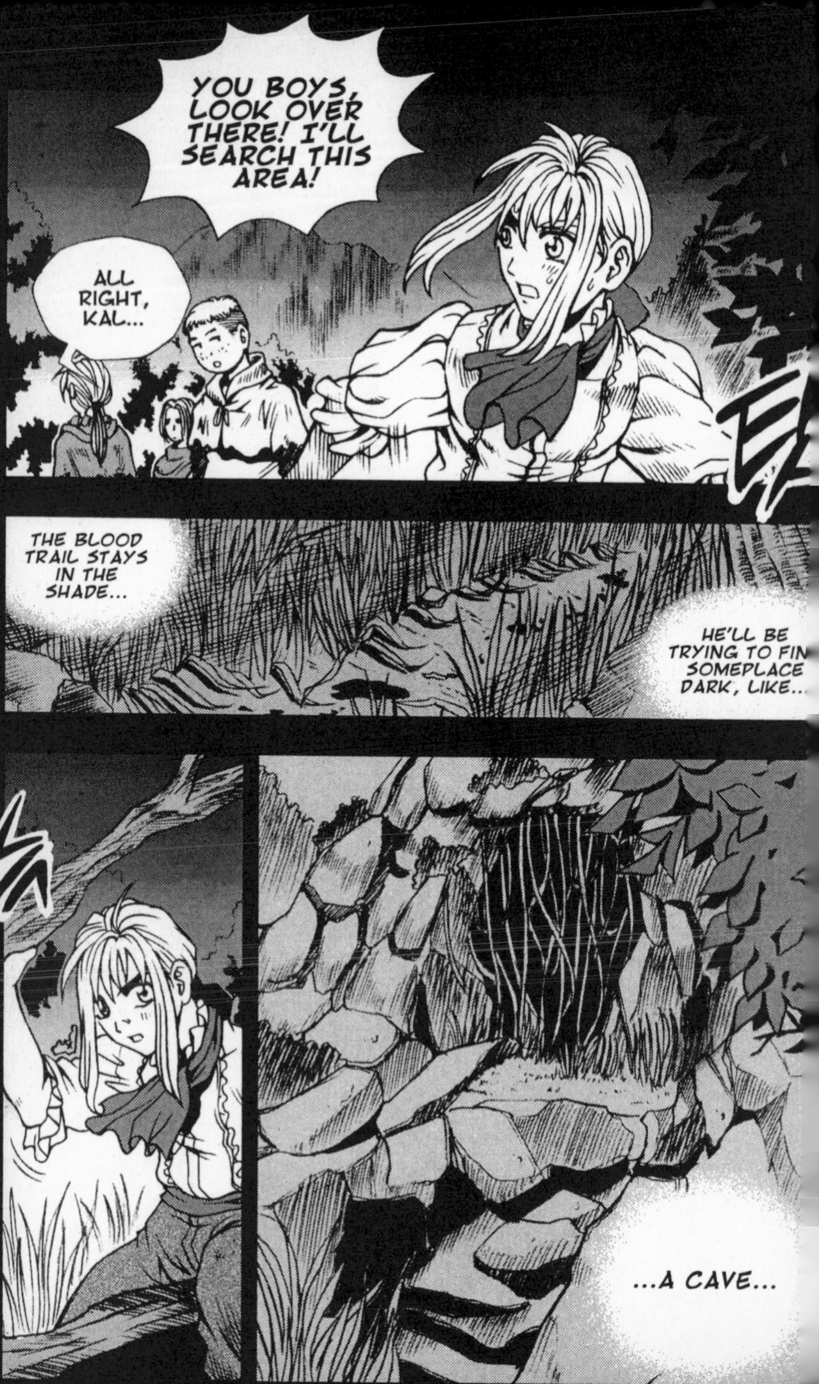
YOU BOYS, LOOK OVER THERE! I'LL SEARCH THIS AREA!
ALL RIGHT, KAL...
THE BLOOD TRAIL STAYS IN THE SHADE...
HE'LL BE TRYING TO FIN SOMEPLACE DARK, LIKE...
...A CAVE...

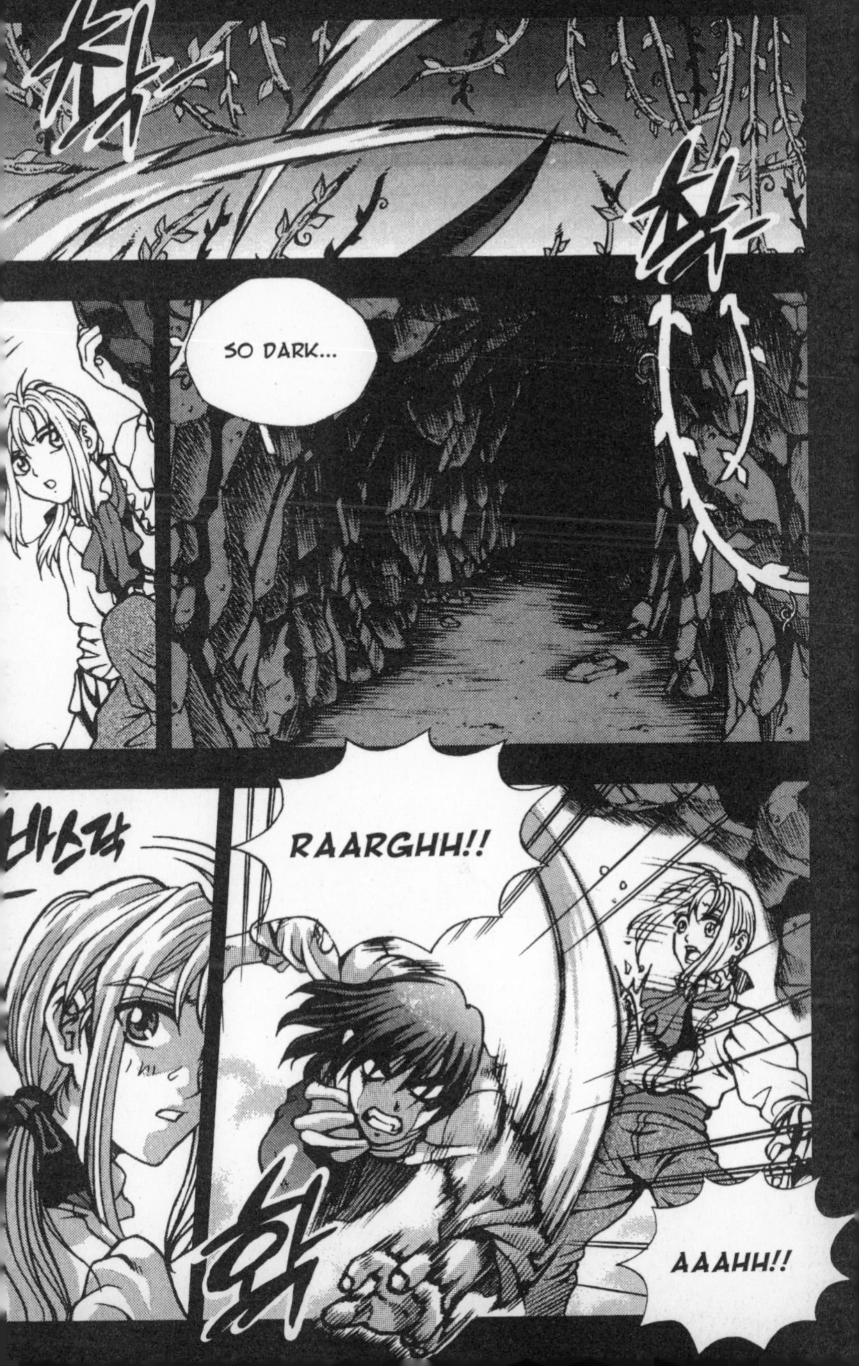
SO DARK...
RAARGHH!!
AAAHH!!

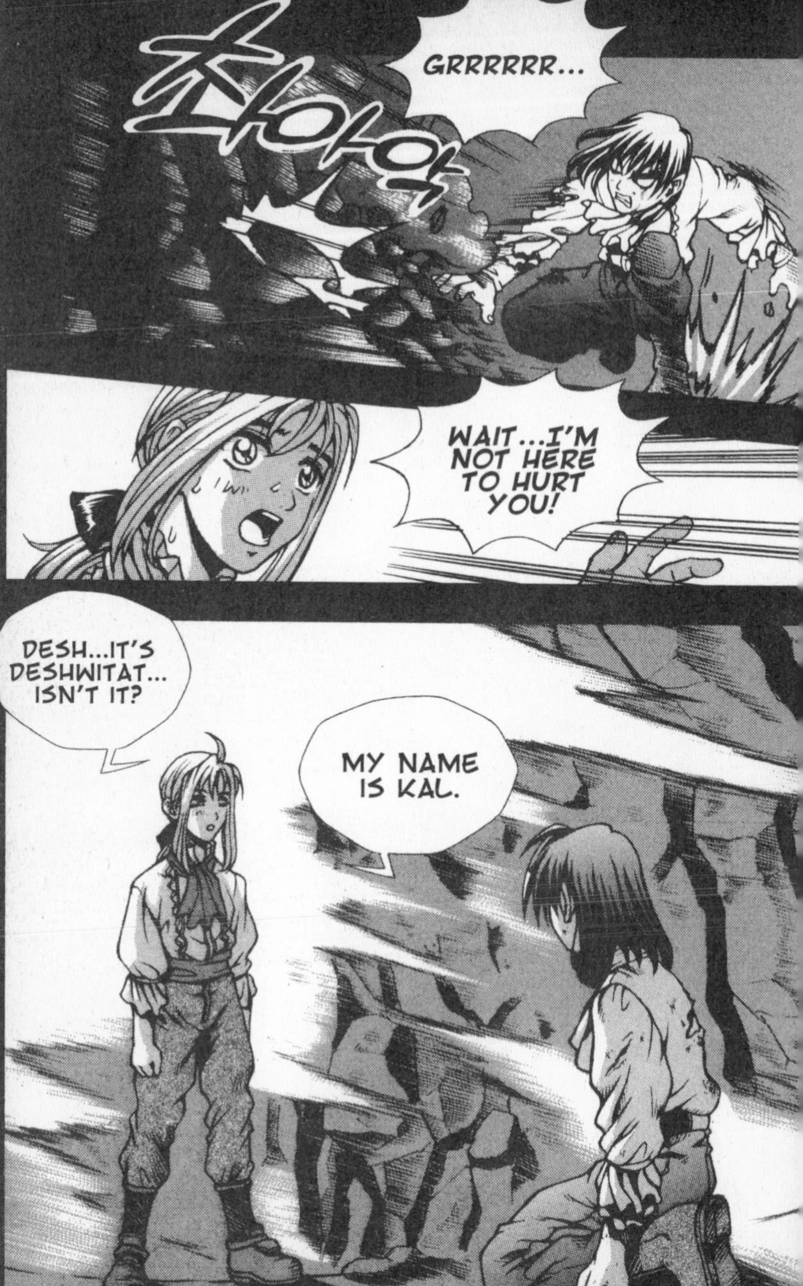
GRRRRRR...
WAIT...I'M NOT HERE TO HURT YOU!
DESH...IT'S DESHWITAT... ISN'T IT?
MY NAME IS KAL.

CHAPTER 24: THE END OF HAPPY DAYS

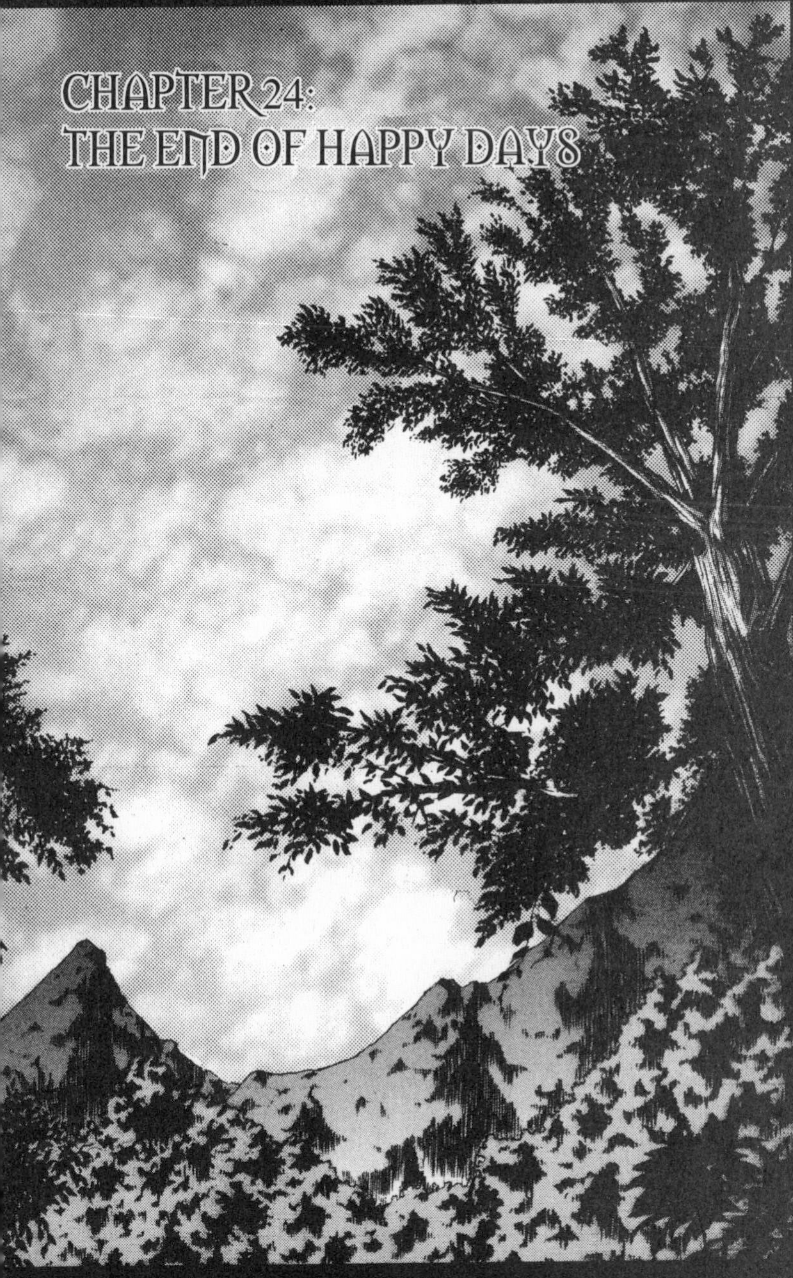

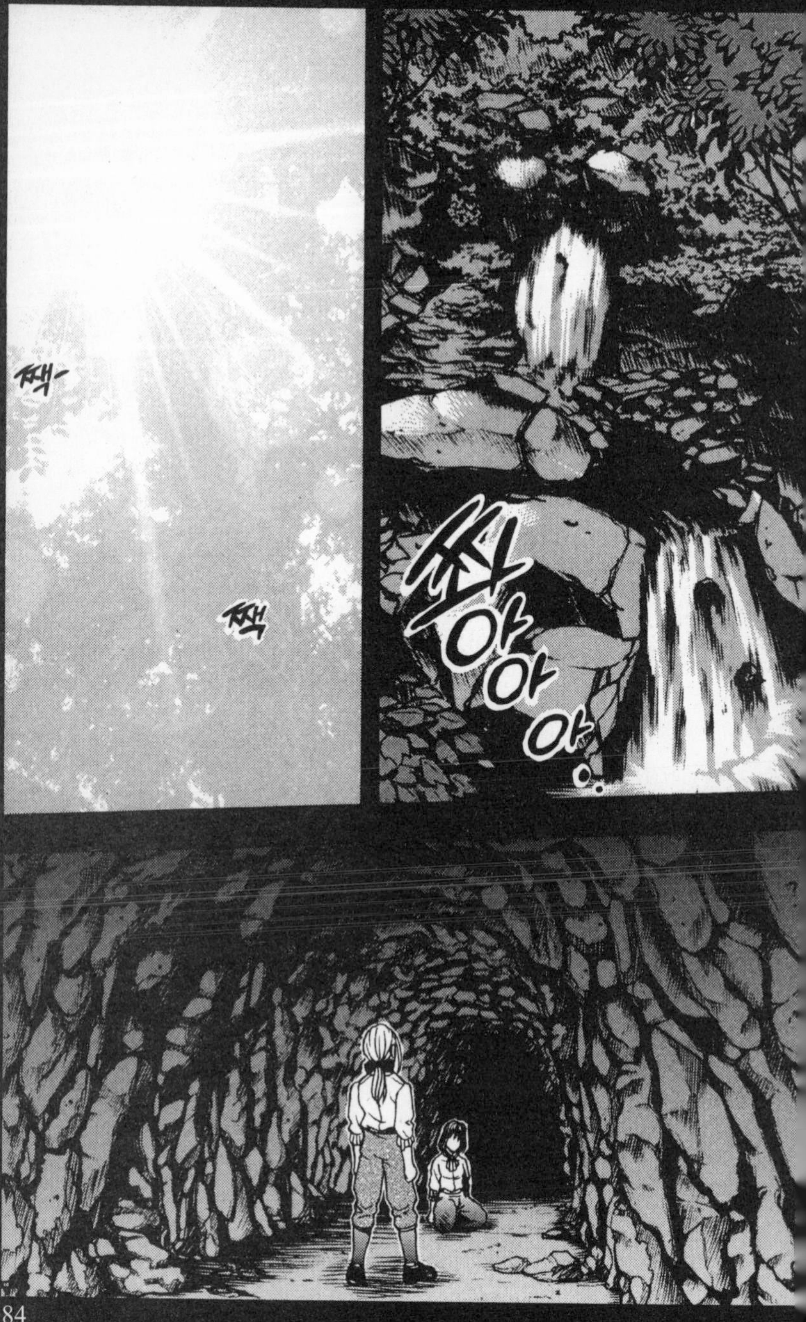
쏴아아아..
짹-
짹

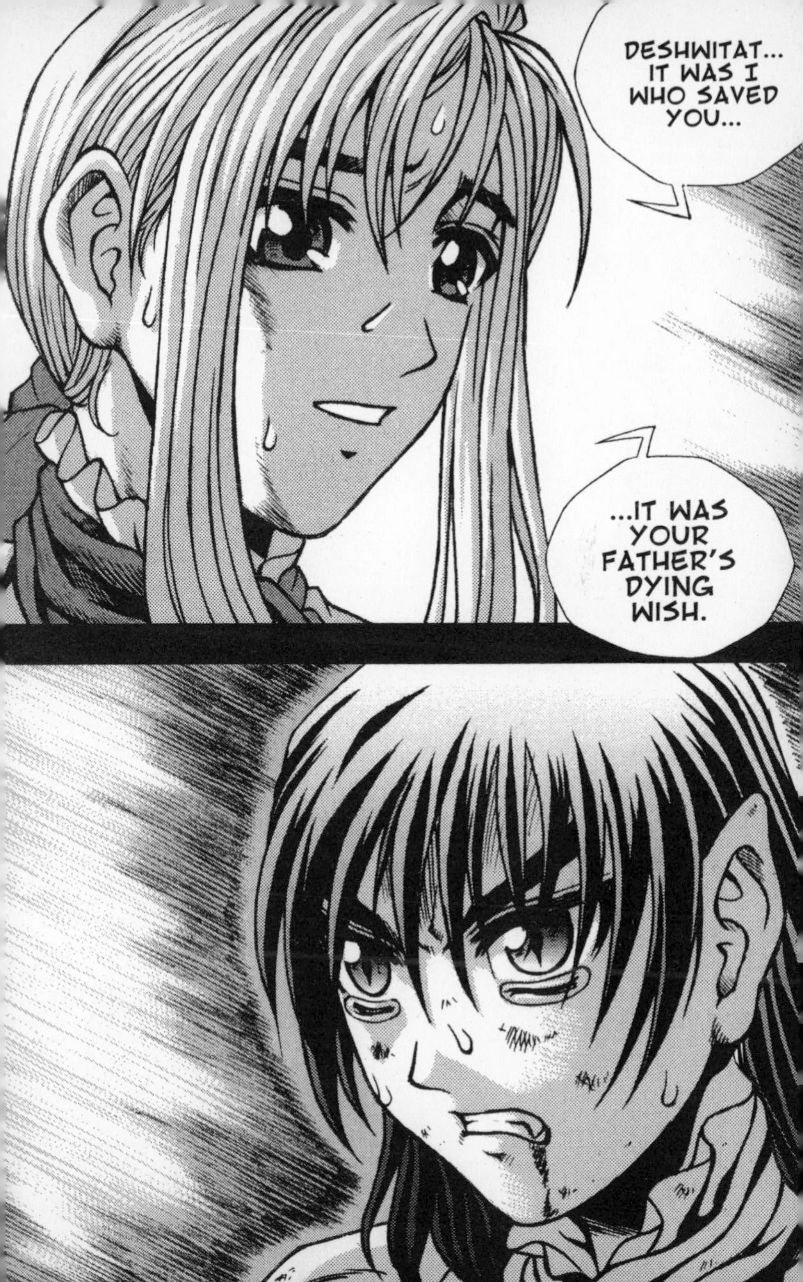
DESHWITAT... IT WAS I WHO SAVED YOU...
...IT WAS YOUR FATHER'S DYING WISH.

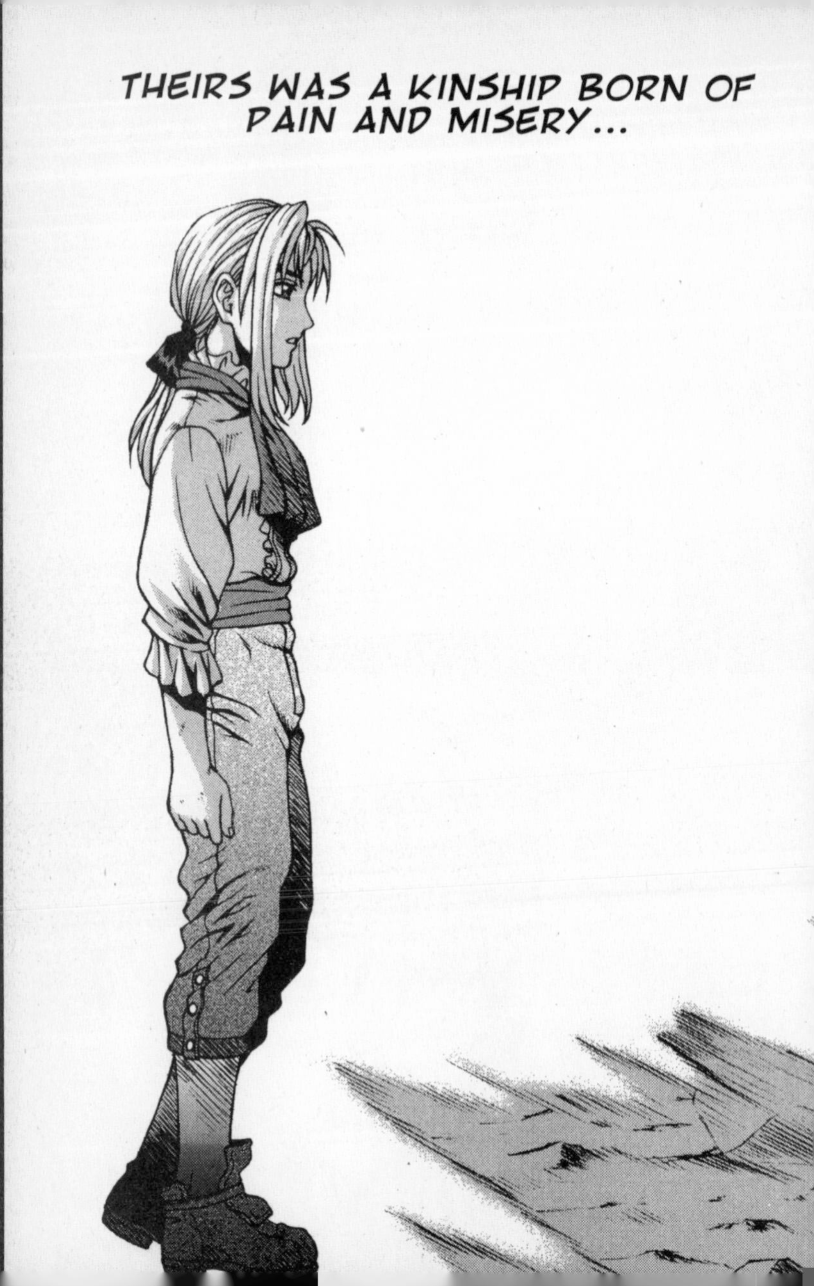
THEIRS WAS A KINSHIP BORN OF PAIN AND MISERY...

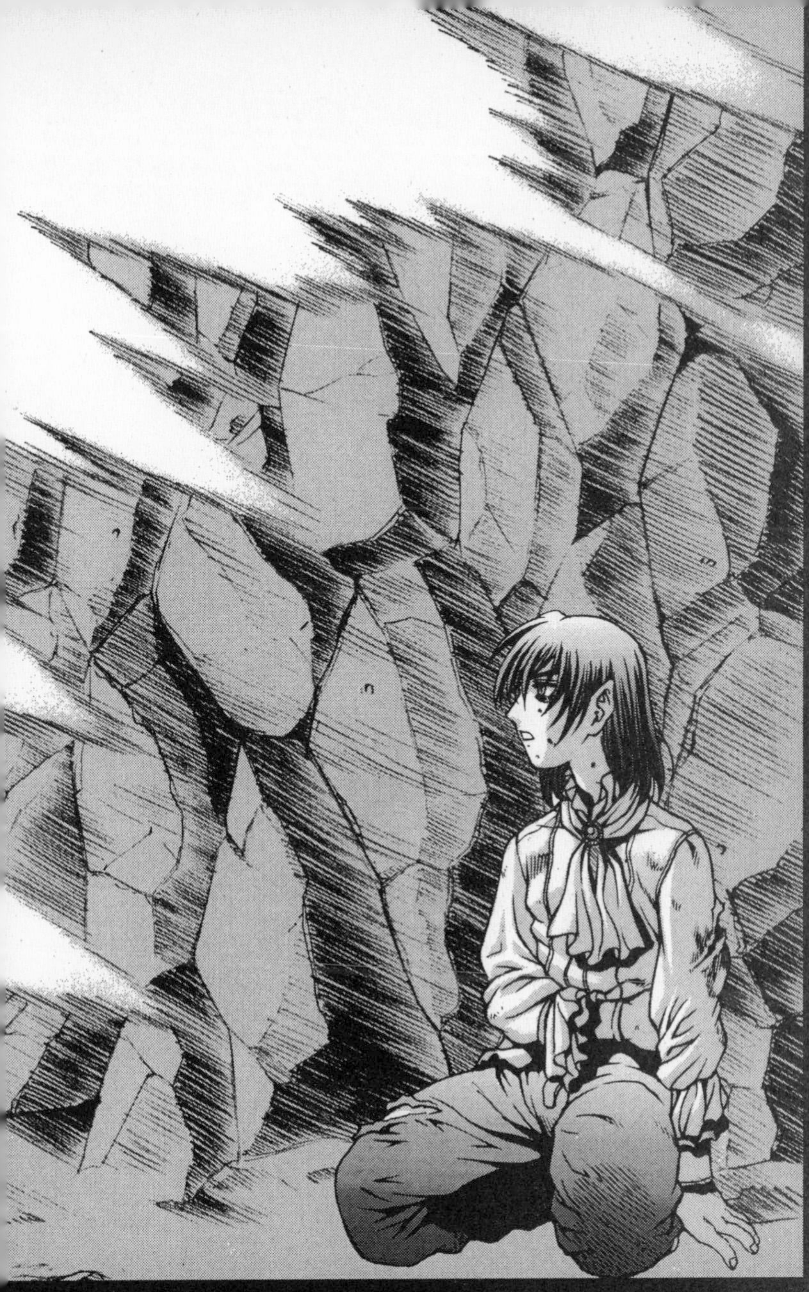

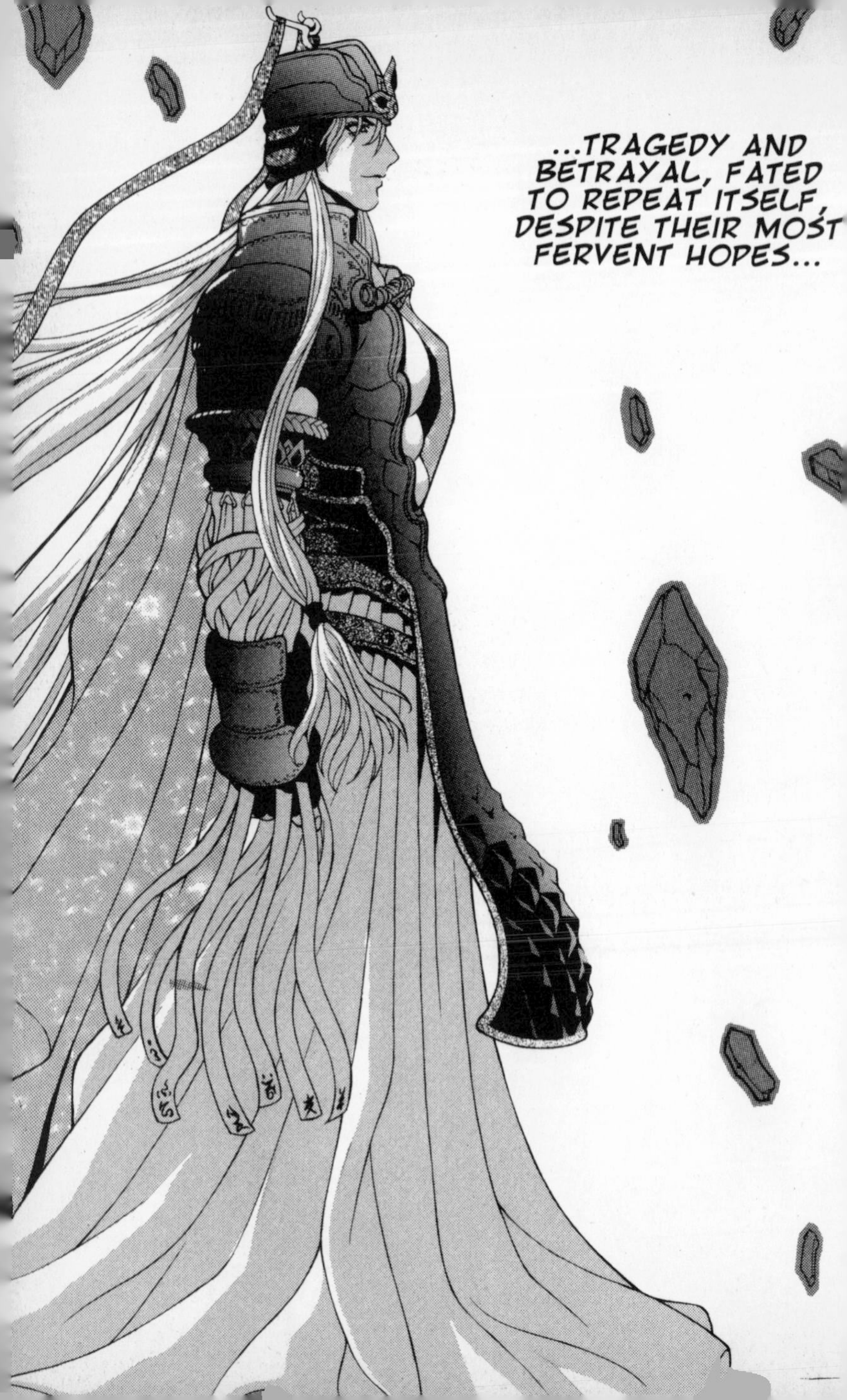
...TRAGEDY AND BETRAYAL, FATED TO REPEAT ITSELF, DESPITE THEIR MOST FERVENT HOPES...

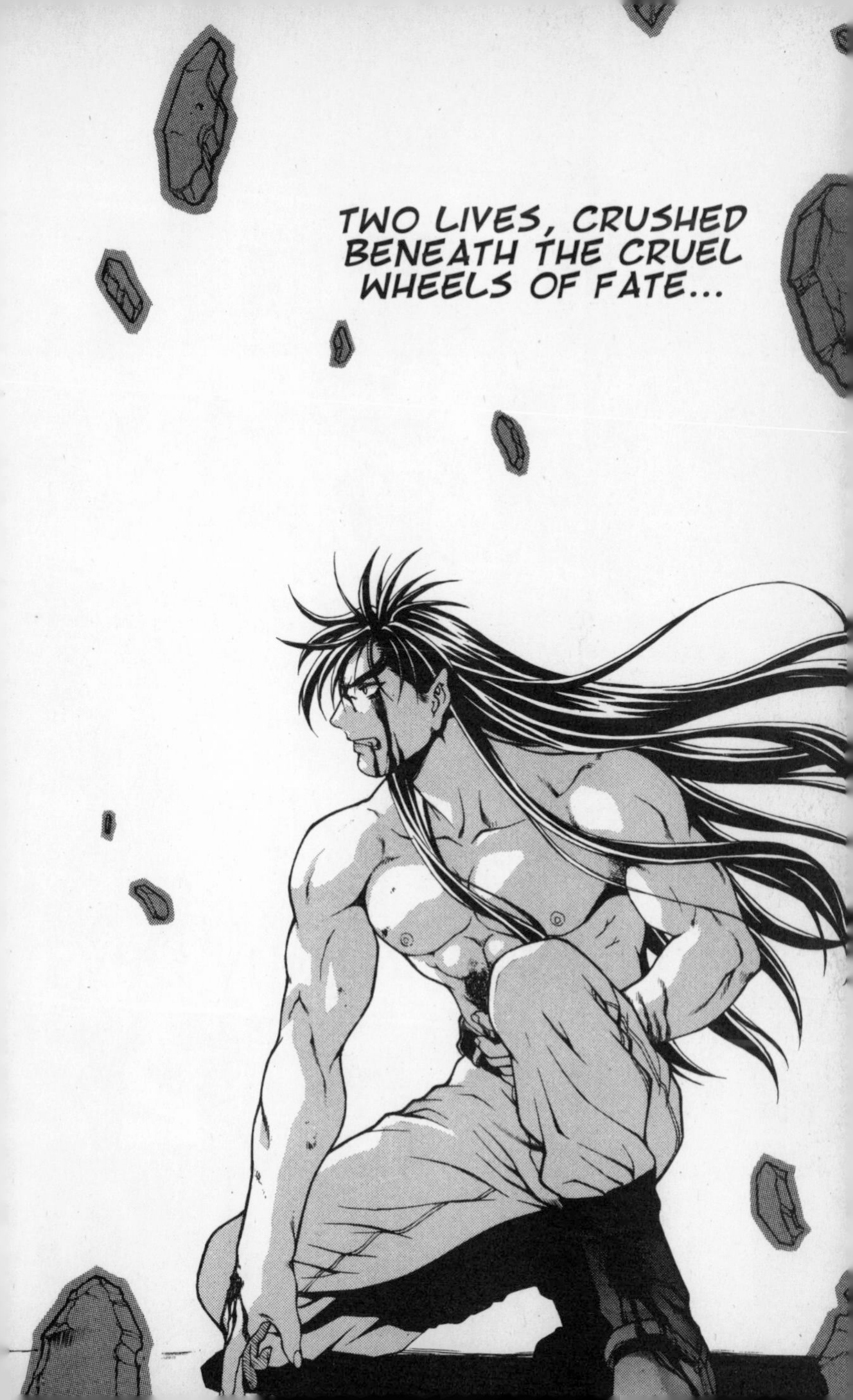
TWO LIVES, CRUSHED BENEATH THE CRUEL WHEELS OF FATE...

REB

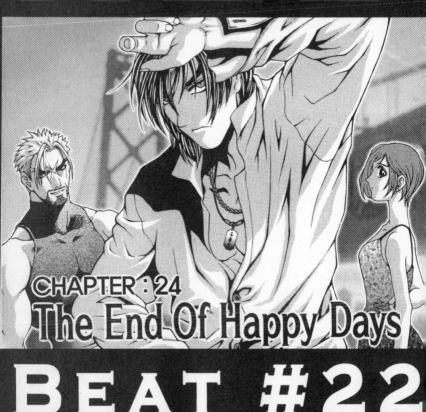

CHAPTER : 24
The End Of Happy Days

BEAT #22
'THE END OF

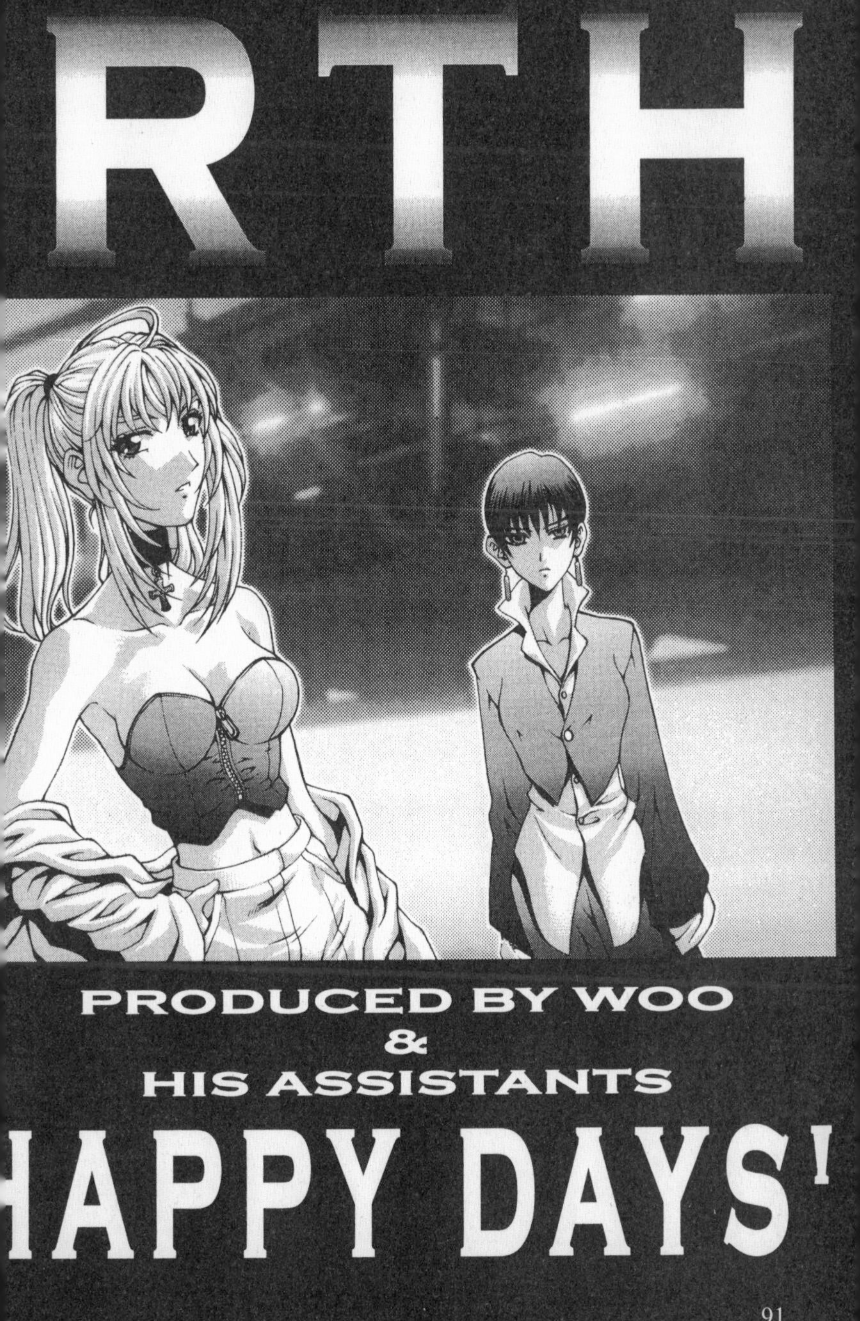
RTH
PRODUCED BY WOO
&
HIS ASSISTANTS
HAPPY DAYS'

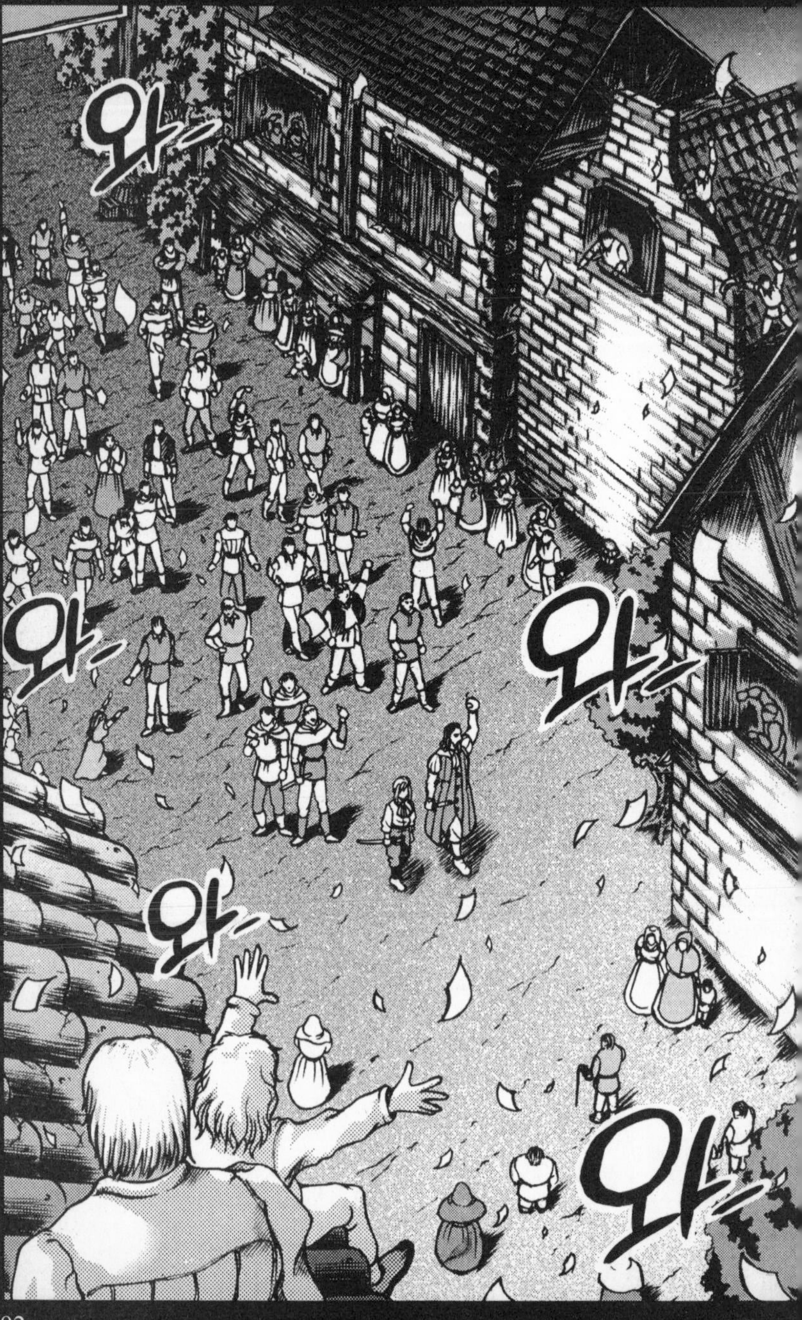
와–
와–
와–
와–
와–

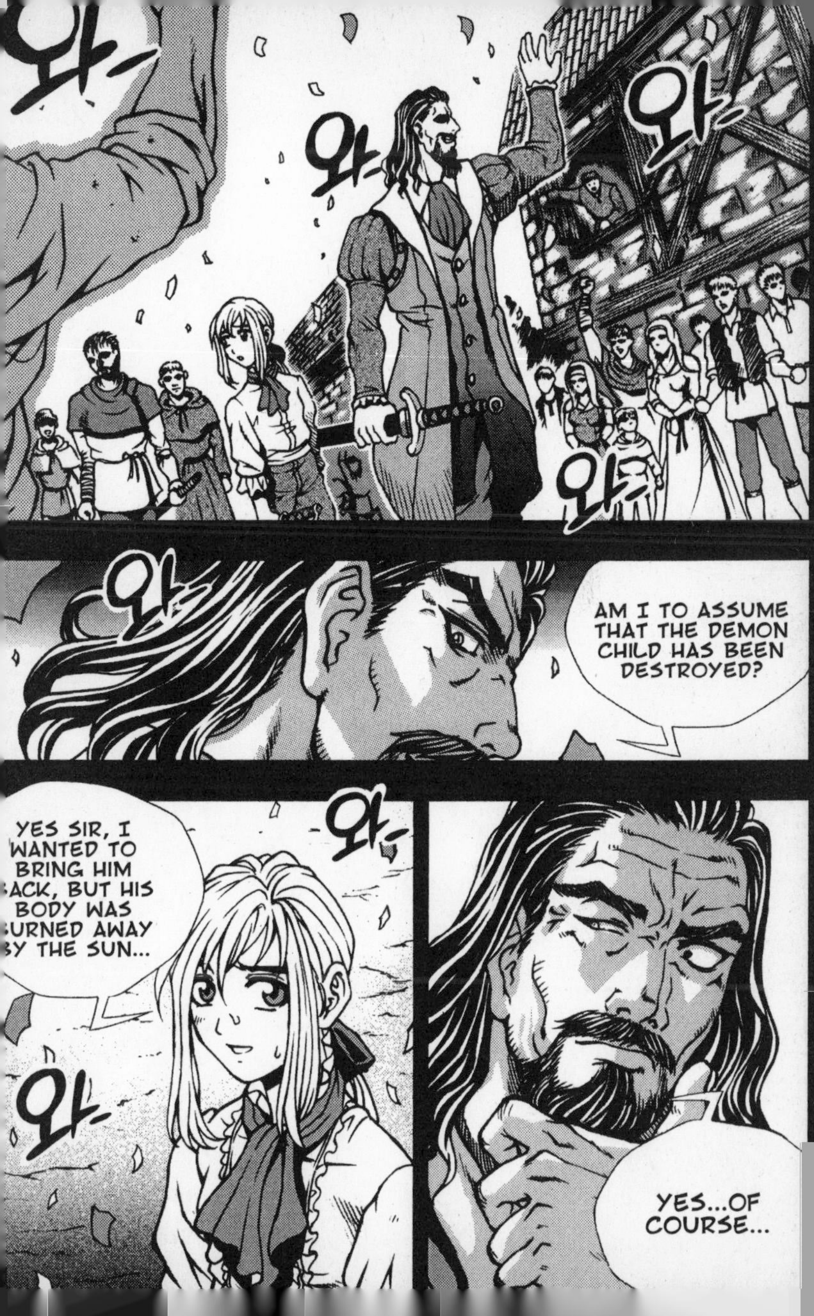
와–
와–
와–
와–
와–
AM I TO ASSUME THAT THE DEMON CHILD HAS BEEN DESTROYED?
와–
YES SIR, I WANTED TO BRING HIM ACK, BUT HIS BODY WAS URNED AWAY Y THE SUN...
와–
YES...OF COURSE...

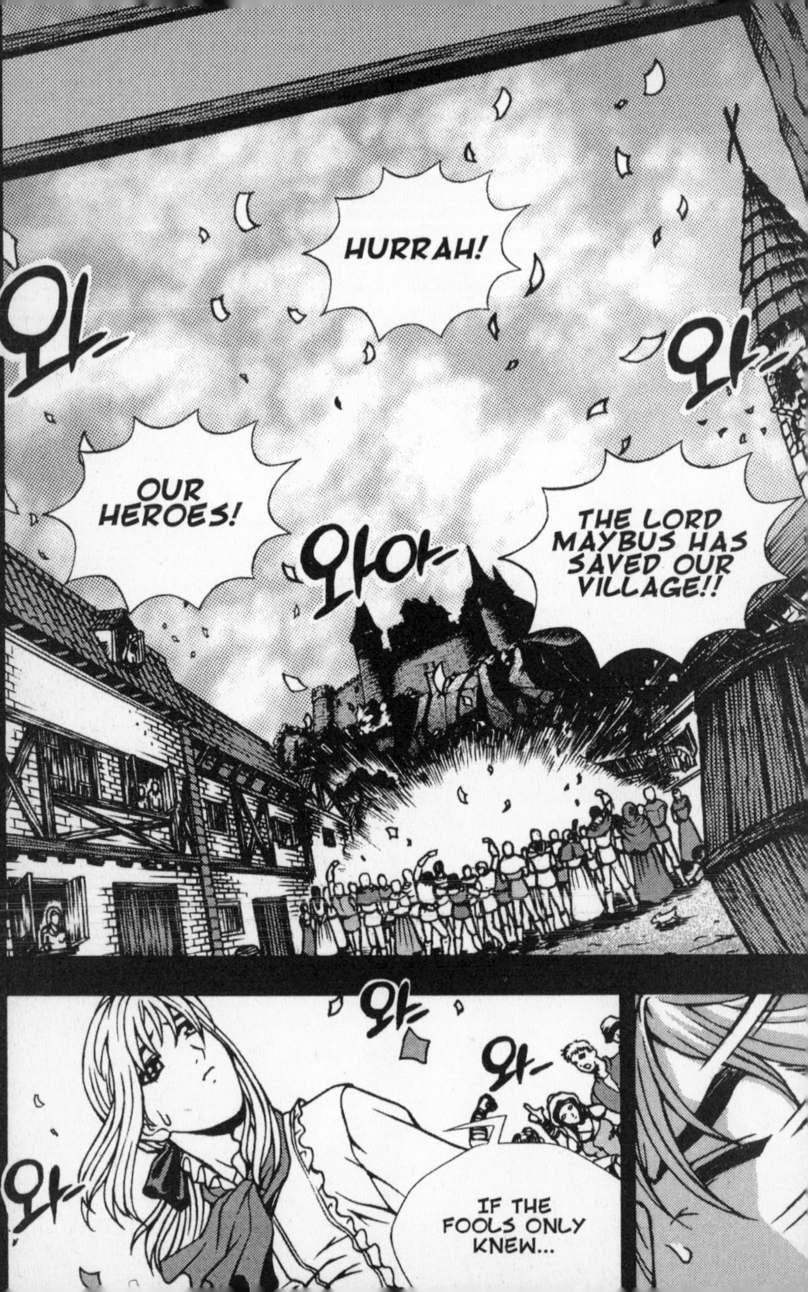
HURRAH!
와-
와-
THE LORD MAYBUS HAS SAVED OUR VILLAGE!!
와아-
OUR HEROES!
와-
와-
IF THE FOOLS ONLY KNEW...
와-

BUT I KNEW.

THEY WERE
FRIGHTENED
AND ANGRY...

THE RUMORS
SURROUNDING
CASTLE LUDBICH
WERE ALL FALSE...
MERELY
SUPERSTITION AND
IGNORANCE, FUELED
BY THE HARSH
REALITIES OF A
CRUEL EXISTENCE...

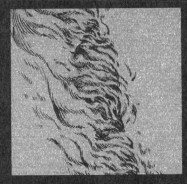

YEARS OF FAMINE,
EXORBITANT TAXATION...
THEY NEEDED A
SCAPEGOAT, A MEANS OF
TAKING CONTROL OF
WHAT WAS BEYOND THEIR
CONTROL. MAN FEARS
WHAT HE DOES NOT
UNDERSTAND...AND SO
THEY SAW CASTLE
LUDBICH AS A THREAT.

AND MY FATHER SEIZED THEIR PANIC AS A MEANS OF
RESURRECTING OUR ONCE POWERFUL FAMILY NAME.

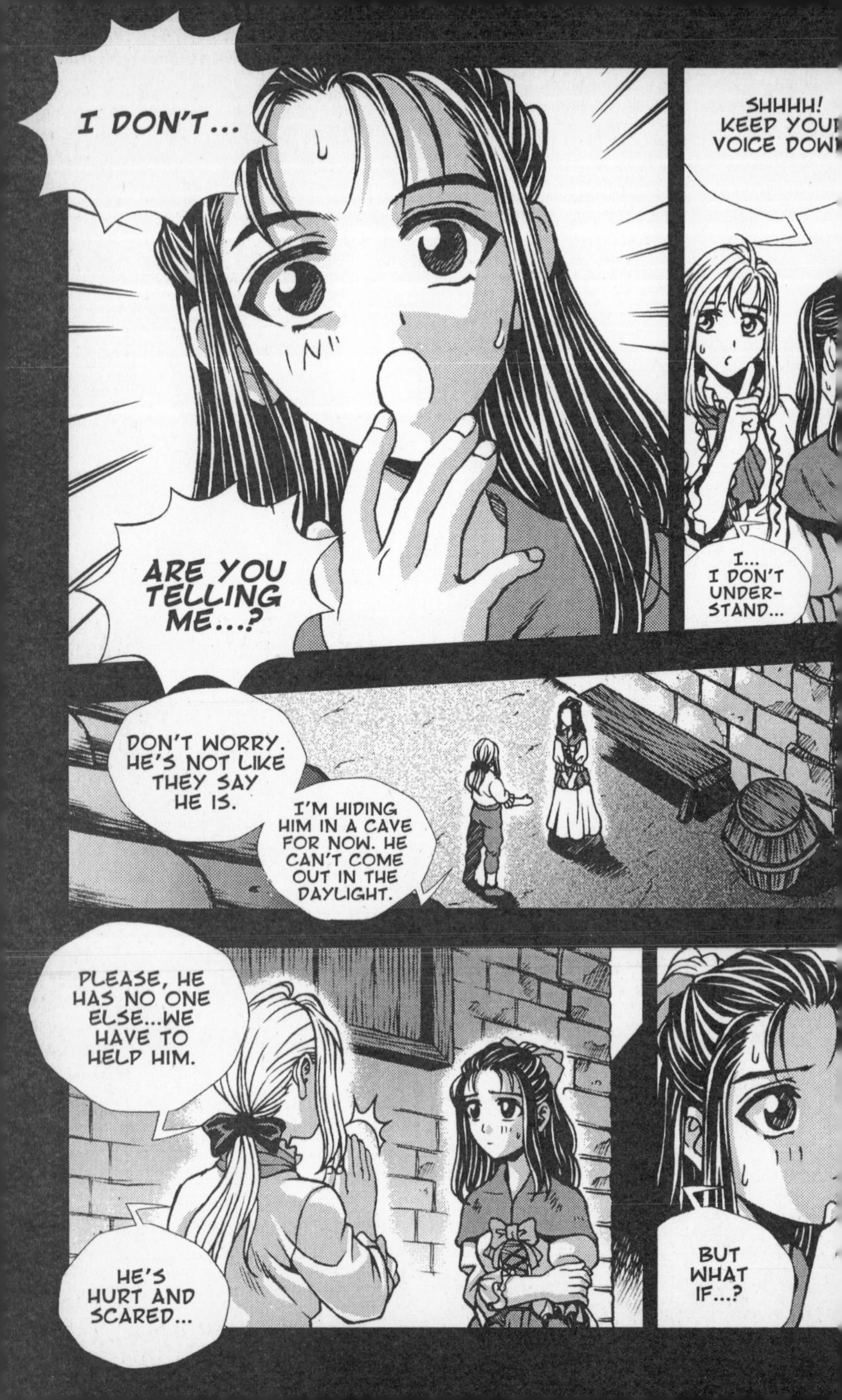
I DON'T...
ARE YOU TELLING ME...?
SHHHH! KEEP YOUR VOICE DOW
I... I DON'T UNDER-STAND...
DON'T WORRY. HE'S NOT LIKE THEY SAY HE IS.
I'M HIDING HIM IN A CAVE FOR NOW. HE CAN'T COME OUT IN THE DAYLIGHT.
PLEASE, HE HAS NO ONE ELSE...WE HAVE TO HELP HIM.
HE'S HURT AND SCARED...
BUT WHAT IF...?

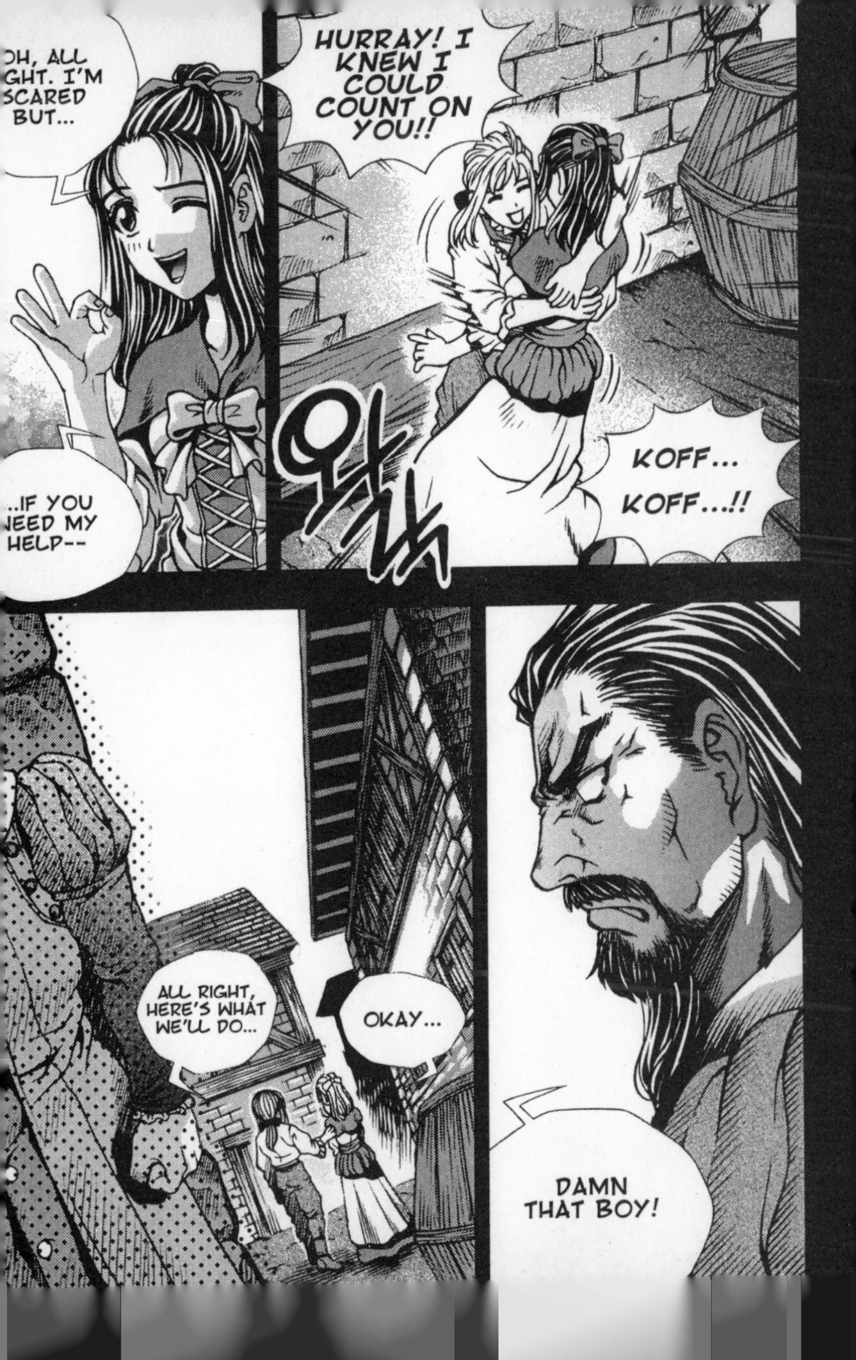
OH, ALL GHT. I'M SCARED BUT...
...IF YOU EED MY HELP--
HURRAY! I KNEW I COULD COUNT ON YOU!!
KOFF... KOFF...!!
ALL RIGHT, HERE'S WHAT WE'LL DO...
OKAY...
DAMN THAT BOY!

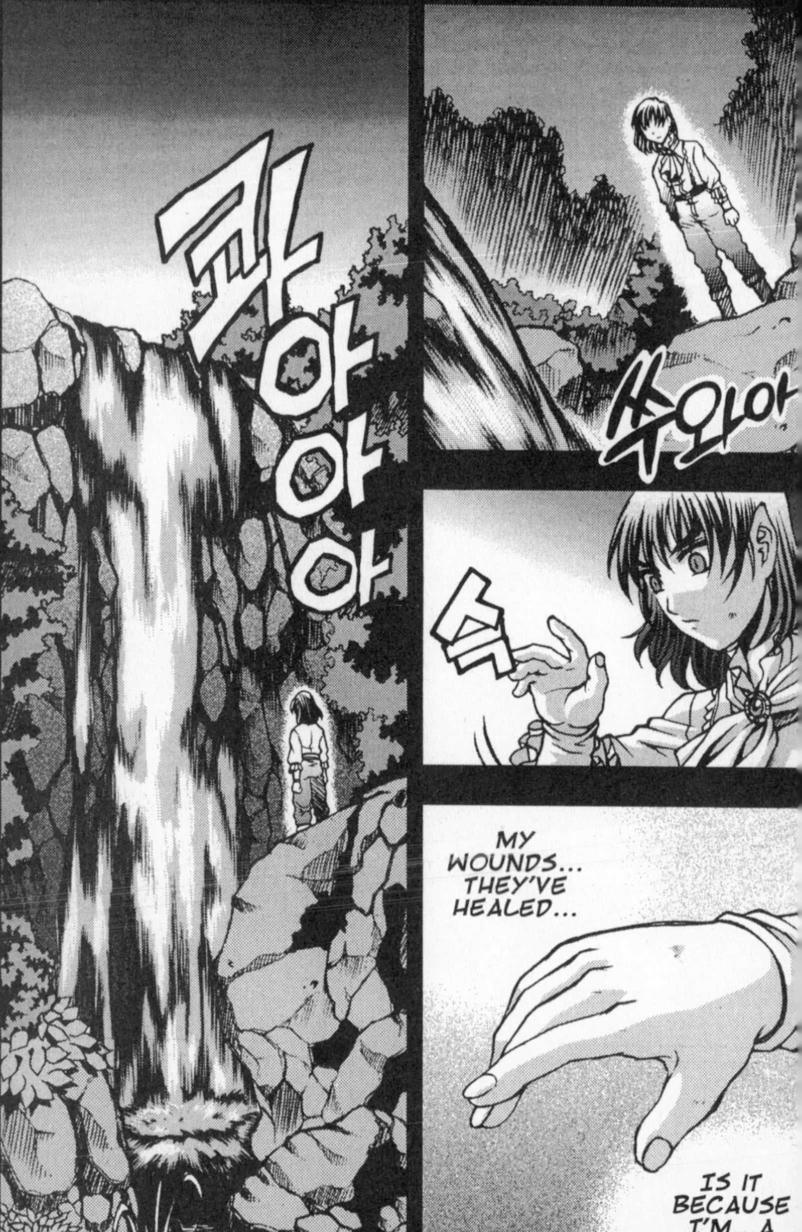
콰아아아
MY WOUNDS... THEY'VE HEALED...
IS IT BECAUSE I'M...A VAMPIRE...?

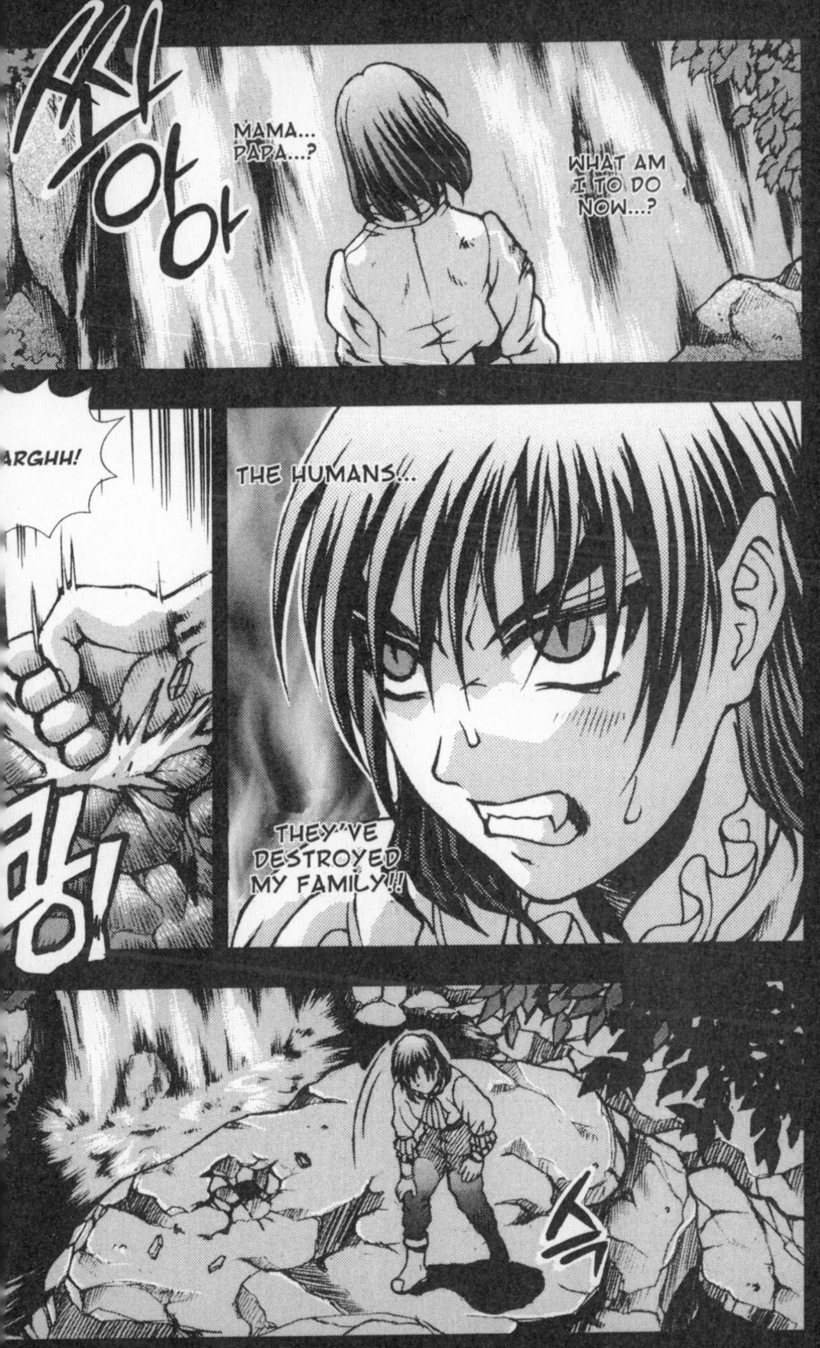
쏴아아
MAMA... PAPA...?
WHAT AM I TO DO NOW...?
ARGHH!
쾅!
THE HUMANS...
THEY'VE DESTROYED MY FAMILY!!

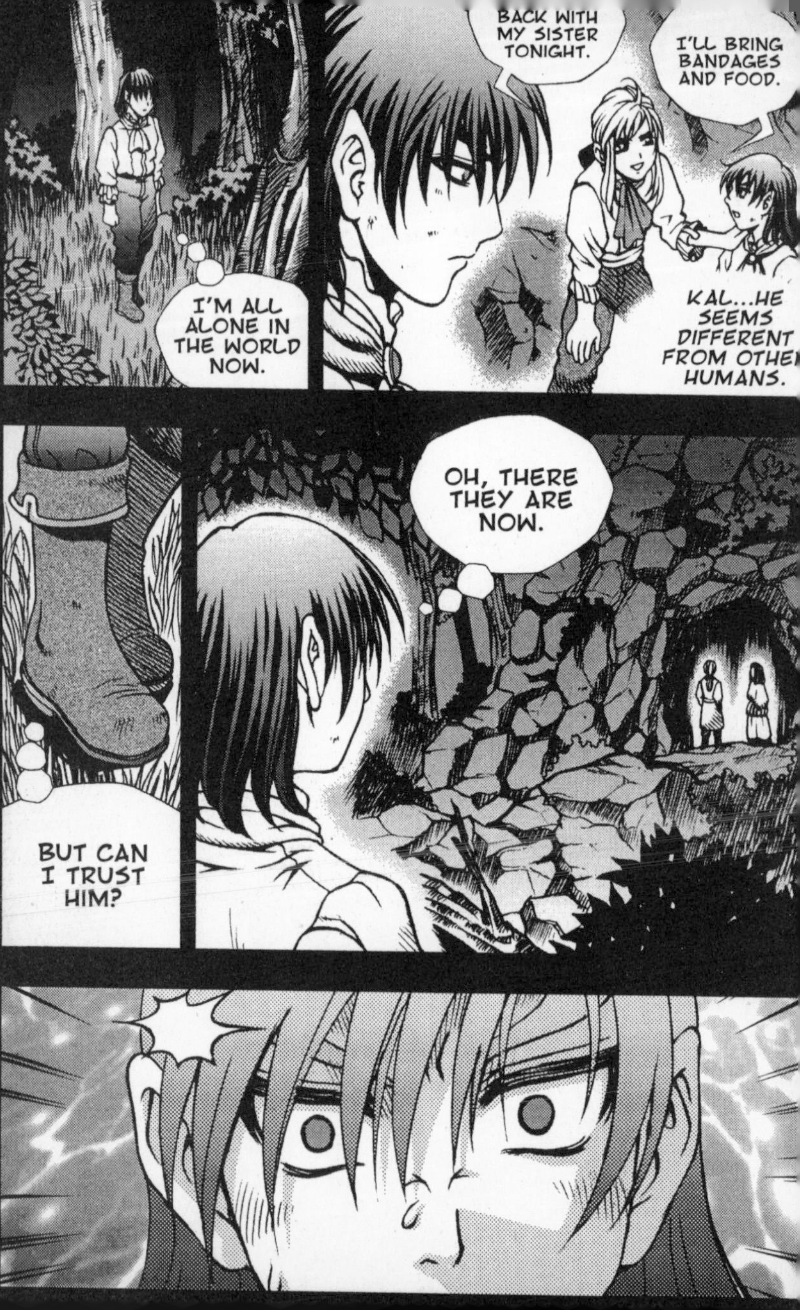

I'M ALL ALONE IN THE WORLD NOW.
BACK WITH MY SISTER TONIGHT.
I'LL BRING BANDAGES AND FOOD.
KAL...HE SEEMS DIFFERENT FROM OTHE HUMANS.
BUT CAN I TRUST HIM?
OH, THERE THEY ARE NOW.

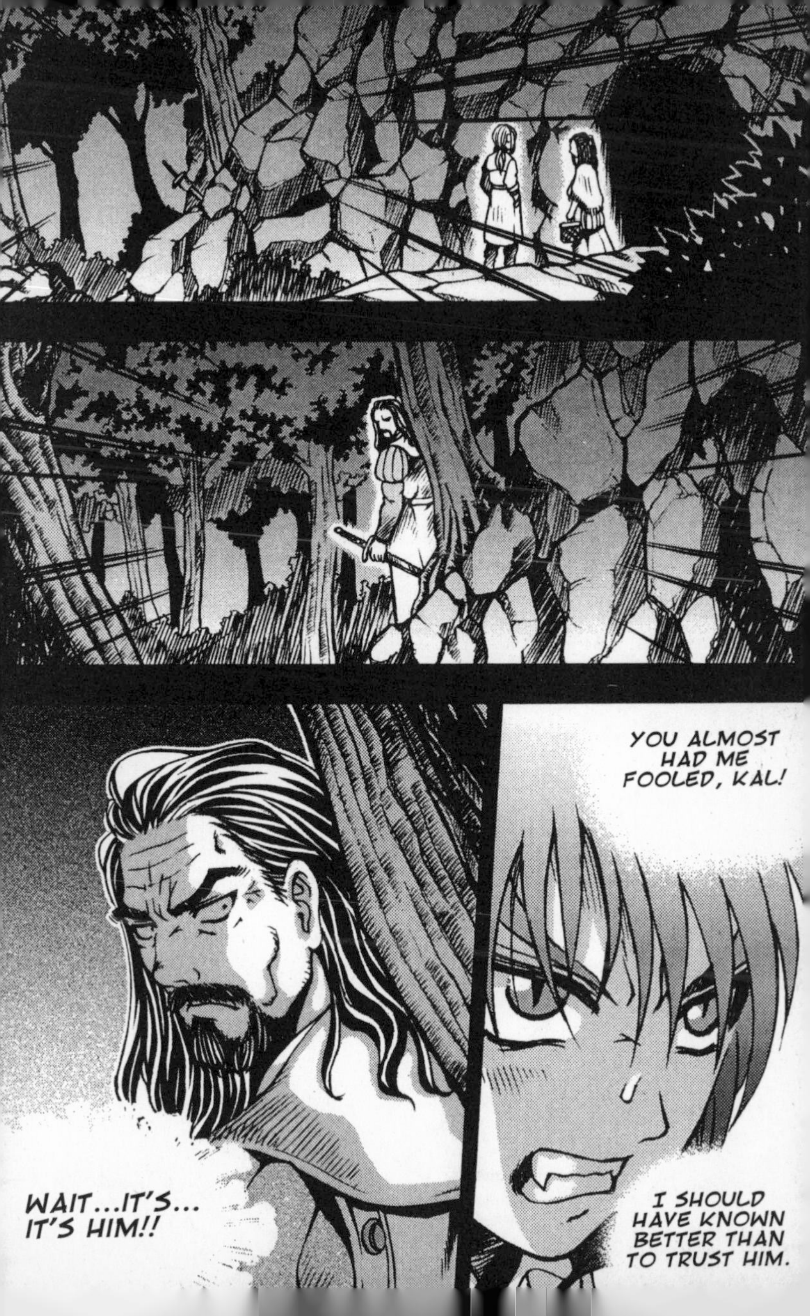
YOU ALMOST HAD ME FOOLED, KAL!
I SHOULD HAVE KNOWN BETTER THAN TO TRUST HIM.
WAIT...IT'S... IT'S HIM!!

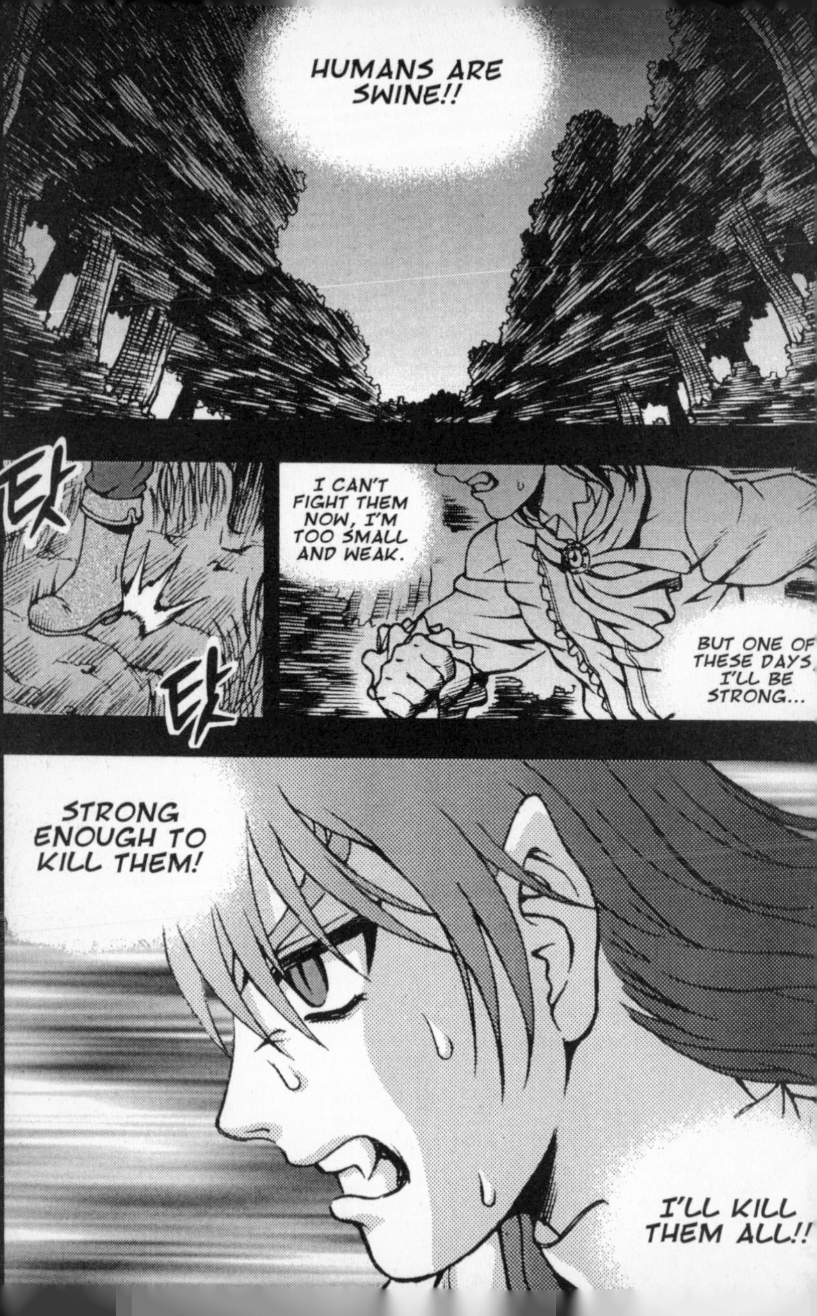
HUMANS ARE SWINE!!
탁
탁
I CAN'T FIGHT THEM NOW, I'M TOO SMALL AND WEAK.
BUT ONE OF THESE DAYS, I'LL BE STRONG...
STRONG ENOUGH TO KILL THEM!
I'LL KILL THEM ALL!!

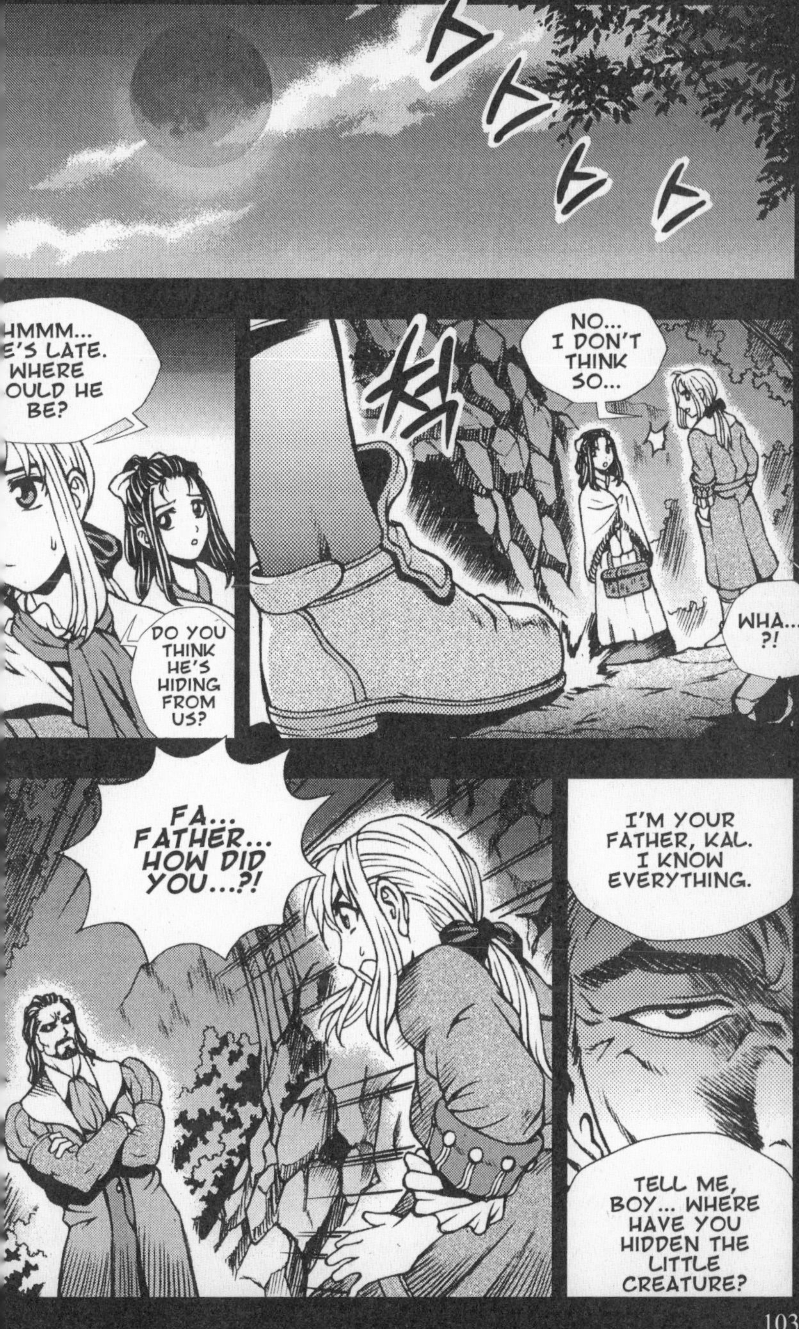
HMMM... E'S LATE. WHERE OULD HE BE?
DO YOU THINK HE'S HIDING FROM US?
NO... I DON'T THINK SO...
WHA... ?!
FA... FATHER... HOW DID YOU...?!
I'M YOUR FATHER, KAL. I KNOW EVERYTHING.
TELL ME, BOY... WHERE HAVE YOU HIDDEN THE LITTLE CREATURE?

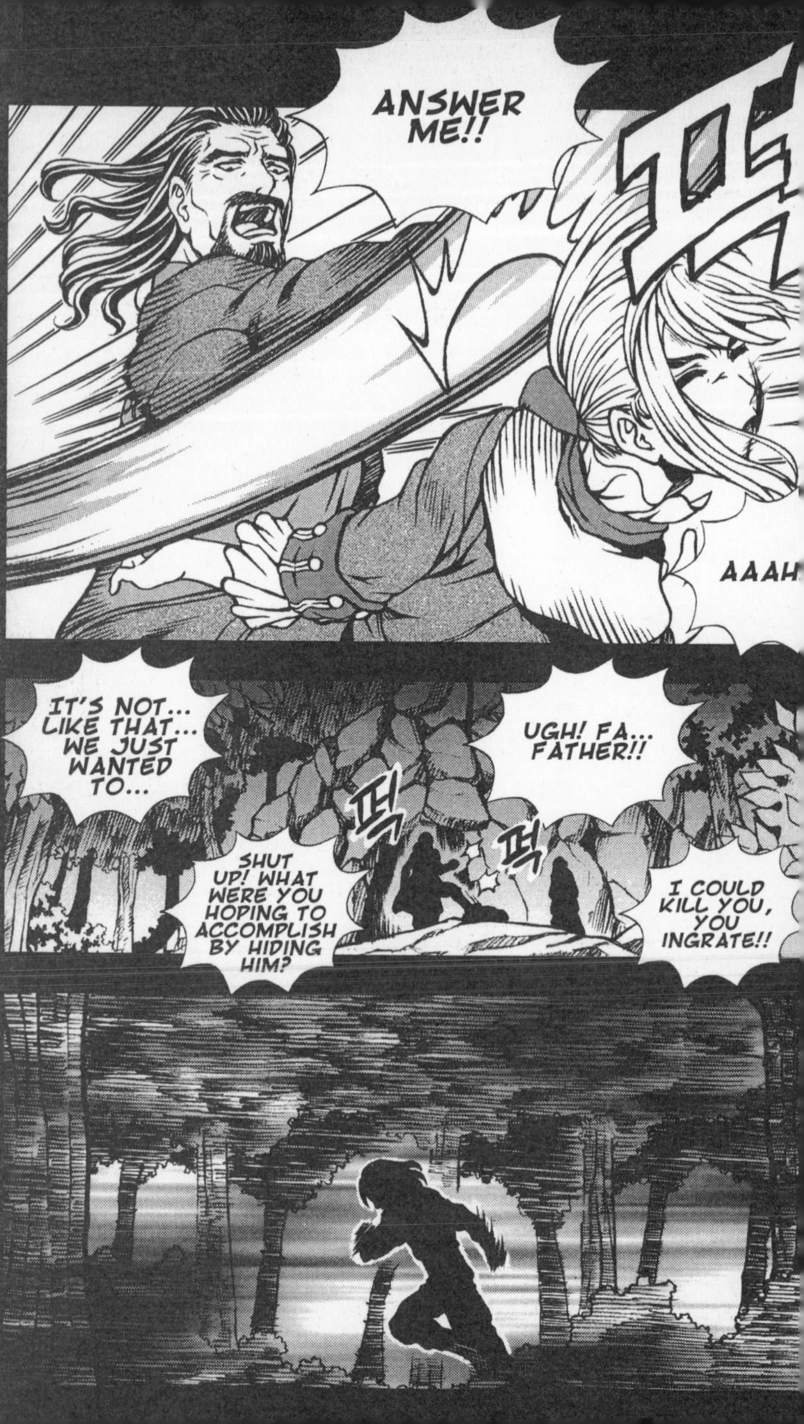
ANSWER ME!!
AAAH
UGH! FA... FATHER!!
IT'S NOT... LIKE THAT... WE JUST WANTED TO...
퍽
퍽
SHUT UP! WHAT WERE YOU HOPING TO ACCOMPLISH BY HIDING HIM?
I COULD KILL YOU, YOU INGRATE!!

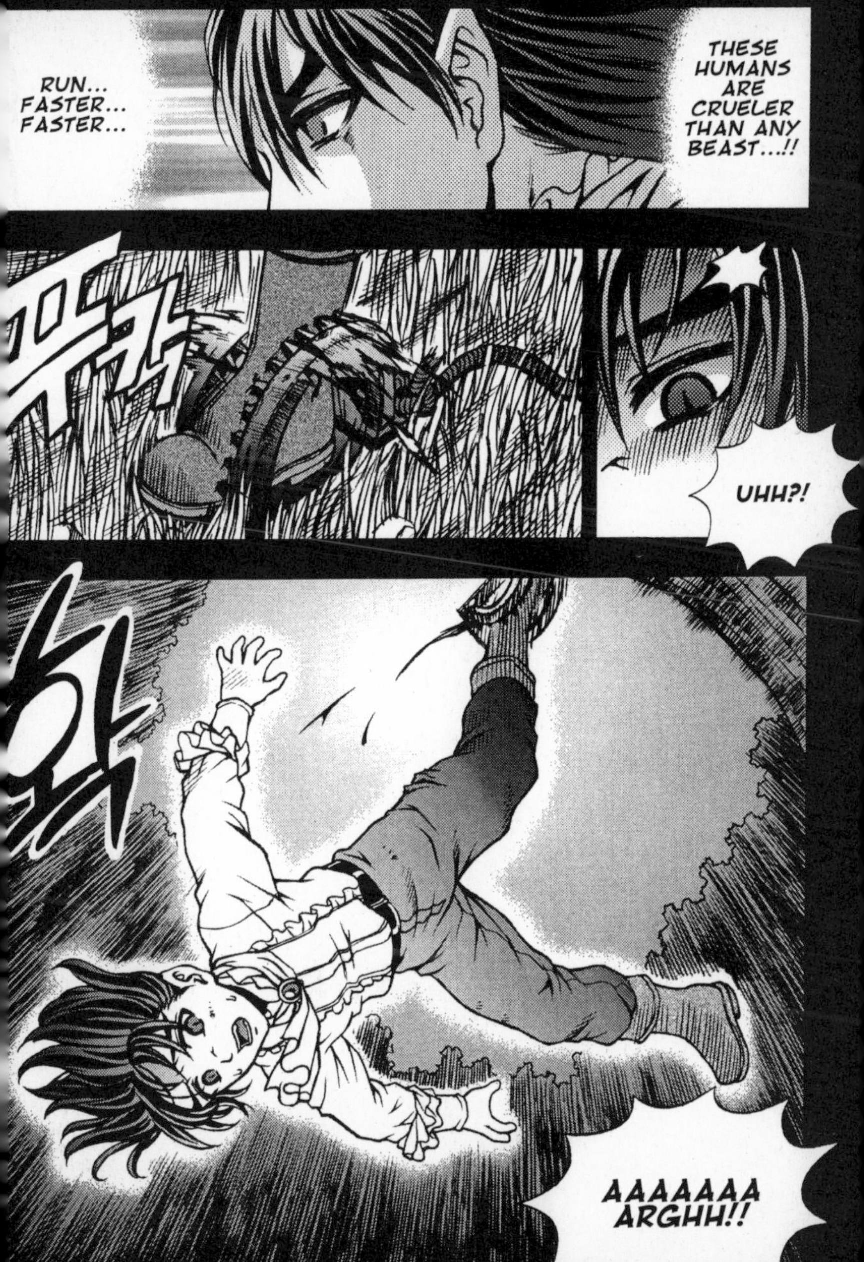
THESE HUMANS ARE CRUELER THAN ANY BEAST...!!
RUN... FASTER... FASTER...
UHH?!
AAAAAAA ARGHH!!

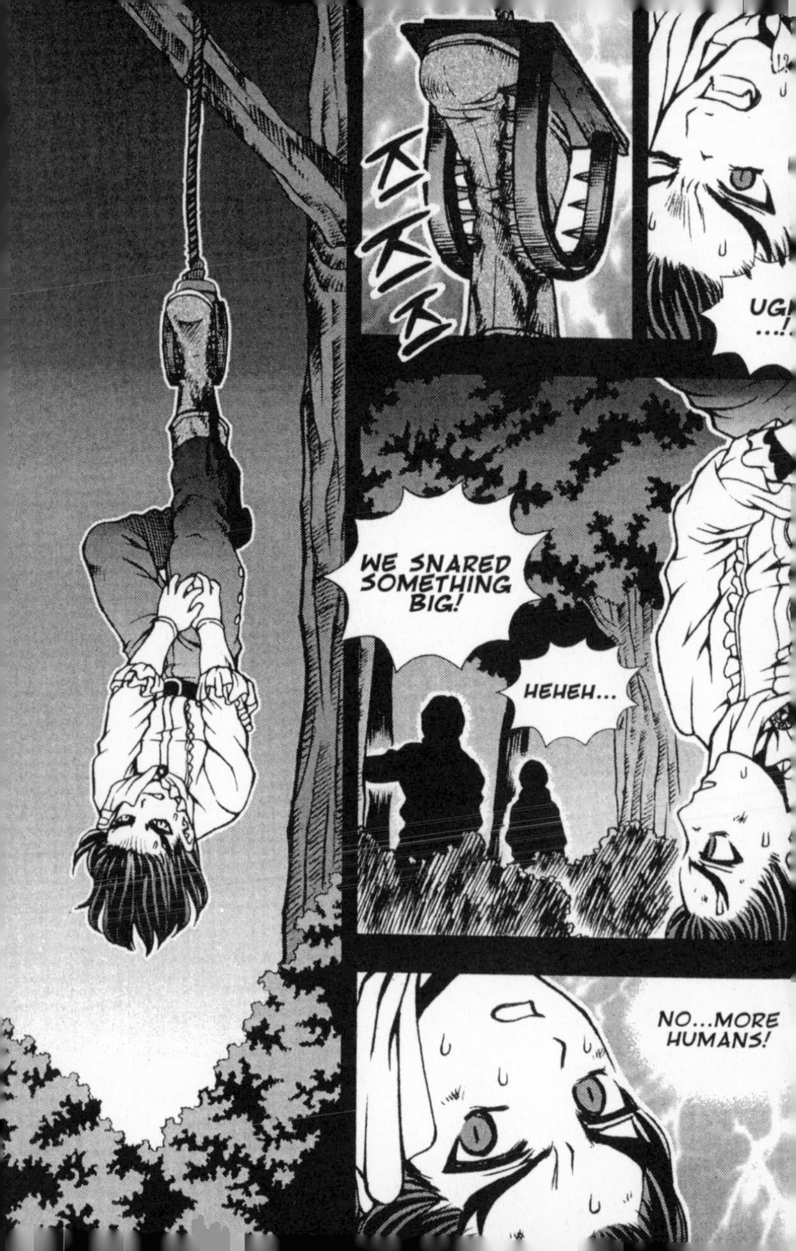
!?
UG ...!
KIKIKI
WE SNARED SOMETHING BIG!
HEHEH...
NO...MORE HUMANS!

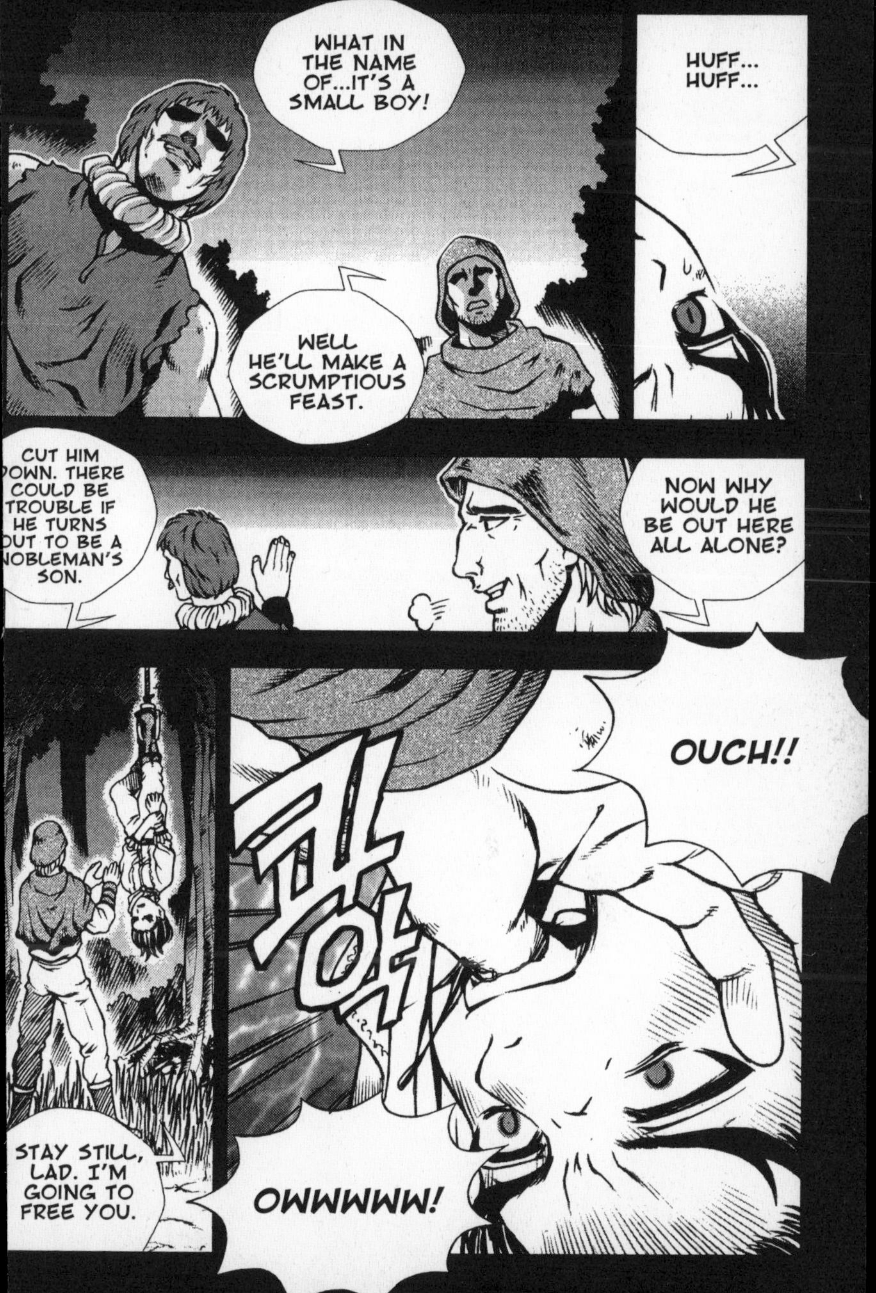
HUFF... HUFF...
WHAT IN THE NAME OF...IT'S A SMALL BOY!
WELL HE'LL MAKE A SCRUMPTIOUS FEAST.
NOW WHY WOULD HE BE OUT HERE ALL ALONE?
CUT HIM DOWN. THERE COULD BE TROUBLE IF HE TURNS OUT TO BE A NOBLEMAN'S SON.
OUCH!!
OWWWWW!
STAY STILL, LAD. I'M GOING TO FREE YOU.

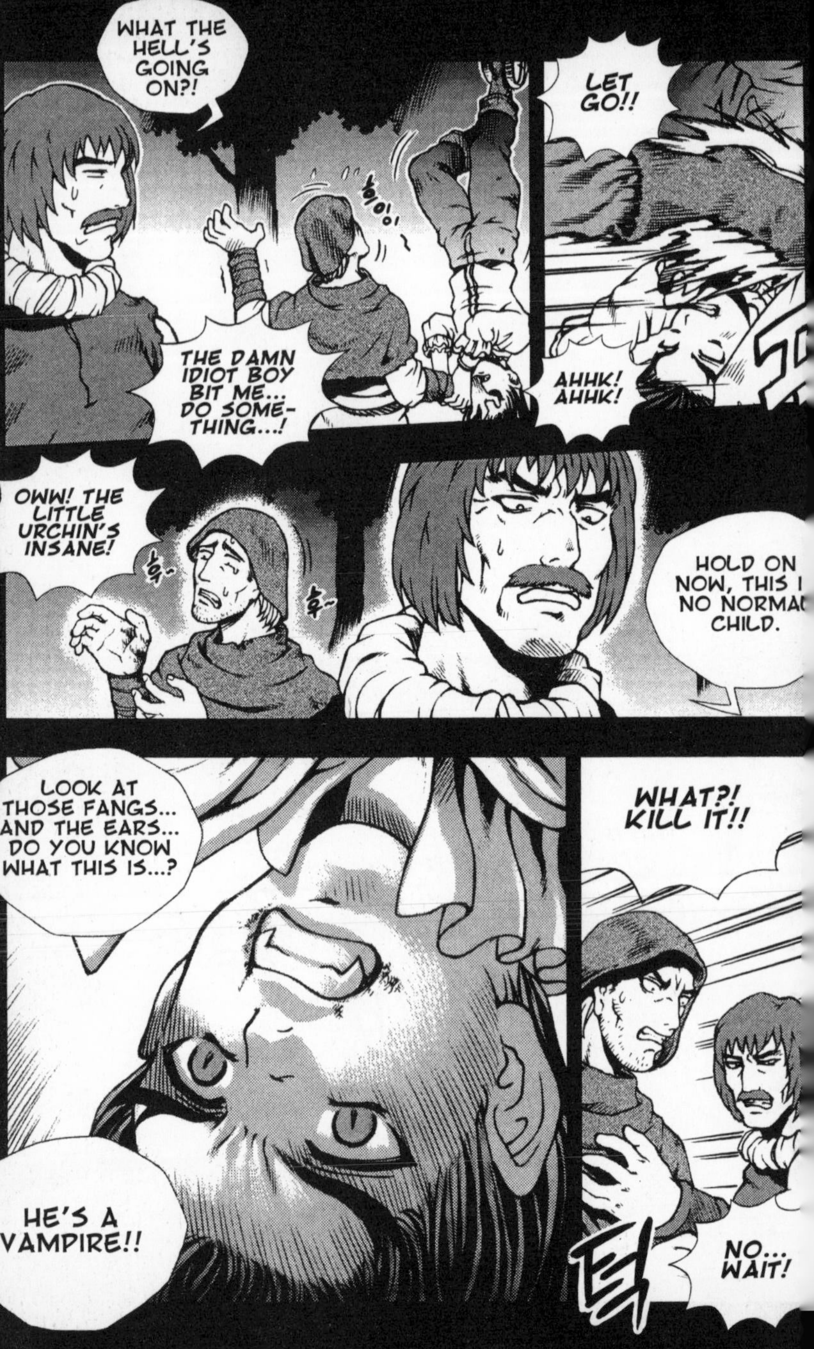
WHAT THE HELL'S GOING ON?!
THE DAMN IDIOT BOY BIT ME... DO SOME-THING...!
LET GO!!
AHHK! AHHK!
OWW! THE LITTLE URCHIN'S INSANE!
HOLD ON NOW, THIS I NO NORMA CHILD.
LOOK AT THOSE FANGS... AND THE EARS... DO YOU KNOW WHAT THIS IS...?
HE'S A VAMPIRE!!
WHAT?! KILL IT!!
NO... WAIT!

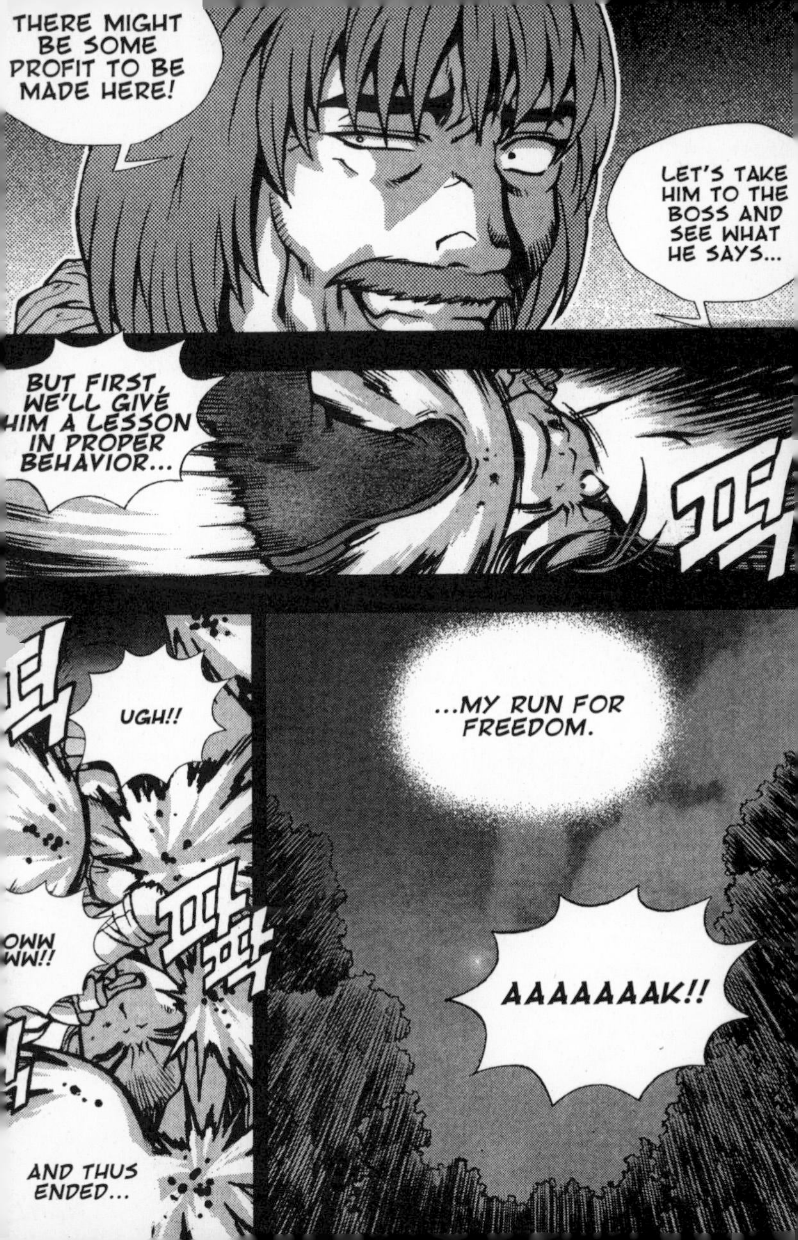
THERE MIGHT BE SOME PROFIT TO BE MADE HERE!
LET'S TAKE HIM TO THE BOSS AND SEE WHAT HE SAYS...
BUT FIRST, WE'LL GIVE HIM A LESSON IN PROPER BEHAVIOR...
UGH!!
OWW WW!!
AND THUS ENDED...
...MY RUN FOR FREEDOM.
AAAAAAAK!!

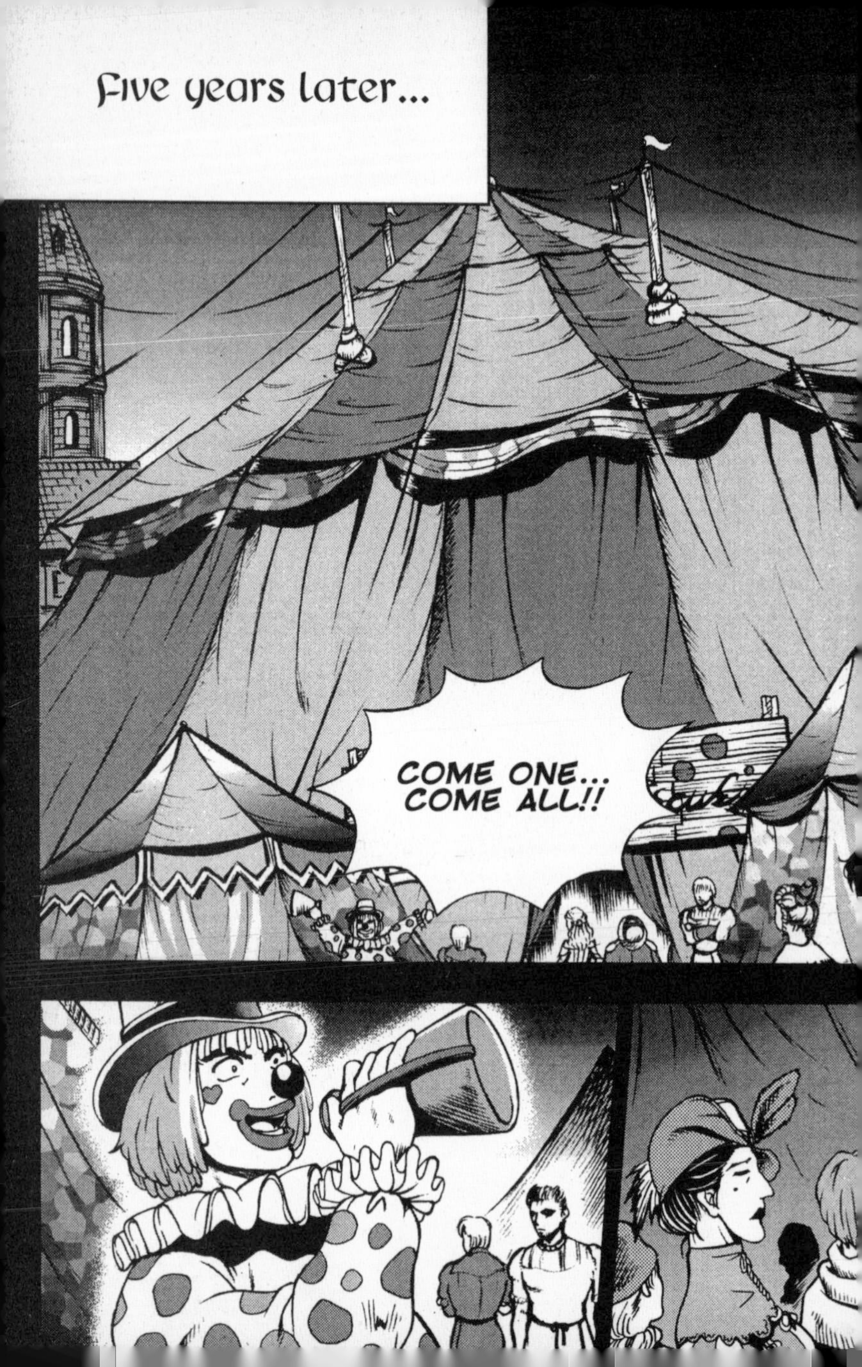
Five years later...
COME ONE... COME ALL!!

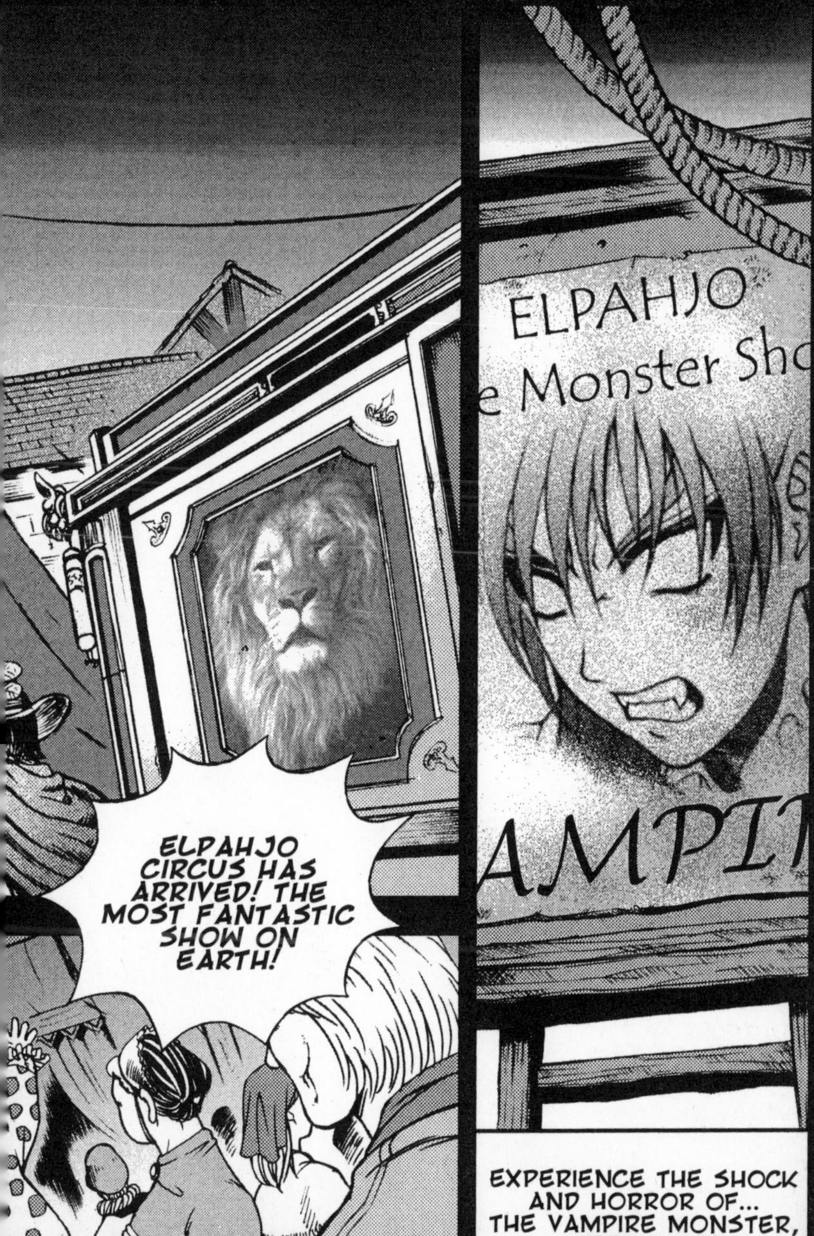
ELPAHJO
e Monster Sho
AMPI
EXPERIENCE THE SHOCK AND HORROR OF... THE VAMPIRE MONSTER, DESHWITAT!
ELPAHJO CIRCUS HAS ARRIVED! THE MOST FANTASTIC SHOW ON EARTH!

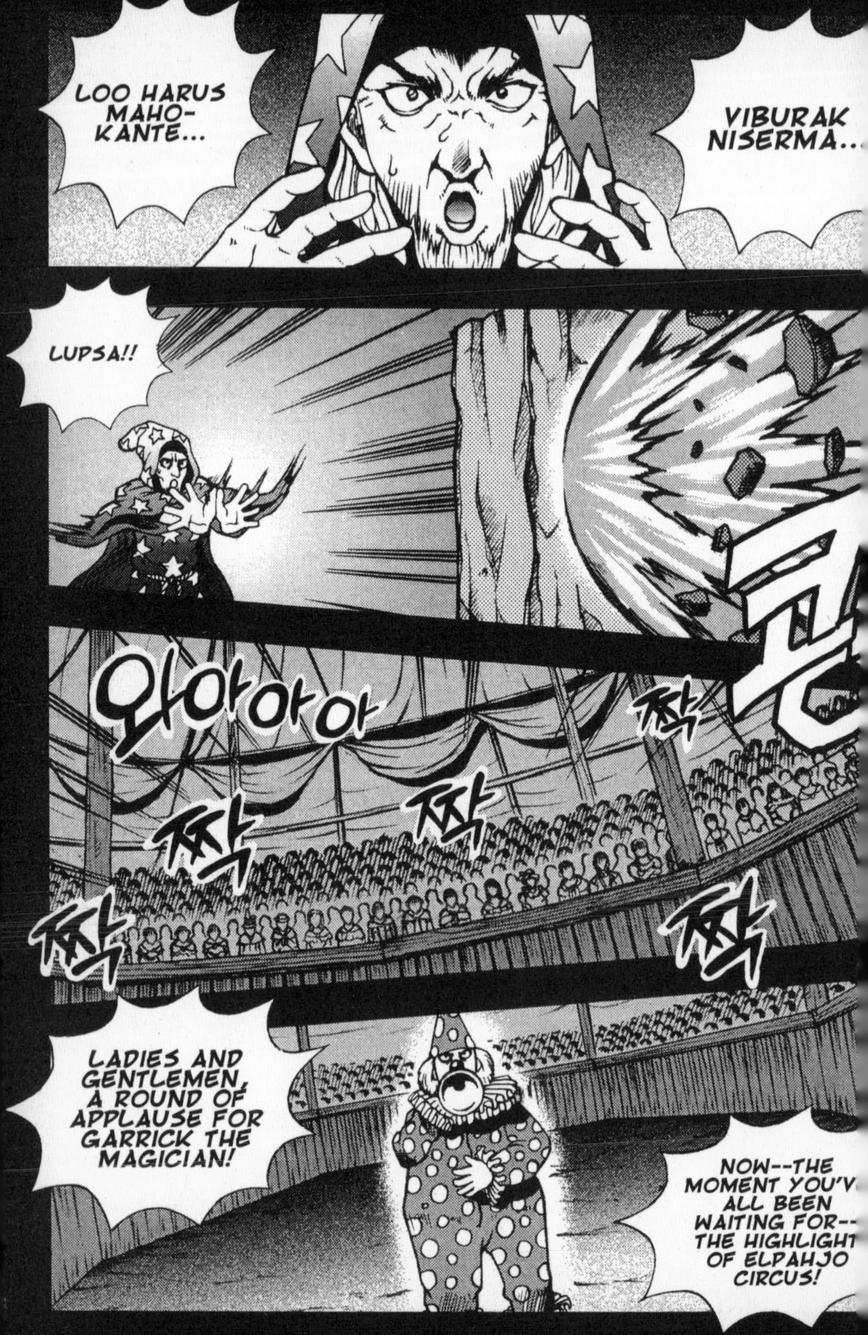
LOO HARUS MAHO-KANTE...
VIBURAK NISERMA...
LUPSA!!
와아아아아
짝
짝
짝
짝
짝
LADIES AND GENTLEMEN, A ROUND OF APPLAUSE FOR GARRICK THE MAGICIAN!
NOW--THE MOMENT YOU'V ALL BEEN WAITING FOR--THE HIGHLIGHT OF ELPAHJO CIRCUS!

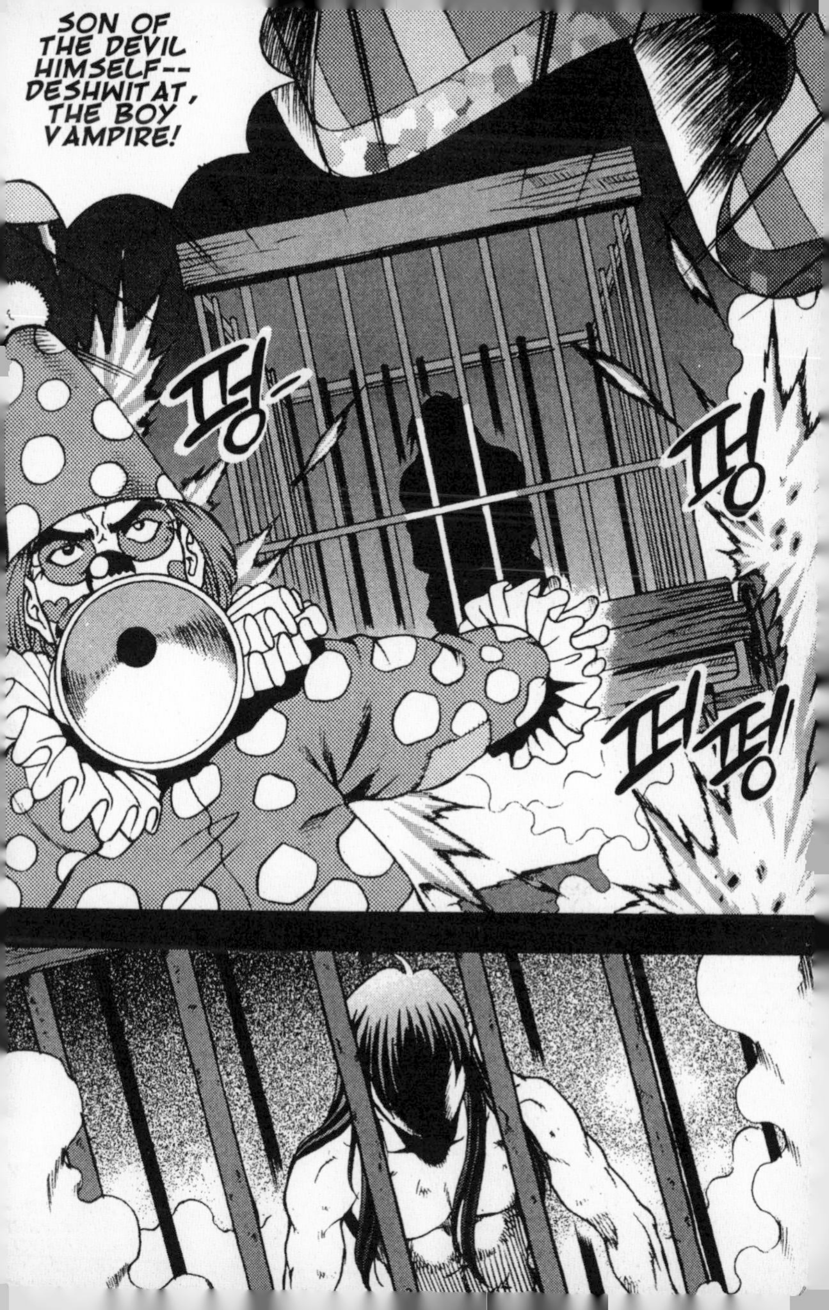
SON OF THE DEVIL HIMSELF-- DESHWITAT, THE BOY VAMPIRE!
펑-
펑
퍼펑!

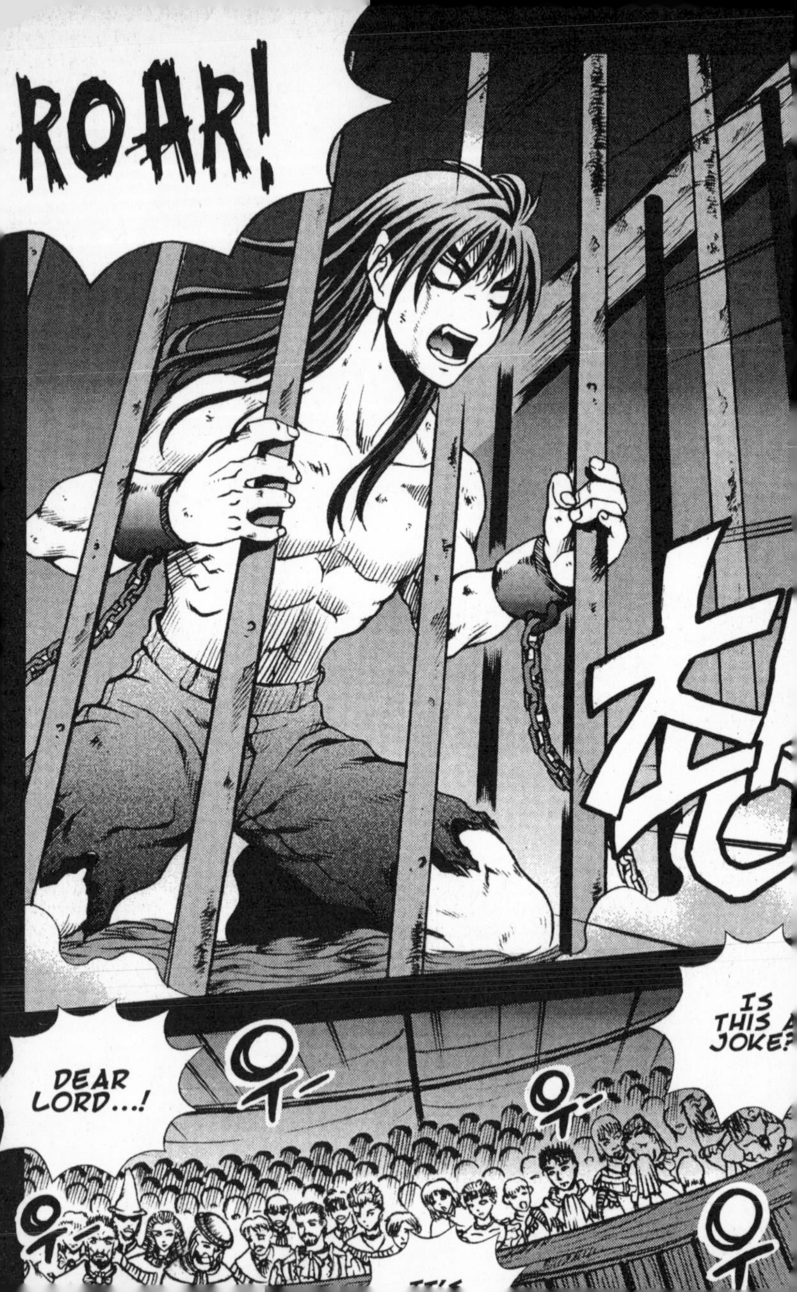
ROAR!
IS THIS A JOKE?
DEAR LORD...!

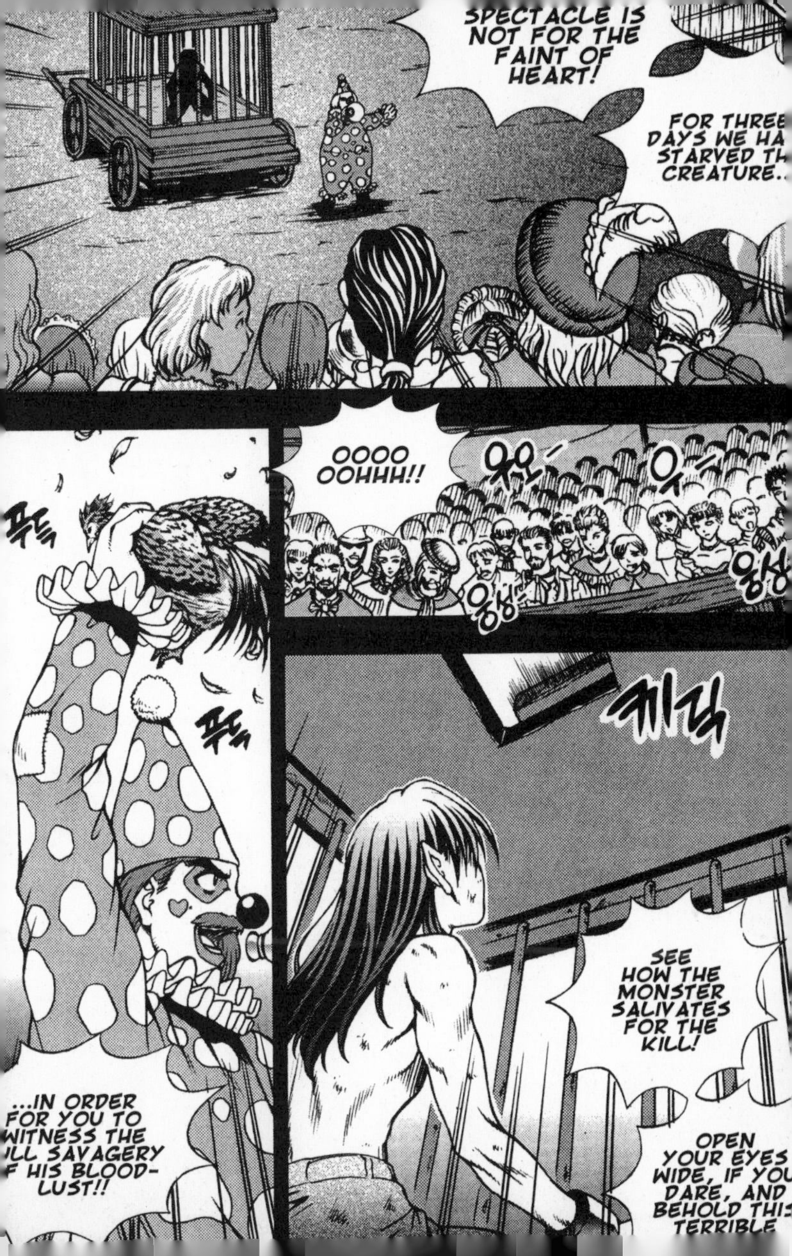
SPECTACLE IS NOT FOR THE FAINT OF HEART!
FOR THREE DAYS WE HA STARVED TH CREATURE..
푸득
푸득
...IN ORDER FOR YOU TO WITNESS THE ULL SAVAGERY F HIS BLOOD-LUST!!
OOOO OOHHHH!!
우오–
와–
웅성
웅성
끼각
SEE HOW THE MONSTER SALIVATES FOR THE KILL!
OPEN YOUR EYES WIDE, IF YOU DARE, AND BEHOLD THIS TERRIBLE

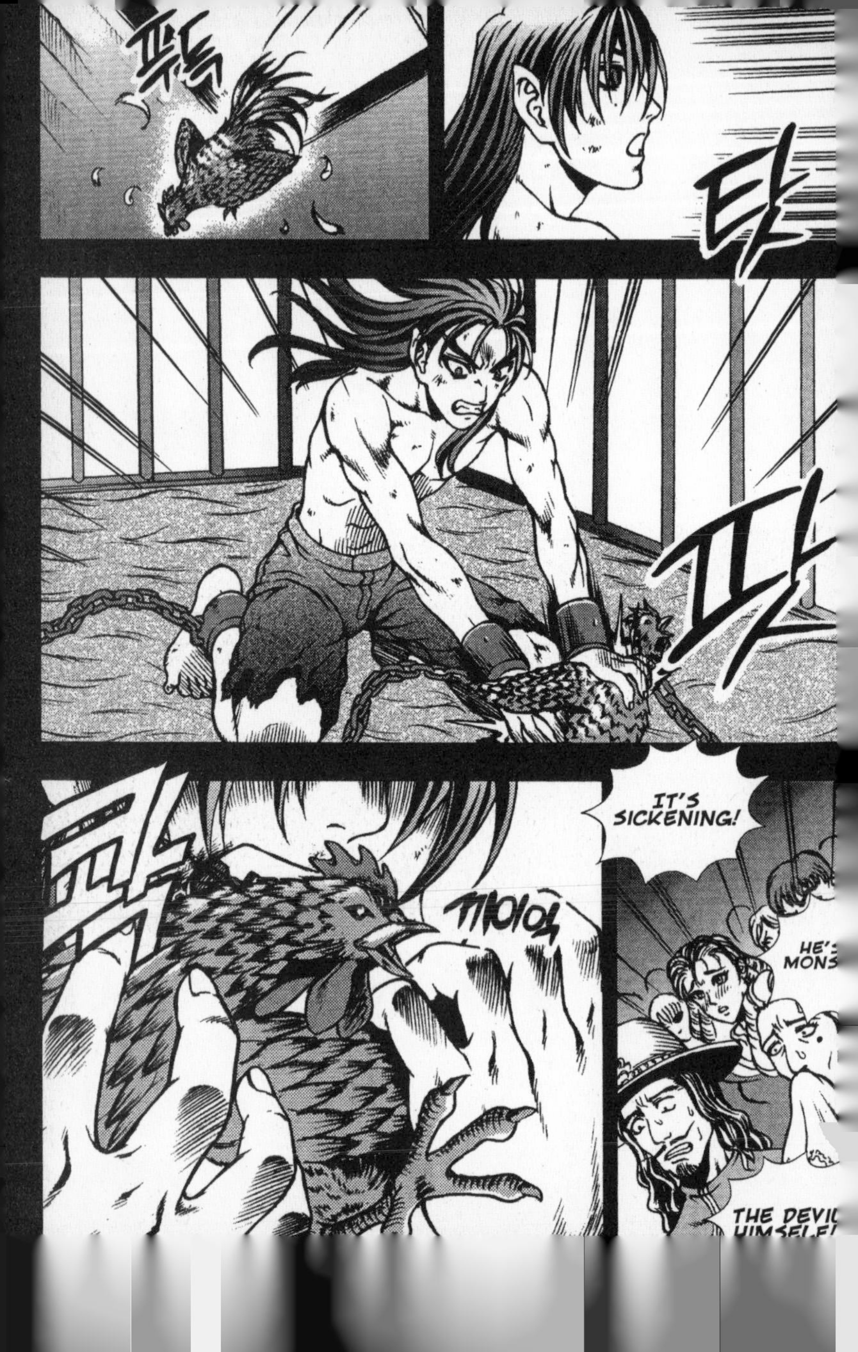

푸드득
탁
끼이이익
IT'S SICKENING!
HE'S MONS
THE DEVIL HIMSELF!

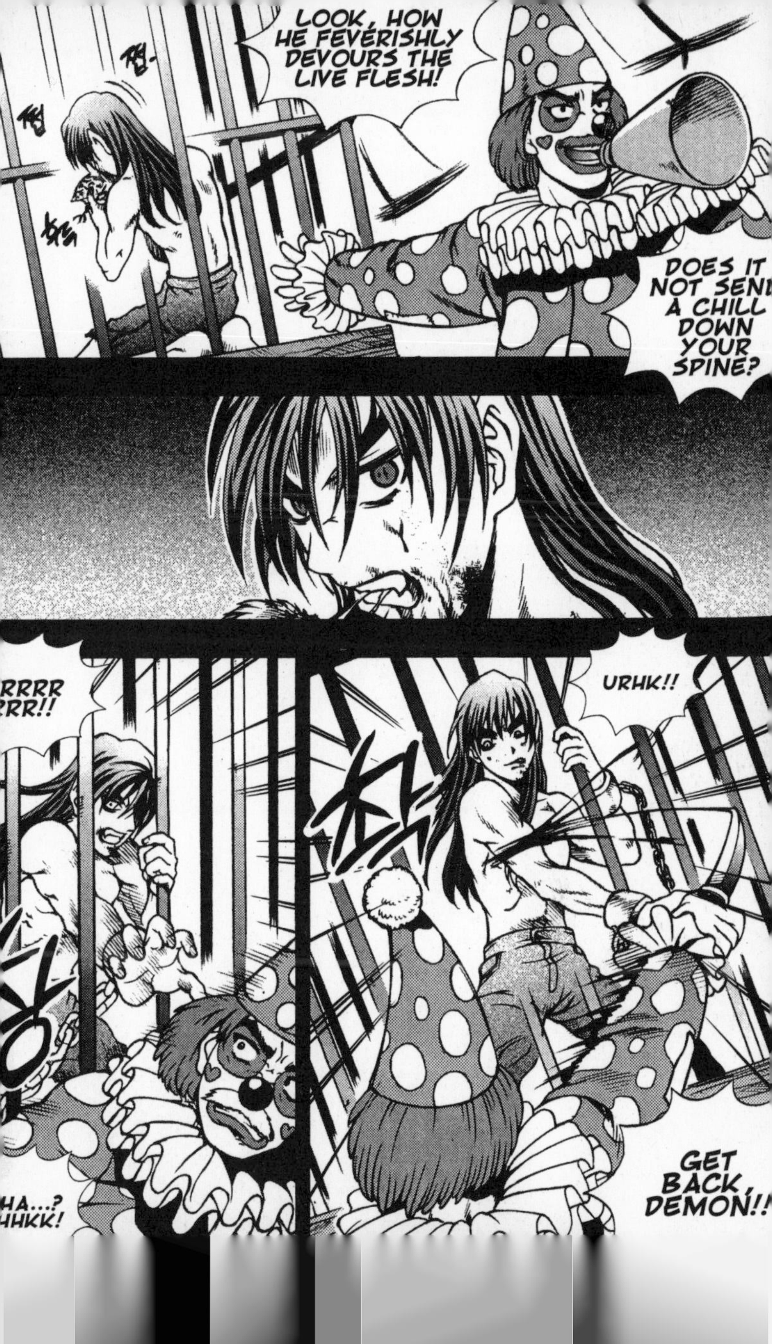
LOOK, HOW HE FEVERISHLY DEVOURS THE LIVE FLESH!
DOES IT NOT SEND A CHILL DOWN YOUR SPINE?
RRRR RR!!
HA...? HHKK!
URHK!!
GET BACK, DEMON!!

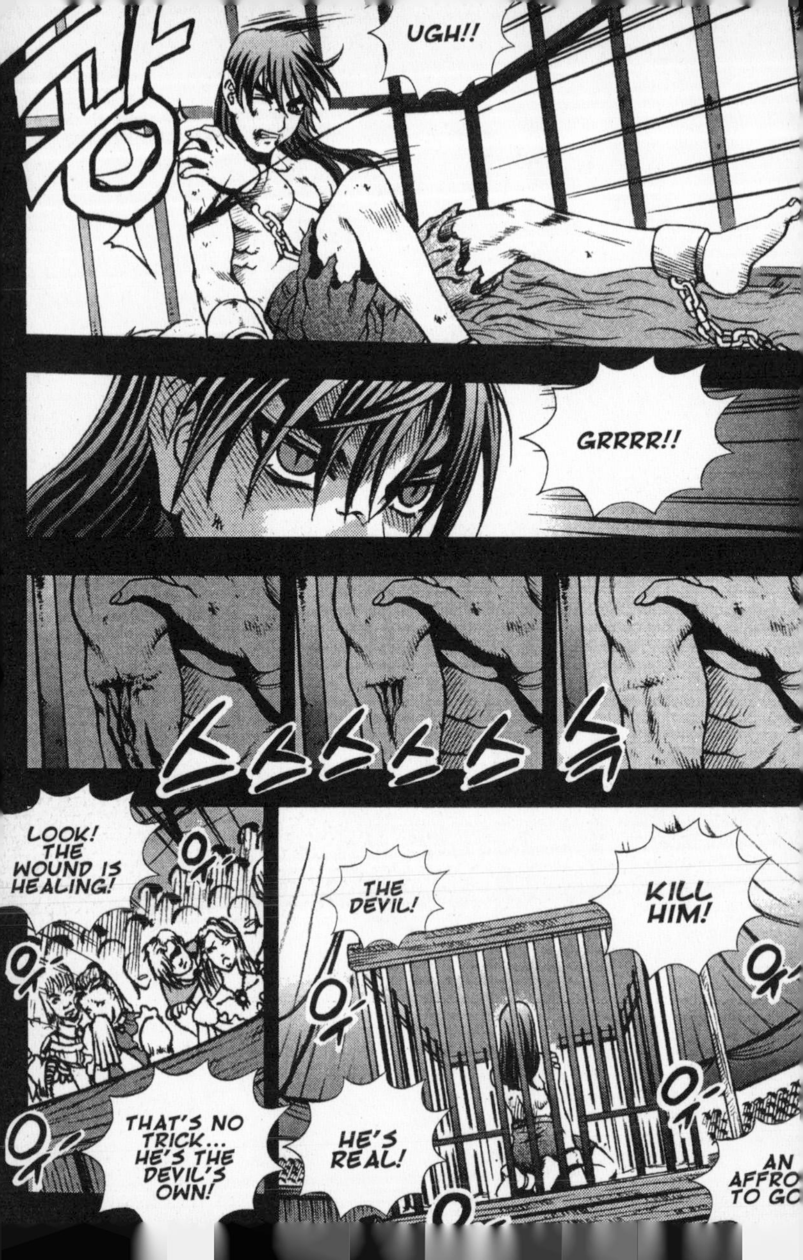
UGH!!
GRRRR!!
KILL HIM!
THE DEVIL!
HE'S REAL!
AN AFFRO TO GO
LOOK! THE WOUND IS HEALING!
THAT'S NO TRICK... HE'S THE DEVIL'S OWN!

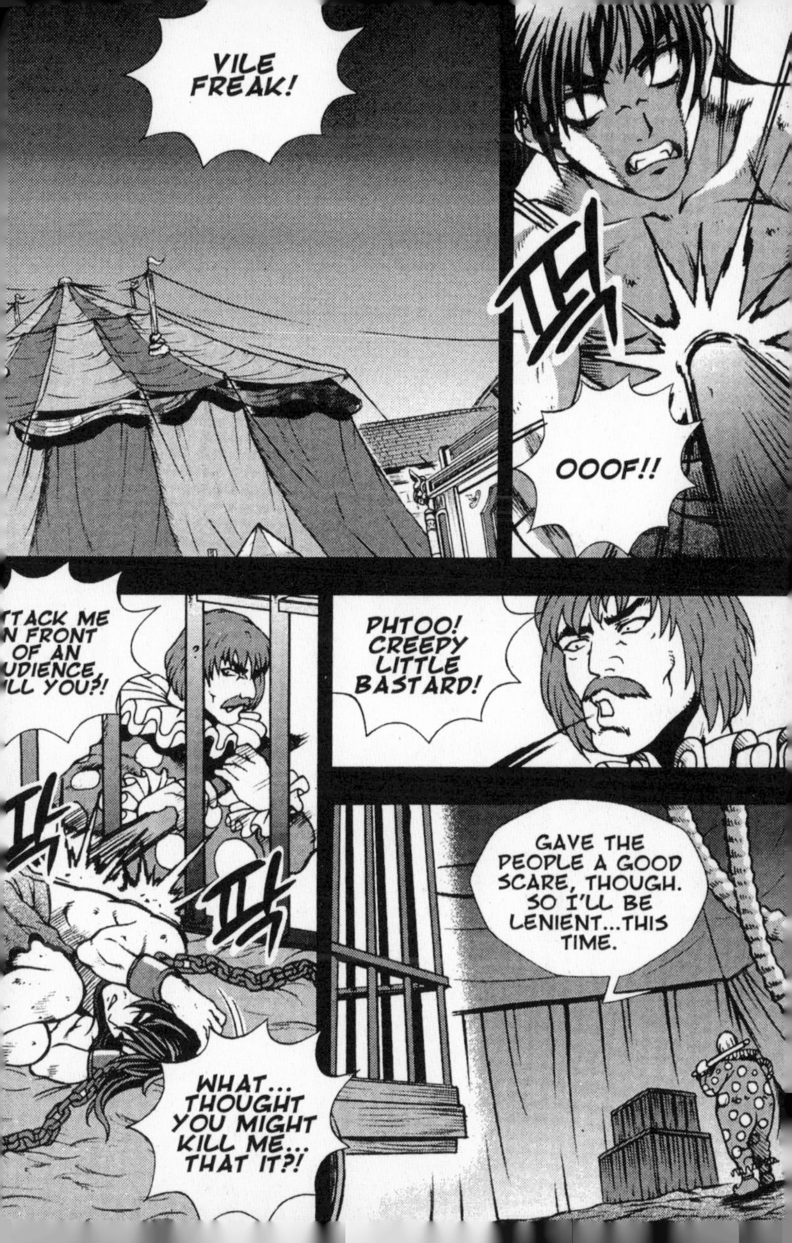
VILE FREAK!
OOOF!!
TTACK ME N FRONT OF AN UDIENCE, ILL YOU?!
PHTOO! CREEPY LITTLE BASTARD!
WHAT... THOUGHT YOU MIGHT KILL ME... THAT IT?!
GAVE THE PEOPLE A GOOD SCARE, THOUGH. SO I'LL BE LENIENT...THIS TIME.

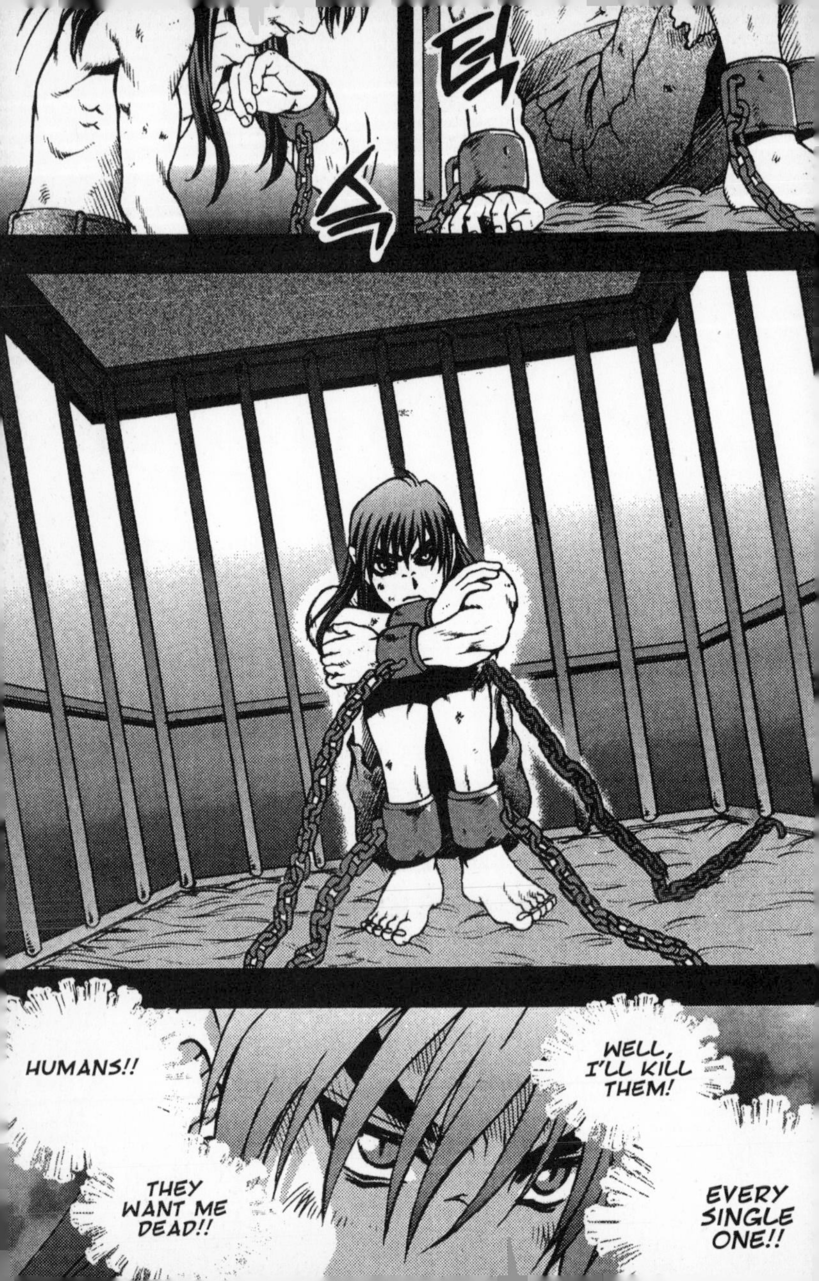
턱
HUMANS!!
THEY WANT ME DEAD!!
WELL, I'LL KILL THEM!
EVERY SINGLE ONE!!

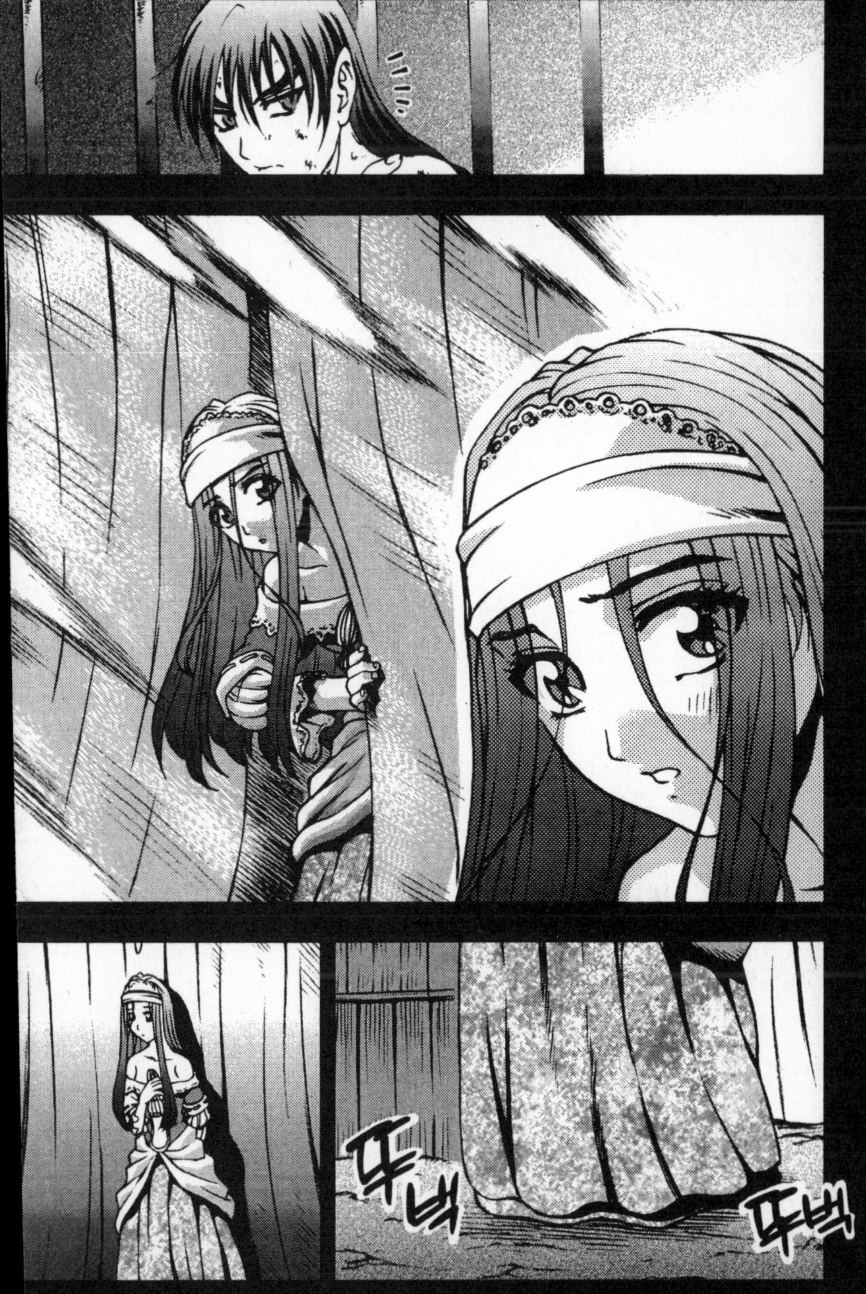
뚜벅
뚜벅

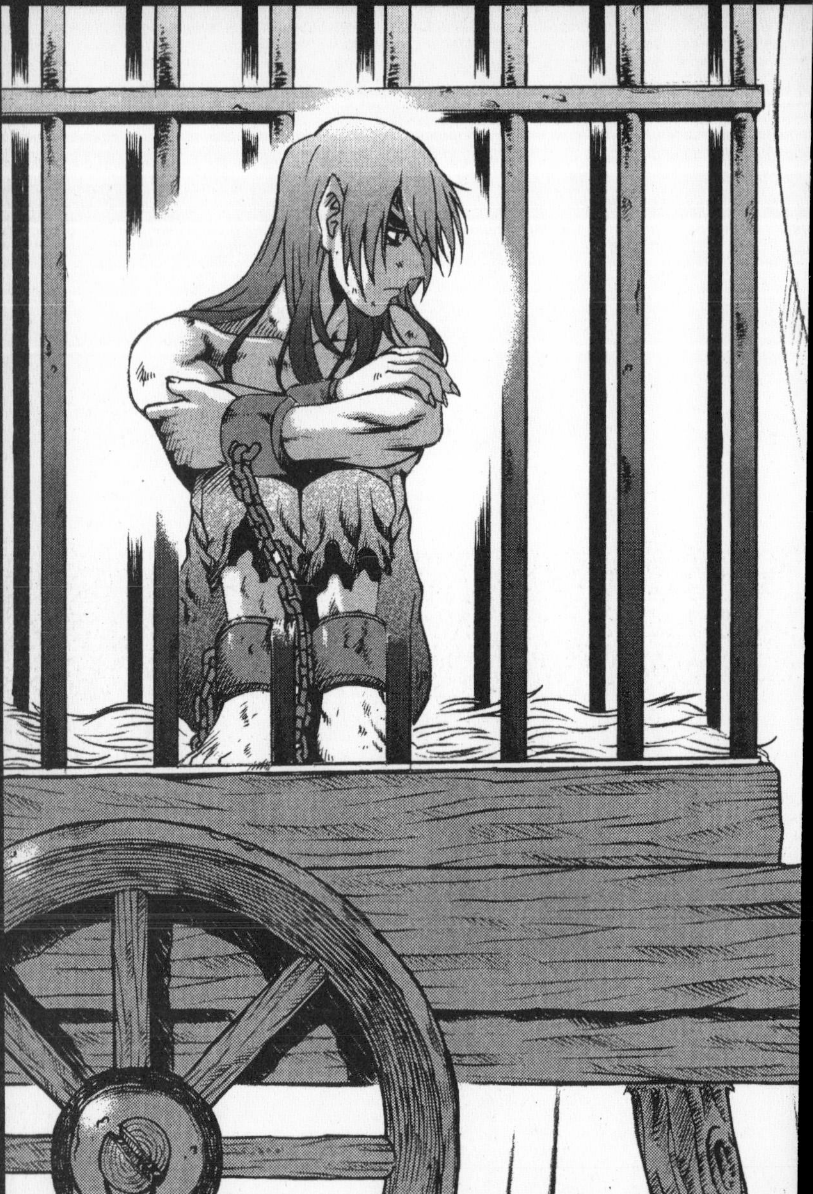

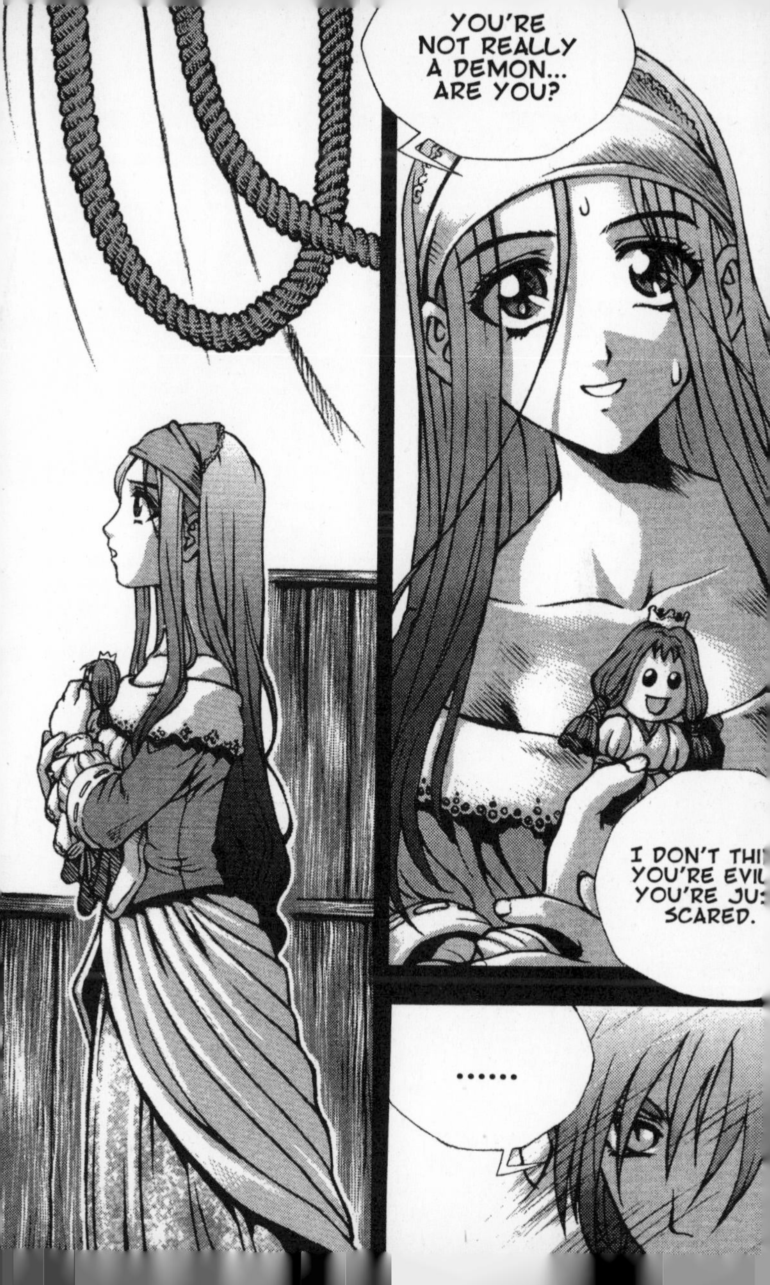
YOU'RE NOT REALLY A DEMON... ARE YOU?
I DON'T THI YOU'RE EVIL YOU'RE JUS SCARED.
......

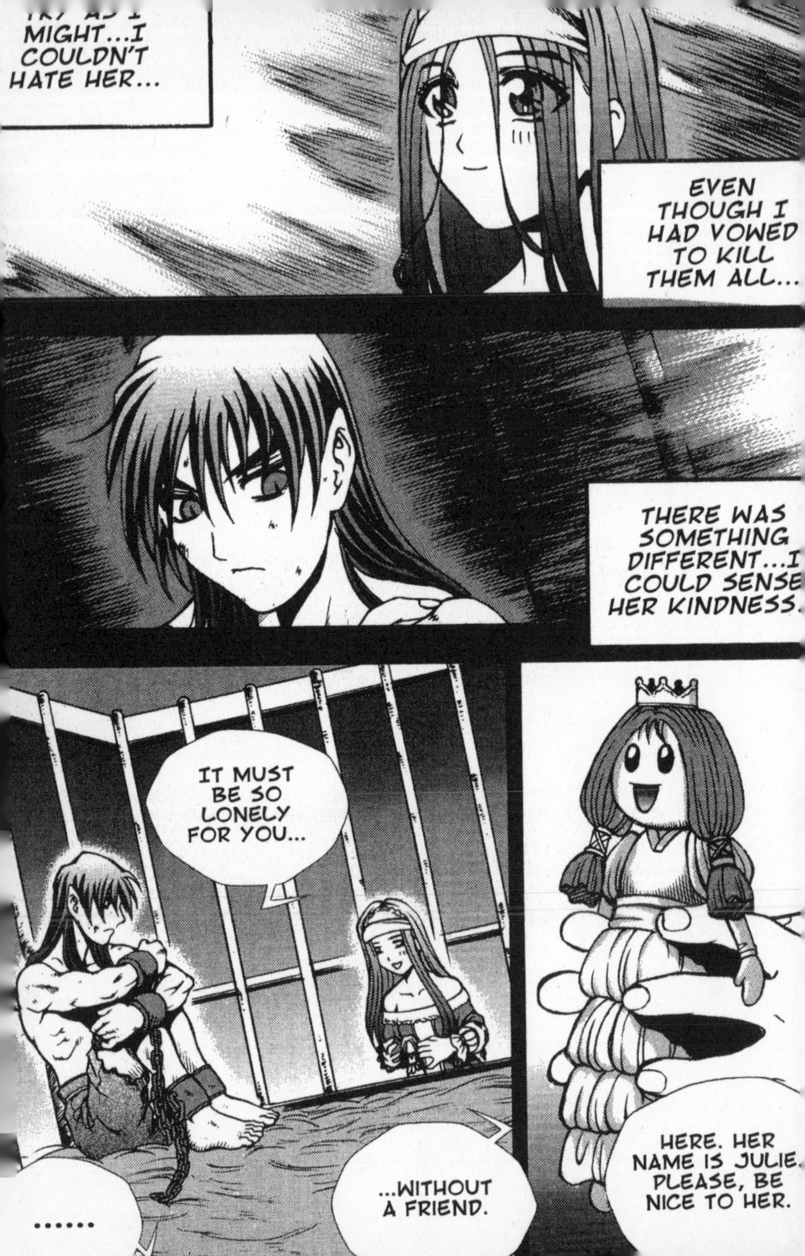
MIGHT...I COULDN'T HATE HER...
EVEN THOUGH I HAD VOWED TO KILL THEM ALL...
THERE WAS SOMETHING DIFFERENT...I COULD SENSE HER KINDNESS.
IT MUST BE SO LONELY FOR YOU...
......
...WITHOUT A FRIEND.
HERE. HER NAME IS JULIE. PLEASE, BE NICE TO HER.

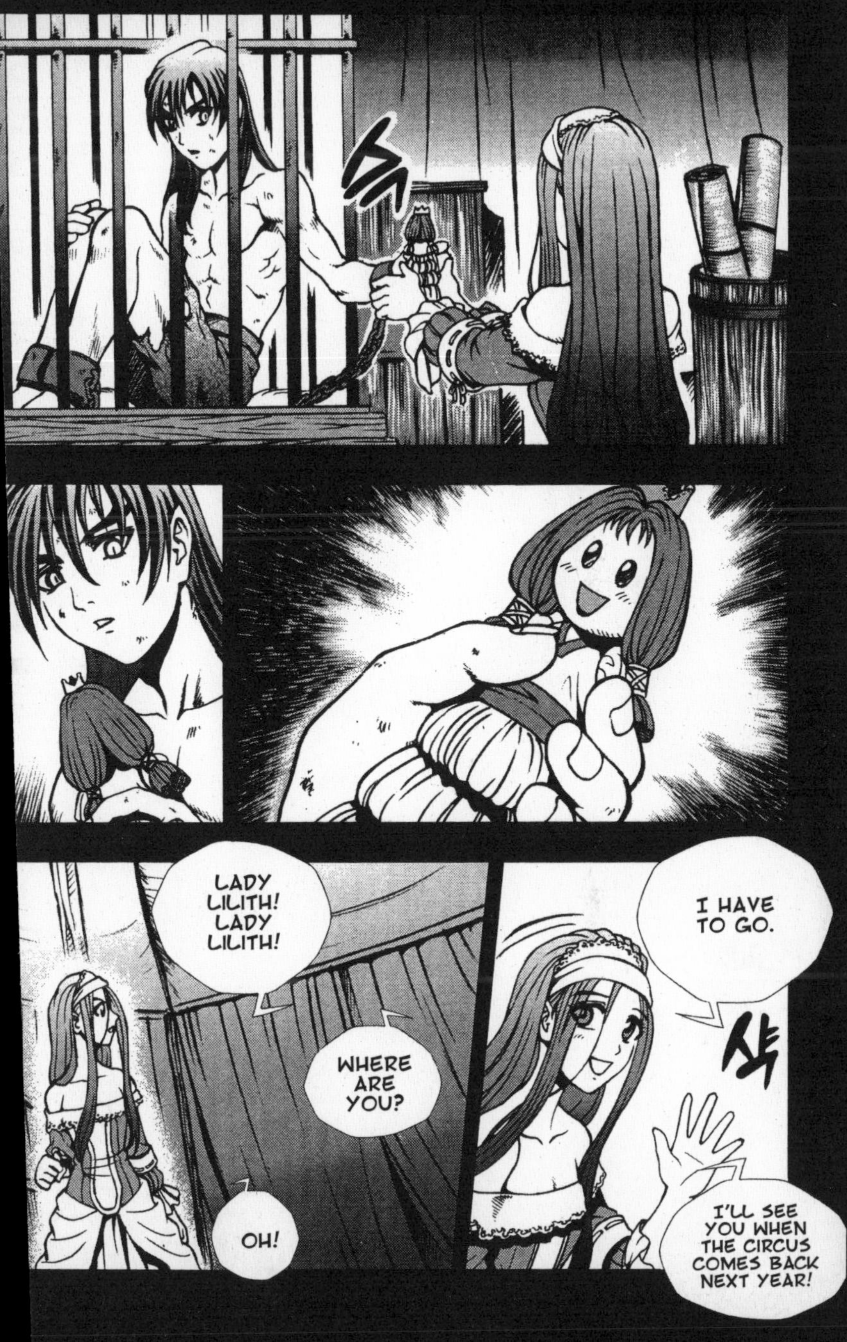
슥
LADY LILITH! LADY LILITH!
WHERE ARE YOU?
OH!
I HAVE TO GO.
샥
I'LL SEE YOU WHEN THE CIRCUS COMES BACK NEXT YEAR!

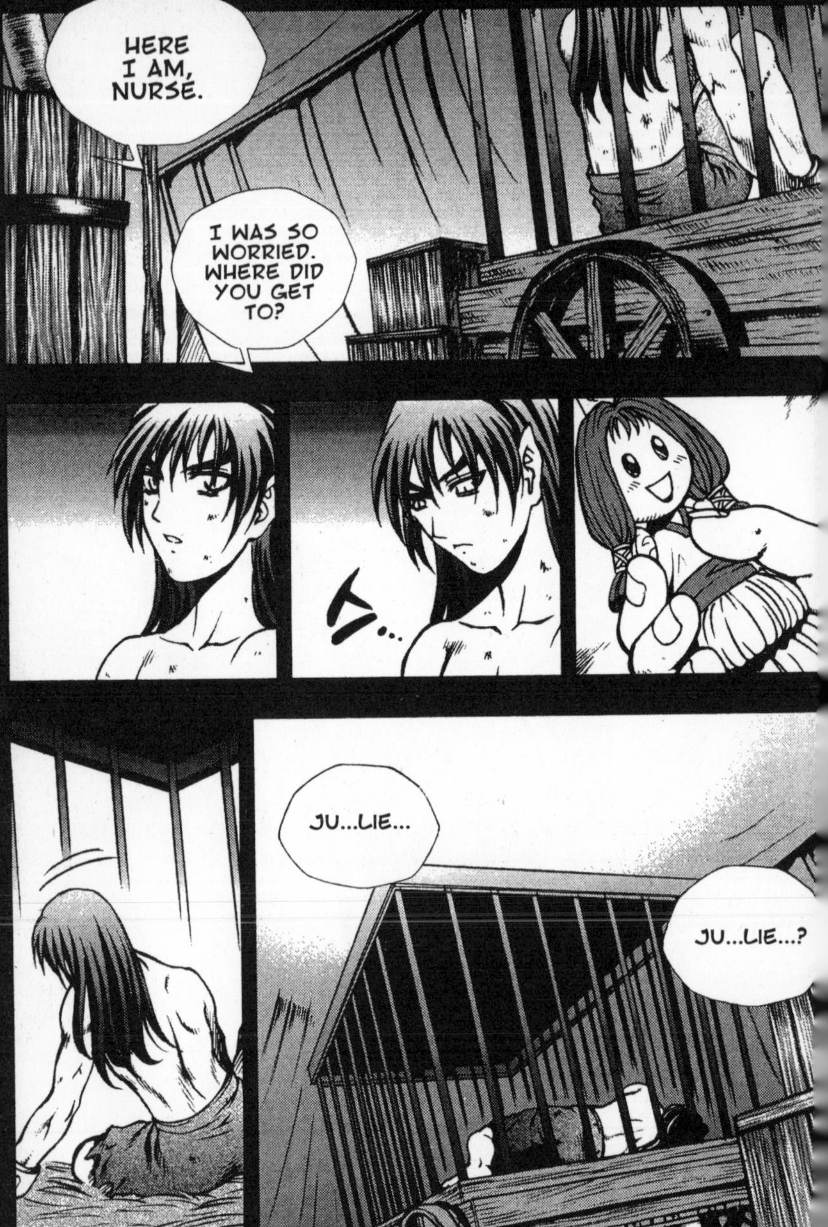
HERE I AM, NURSE.
I WAS SO WORRIED. WHERE DID YOU GET TO?
JU...LIE...
JU...LIE...?

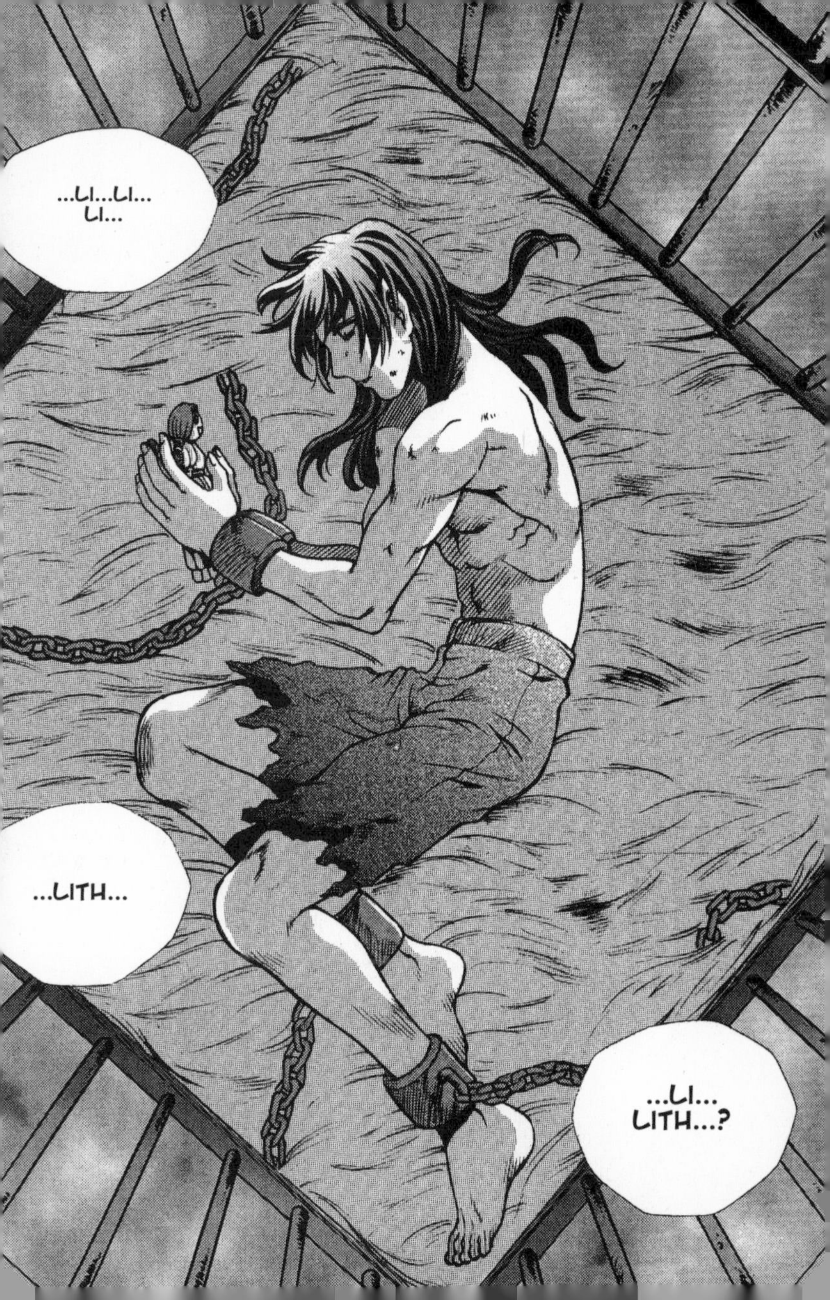
...LI...LI... LI...
...LITH...
...LI... LITH...?

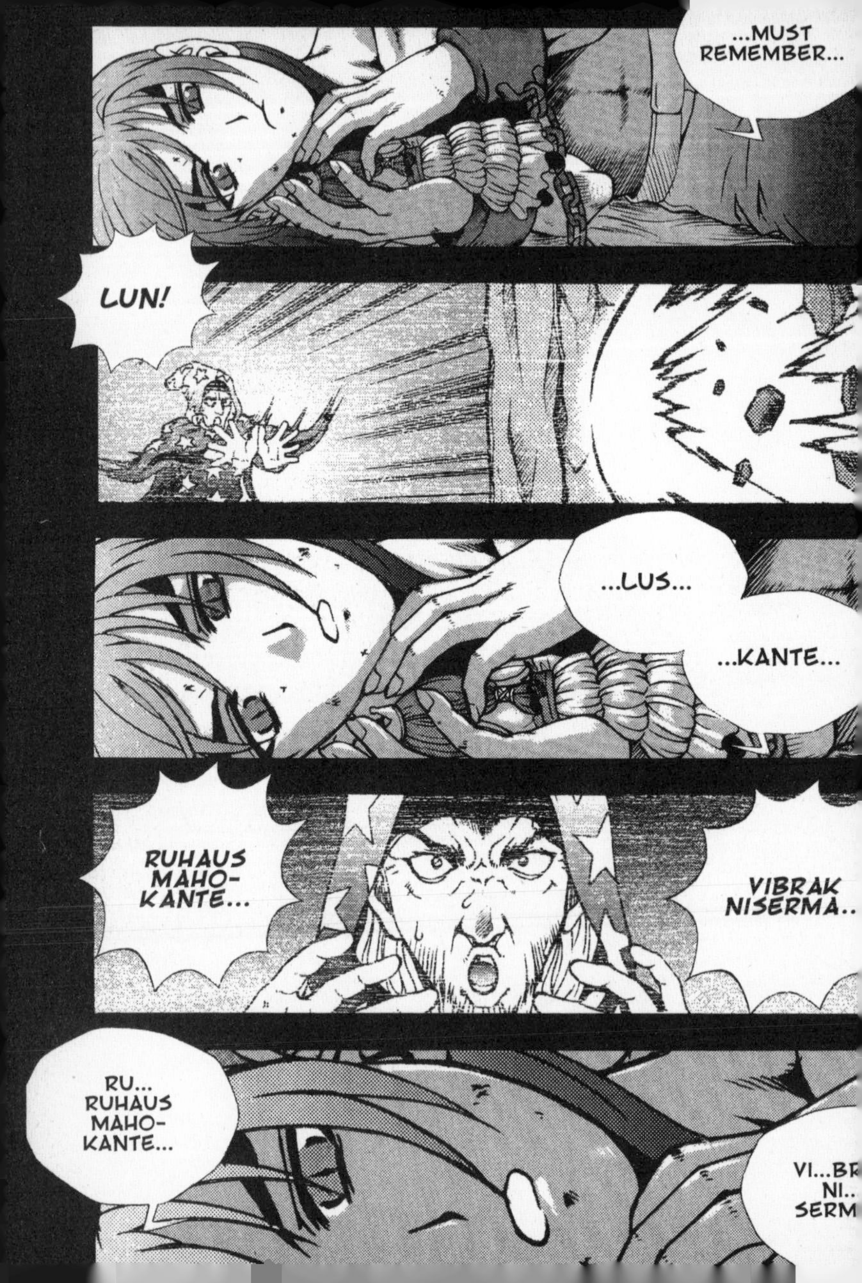
...MUST REMEMBER...
LUN!
...LUS...
...KANTE...
VIBRAK NISERMA...
RUHAUS MAHO-KANTE...
VI...BR NI... SERM
RU... RUHAUS MAHO-KANTE...

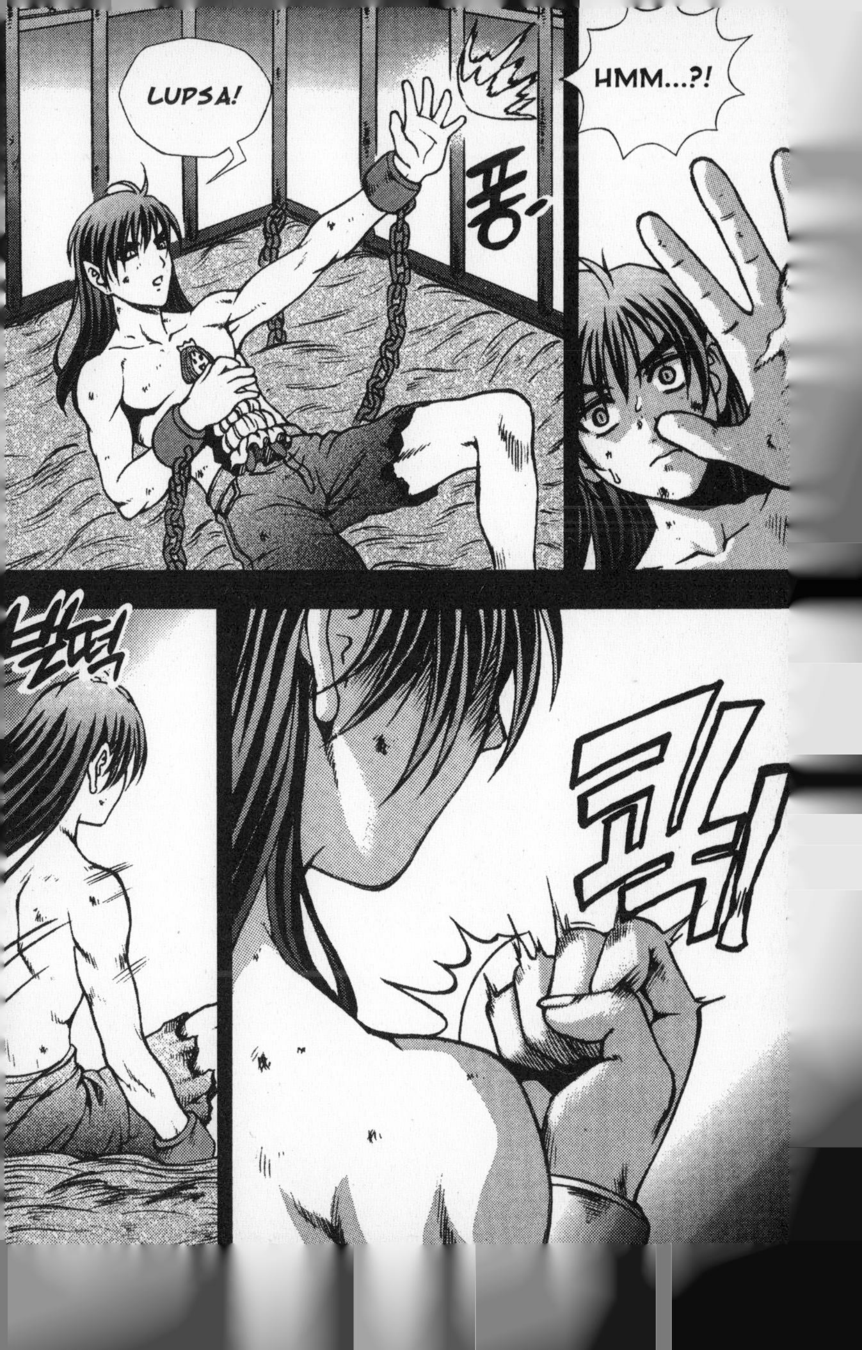
LUPSA!
퐁-
HMM...?!
꽉!

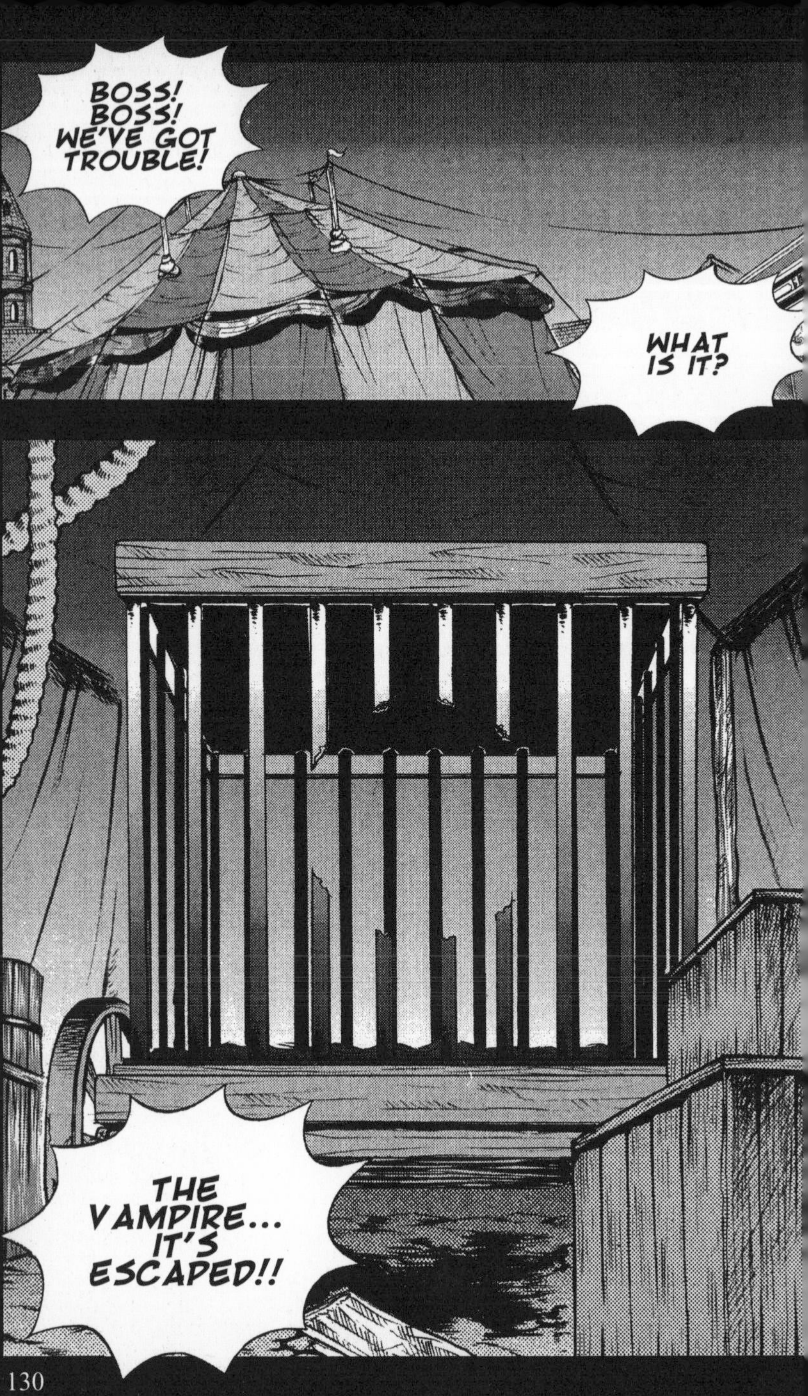
BOSS! BOSS! WE'VE GOT TROUBLE!
WHAT IS IT?
THE VAMPIRE... IT'S ESCAPED!!

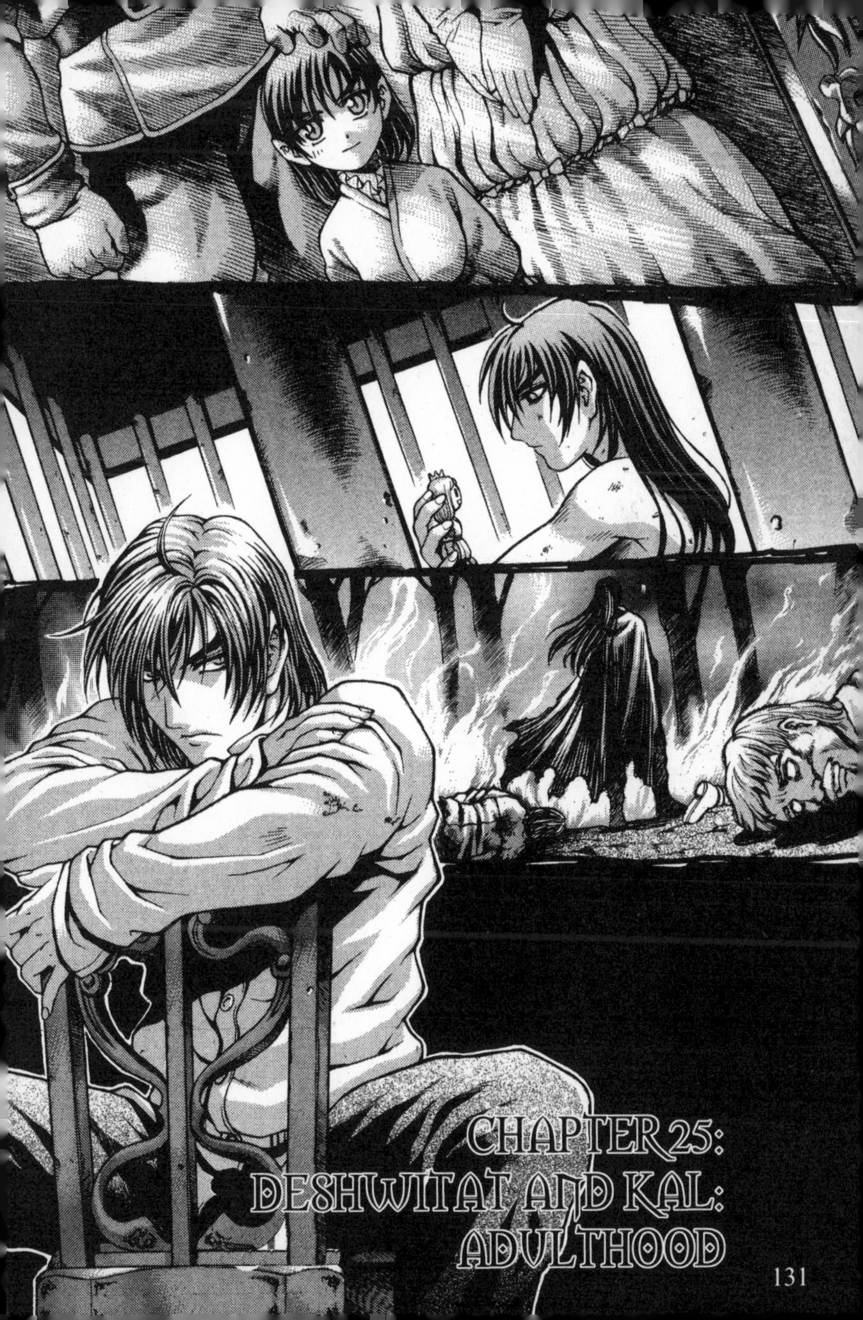
CHAPTER 25:
DESHWITAT AND KAL:
ADULTHOOD

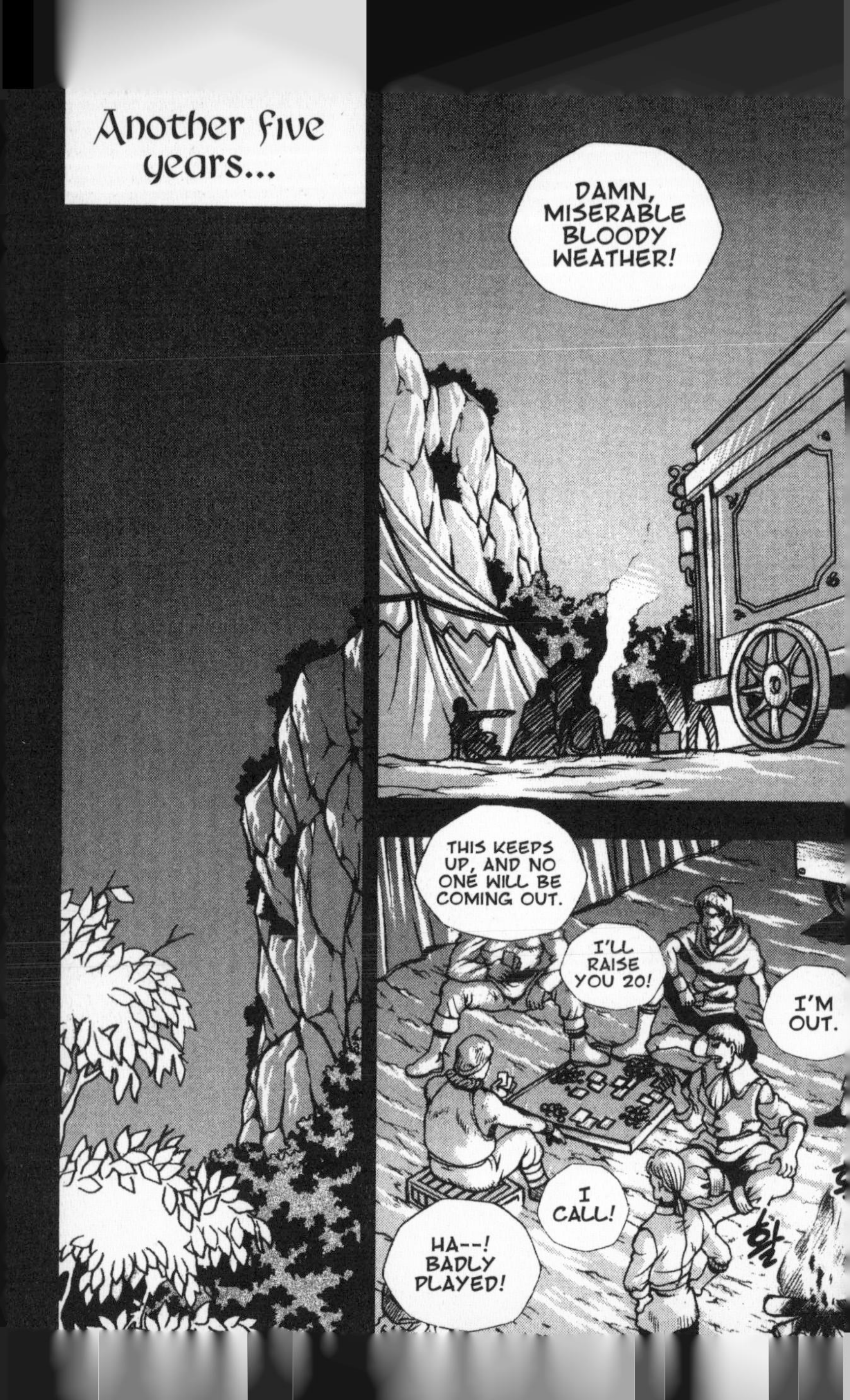
Another five years...
DAMN, MISERABLE BLOODY WEATHER!
THIS KEEPS UP, AND NO ONE WILL BE COMING OUT.
I'LL RAISE YOU 20!
I'M OUT.
I CALL!
HA--! BADLY PLAYED!

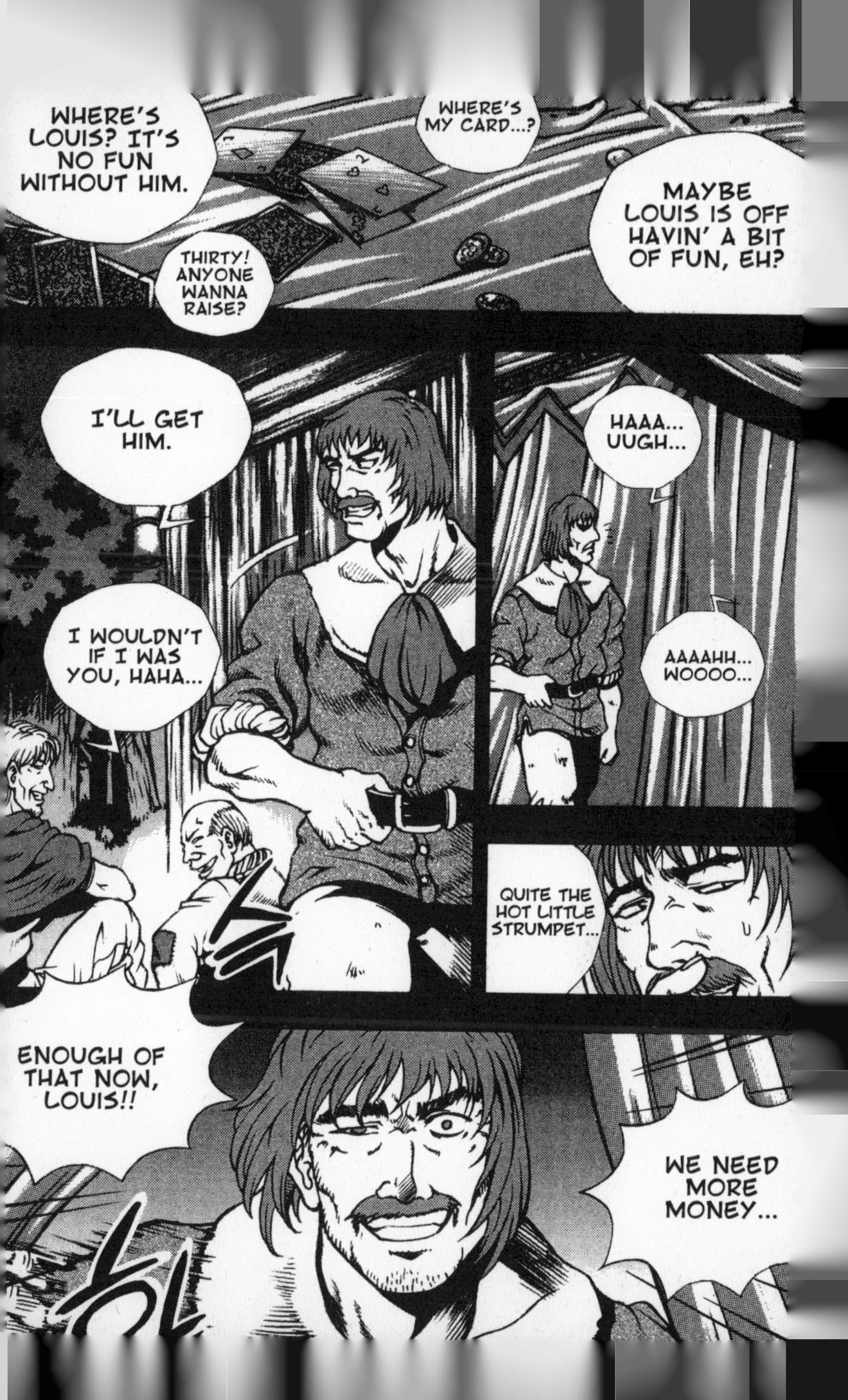
WHERE'S LOUIS? IT'S NO FUN WITHOUT HIM.
WHERE'S MY CARD...?
THIRTY! ANYONE WANNA RAISE?
MAYBE LOUIS IS OFF HAVIN' A BIT OF FUN, EH?
I'LL GET HIM.
I WOULDN'T IF I WAS YOU, HAHA...
HAAA... UUGH...
AAAAHH... WOOOO...
QUITE THE HOT LITTLE STRUMPET...
ENOUGH OF THAT NOW, LOUIS!!
WE NEED MORE MONEY...

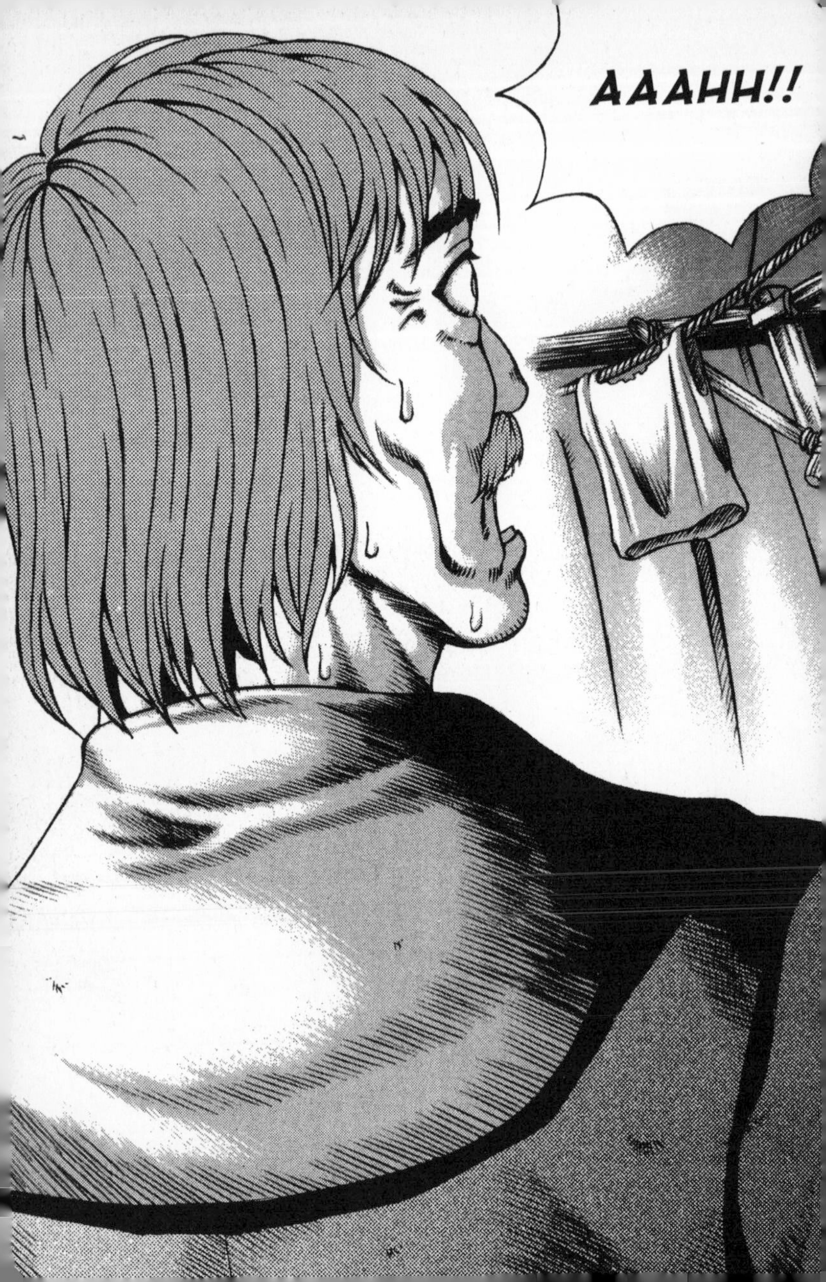
AAAHH!!

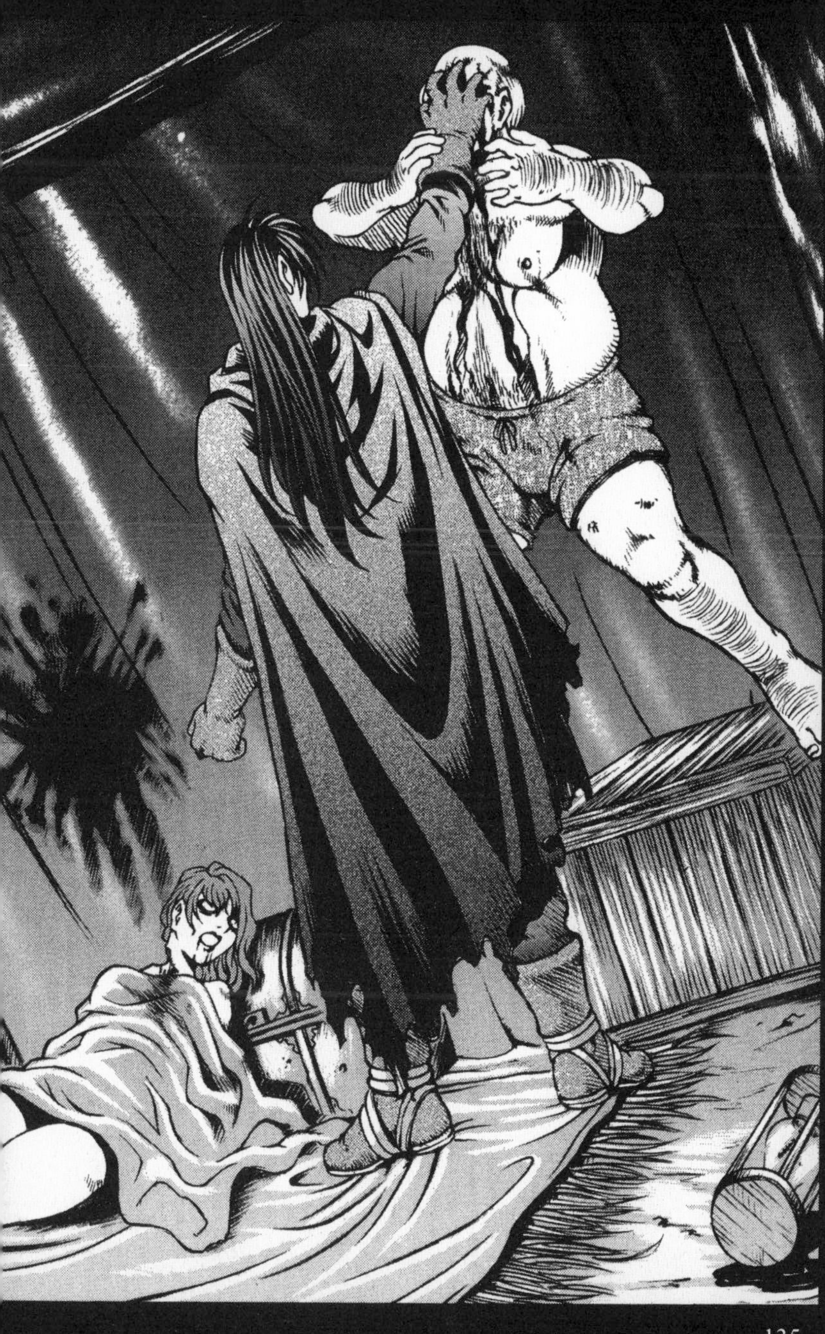

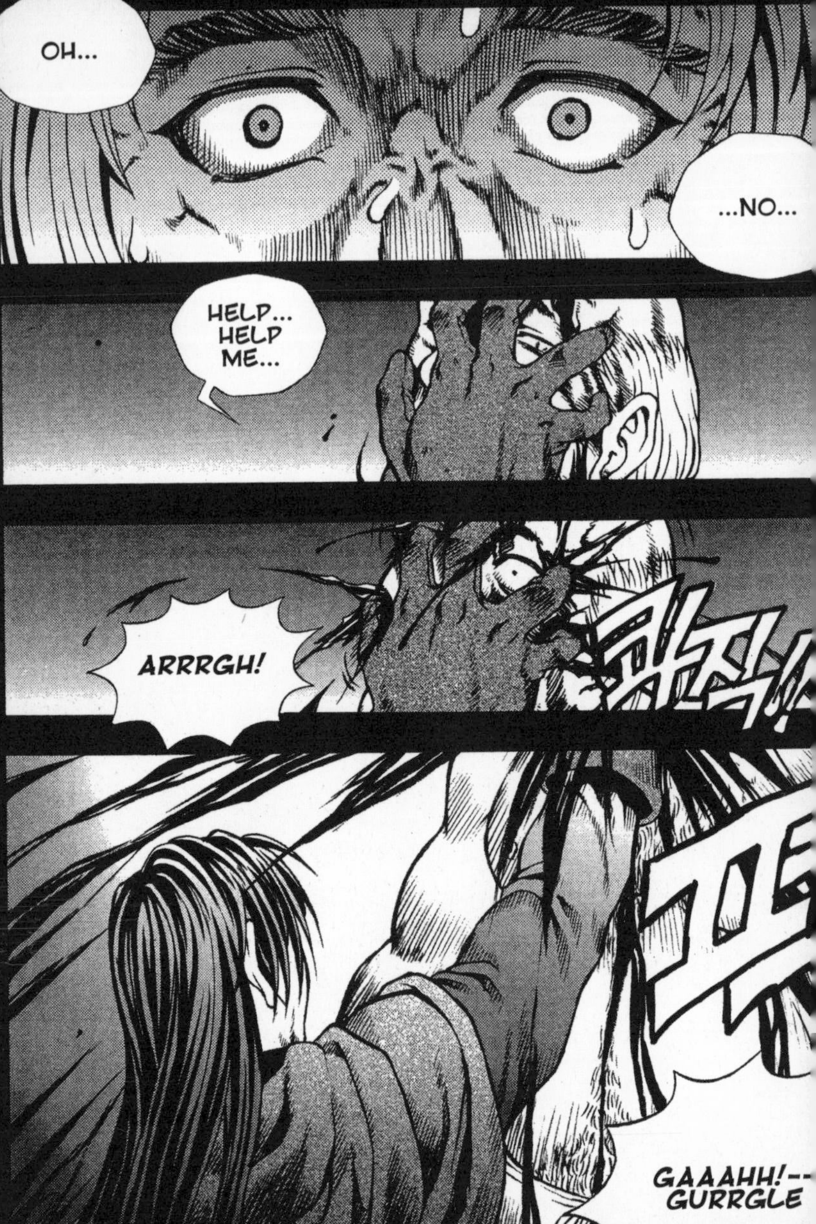
OH...
...NO...
HELP... HELP ME...
ARRRGH!
GAAAHH!-- GURRGLE

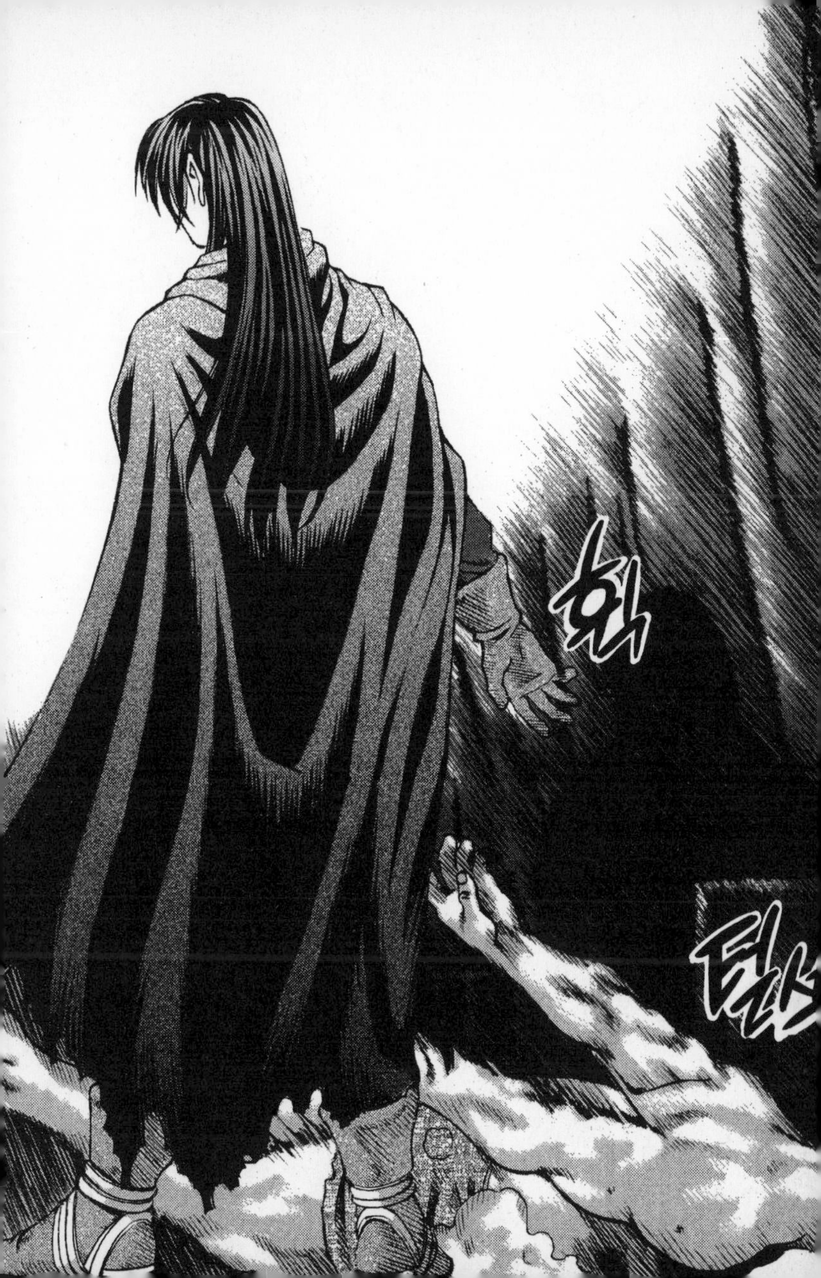

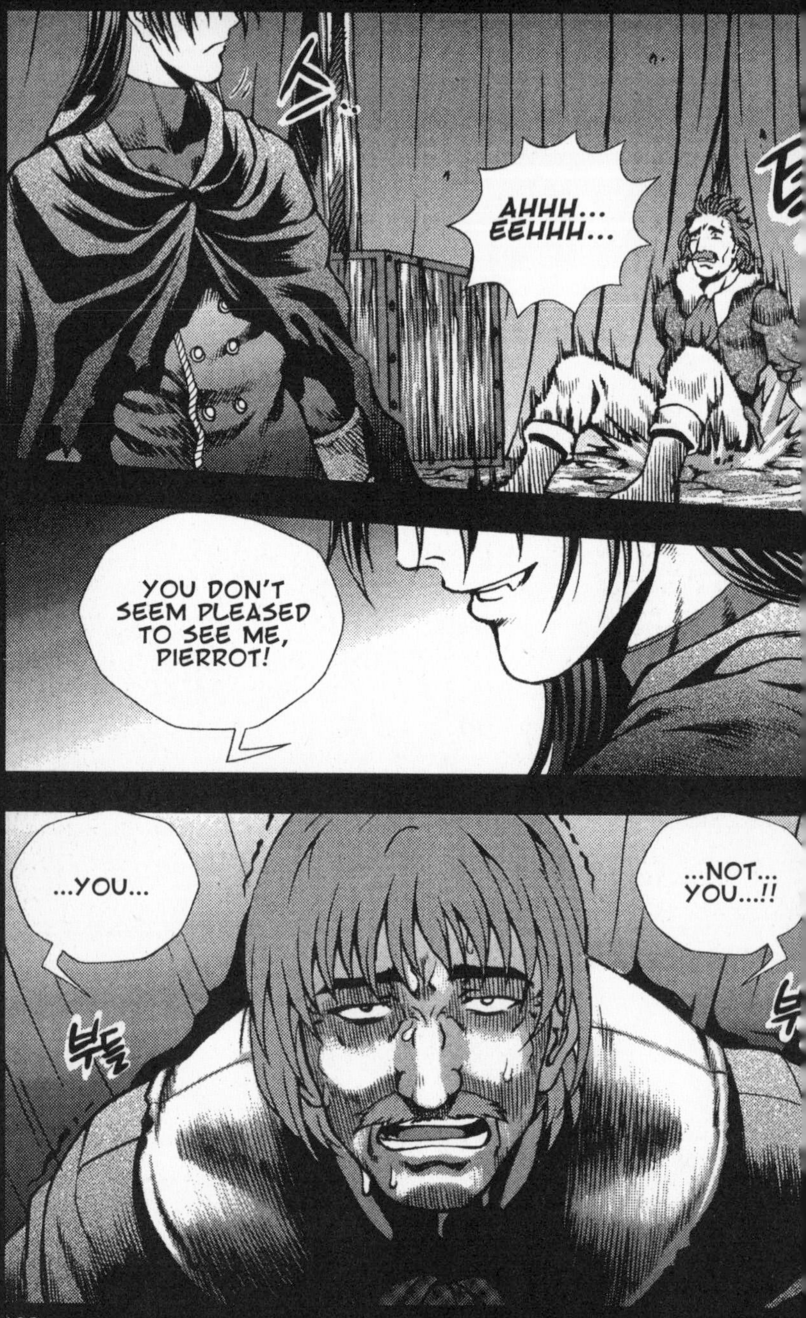
AHHH... EEHHH...
YOU DON'T SEEM PLEASED TO SEE ME, PIERROT!
...YOU...
...NOT... YOU...!!
부들

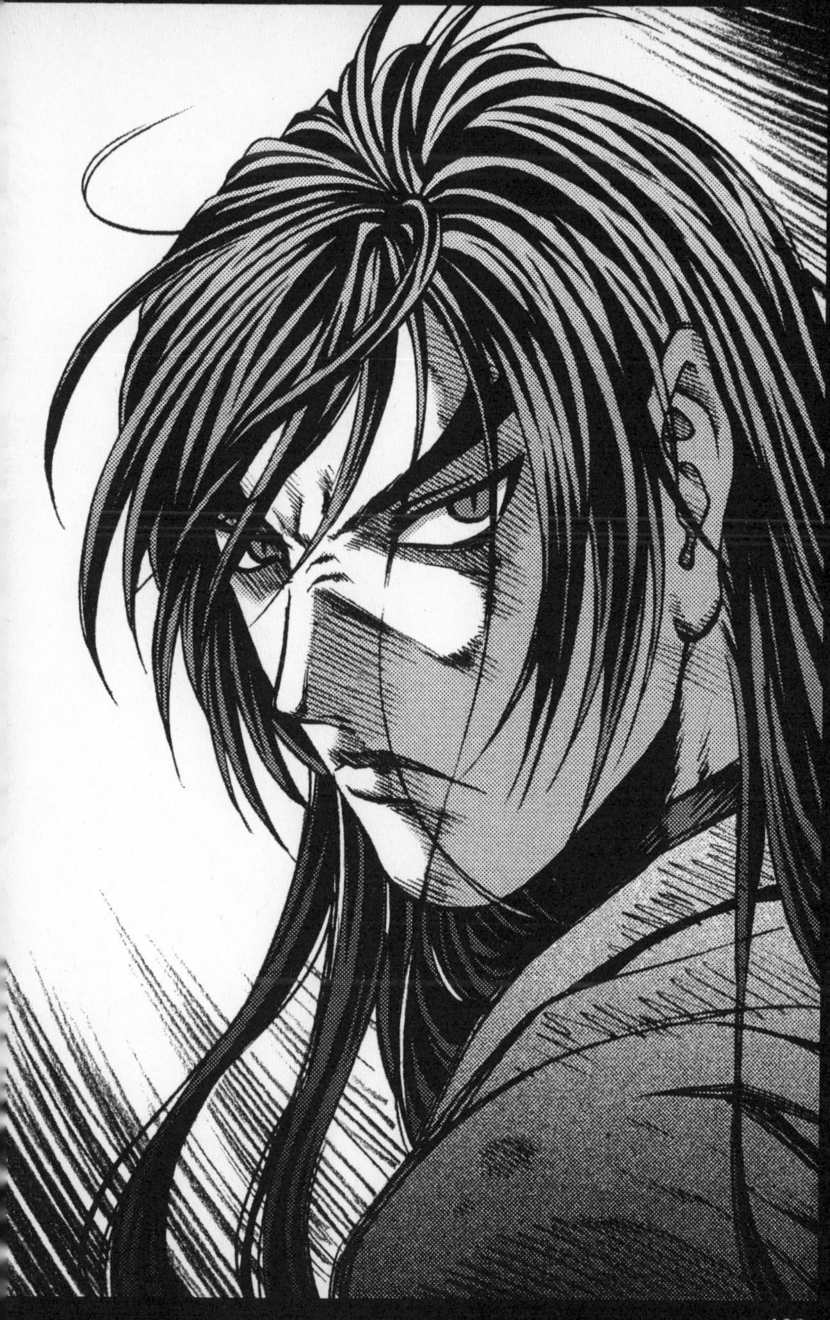

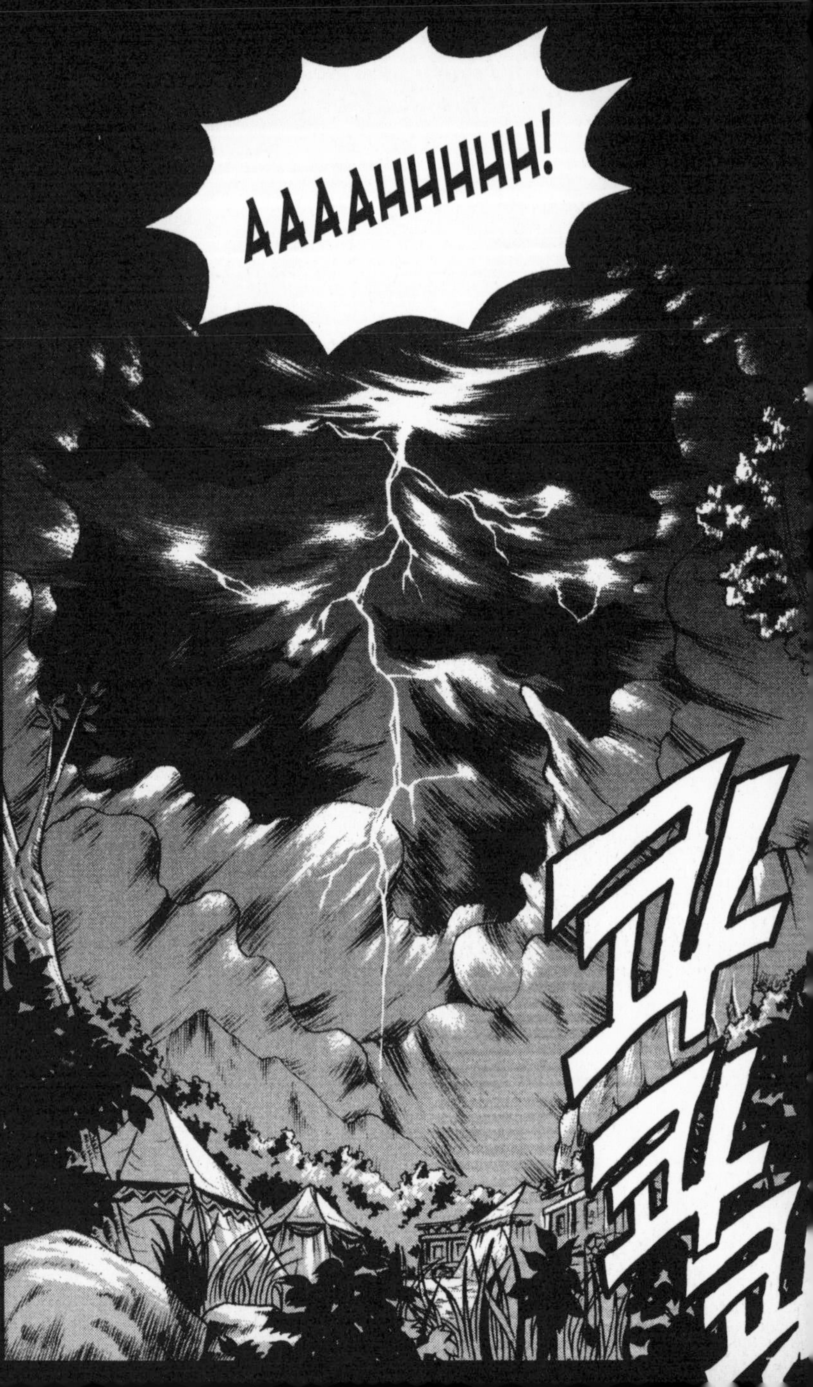
AAAAHHHHHH!

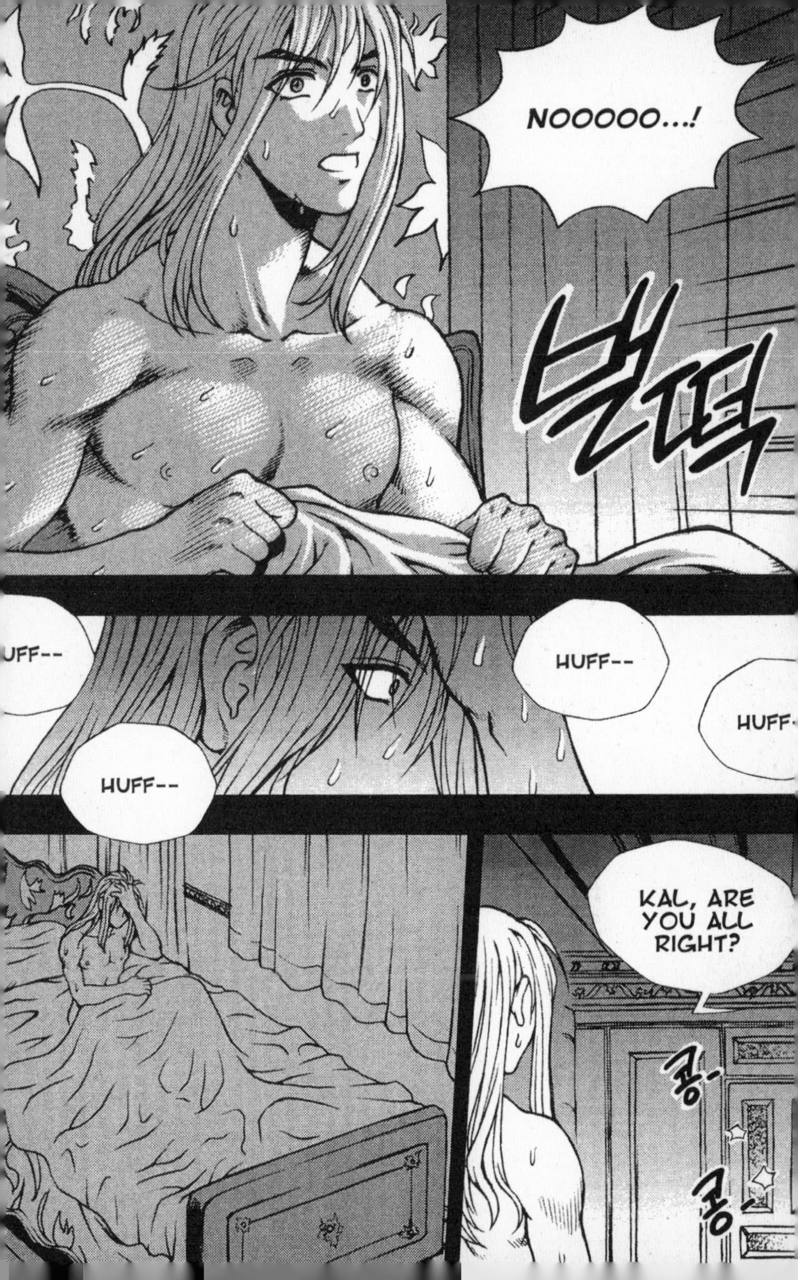
NOOOOO...!
벌떡
UFF--
HUFF--
HUFF--
HUFF-
KAL, ARE YOU ALL RIGHT?
콩
콩

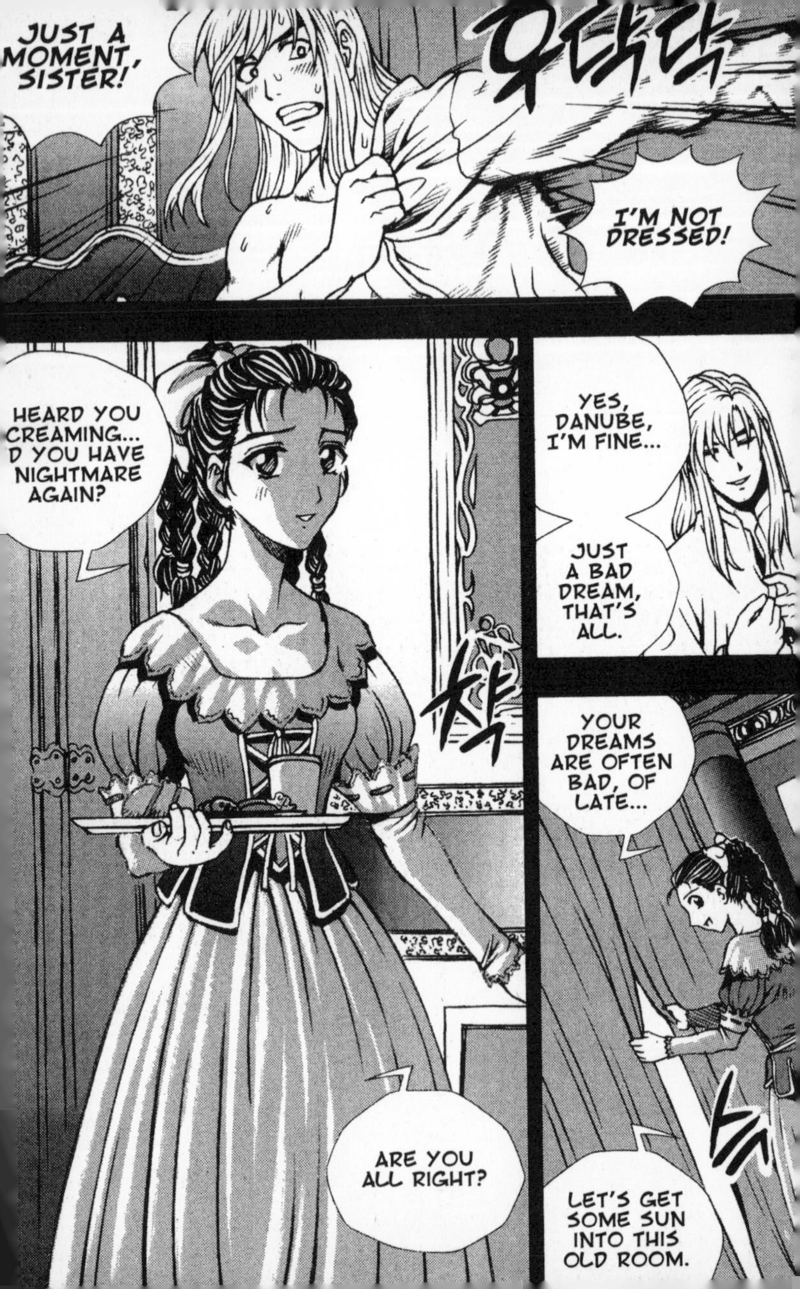
JUST A MOMENT, SISTER!
우다닥
I'M NOT DRESSED!
HEARD YOU CREAMING... D YOU HAVE NIGHTMARE AGAIN?
착
ARE YOU ALL RIGHT?
YES, DANUBE, I'M FINE...
JUST A BAD DREAM, THAT'S ALL.
YOUR DREAMS ARE OFTEN BAD, OF LATE...
LET'S GET SOME SUN INTO THIS OLD ROOM.

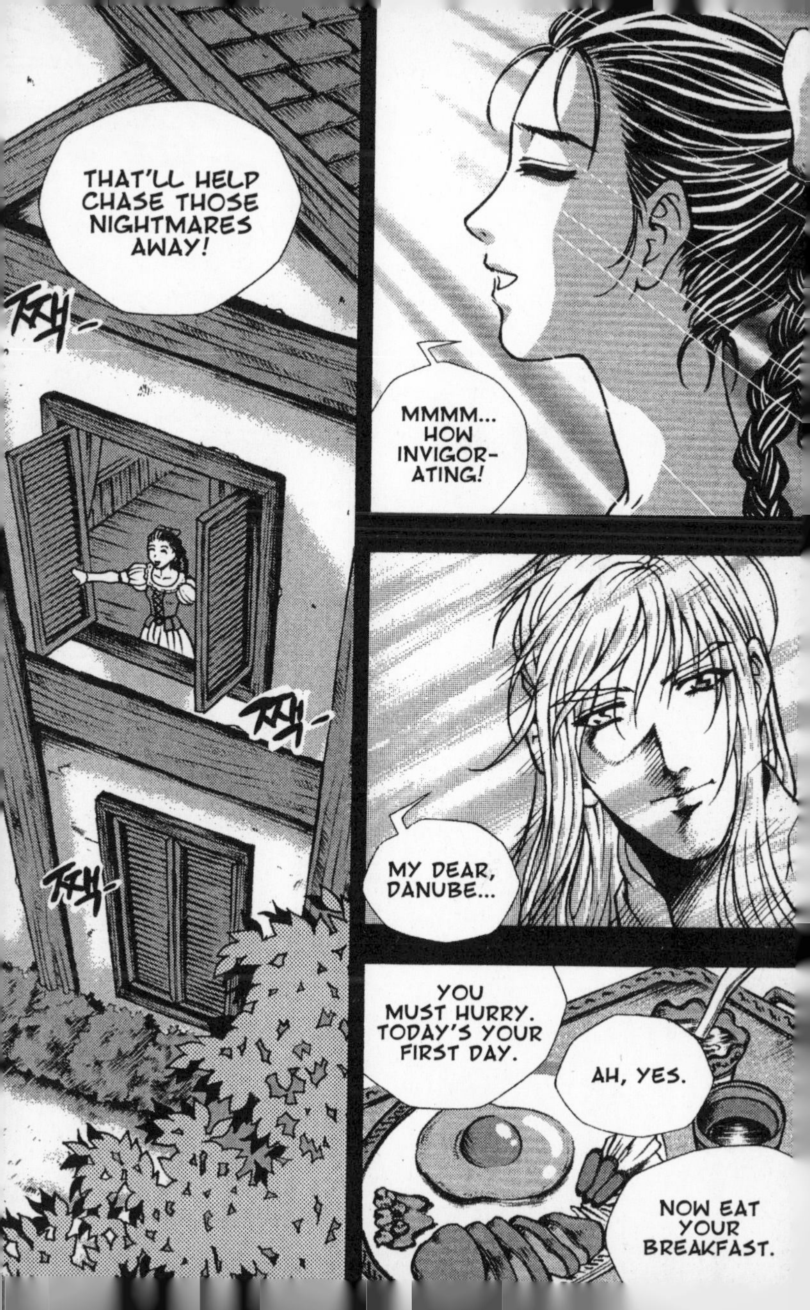
THAT'LL HELP CHASE THOSE NIGHTMARES AWAY!
MMMM... HOW INVIGOR-ATING!
MY DEAR, DANUBE...
YOU MUST HURRY. TODAY'S YOUR FIRST DAY.
AH, YES.
NOW EAT YOUR BREAKFAST.

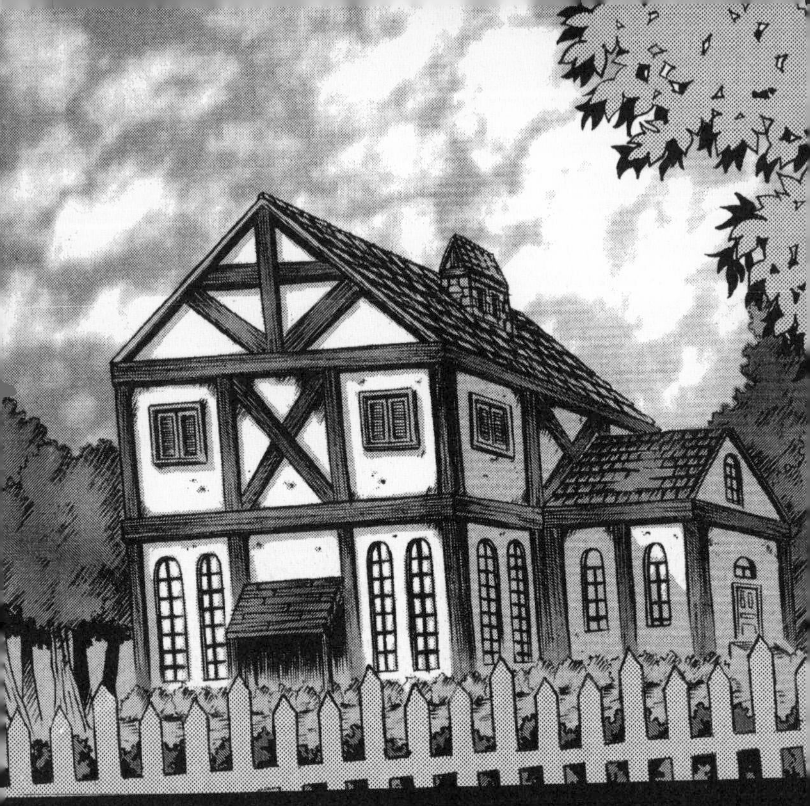
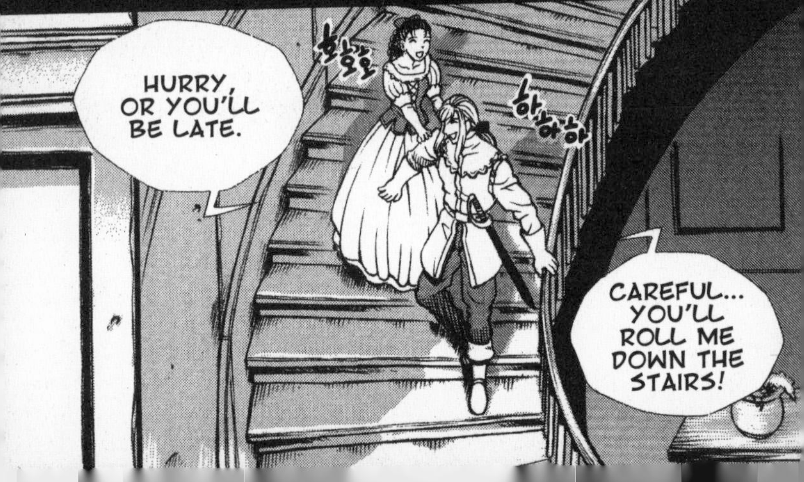
HURRY, OR YOU'LL BE LATE.
호호호
하하하
CAREFUL... YOU'LL ROLL ME DOWN THE STAIRS!

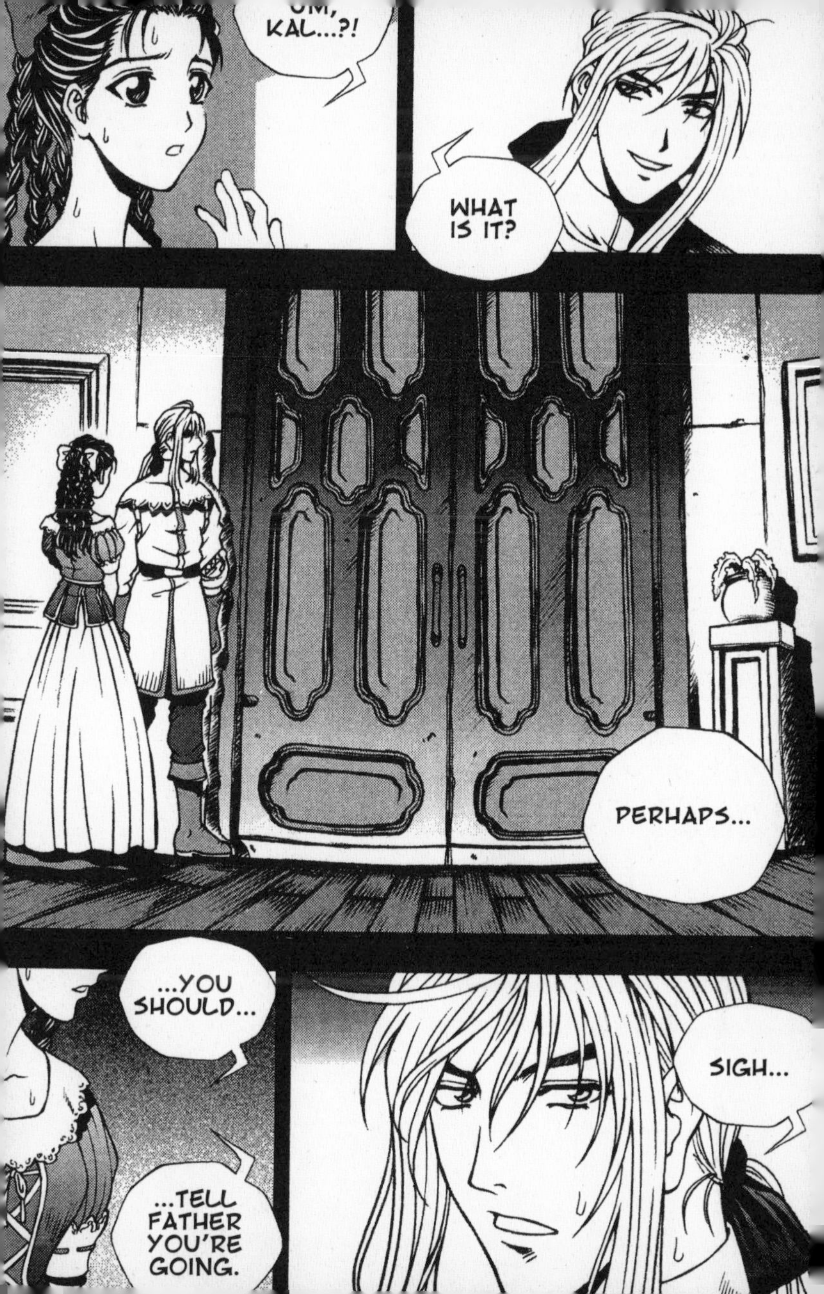
UM, KAL...?!
WHAT IS IT?
PERHAPS...
...YOU SHOULD...
...TELL FATHER YOU'RE GOING.
SIGH...

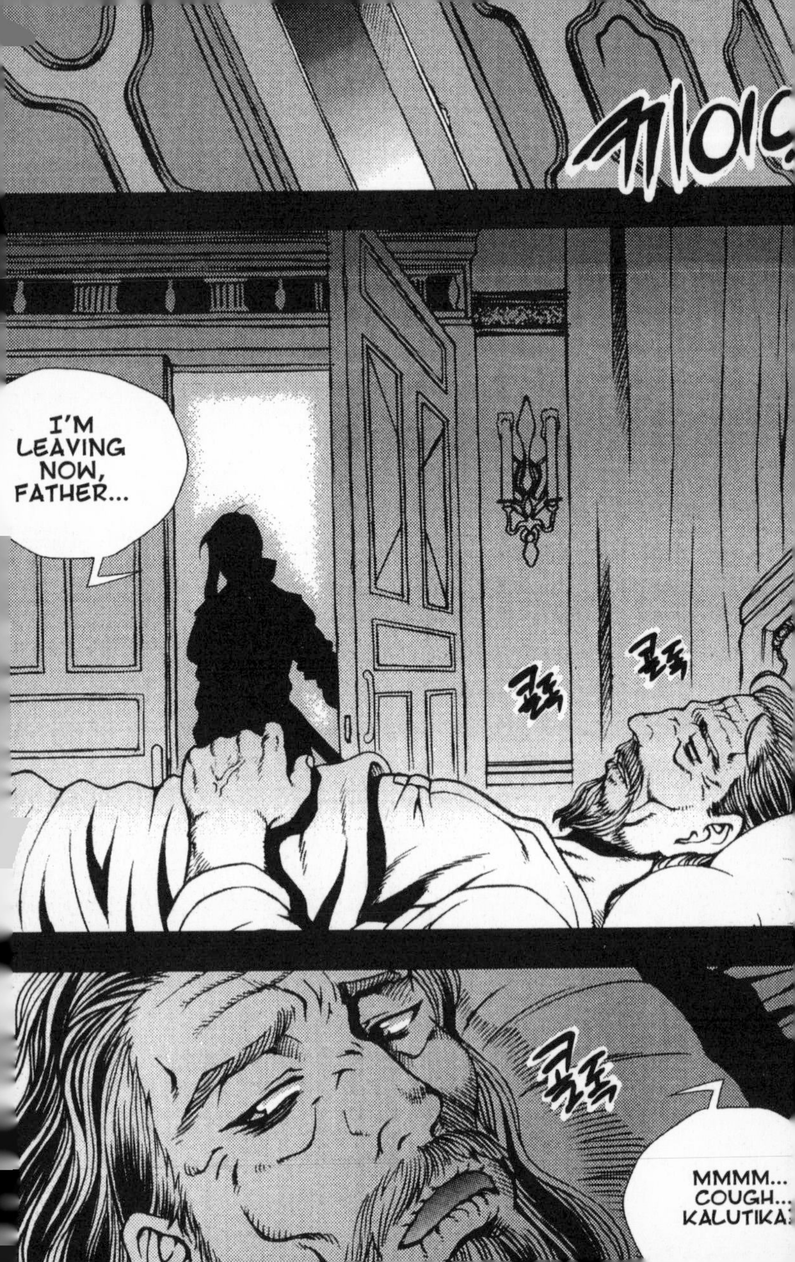
I'M LEAVING NOW, FATHER...
콜록
콜록
콜록
MMMM... COUGH... KALUTIKA

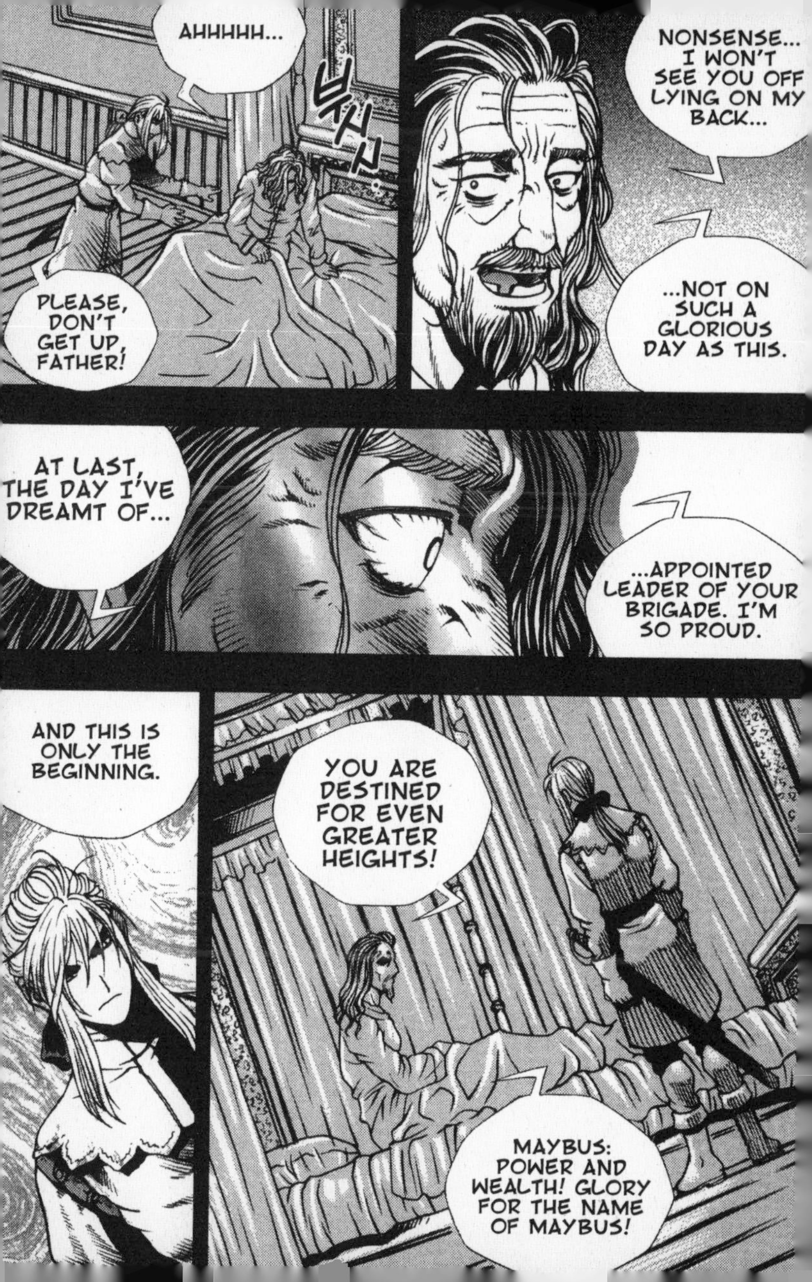
AHHHHH...
PLEASE, DON'T GET UP, FATHER!
NONSENSE... I WON'T SEE YOU OFF LYING ON MY BACK...
...NOT ON SUCH A GLORIOUS DAY AS THIS.
AT LAST, THE DAY I'VE DREAMT OF...
...APPOINTED LEADER OF YOUR BRIGADE. I'M SO PROUD.
AND THIS IS ONLY THE BEGINNING.
YOU ARE DESTINED FOR EVEN GREATER HEIGHTS!
MAYBUS: POWER AND WEALTH! GLORY FOR THE NAME OF MAYBUS!

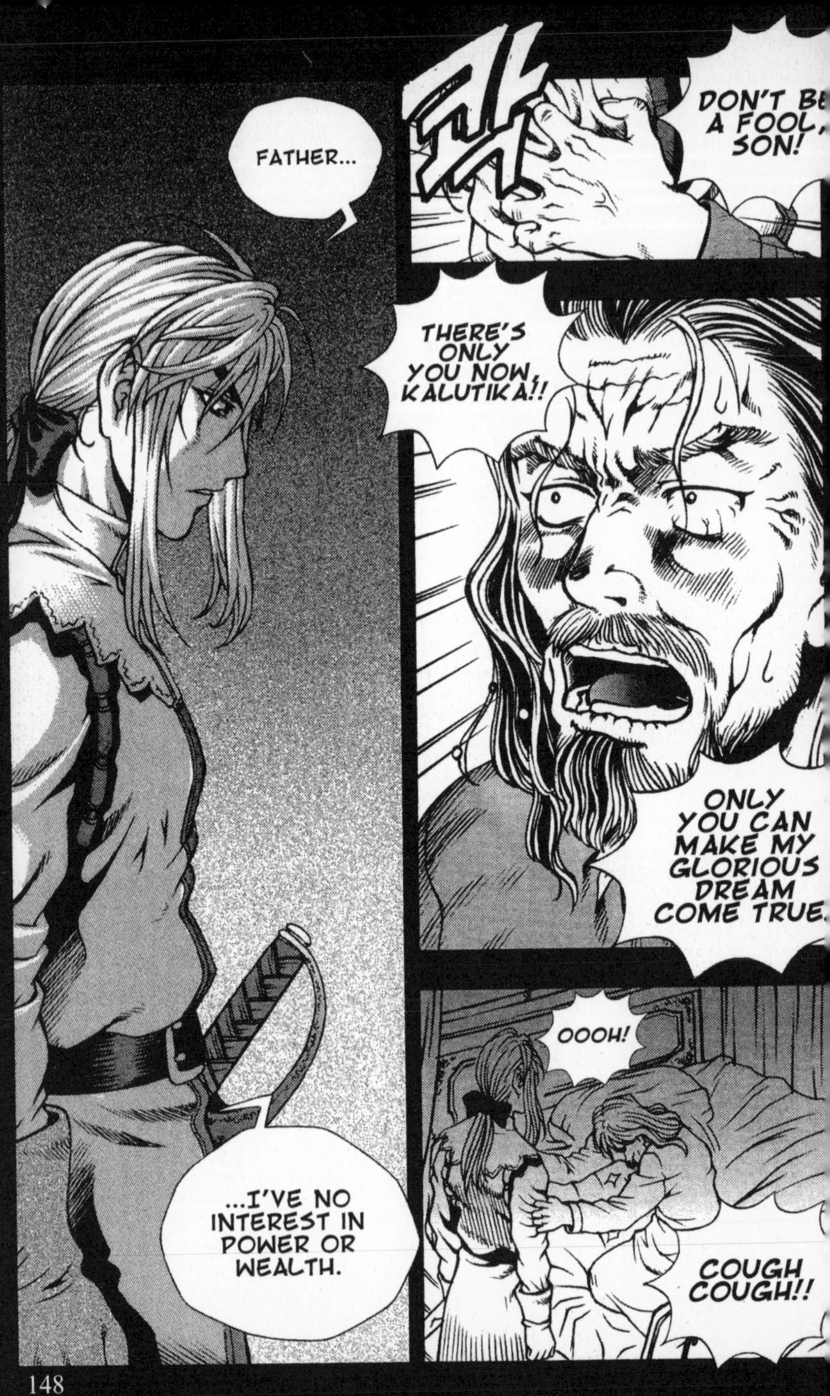
FATHER...
...I'VE NO INTEREST IN POWER OR WEALTH.
DON'T BE A FOOL, SON!
THERE'S ONLY YOU NOW, KALUTIKA!!
ONLY YOU CAN MAKE MY GLORIOUS DREAM COME TRUE.
OOOH!
COUGH COUGH!!

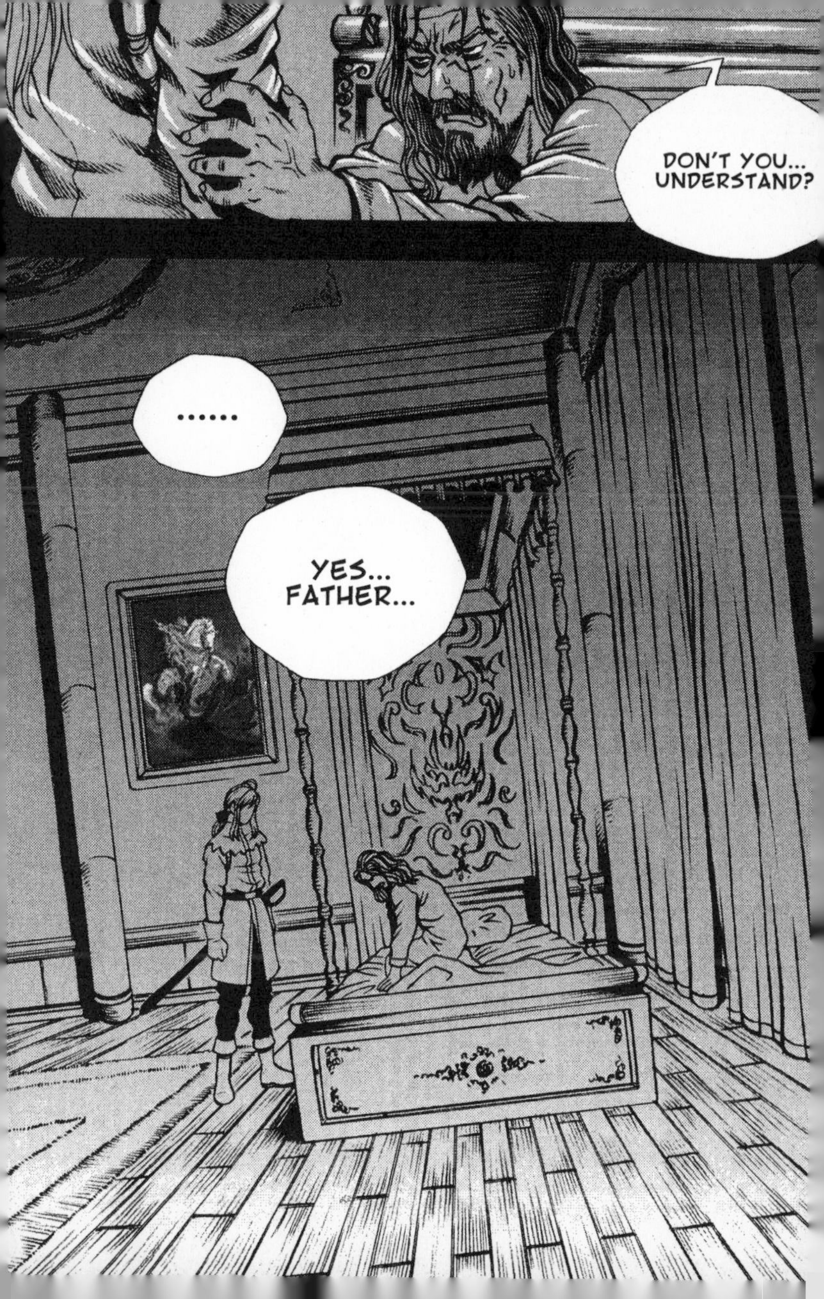
DON'T YOU... UNDERSTAND?
......
YES... FATHER...

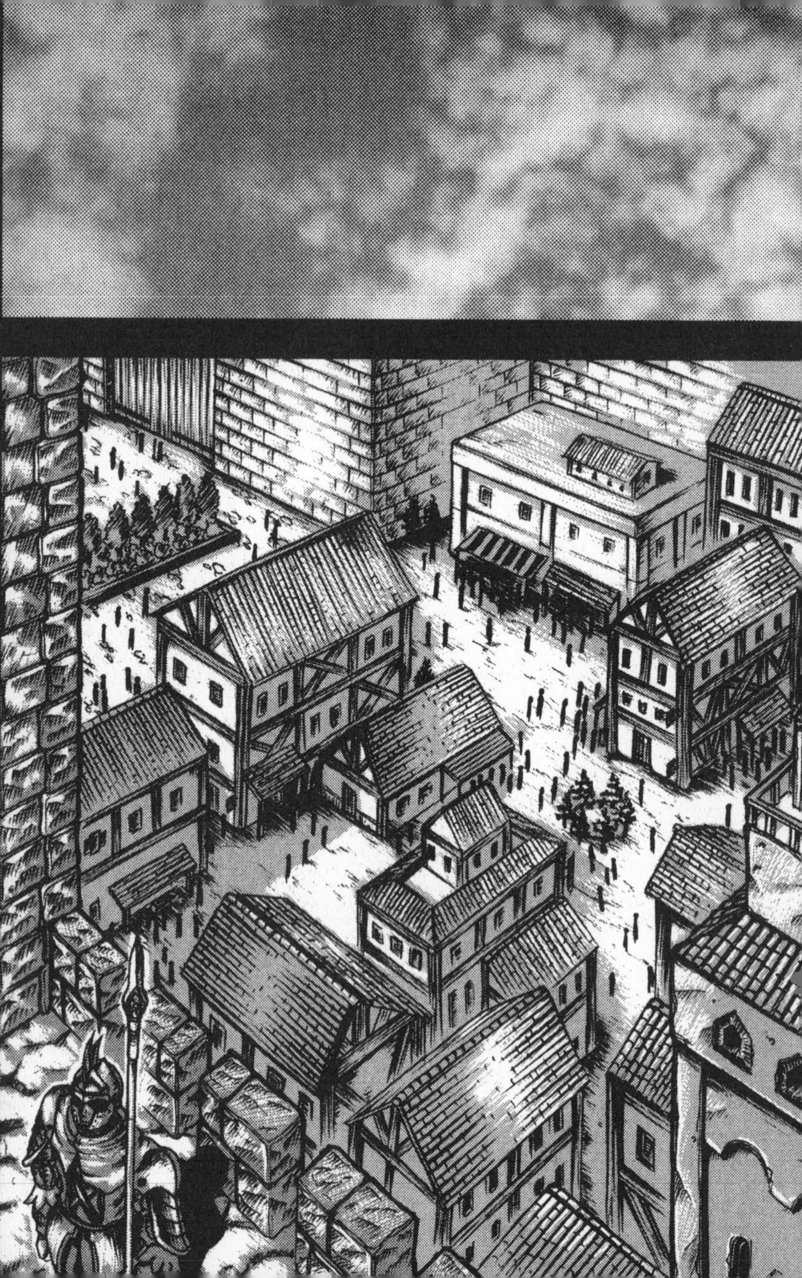

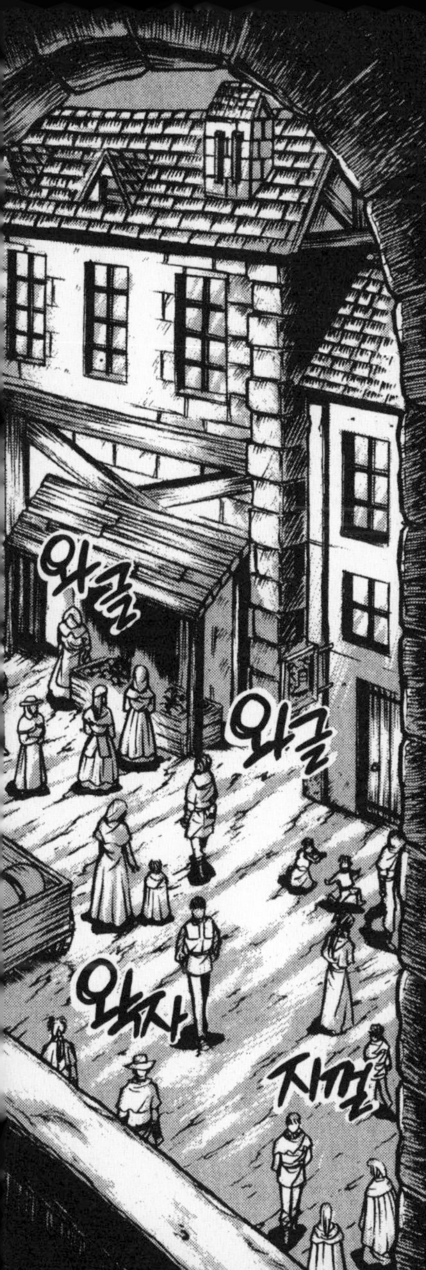
와글
와글
와자
지껄
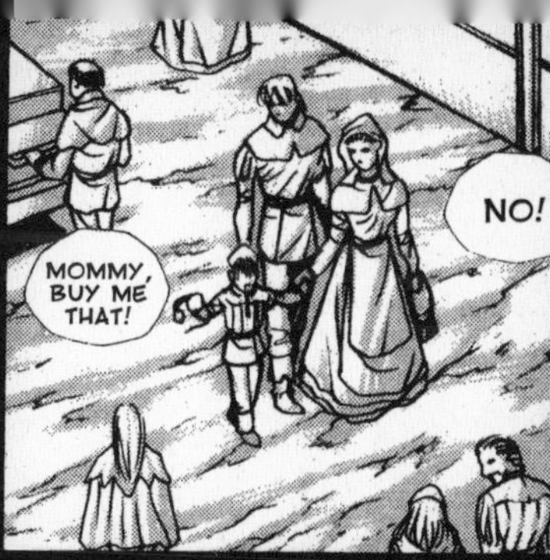
MOMMY, BUY ME THAT!
NO!
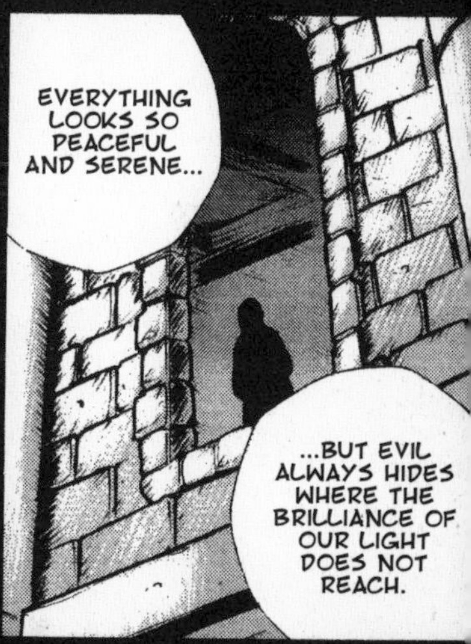
EVERYTHING LOOKS SO PEACEFUL AND SERENE...
...BUT EVIL ALWAYS HIDES WHERE THE BRILLIANCE OF OUR LIGHT DOES NOT REACH.
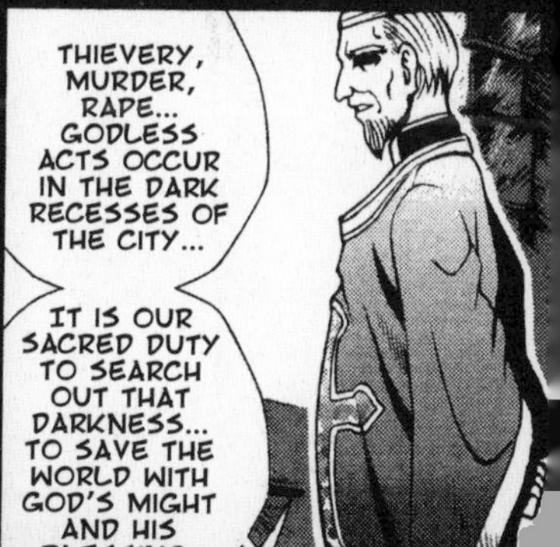
THIEVERY, MURDER, RAPE... GODLESS ACTS OCCUR IN THE DARK RECESSES OF THE CITY...
IT IS OUR SACRED DUTY TO SEARCH OUT THAT DARKNESS... TO SAVE THE WORLD WITH GOD'S MIGHT AND HIS BLESSING.

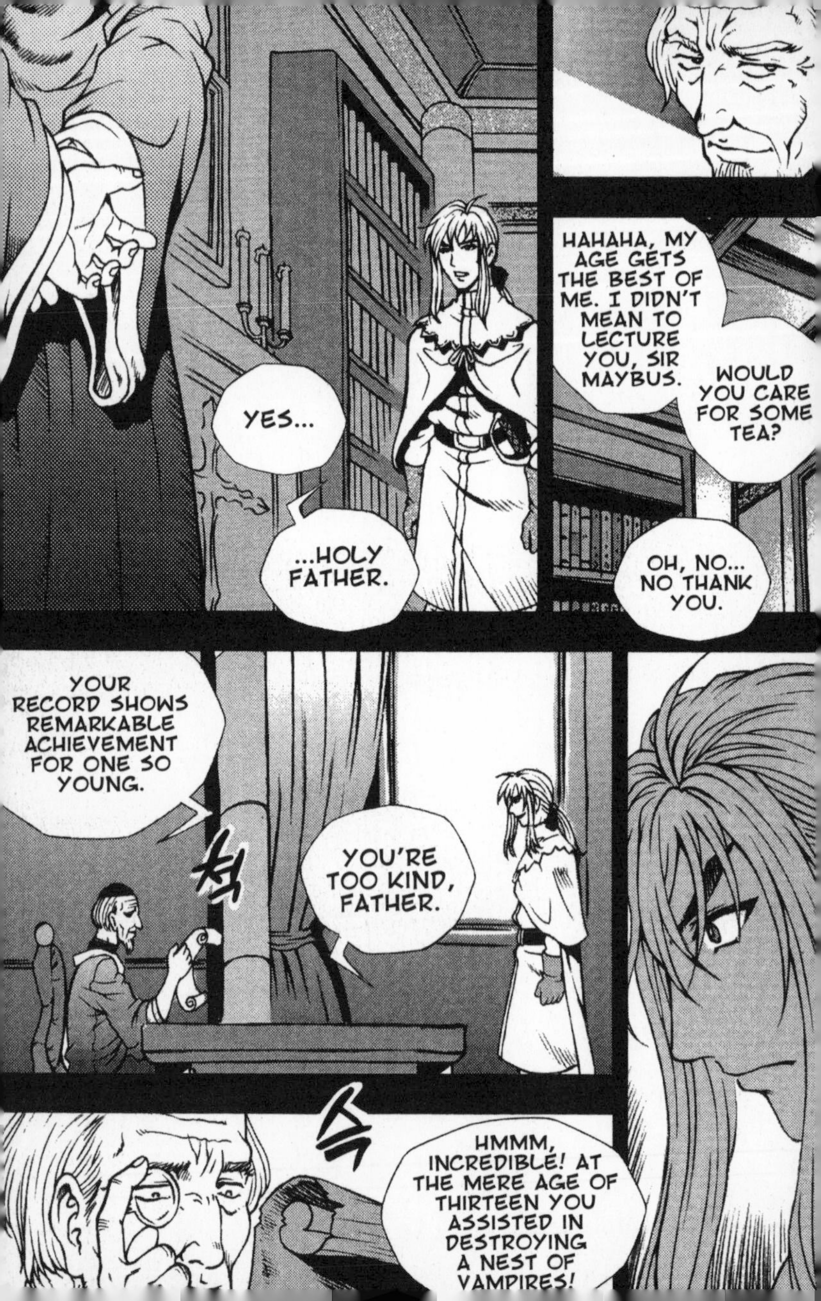
YES...
...HOLY FATHER.
HAHAHA, MY AGE GETS THE BEST OF ME. I DIDN'T MEAN TO LECTURE YOU, SIR MAYBUS.
WOULD YOU CARE FOR SOME TEA?
OH, NO... NO THANK YOU.
YOUR RECORD SHOWS REMARKABLE ACHIEVEMENT FOR ONE SO YOUNG.
YOU'RE TOO KIND, FATHER.
HMMM, INCREDIBLE! AT THE MERE AGE OF THIRTEEN YOU ASSISTED IN DESTROYING A NEST OF VAMPIRES!

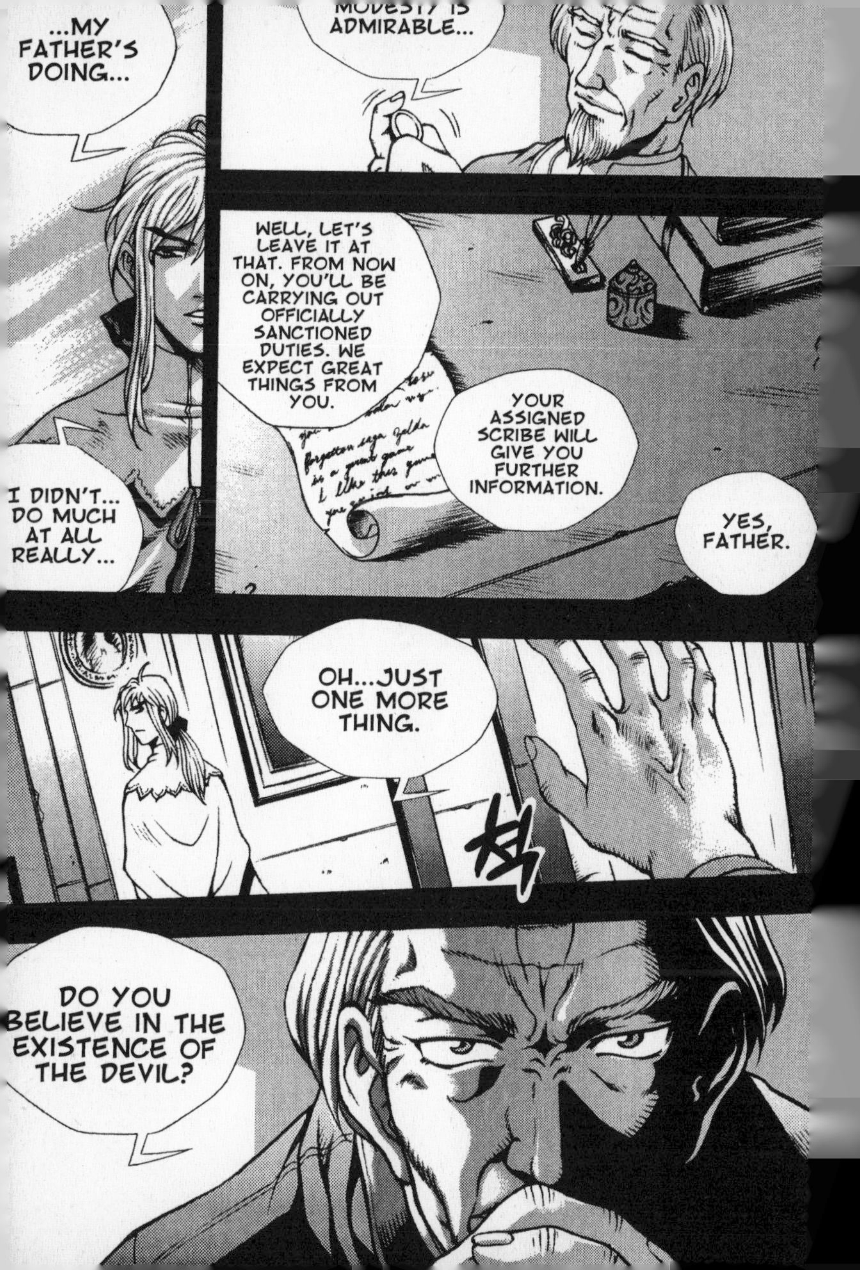
MODESTY IS ADMIRABLE...
WELL, LET'S LEAVE IT AT THAT. FROM NOW ON, YOU'LL BE CARRYING OUT OFFICIALLY SANCTIONED DUTIES. WE EXPECT GREAT THINGS FROM YOU.
YOUR ASSIGNED SCRIBE WILL GIVE YOU FURTHER INFORMATION.
YES, FATHER.
...MY FATHER'S DOING...
I DIDN'T... DO MUCH AT ALL REALLY...
OH...JUST ONE MORE THING.
DO YOU BELIEVE IN THE EXISTENCE OF THE DEVIL?

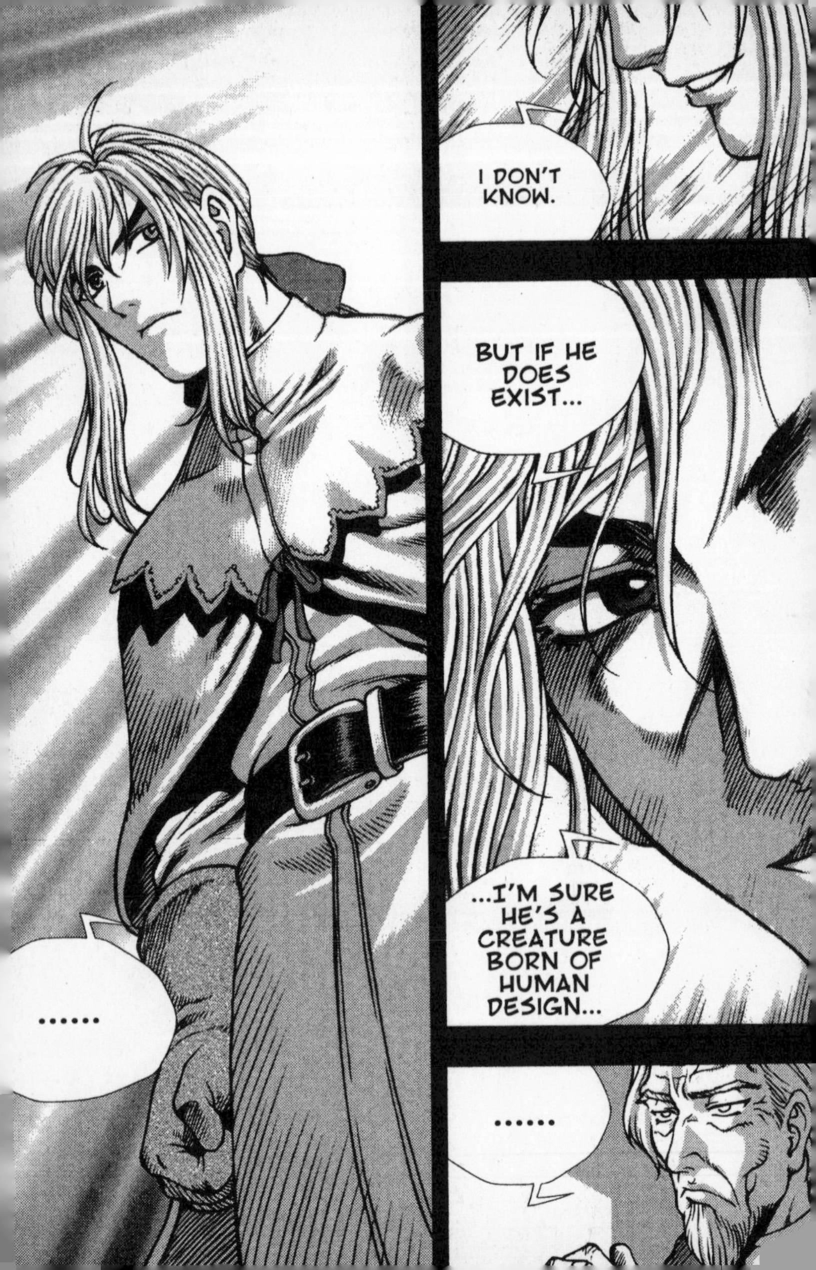
I DON'T KNOW.
BUT IF HE DOES EXIST...
...I'M SURE HE'S A CREATURE BORN OF HUMAN DESIGN...
......
......

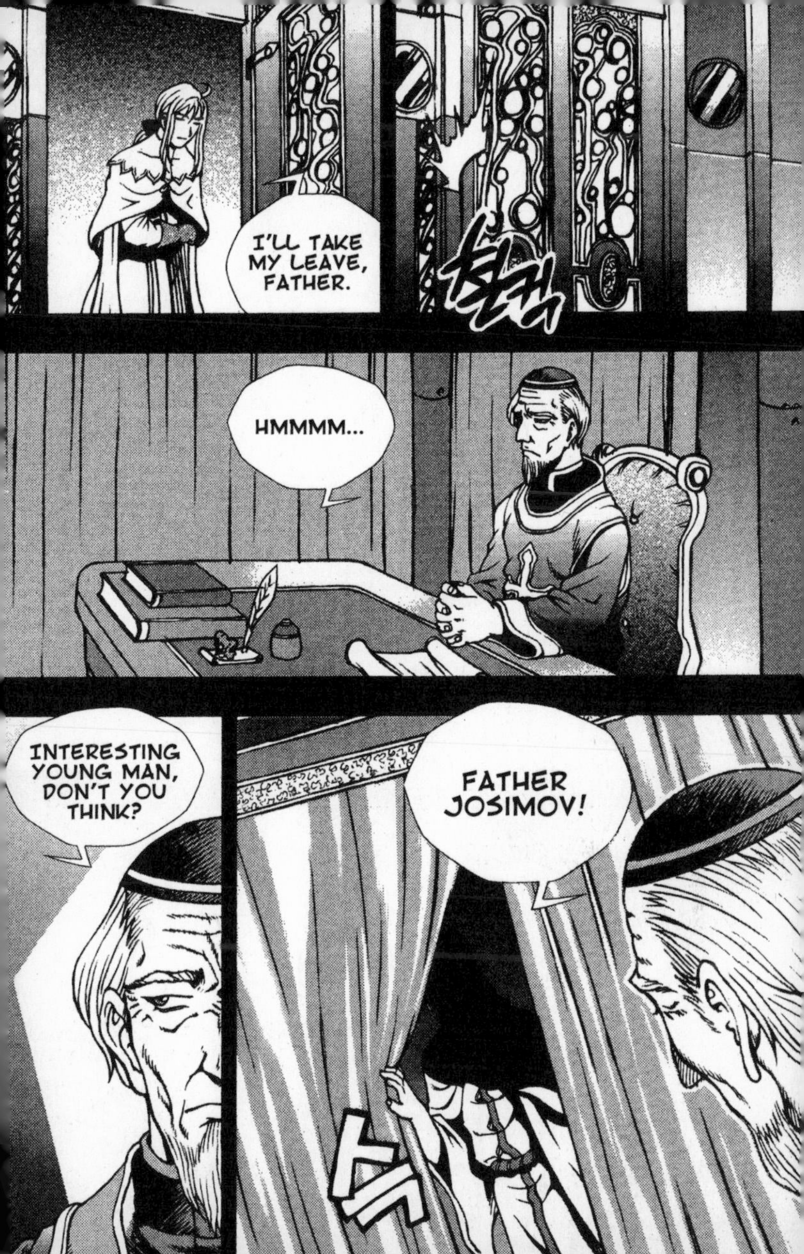
I'LL TAKE MY LEAVE, FATHER.
HMMMM...
INTERESTING YOUNG MAN, DON'T YOU THINK?
FATHER JOSIMOV!

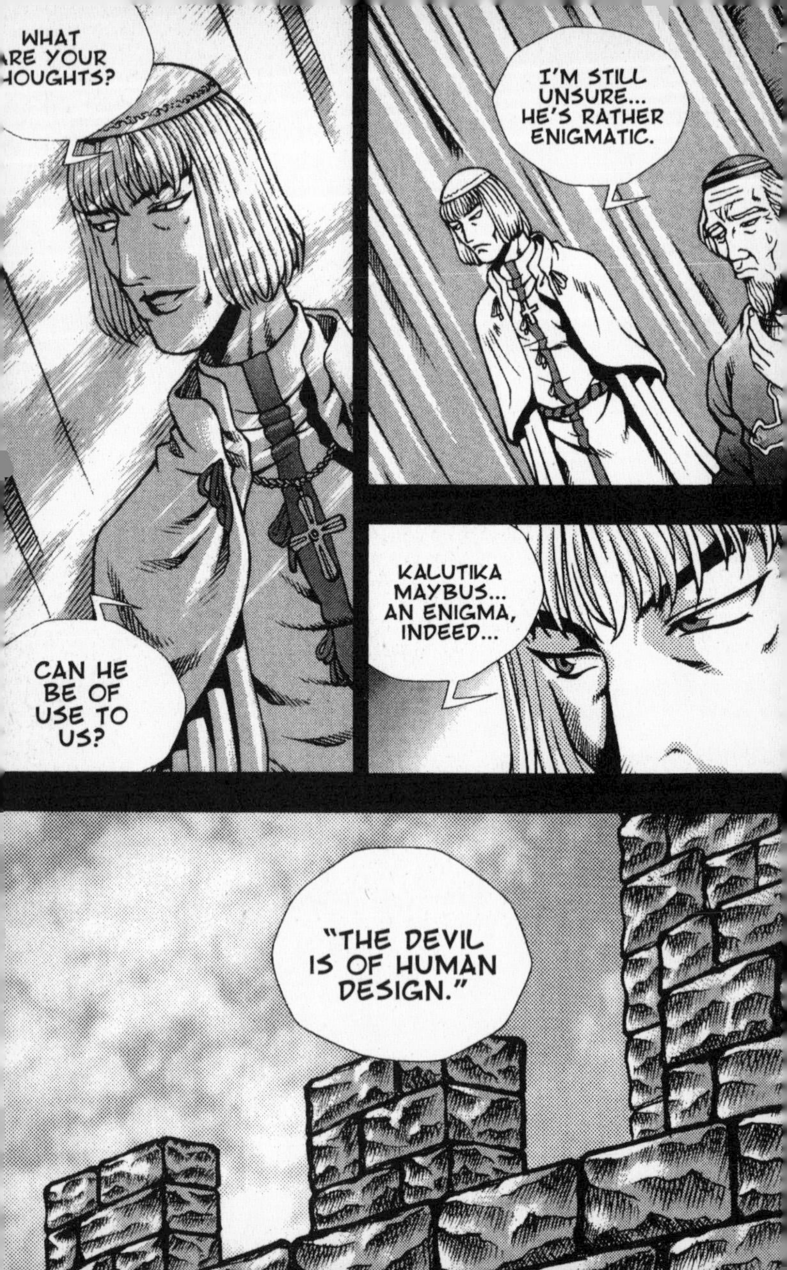
WHAT ARE YOUR THOUGHTS?
CAN HE BE OF USE TO US?
I'M STILL UNSURE... HE'S RATHER ENIGMATIC.
KALUTIKA MAYBUS... AN ENIGMA, INDEED...
"THE DEVIL IS OF HUMAN DESIGN."

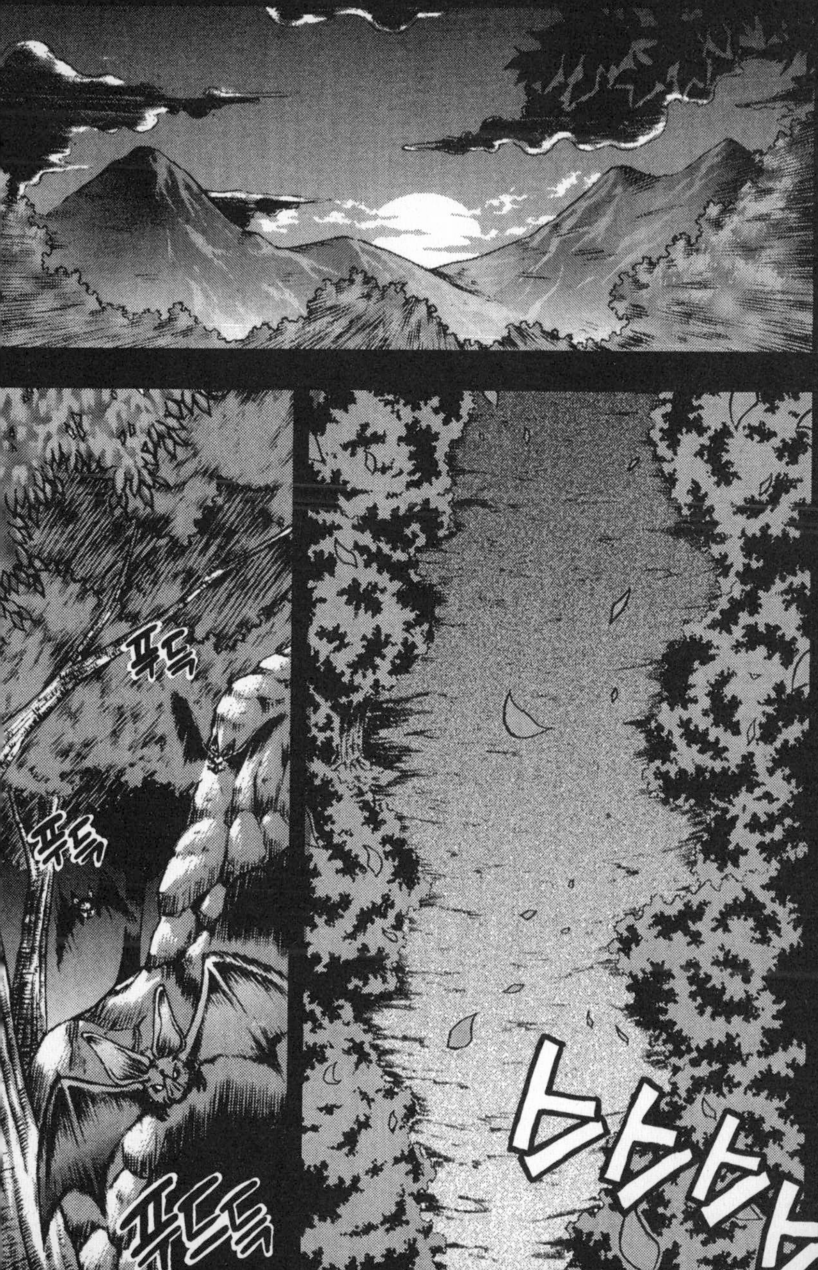
푸드득
푸드득
푸드드득

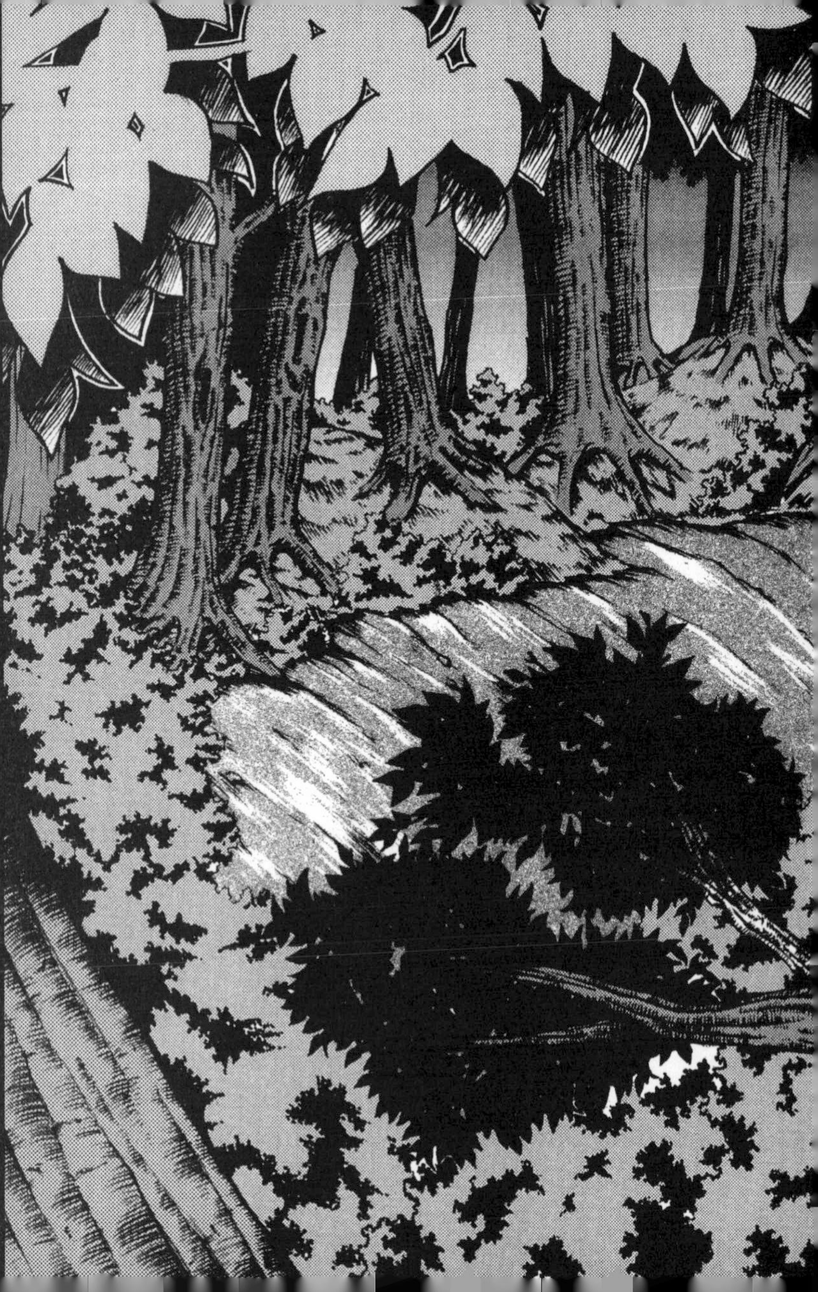

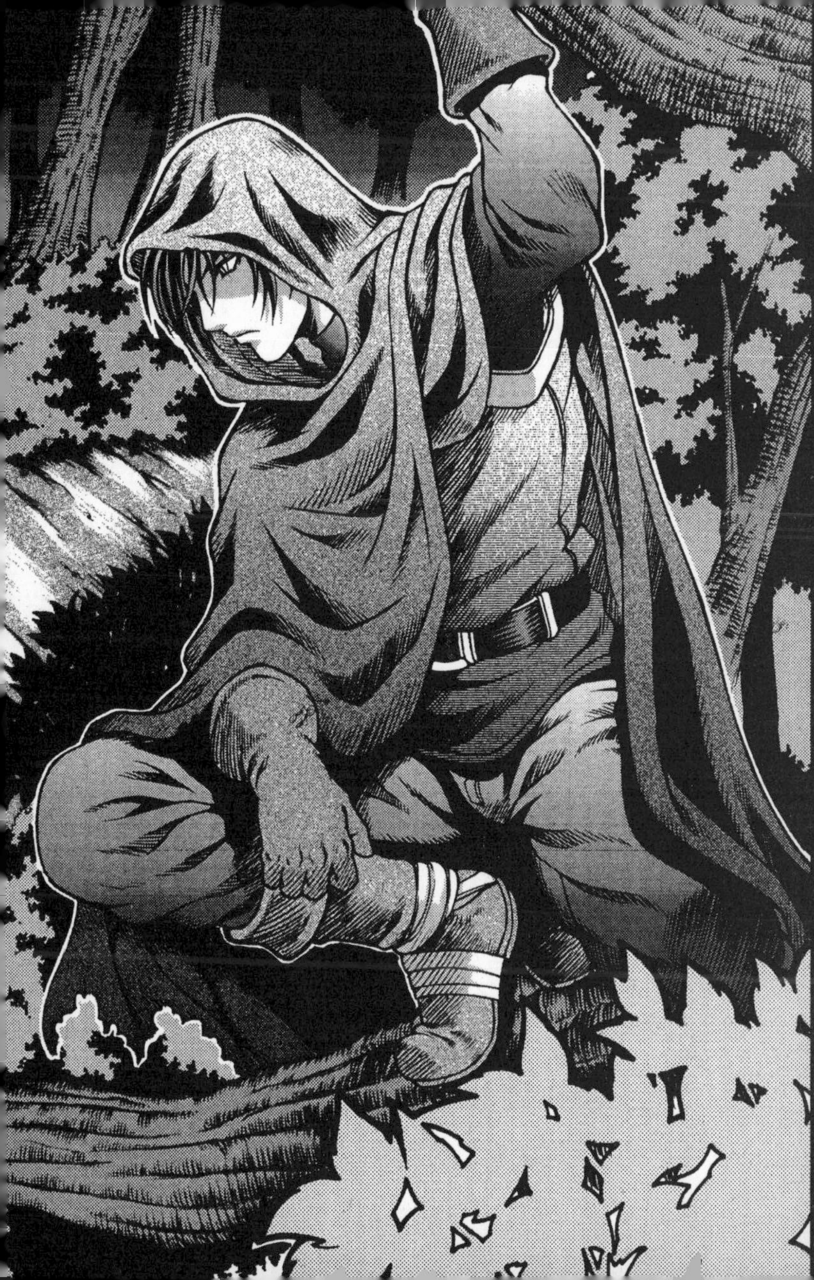

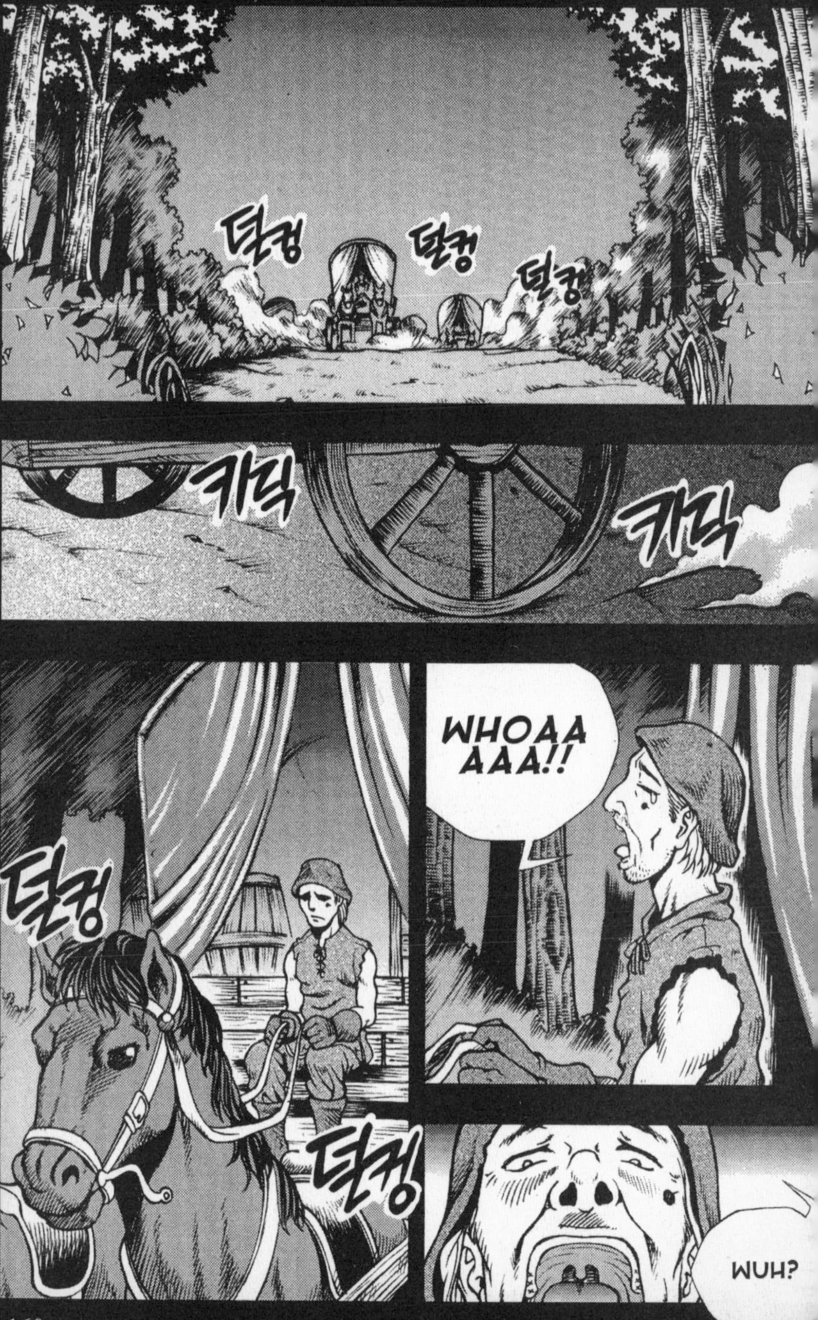
덜컹
덜컹
덜컹
카닥
카닥
덜컹
덜컹
WHOAA AAA!!
WUH?

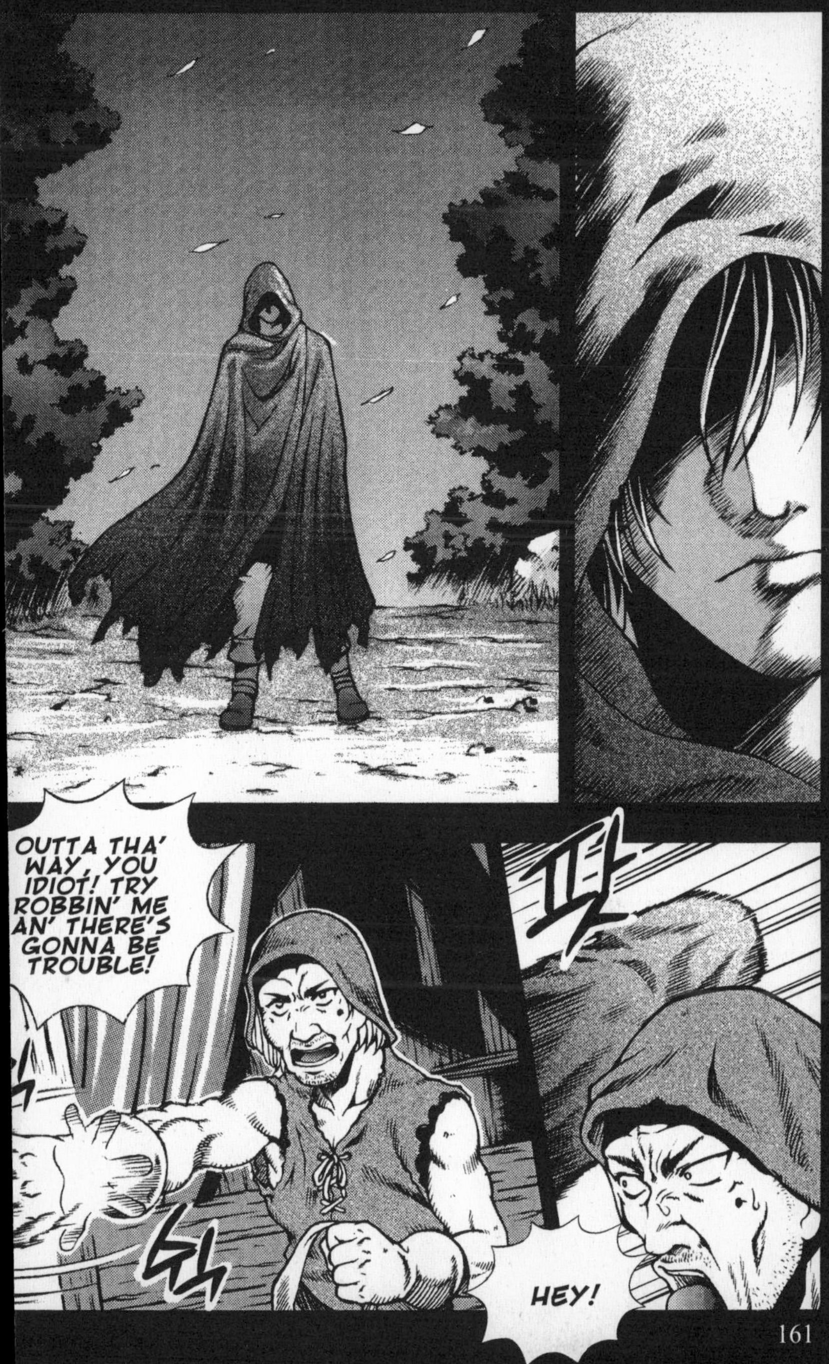
HEY!
OUTTA THA' WAY, YOU IDIOT! TRY ROBBIN' ME AN' THERE'S GONNA BE TROUBLE!

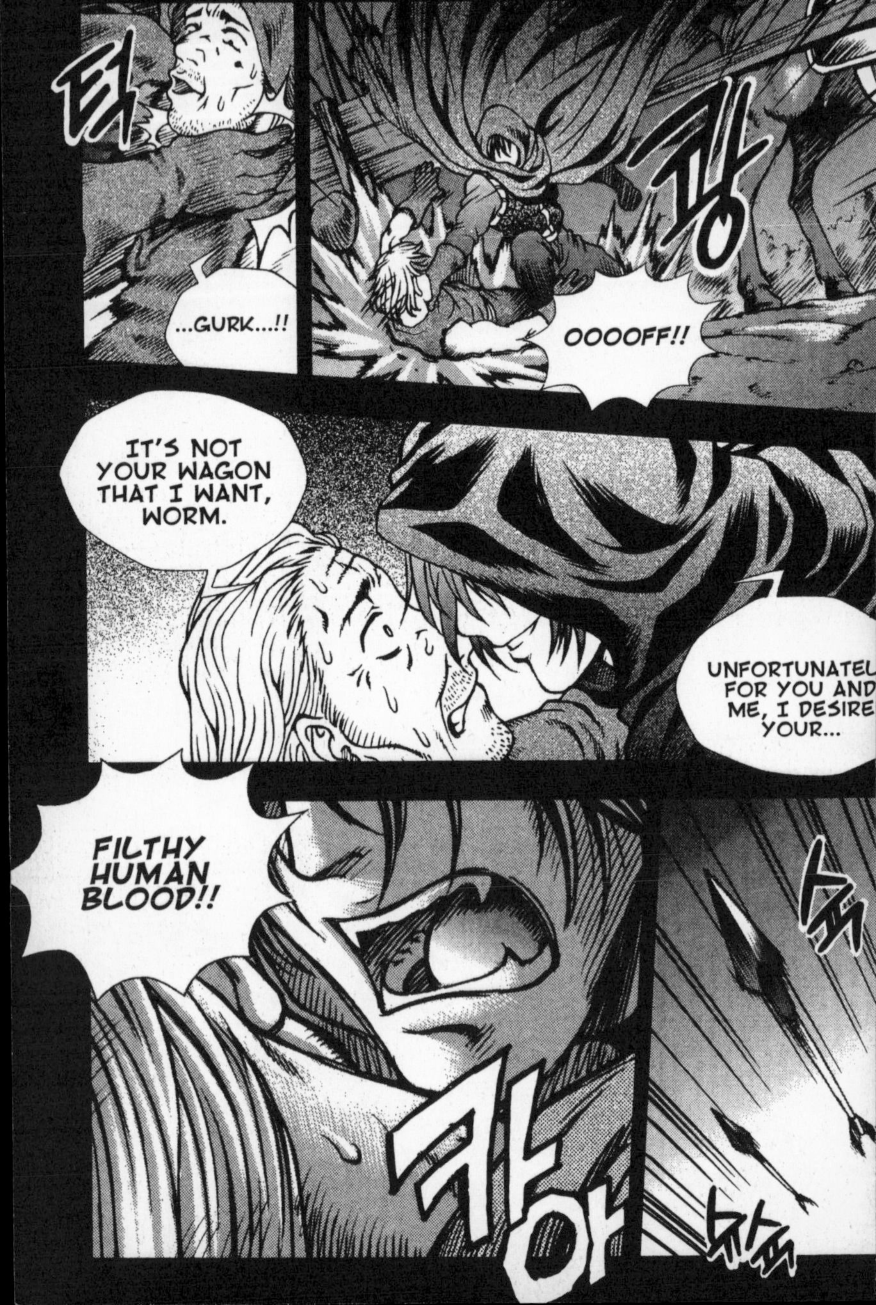
...GURK...!!
OOOOFF!!
IT'S NOT YOUR WAGON THAT I WANT, WORM.
UNFORTUNATEL FOR YOU AND ME, I DESIRE YOUR...
FILTHY HUMAN BLOOD!!

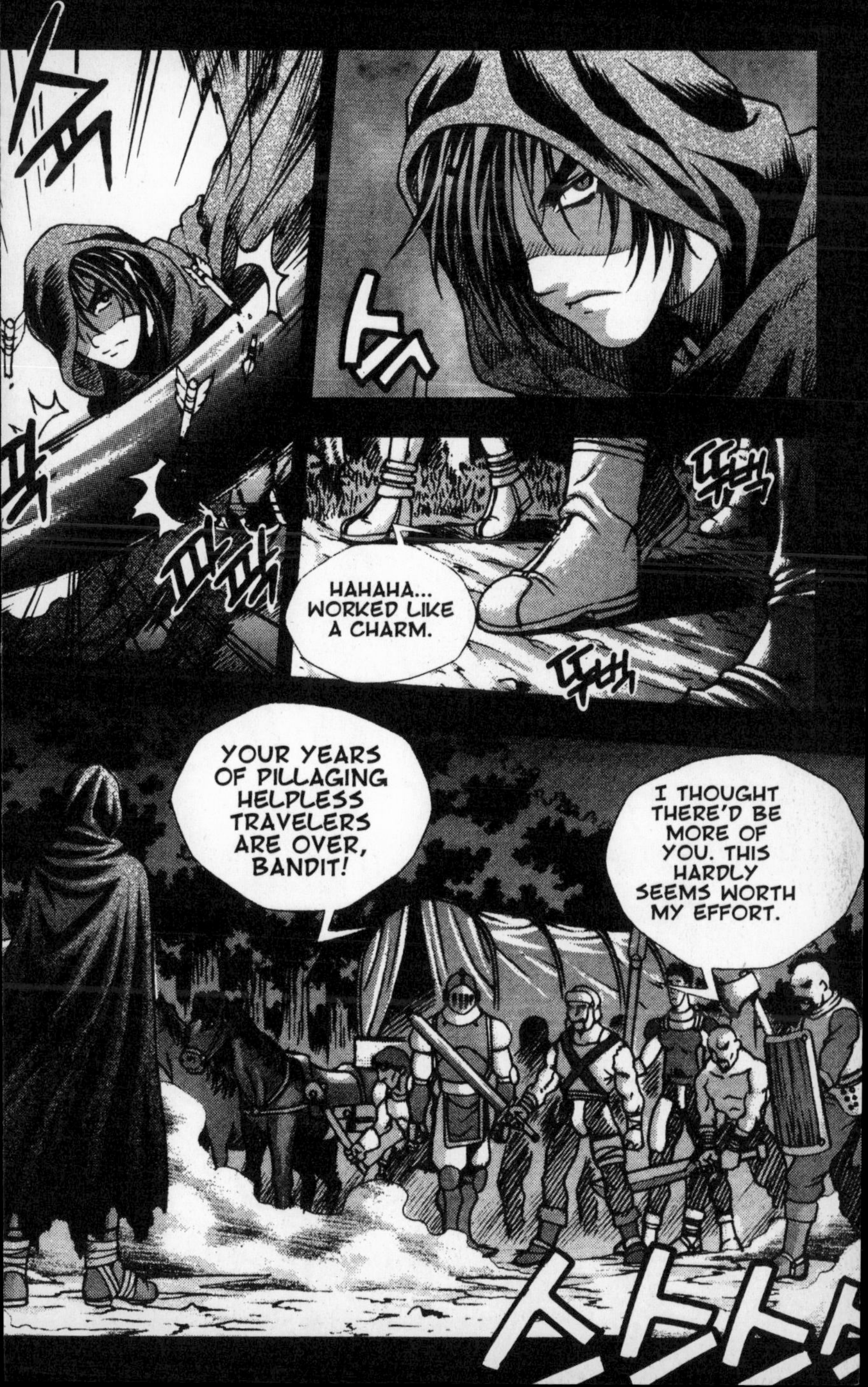
HAHAHA... WORKED LIKE A CHARM.
I THOUGHT THERE'D BE MORE OF YOU. THIS HARDLY SEEMS WORTH MY EFFORT.
YOUR YEARS OF PILLAGING HELPLESS TRAVELERS ARE OVER, BANDIT!

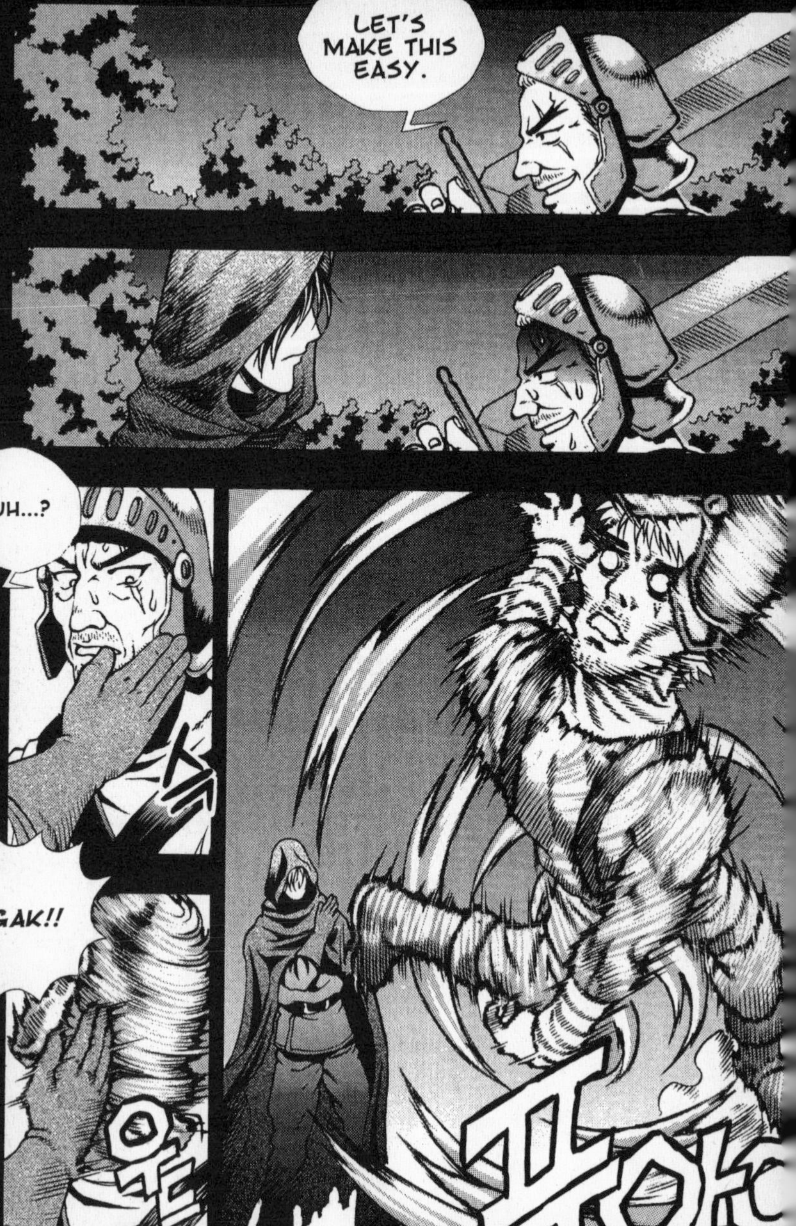
LET'S MAKE THIS EASY.
TOKO
UH...?
GAK!!

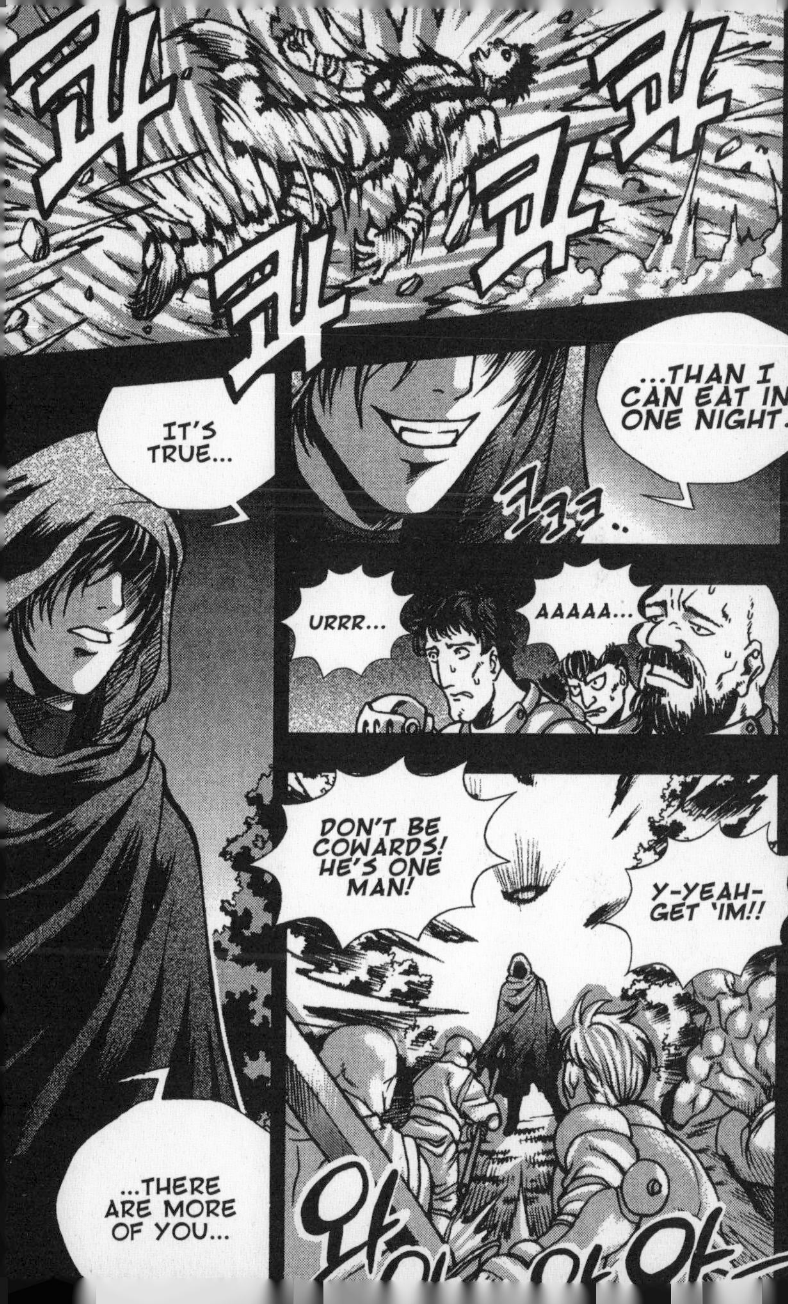
IT'S TRUE...
...THAN I CAN EAT IN ONE NIGHT.
URRR...
AAAAA...
...THERE ARE MORE OF YOU...
DON'T BE COWARDS! HE'S ONE MAN!
Y-YEAH-GET 'IM!!

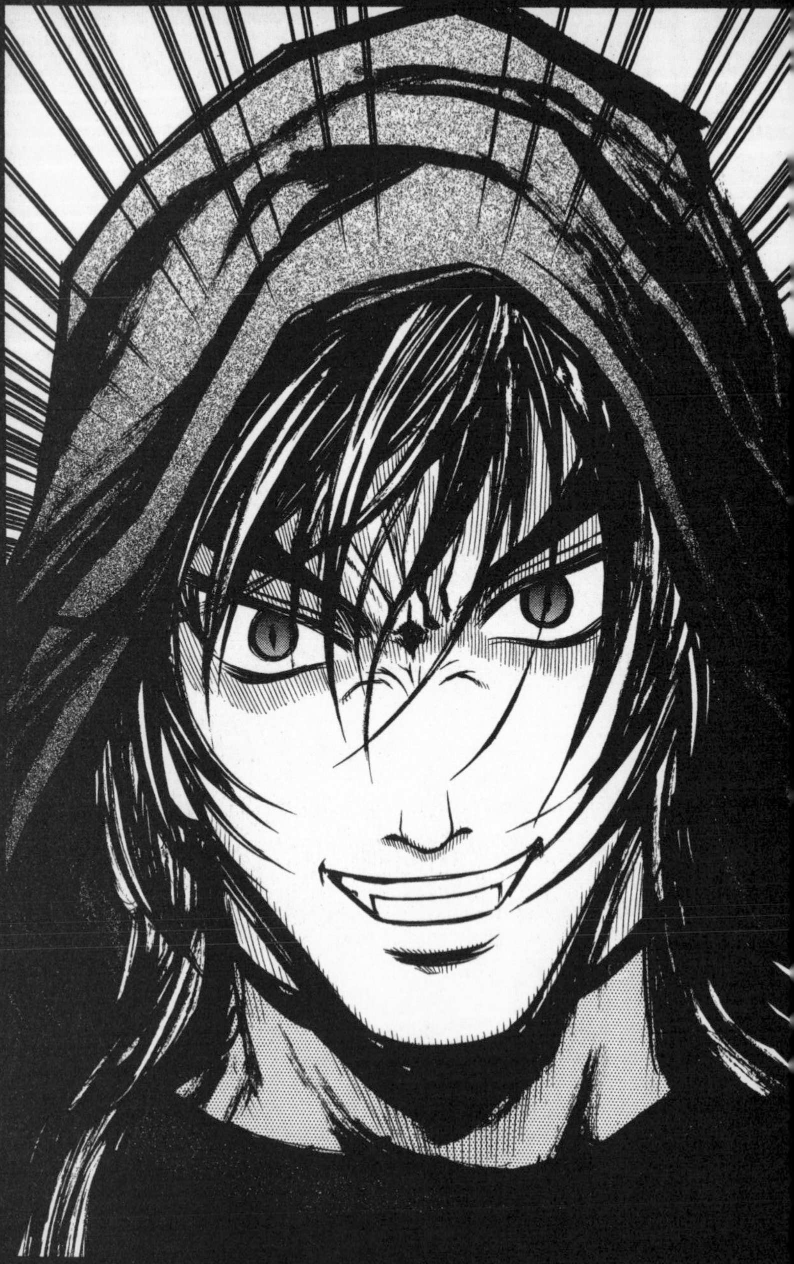

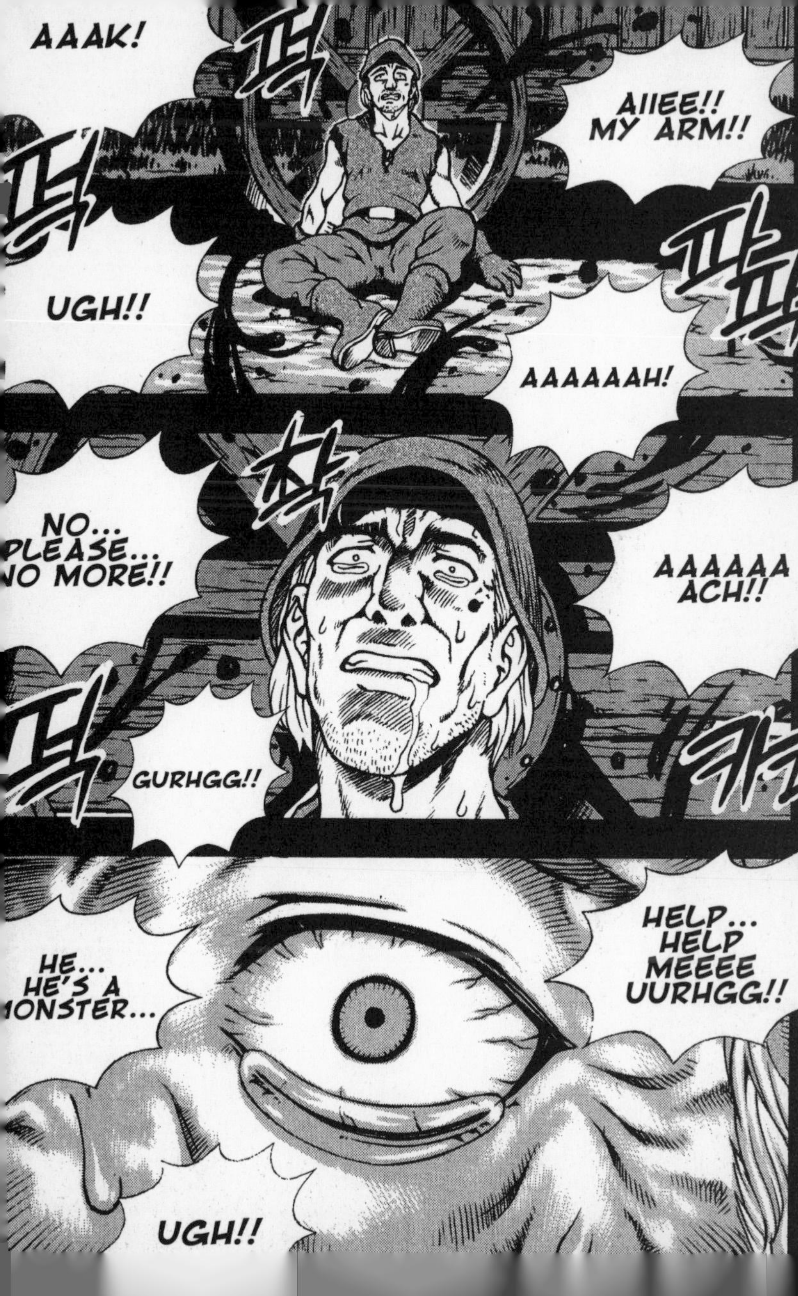
AAAK!
퍽
퍽
AIIEE!! MY ARM!!
UGH!!
AAAAAAH!
NO... PLEASE... NO MORE!!
AAAAAA ACH!!
퍽
GURHGG!!
HE... HE'S A MONSTER...
HELP... HELP MEEEE UURHGG!!
UGH!!

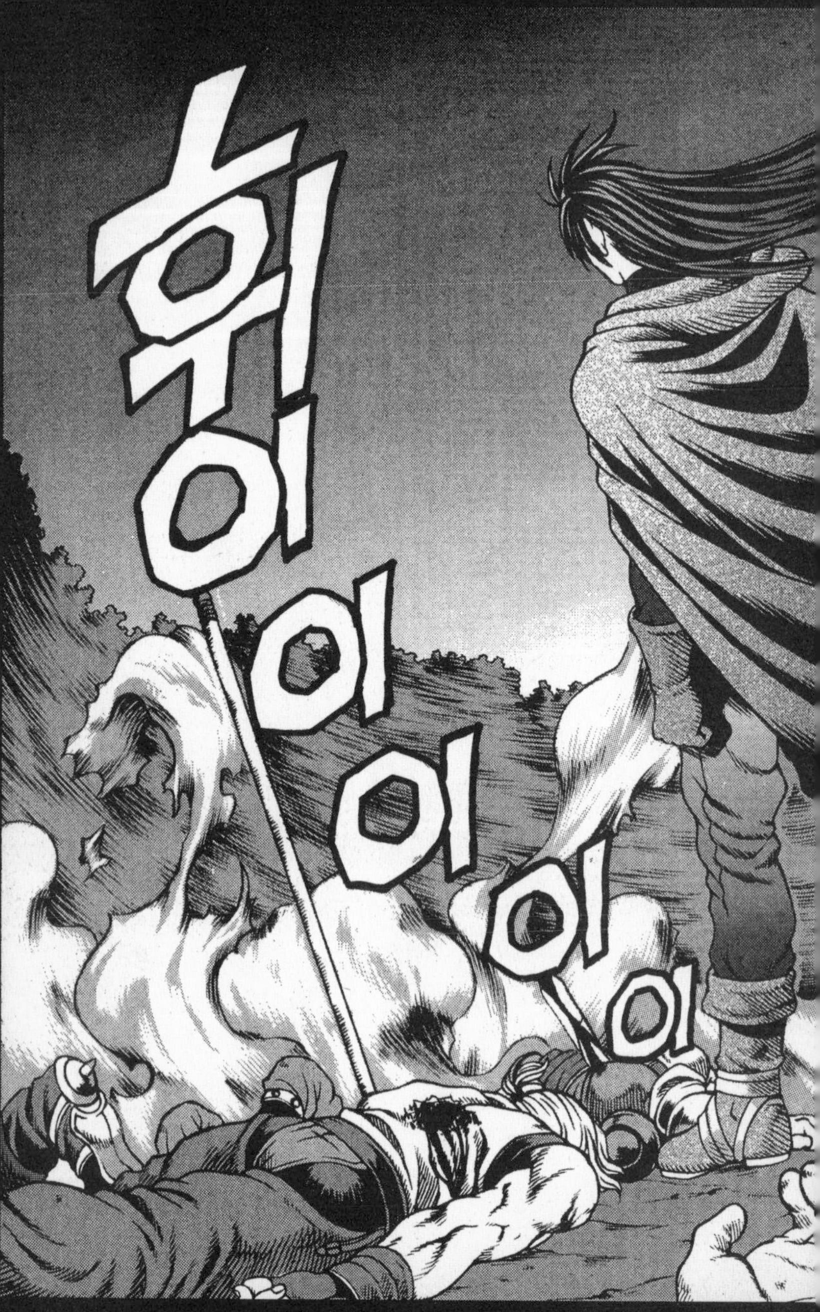
휘이이이이이

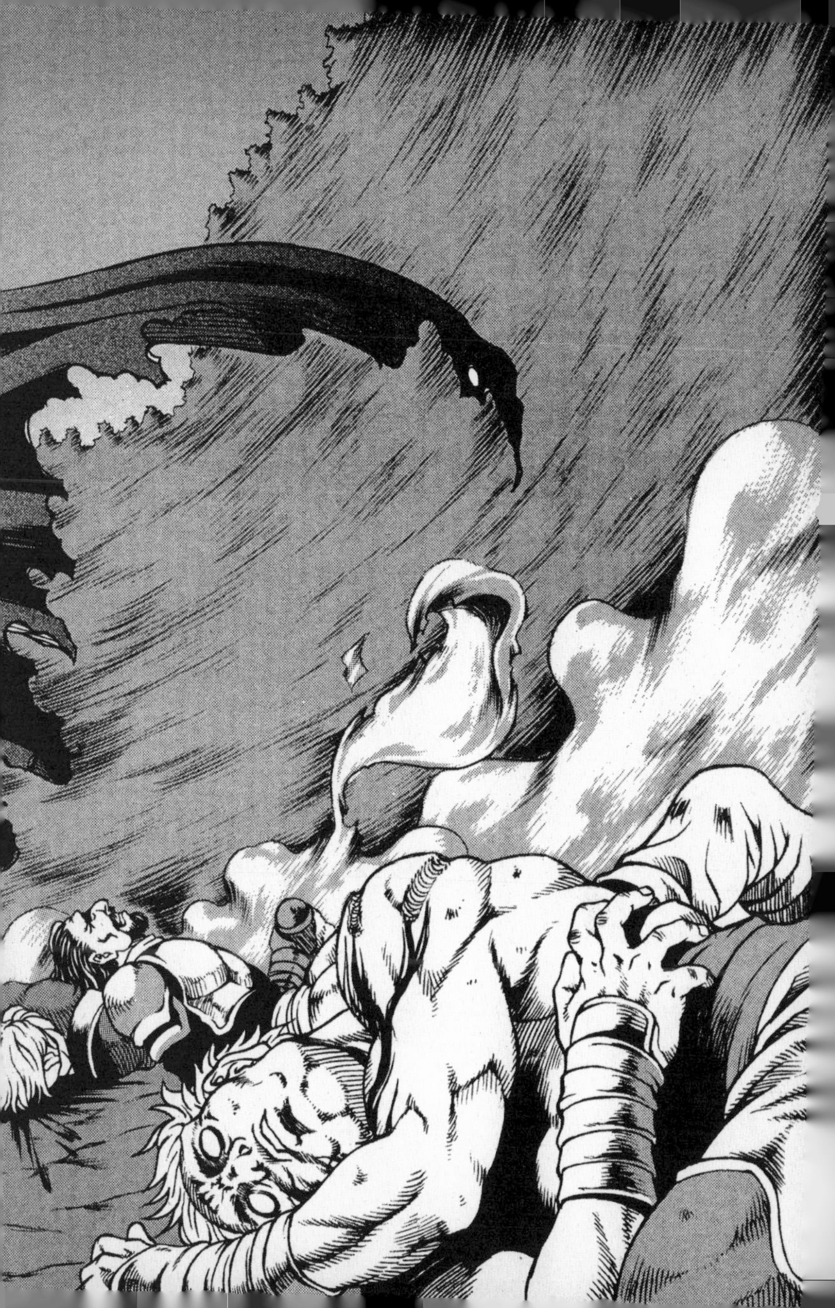

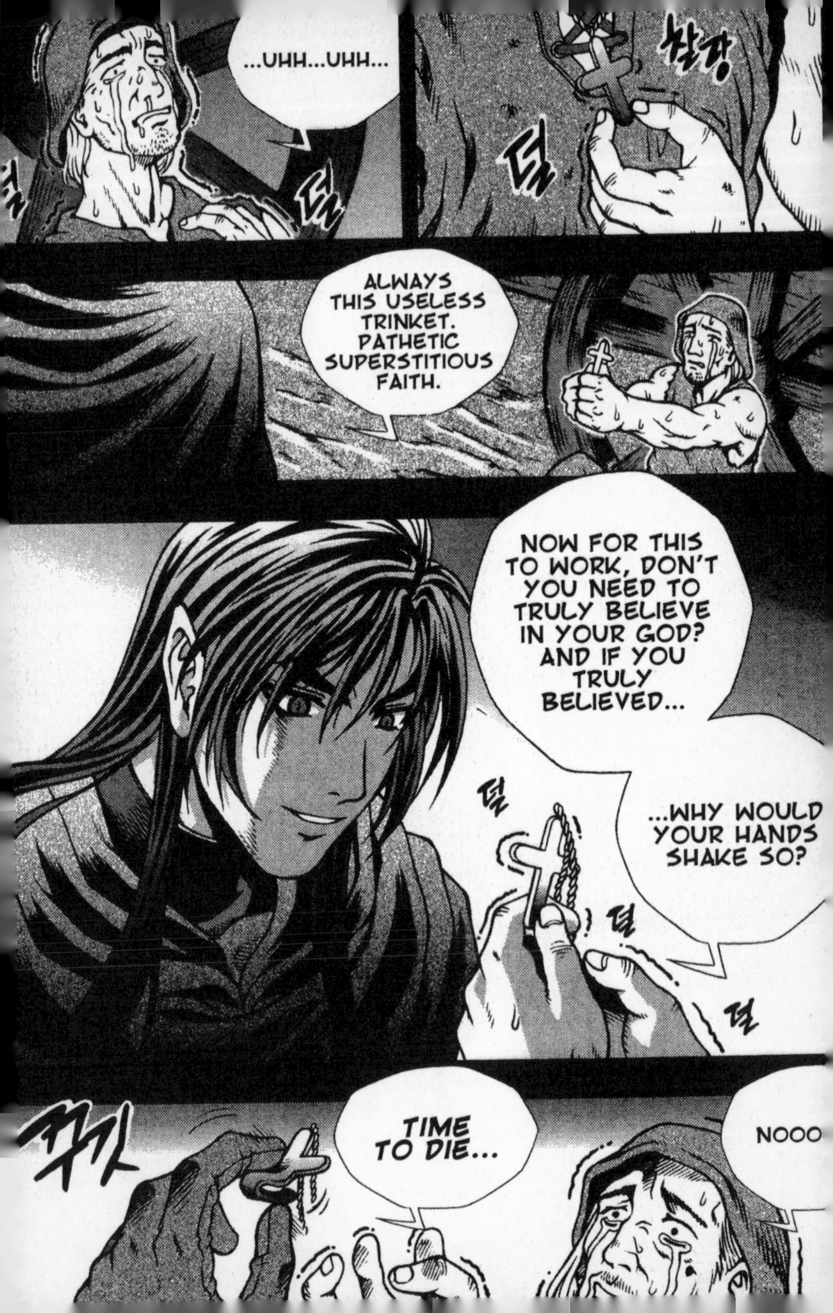
...UHH...UHH...
ALWAYS THIS USELESS TRINKET. PATHETIC SUPERSTITIOUS FAITH.
NOW FOR THIS TO WORK, DON'T YOU NEED TO TRULY BELIEVE IN YOUR GOD? AND IF YOU TRULY BELIEVED...
...WHY WOULD YOUR HANDS SHAKE SO?
TIME TO DIE...
NOOO

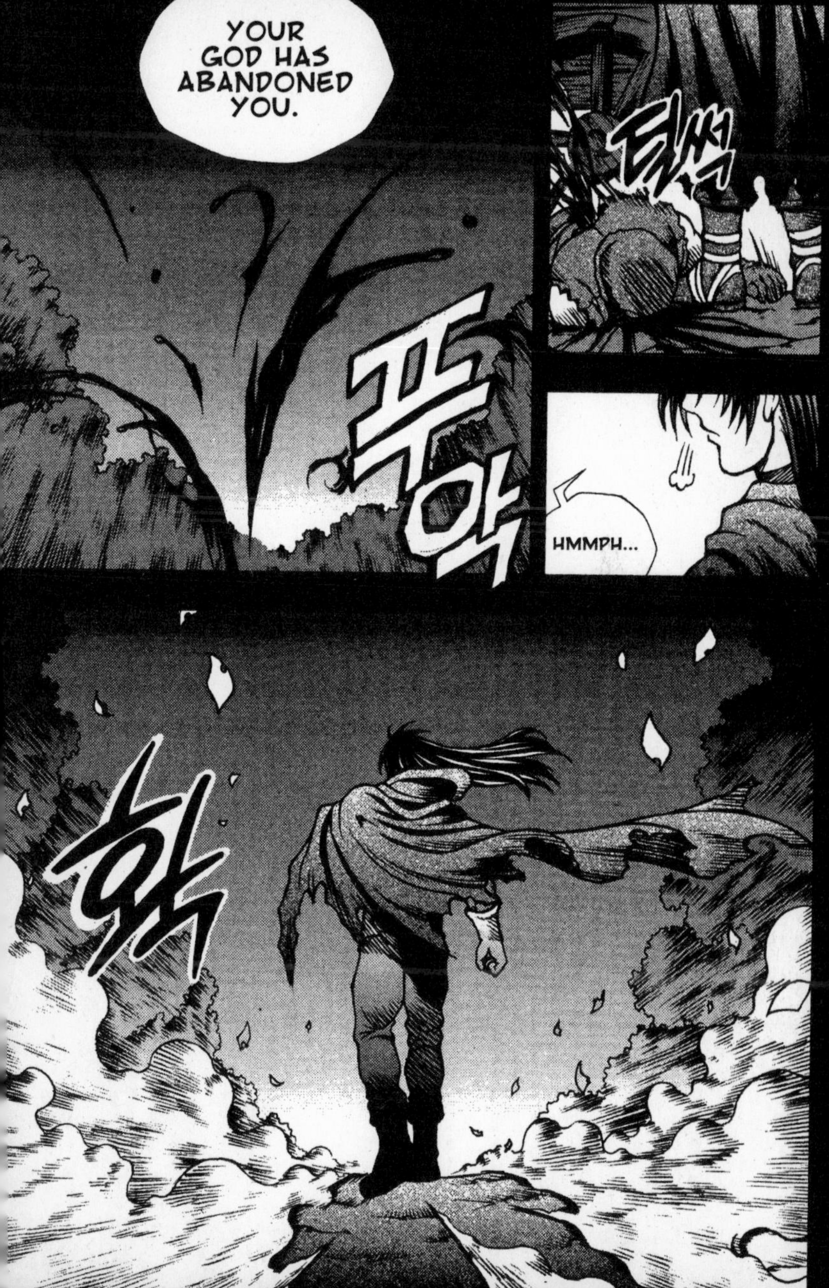
YOUR GOD HAS ABANDONED YOU.
HMMPH...

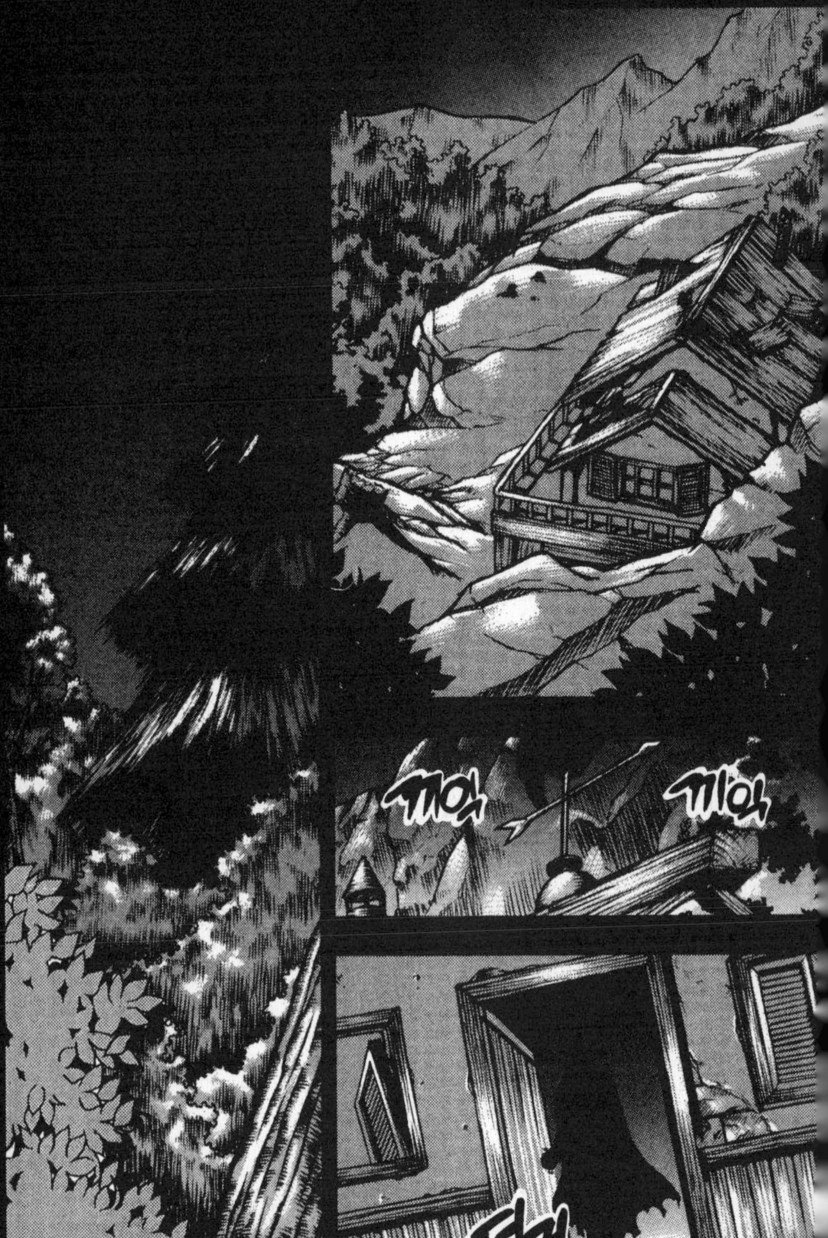
끼익
끼익
덜컹

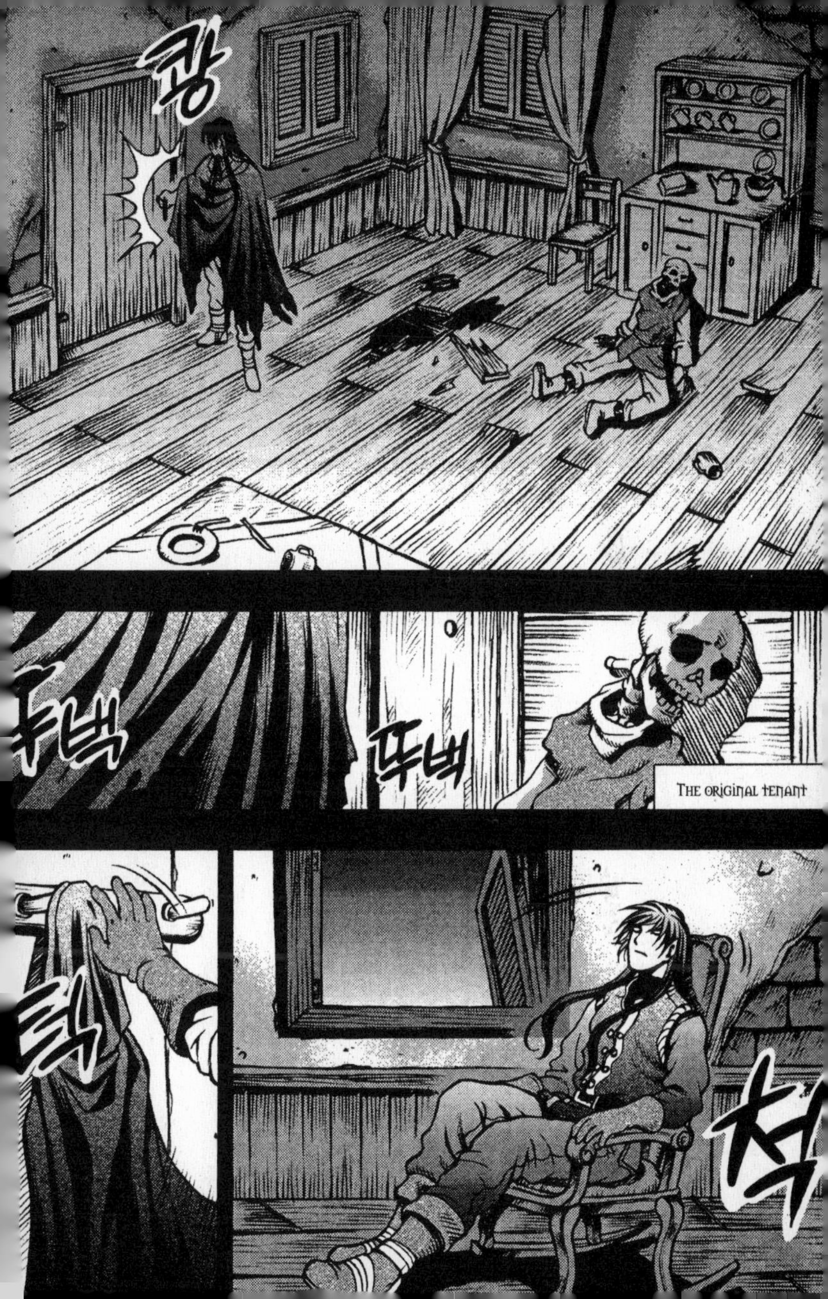
쾅
뚜벅
뚜벅
THE ORIGINAL TENANT
척

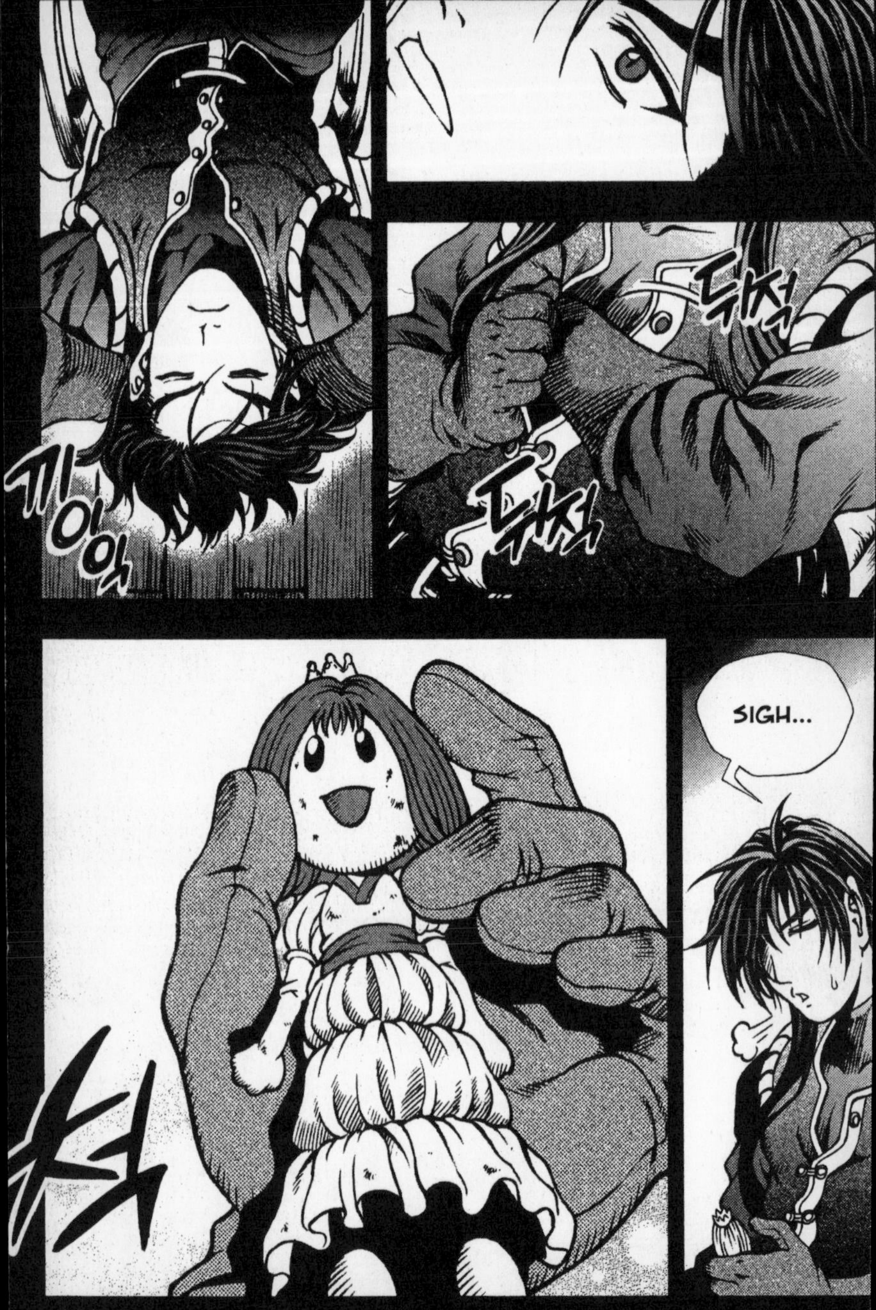
찌이익
SIGH...
척

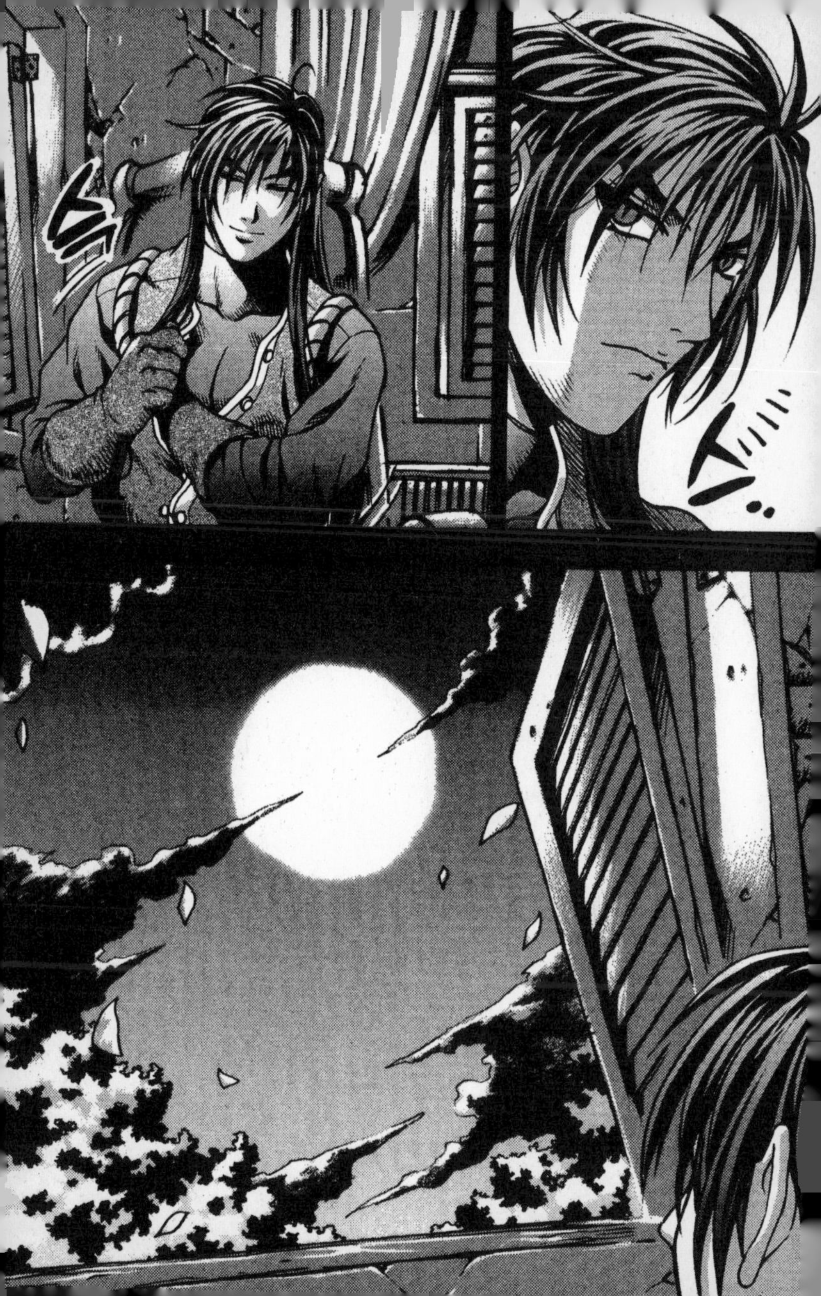

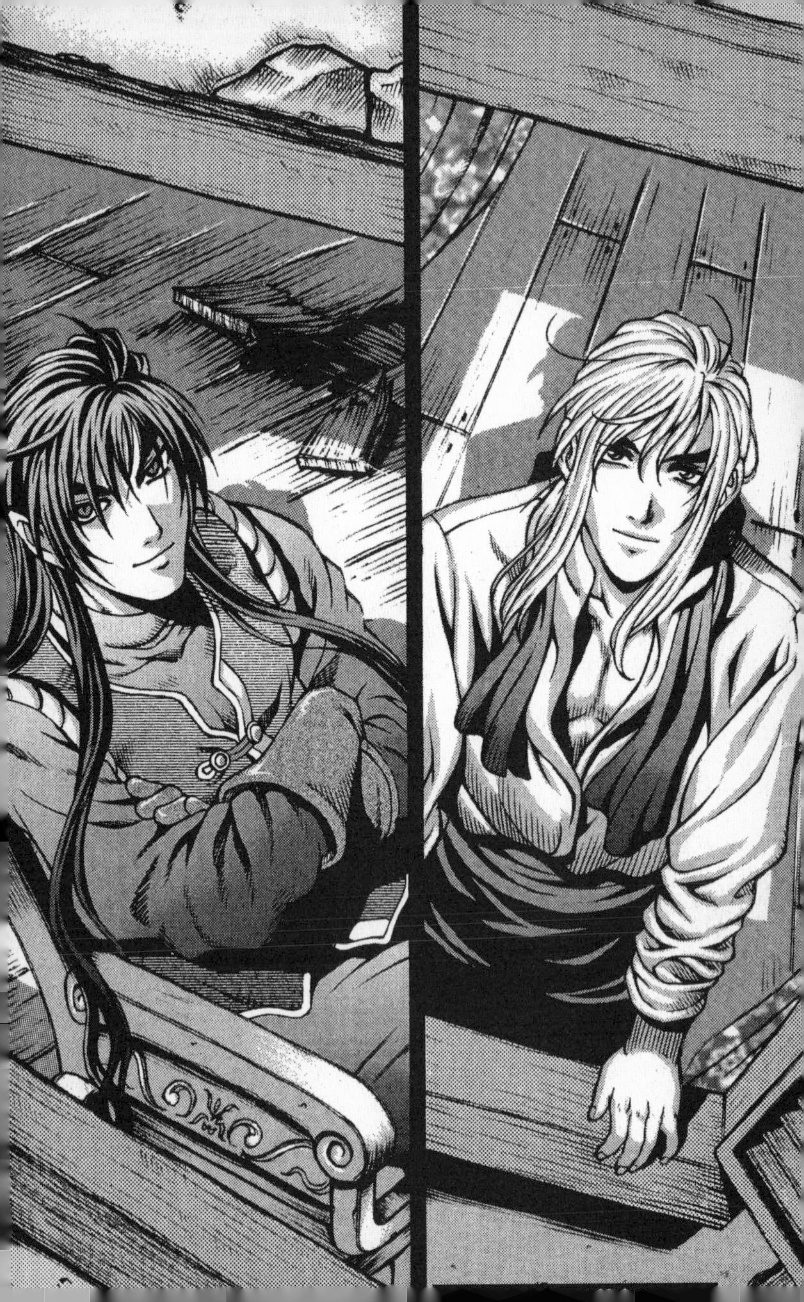

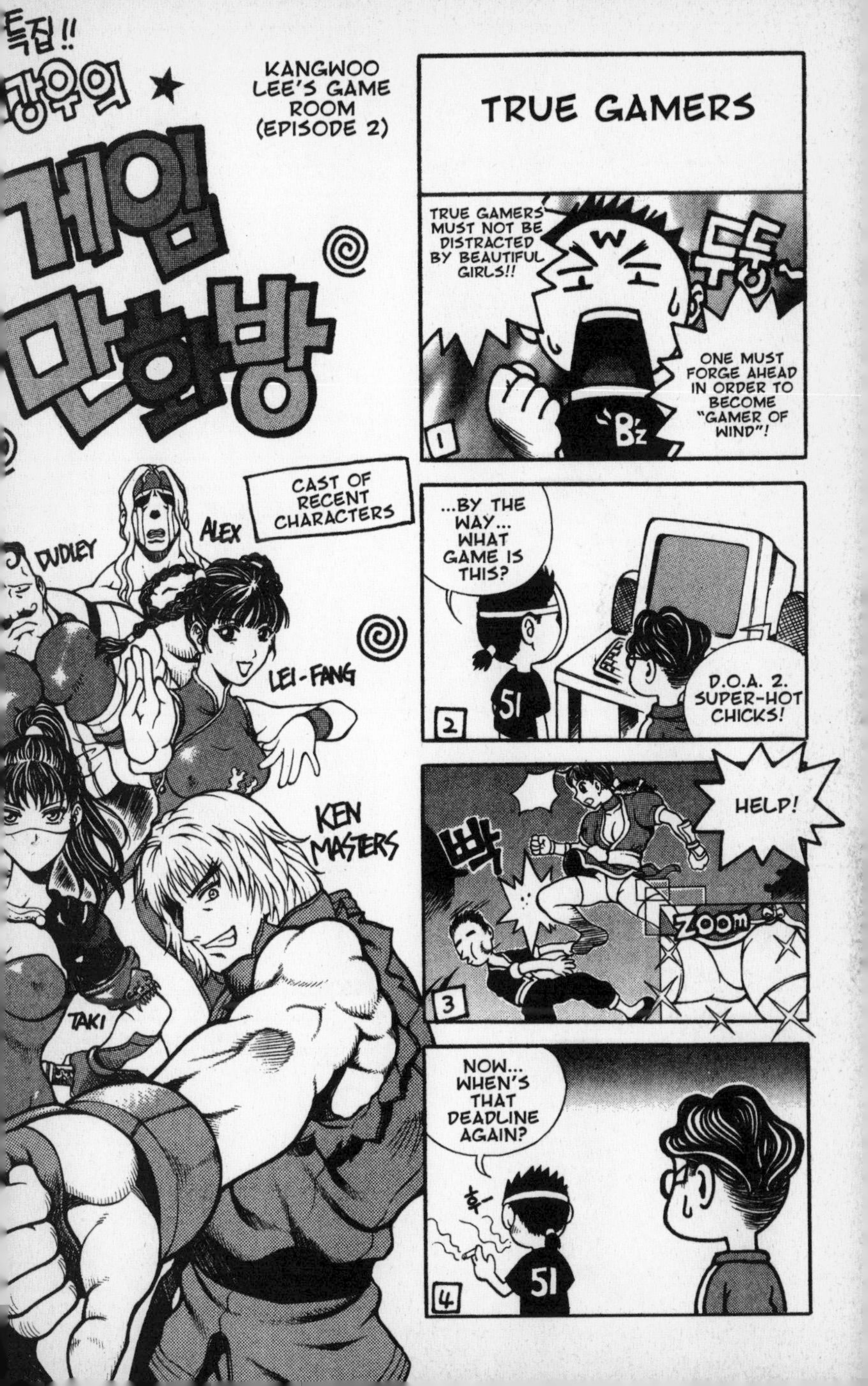

특집!!
강우의 ★
게임 만화방
KANGWOO LEE'S GAME ROOM (EPISODE 2)
CAST OF RECENT CHARACTERS
ALEX
DUDLEY
LEI-FANG
KEN MASTERS
TAKI
TRUE GAMERS
TRUE GAMERS MUST NOT BE DISTRACTED BY BEAUTIFUL GIRLS!!
두둥~
ONE MUST FORGE AHEAD IN ORDER TO BECOME "GAMER OF WIND"!
...BY THE WAY... WHAT GAME IS THIS?
D.O.A. 2. SUPER-HOT CHICKS!
HELP!
빡
ZOOM
NOW... WHEN'S THAT DEADLINE AGAIN?
후-

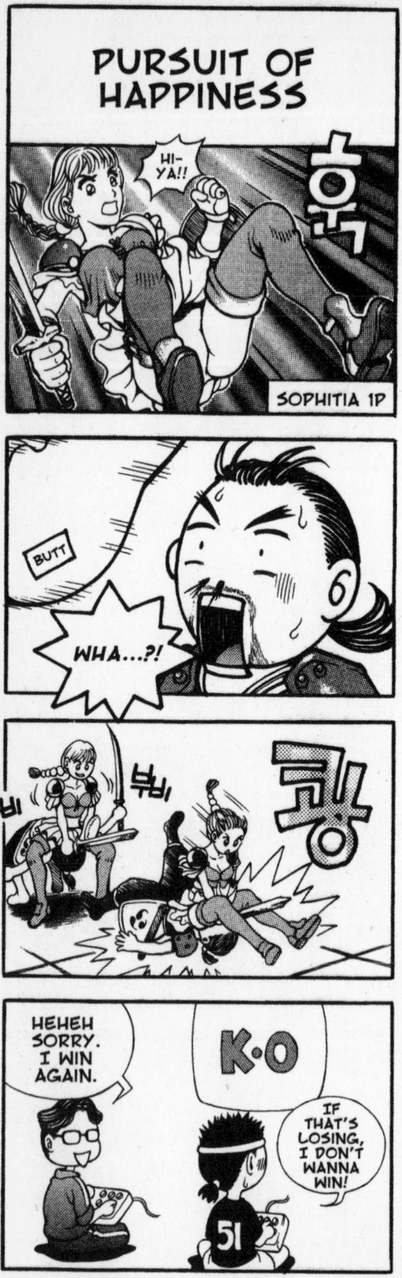
PURSUIT OF HAPPINESS
HI-YA!!
후
SOPHITIA 1P
BUTT
WHA...?!
부비
부비
쾅
HEHEH SORRY. I WIN AGAIN.
K·O
IF THAT'S LOSING, I DON'T WANNA WIN!

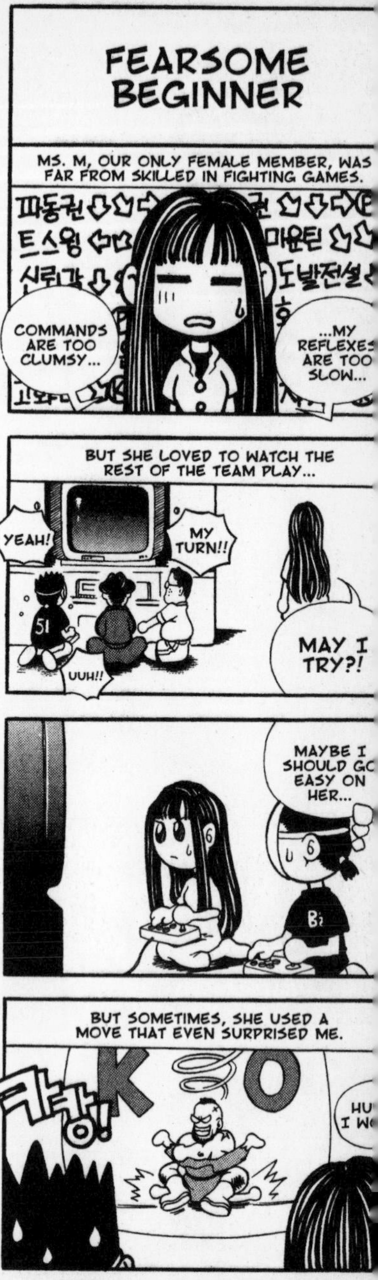
FEARSOME BEGINNER
MS. M, OUR ONLY FEMALE MEMBER, WAS FAR FROM SKILLED IN FIGHTING GAMES.
COMMANDS ARE TOO CLUMSY...
...MY REFLEXES ARE TOO SLOW...
BUT SHE LOVED TO WATCH THE REST OF THE TEAM PLAY...
YEAH!
MY TURN!!
UUH!!
MAY I TRY?!
MAYBE I SHOULD GO EASY ON HER...
BUT SOMETIMES, SHE USED A MOVE THAT EVEN SURPRISED ME.
카캉!
K O

* FINAL ATOMIC BUSTER: JOYSTICK (TWO FULL CIRCLES) + P

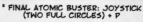

Preview: Vol. 7

In the next blood-soaked installment of Rebirth...

Deshwitat wasn't the only immortal to have once counted the treacherous Kalutika Maybus among his allies. Enter that incorrigible rogue and swordsman supreme—Rett Butler!

As he rises through the ranks of The Church's Sacred Knights, young Kal finds that he'll need a man of action at his side. And who better fit to lend his sword than the Robin Hood-esque Rett, a hell-raising scoundrel with nothing to lose.

When Kal and Rett investigate reports of missing villagers in a nearby forest, they ride straight into a nightmarish scene of unimaginable horror— and face to face with the savage vampire, Deshwitat.

ALSO AVAILABLE FROM TOKYOPOP®

MANGA

.HACK//LEGEND OF THE TWILIGHT
@LARGE
A.I. LOVE YOU
AI YORI AOSHI
ANGELIC LAYER
ARM OF KANNON May 2004
BABY BIRTH
BATTLE ROYALE
BATTLE VIXENS April 2004
BRAIN POWERED
BRIGADOON
B'TX
CANDIDATE FOR GODDESS, THE April 2004
CARDCAPTOR SAKURA
CARDCAPTOR SAKURA - MASTER OF THE CLOW
CARDCAPTOR SAKURA AUTHENTIC May 2004
CHOBITS
CHRONICLES OF THE CURSED SWORD
CLAMP SCHOOL DETECTIVES
CLOVER
COMIC PARTY June 2004
CONFIDENTIAL CONFESSIONS
CORRECTOR YUI
COWBOY BEBOP
COWBOY BEBOP: SHOOTING STAR
CRESCENT MOON May 2004
CYBORG 009
DEMON DIARY
DEMON ORORON, THE April 2004
DEUS VITAE June 2004
DIGIMON
DIGIMON ZERO TWO
DIGIMON SERIES 3 April 2004
DNANGEL April 2004
DOLL - HARDCOVER May 2004
DRAGON HUNTER
DRAGON KNIGHTS
DUKLYON: CLAMP SCHOOL DEFENDERS
ERICA SAKURAZAWA WORKS
FAERIES' LANDING
FAKE
FLCL
FORBIDDEN DANCE
FRUITS BASKET
G GUNDAM
GATE KEEPERS
GETBACKERS
GHOST! March 2004
GIRL GOT GAME
GRAVITATION
GTO
GUNDAM WING

GUNDAM WING: BATTLEFIELD OF PACIFISTS
GUNDAM WING: ENDLESS WALTZ
GUNDAM WING: THE LAST OUTPOST (G-UNIT)
HAPPY MANIA
HARLEM BEAT
I.N.V.U.
IMMORTAL RAIN June 2004
INITIAL D
ISLAND
JING: KING OF BANDITS
JULINE
JUROR 13 Coming Soon
KARE KANO
KILL ME, KISS ME
KINDAICHI CASE FILES, THE
KING OF HELL
KODOCHA: SANA'S STAGE
LAMENT OF THE LAMB May 2004
LES BIJOUX
LOVE HINA
LUPIN III
MAGIC KNIGHT RAYEARTH I
MAGIC KNIGHT RAYEARTH II
MAHOROMATIC: AUTOMATIC MAIDEN May 2004
MAN OF MANY FACES
MARMALADE BOY
MARS
MINK April 2004
MIRACLE GIRLS
MIYUKI-CHAN IN WONDERLAND
MODEL May 2004
ONE April 2004
PARADISE KISS
PARASYTE
PEACH GIRL
PEACH GIRL: CHANGE OF HEART
PEACH GIRL: AUTHENTIC COLLECTORS BOX SET May 2004
PET SHOP OF HORRORS
PITA-TEN
PLANET LADDER
PLANETES
PRIEST
PSYCHIC ACADEMY March 2004
RAGNAROK
RAVE MASTER
REALITY CHECK
REBIRTH
REBOUND
REMOTE June 2004
RISING STARS OF MANGA
SABER MARIONETTE J
SAILOR MOON
SAINT TAIL

11.20.03 T

ALSO AVAILABLE FROM TOKYOPOP®

SAIYUKI March 2004
SAMURAI DEEPER KYO
SAMURAI GIRL REAL BOUT HIGH SCHOOL
SCRYED
SEIKAI TRILOGY, THE CREST OF THE STARS June 2004
SGT. FROG March 2004
SHAOLIN SISTERS
SHIRAHIME-SYO: SNOW GODDESS TALES HARDCOVER
SHIRAHIME-SYO: SNOW GODDESS TALES SOFTCOVER
June 2004
SHUTTERBOX
SKULL MAN, THE
SNOW DROP
SOKORA REFUGEES Coming Soon
SORCERER HUNTERS
SUIKODEN III May 2004
SUKI
TOKYO BABYLON May 2004
TOKYO MEW MEW
UNDER THE GLASS MOON
VAMPIRE GAME
VISION OF ESCAFLOWNE, THE
WILD ACT
WISH
WORLD OF HARTZ Coming Soon
X-DAY
ZODIAC P.I.

NOVELS
KARMA CLUB Coming Soon
SAILOR MOON

ART BOOKS
CARDCAPTOR SAKURA
MAGIC KNIGHT RAYEARTH
PEACH GIRL ART BOOK April 2004

ANIME GUIDES
COWBOY BEBOP ANIME GUIDES
GUNDAM TECHNICAL MANUALS
SAILOR MOON SCOUT GUIDES

TOKYOPOP KIDS
STRAY SHEEP

CINE-MANGA™
CARDCAPTORS
FAIRLY ODDPARENTS March 2004
FINDING NEMO
G.I. JOE SPY TROOPS
JACKIE CHAN ADVENTURES
JIMMY NEUTRON BOY GENIUS, THE ADVENTURES OF
KIM POSSIBLE
LIZZIE MCGUIRE
POWER RANGERS: NINJA STORM
SHREK Coming Soon
SPONGEBOB SQUAREPANTS
SPY KIDS 2
SPY KIDS 3-D Game Over March 2004
TRANSFORMERS: ARMADA
TRANSFORMERS: ENERGON May 2004

For more
information visit
www.TOKYOPOP.com

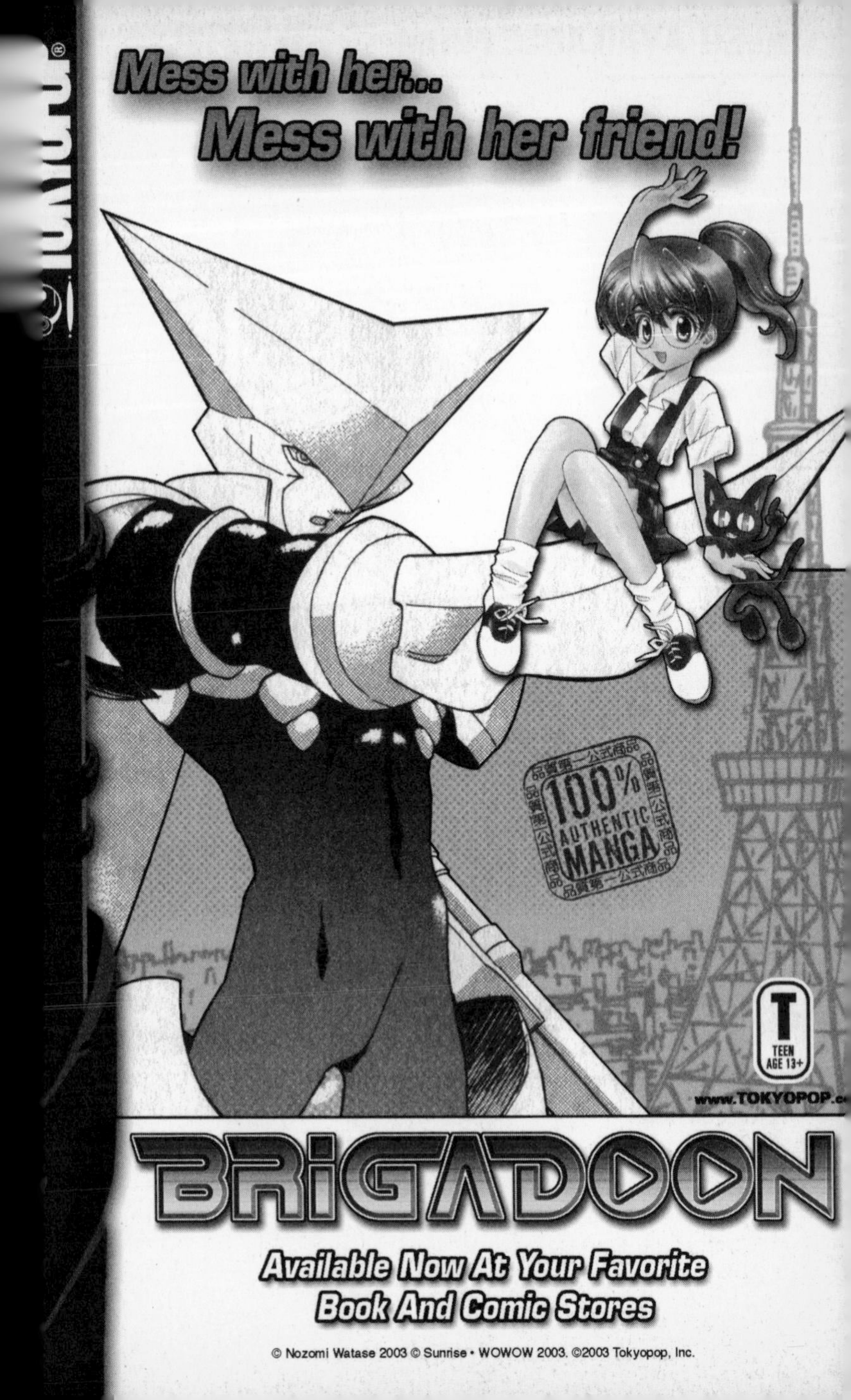
TOKYOPOP®
Mess with her...
Mess with her friend!
100% AUTHENTIC MANGA
品質第一公式商品
T
TEEN AGE 13+
www.TOKYOPOP.co
BRIGADOON
Available Now At Your Favorite
Book And Comic Stores
© Nozomi Watase 2003 © Sunrise • WOWOW 2003. ©2003 Tokyopop, Inc.

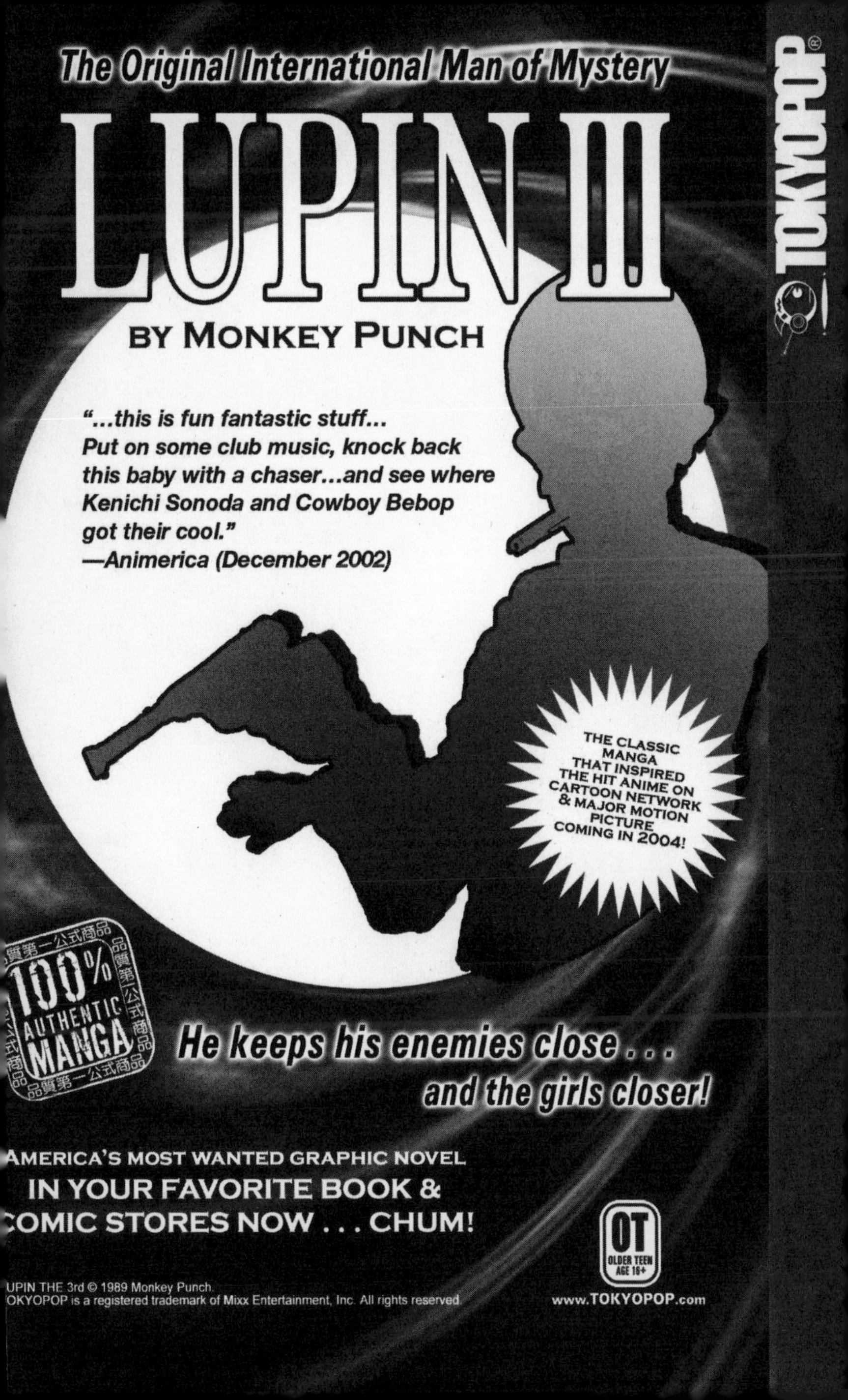

The Original International Man of Mystery
LUPIN III
BY MONKEY PUNCH
"...this is fun fantastic stuff... Put on some club music, knock back this baby with a chaser...and see where Kenichi Sonoda and Cowboy Bebop got their cool."
—Animerica (December 2002)
THE CLASSIC MANGA THAT INSPIRED THE HIT ANIME ON CARTOON NETWORK & MAJOR MOTION PICTURE COMING IN 2004!
TOKYOPOP®
100% AUTHENTIC MANGA
品質第一公式商品
He keeps his enemies close . . .
and the girls closer!
AMERICA'S MOST WANTED GRAPHIC NOVEL
IN YOUR FAVORITE BOOK &
OMIC STORES NOW . . . CHUM!
OT OLDER TEEN AGE 16+
UPIN THE 3rd © 1989 Monkey Punch.
OKYOPOP is a registered trademark of Mixx Entertainment, Inc. All rights reserved.
www.TOKYOPOP.com

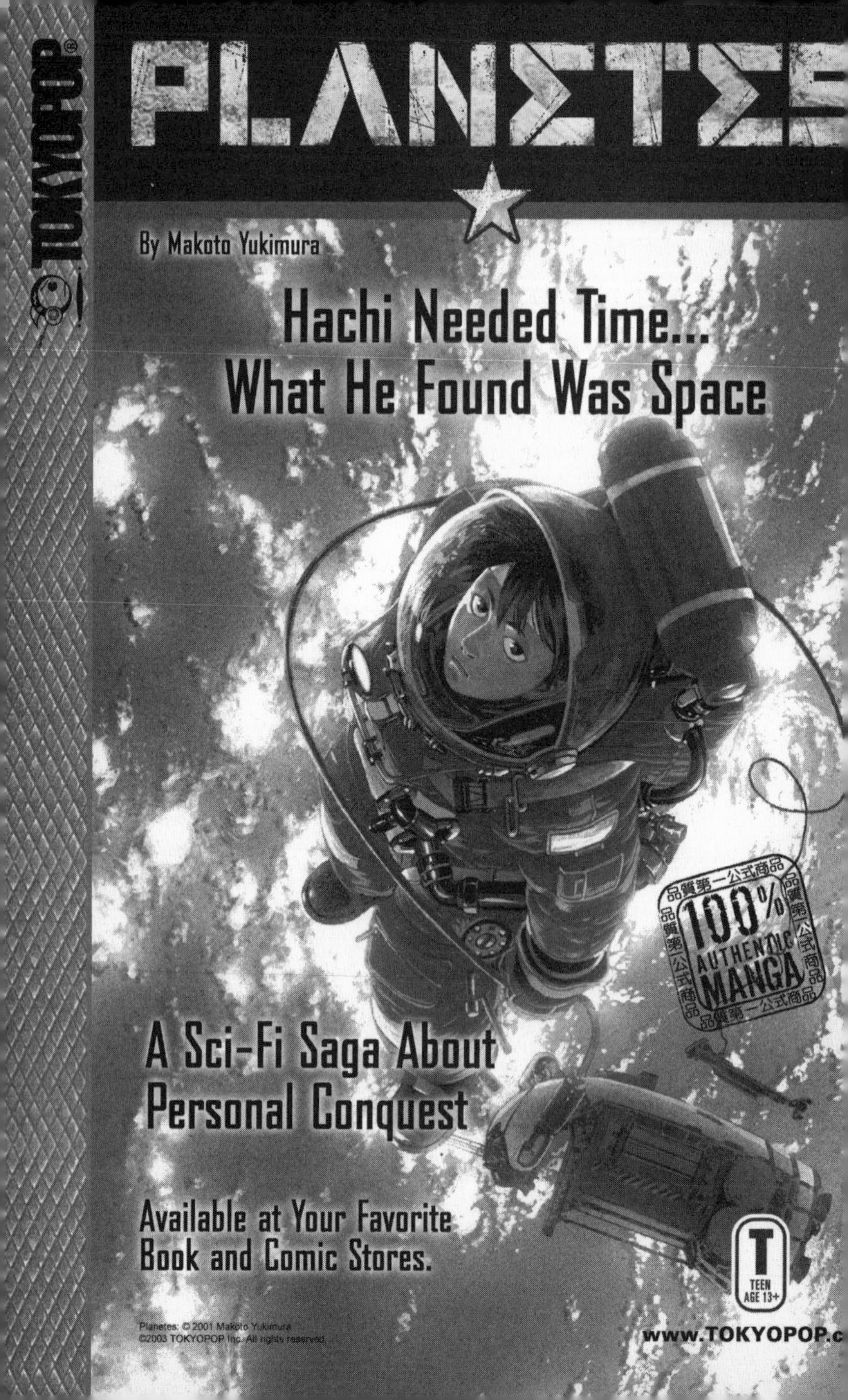
TOKYOPOP®
PLANETES
By Makoto Yukimura
Hachi Needed Time...
What He Found Was Space
品質第一公式商品
100%
AUTHENTIC
MANGA
A Sci-Fi Saga About
Personal Conquest
Available at Your Favorite
Book and Comic Stores.
T
TEEN
AGE 13+
Planetes: © 2001 Makoto Yukimura
©2003 TOKYOPOP Inc. All rights reserved.
www.TOKYOPOP.c